MAR

To: my Lotta-Bu'
Pal -
From: Rusty

Enjoy !

The Margin

Outskirts Press, Inc.
Denver, Colorado

This is a work of fiction. The events and characters described here are imaginary and are not intended to refer to specific places or living persons. The opinions expressed in this manuscript are solely the opinions of the author and do not represent the opinions or thoughts of the publisher.

The Margin
All Rights Reserved
Copyright © 2007 Marvin Wiebener
V 3.0R1.0

Cover Image © 2007 JupiterImages Corporation
All Rights Reserved. Used With Permission.

This book may not be reproduced, transmitted, or stored in whole or in part by any means, including graphic, electronic, or mechanical without the express written consent of the publisher except in the case of brief quotations embodied in critical articles and reviews.

Outskirts Press
http://www.outskirtspress.com

ISBN-13: 978-1-4327-0815-3

Outskirts Press and the "OP" logo are trademarks belonging to Outskirts Press, Inc.

Printed in the United States of America

DEDICATION

To my wife Peggy for her endless support and encouragement.

CHAPTER 1

Fred Gray stepped out the back door of his sprawling ranch house, coffee cup in hand. "Bear," he called. Nothing. The rancher took another sip, scanning the countryside. "Bear!" This time he shouted. The big German shepherd/ Border collie mix came sauntering to his side from the pasture north of the house. Fred sat down on a homemade wooden bench and motioned for Bear. The dog sniffed the coffee cup and plopped down at Fred's feet. The usual morning routine. Next to spending time with Helen, his wife of nearly 50 years, having coffee and a morning chat with Bear was just about his favorite pastime. "Bear, you been chasing deer this morning or just set'n on your lazy ass?"

She didn't answer, just rolled her dark eyes in Fred's direction. He reached down and gave her a pat. "It's okay, Bear. You and me get'n too damn old to chase anything." The two old-timers sat in silence for a while, enjoying each other's company. No pressure, no arguments—just a friendship that started ten years earlier when Fred found what was left of a litter of pups some son of a bitch had dumped on a county road near his ranch. Two of the four pups had been run over and were being picked over by buzzards. Another died at the vet's from malnutrition, the doc thought. Bear spent three days at the vet clinic to the tune of a hundred bucks and survived.

She had a small white spot on one side, some brown under her snout, chest, and front paws. The rest, including her eyes, was black as coal. At about eight weeks she looked like a bear cub.

Fred finished off half his coffee and set the tin drinking cup down next to the dog. Bear lapped up the rest. The rancher leaned to his left and pulled a Redman Golden Select tobacco pouch from his back pocket, pulled the soft "freshness guaranteed" pocket open, and tore off a leaf. He rolled the leaf around between the palms of his hands, stuck the ball between his back teeth, and clamped down hard, allowing saliva to mix with the juice from the leaf. He knew it was a bad habit—hell, it might even kill him someday, but Fred figured he'd earned the right to a bad habit or two.

"Bear, it's get'n late, nearly seven. I'm gonna send the hands out to fix the fence over by the Eagle Chief; then I got an important phone call to make. Your assignment today is to keep the desperados away. Think you can handle that?" She slept.

Fred spit juice into the grass, then the whole wad, wiped the spit off his whiskered chin, and headed back into the house to brush his teeth and gargle. Helen wouldn't let him get within ten feet of her with tobacco smell on his breath.

* * *

"Dr. Bethel, you have a call on line one," the receptionist said over the intercom.

"Take a message."

"It's Fred Gray."

"Take a message!"

Lee Bethel grabbed his briefcase and a stack of graduate essays he'd just graded and was halfway out his office door.

"He says it's urgent!"

Lee met Fred Gray five years earlier after the rancher had discovered a pile of bones at the bottom of a box canyon. A spring downpour had eroded just enough soil to expose the bones. Fred knew they weren't cattle bones, and they were too large for deer. In a casual conversation with the local county extension agent, Fred mentioned his discovery. The agent suggested he call in an expert and gave him the number of the Oklahoma Anthropological Society. After a couple of weeks of being passed from one department to another and playing phone tag, Fred and Lee Bethel finally connected. Dr. Bethel, an archaeologist from the university, and two graduate students visited the site that summer. A bison skull, a femur, and an arrow point were excavated initially from the site. Later, Bethel called the rancher with the news that the skull and femur were old, very old. Arrangements were finalized for Dr. Bethel to bring his graduate students and a few volunteers to begin a thorough excavation. Bethel and his students had been there every summer since, and the plan was to return again this year.

"Marlene, would you go to room 220 and tell my students that I'll be ten minutes late? I'll take Fred's call."

Bethel had worked with several landowners in northwest Oklahoma over the years. Wind and rain erosion over the last century or two had exposed remnants of past

Indian cultures, some as old as 11,000 years. Lee had received many calls from landowners about possible archaeological discoveries, but he had never received an *urgent* call from one of them.

"Fred, this is Lee, what's going on?"

The rancher dispensed with the usual small talk about families, weather, and the like. "When can you come out?"

"In a few weeks, like we'd originally planned. Why?"

"Can't you come this week?"

"Of all the times I can't come, this is the worst time. I got end of semester essays to grade and dissertations to review, then graduation functions I'm required to attend."

"Yeah, guess this is a bad time, but if you'd seen what I've seen you'd be here tonight, guaranteed!"

"Can't you tell me on the phone?"

"Hell, no!"

"Why?"

"'Cause I think someone's watching me! They might even be listening."

"Fred, you're scaring me! Who's watching and why? What does Helen think?"

"Don't know who or why. The county clerk gave me a courtesy call last week, told me that two different men requested to look at the old courthouse journals, Book Five specifically."

"Slow down, Fred. What old journals, and what's Book Five?"

"Historical journals, turn of the century stuff about the Cherokee outlet, the land run of 1893, and Oklahoma statehood. Book Five contains entries my grandparents made a hundred years ago."

"How do you know they were looking at the same thing?"

"'Cause they asked the clerk to make copies of the

same page."

"What page?"

"The page my grandfather had written an entry in. The clerk said both guys claimed to be representatives of gas exploration companies."

"So maybe someone wants to drill a well on your place."

"Nope, the clerk said they've never had a company ask for the old journals. They're of no commercial use. They just want the land descriptions with current owner names, and those are found in county records, not the old historical journals. As for telling Helen, I haven't yet."

"Why?"

"I think she and Robert think I'm losing it. Lee, I'll tell all of you, hell, I'll even show you, just get out here."

"Is this related to archaeology?"

"Partly. Lee, I'm going to hang up now. Please, first chance you get come out."

"It'll be two weeks, Fred. I'm sorry but it's the best I can do."

"Okay. Two weeks."

Lee looked at his watch; by the time he got to his class, he'd be fifteen minutes late. He rushed into the amphitheater mindful of his professorial responsibilities but oblivious to his surroundings. His mind was on the phone call. He pointed to a student on the first row. "I'm sorry, I can't remember your name."

"Debra," she answered. She looked hurt. After all, she'd perched herself on the kiss-ass row to make an impression, and the louse couldn't remember her name.

"Debra, do me a favor and run to my office and get my briefcase and the stack of graded essays."

There was a soft chuckle from somewhere in the back as Debra exited the class. Lee didn't hear the chuckle and was unaware he'd pissed Debra off. He wouldn't have cared even if he had known—as far as he was concerned, students were there to learn, and he didn't have the time or the inclination to play nursemaid or to care about their individual emotional ups and downs. Lee had been a student once, and he did know why most students, particularly the pretty, empty-headed ones, sat in the first row. That's not rocket science.

The call from Gray was a distraction; it had ruined Lee's day. A chance to get ahead of the paper game was now a far-fetched plan. He hated teaching. He hated grading tests, papers, and essays—dissertations were the worst. Listening to doctoral candidates defend their dissertations was a nightmare, but he loved the fieldwork. Living out of a tent and excavating a bison kill site or a Plains Indian camp eight hundred years old was why he tolerated the university crap. The *dig* was where the action was. That's where education took place.

Dr. Bethel returned to his office with a briefcase packed and arms full of more papers. Marlene was coming down the hall and opened the door to his office for him.

"Thanks, Marlene. Don't know what we'd do without you."

"Yeah, yeah, I've heard that before. Just remember this favor during the next round of budget cuts."

"You don't have to worry, Marlene; I'd be cut long before you." Lee smiled reassuringly.

He laid the stack on his credenza and cleared his desktop of bone fragments and two bags of dirt ready for sifting that he'd marked to coincide with the excavation site it was taken from. He sat down in his 35-year-old executive chair that had originally been covered in some kind of brown artificial leather. Black duct tape now kept what was left of the stuffing inside. He rolled his chair over the carpet protector to a short refrigerator next to his computer desk and took out a cold 16-ounce can of Coca-Cola's most potent energy drink. Lee had already hung a sign on his door that warned certain catastrophic events would occur to anyone who disturbed the office inhabitant. He leaned back and took a long draw from the can, thinking he'd need another to get him through the night of reading one boring paper after another. Better check in before he got to having too much fun.

"Hello."

"Honey, it's your lover boy."

"Oh, which one?"

"Funny. That's really funny. You're a real comedian."

"It's necessary being married to you, lover boy. Hey, what's going on?"

"It's that time of year, you know. Won't be home till midnight or after. Lock the doors and don't wait up. Okay?"

Lee finished off the energy drink and immediately had to pee. The bathroom was at the other end of the building, and he knew if he stepped outside the confines of his office he was fair game for every student who wanted to try their hand, at the last minute, to influence him. He'd made provision for that inevitability and pulled a brown paper bag from under his desk. He took a $3.00 hospital urinal from the sack, opened the plastic lid, and relieved himself.

Lee took the first ten-page essay from the stack, read the author's name, paper title, and word count. Twenty-five hundred words each and 20 more just like it. He grimaced, stretched his neck forward to relieve the tightness he could feel setting in, and groaned.

"Shit!" he mumbled.

CHAPTER 2

Friday, May 19, 9:20 a.m.

Fred was disappointed, more in himself than in Dr. Bethel. He knew Lee had obligations and couldn't come at the drop of a hat, especially not knowing what it was Fred wanted him to see. This was something big, maybe very big, and he needed Lee's help. The rancher stuck his head out the den entry and called down the short hall to the kitchen.

"Helen."

"What, honey?" She stepped back from the cabinet to make eye contact.

"Goin' out to see how Robert's doing repairing that pond dam. Be back later."

"Make sure your two-way is on and the volume up in case I need you."

Helen wasn't concerned about needing her husband; she was worried about him needing her. He'd acted strange since March, she thought. Most days he seemed distant, lost in his own thoughts. Helen had talked to their oldest son, who actually operated the ranch since Fred's retirement, about his father's behavior. Robert had noticed some forgetfulness as well as more than the usual amount of worry. Both hoped and prayed it wasn't one of those awful old-age diseases that robbed people first of their memory then their personality.

Fred called Bear and headed to the barn. He wasn't sure the old flatbed would start, but he wanted to give it a try, assuming one of the hands hadn't taken the battery. Fred opened the hood. It was still there; the posts had even been wire-brushed. There was coolant in the radiator, and the oil looked clean, measuring full on the stick. The key was in the ignition. He turned it and the powerful engine roared to life. Fred let it idle while he filled the feeder with cottonseed cake. He might as well make himself useful for the next two weeks, he thought. He backed out of the barn and whistled for Bear to load up. She always rode standing on the flatbed, but today she just sat looking at Fred.

"Arthritis got ya?"

Bear gave a low muffled bark followed by a short whine. Fred reached across the seat and opened the passenger side door.

"In, girl!"

Bear slipped up on the seat, put her paws on the dash, and barked.

"Is that your way of saying you're ready to go?" Fred pulled the snake catcher off the gun rack, hooked it under the door latch, and yanked the door shut. Fifteen minutes later, a herd of black Angus was following the truck as the feeder dispensed the cake. Cattle fed, Fred parked the old truck on a slope overlooking a shallow canyon, shut the engine off, and got out.

"Time for another chew, Bear." Fred pulled the

Redman package out again. He walked around to the front of the truck, leaned against the fender, and cocked his sweat-stained Stetson back on his head. Fred untied the red bandana from around his neck and doused it good with water from a gallon thermos and wiped his face. He took a long drink and poured some into the thermos lid so Bear could lap.

He thought back to 1952, fresh home from the Korean War. Memories he wanted to forget but couldn't. Memories of fallen comrades haunted him. Some died directly from the warfare, while others who were not so lucky froze to death. Sometimes the images would fade, but then some benign word or event would bring them back with a vengeance. He even had twinges of guilt that he'd survived and so many of his friends hadn't—this was something Fred had never shared with anyone, not even Helen.

Fred brushed the moisture from his eyes and stared out over a small rise toward the sandstone outcropping not more than 50 yards to the south, the place that had captured his undivided attention for the past three months. Bear had found a shady spot just under the fender Fred was leaning against and was asleep. The afternoon sun was bearing down hard, and her black coat absorbed the heat like a sponge in water.

It was 1956, shortly after his mother's death from a long torturous battle with cancer, when his father, Isaac, sent him into Buffalo, the county seat, to research old land records. Fred's younger brother and sister were attending a nearby state college, and Isaac needed to sell off some land to pay the tuition. Fortunately, a neighbor needed two hundred acres of pastureland, but before the sale could be completed, an accurate land description had to be located and made a part of the new abstract. That was the first time he had seen the old journals, dating back before the Oklahoma land run of 1893. Anything of importance occurring in that region of Indian Territory was recorded in those journals. Cavalry movements, Indian battles, births, deaths, criminal arrests, hangings, wagon train and supply lines were part of the entries. Some were obviously made by government officials, but others were made by pioneers themselves, as was the case of his grandfather's original purchase of an adjoining claim. The neighbor, according to Isaacs's entry, "couldn't take the hard life no more," so Jeremiah offered to buy his land for 50 cents an acre plus a wagon and a two-year-old mule named Dolly. That was the first time he'd noticed that next to his grandfather's entry, in the margin of the journal, was a drawing, maybe a map, he remembered thinking. It took three more trips to the county courthouse that month to gather all the information about the land so that the lawyer could prepare a legal bill of sale. On each visit he studied the drawing and wondered about its significance. Seemed like a lifetime ago, he thought.

"Get'n hot, Bear. Guess we'd better find some permanent shade."

Bear woofed without raising her snout off the ground. Fred opened the passenger door and the dog got in. They headed down the slope and into the bone-dry creek bed that hadn't seen water in three months. Fred slowed the truck and looked at the outcropping, again calculating the distance from where he'd parked two months earlier, to the other side of the ravine. "Between a quarter and half mile I'd guess," he said aloud. "Bear," Fred paused, "there's something inside that cave!" Bear woofed.

Fred shifted into four-wheel drive and eased over the rocks into the creek bed and up a steep incline, trying to avoid as much cactus as possible. He parked the truck back in the barn and headed to the house. Bear stretched out on the cool concrete driveway under the protection of a maple tree and went back to sleep.

"Been looking for you, Mr. Gray," Helen said when Fred came through the back door, trying to mask her worry with a cheery greeting.

"Oh, how come?"

"Said you were going to check on Robert, and he said he hadn't seen you all afternoon. I was beginning to worry."

"Yeah, remember saying that, but changed my mind and fed cows instead."

"Do you remember me asking you to make sure the two-way was on and volume up in case I needed you?"

"No. Guess I didn't hear you. Sorry." Fred poured some sun tea Helen had made earlier in the day over a quart jug of ice and loaded it with sugar. Without saying anything else, he went back to the adjoining den and shut the door. He hadn't even made eye contact with his wife.

Helen brushed a lock of her graying auburn hair away from her cheek and dabbed the tears with a lace handkerchief she kept stuffed in her apron pocket. *He's just so different*, she thought. She had tried talking to him about her concerns, but he would just reassure her everything was alright and not to worry.

CHAPTER 3

Friday, June 2, 7:04 p.m.

D r. Bethel finished the five-page single-spaced evaluation of the last PhD candidate. After running it through spell-check, he clicked print. He laced his fingers behind his head, leaned back, and listened to the final stanza of his favorite Mozart piece. Classical music was not what he normally chose to listen to, but this particular piece was somehow soothing. There was no distracting beat or lyrics to sort through; it was just calming, orchestrated music that held other noises at bay.

The music came to a close. Lee phoned his wife. "Ready?"

"Ready as I'll ever be."

"See you in ten." Lee hung the phone up, shut the light off, and hurried on to his car. The academic drudgery was over for another semester. The summer dig was ahead. Then, there was Fred Gray's strange phone call. Tonight he would put all of it aside. The evening, or what was left of it, belonged only to him and his wife. Lee had only seen Beverly in passing during the last two weeks, and he had missed her. Their date night was her meager payback for keeping all distractions away while he needed privacy the most. She deserved more, maybe a dozen roses to accompany the evening he had planned. There was a florist just down the street that stayed open until eight. If he hurried he could just make it.

Beverly Bethel had put her career on hold shortly after they decided to start a family. After two miscarriages and a failed in vitro, Beverly began having episodes of depression, the longest lasting several months. Lee could not get her to leave the house. Finally, after she'd lost 20 pounds from her already trim frame, he coaxed her into seeing a doctor. Four months later, after weeks of trying one anti-depressant after another, she began to feel better. Still disappointed that she could not get pregnant, Beverly decided to return to teaching part-time and finish her PhD dissertation in anthropology. Her interest in human evolution and Lee's in ancient civilizations was the common thread that brought them together in the first place.

"Red roses!" Beverly said, smiling as she watched Lee struggle through the back door, trying not to spill the water.

"Red roses for my lady." Lee was trying to sound romantic, even passionate. She appreciated the attempt.

"Where are you taking me?"

"You love fries so much, I thought McDonald's on Lindsey."

"Well, my dear, you thought wrong. What's your plan B?"

"We have reservations at Morgan's for eight."

"My favorite! What's the occasion?"

"You're the occasion, my dear!"

Beverly smiled.

* * *

It was 11:00 p.m. The jazz band was packing their instruments; Lee and Beverly were still standing on the dance floor holding each other, oblivious to their surroundings.

"Guess we should let these people go home," Lee whispered.

Beverly pulled Lee's head close so her lips were touching the lobe of his ear. "Yeah, we can pick up where we left off when we get home." The warmth of her breath against his cheek sent waves of ecstasy through him. He was ready.

They hurried through the back door. Beverly switched the kitchen light off on the way to the bedroom. "Got a message," she said.

Lee looked back. "Forget it."

"Might be important." She was talking to an empty hallway.

Beverly hit the button on the machine and listened. "Lee, it's been two weeks. Call me as soon as you get this message. I don't care what time it is." The caller left no number or name, but Beverly could tell who it was from. "Honey, better listen to this message." Lee was already in bed. He rose up on his elbows. "This isn't good for the body or soul."

She handed him his robe, smiling. "I'll be waiting."

Lee listened to the message, settled back in his chair, and called Fred Gray. The phone rang once.

"Hello."

Lee didn't recognize the raspy whisper on the other end. Maybe it wasn't the rancher, he thought.

"Mr. Gray?"

"Yeah, Lee, it's Fred. I disconnected the phone in the

bedroom so's not to wake Helen. Been set'n here wait'n on your call. Sometimes my voice carries down the hall—that's why I'm whispering."

"Oh, so what's going on?" Lee sensed desperation in the old man's voice. He wasn't a psychologist, but Fred's behavior was beginning to concern him. Secretive, deceiving behavior wasn't at all Fred's style.

"Thanks for calling back. Just want to confirm when you'd be out. It's been two weeks."

"I was going to call first thing in the morning. Wanted to finalize details of the summer excavation at the kill site, thought we'd firm a date then."

"Let's firm it right now, that's if you don't mind."

Lee pulled his day planner out of the desk drawer. "Fred, I can be there Monday at ten a.m."

"That's June fifth, right?" the rancher asked.

"Right."

The two said their good-byes, and Lee hurried down the hall.

CHAPTER 4

Friday, May 26, 1:45 p.m.

Tobias Henry passed through Buffalo, Oklahoma, late that afternoon, headed north on highway 183. In ten minutes he would be home, first time since Christmas break. He had the usual mixed feelings about spending the next two and a half months under the same roof with his parents. He loved them and they loved him, no question in his mind about that. His father was a prominent cattleman, but Tobias grew up knowing the cattle business was not for him. He had shunned invitations to belong to the local 4H chapter and the Future Farmers of America organization in high school, which disappointed his parents very much. Being the only child of that branch of the Henry family tree meant he was destined to inherit a sizable ranching and cattle feedlot operation, as well as the responsibilities that accompanied it.

Tobias turned off 183 onto the gravel road headed west. A swirl of dust followed, announcing to everyone within a mile radius who happened to be looking that a car was approaching. Nearly five months since he had seen his parents, the longest period of separation from them in his 21 years. Surely they would be able to get along, he prayed. This summer would be the first since Tobias was 13 that he would not be helping his dad with the feedlot operation.

Tobias topped a rise and could see his home two miles ahead. The quarter mile tree-lined drive was distinctive, since there were no other trees within a mile. The house had been built in the '40s, just after the war, by his grandfather. Two additions to the main house had been built on in the early '80s after natural gas had been discovered on the property. The feedlot, west of the ranch headquarters a half mile, encompassed about 20 acres, and from the hill he had just crested, it looked like a small town. Bull-wagon semis were leaving and entering the feedlot, and the dust from the 18-wheelers was a constant reminder of the Oklahoma drought. If the wind came from a westerly direction, the odor from a high concentration of cattle urine and manure, particularly on a hot day, was overwhelming at the ranch house. Tobias and his mother called it disgusting; Clark Henry would just smile and say it smelled like money to him. Another reminder of why Tobias didn't want to be a cowboy.

Tobias pulled his car under an elm tree that provided some shade to the east side of the house where the long screened-in porch was located. The ranch house had a seldom used front door located on the north that led directly into a foyer, still decorated in the original richly stained oak flooring and door frames. The main living room was to the right and was decorated in moderate southwest style. To the left of the foyer was the dining room that could seat 14 comfortably. The large kitchen joined the dining room to the south with a door leading to the porch on the east. This, in years past, was the only entrance ranch hands were allowed to use, when meals were served at the house. No matter how cold it was, the cowboys always kicked their boots off on the porch before coming in to eat. Feeding the hands in the house was a practice that had ended years earlier when the feedlot was built. Clark's dad, under his wife's direction, constructed a fully equipped dining hall near the cattle pens and hired a short-order cook to operate it. Clark claimed building the dining hall was probably the smartest thing his dad ever did. It saved his folks' marriage and probably his, too. Tobias's mother had worked hard to earn a law degree, and while cooking was something she did well, it was not a chore she enjoyed.

Tobias honked his horn twice, his customary warning that he was home. His mother was already out the side door waving.

"Tobias!"

"Mom."

"Oh, it's so good to see you," she said, hugging him tightly and kissing his cheek, tears coming down hers. "Get your things in the house. I've just put supper on; it'll be ready by the time your dad gets in."

"Where's he at?"

"The lot. Two cows are sick, and with this mad cow disease scare going around, every sick one gets government attention. Soon as the inspector's gone, he'll be up."

"I'll wash up and be back in a second."

"Yes, I'm anxious to hear about school."

That's surprising, he thought, dragging two duffle bags upstairs to his room. The last time he was face to face with his parents they were still trying to get him to change his mind about ranching. The true test would be at supper. His dad usually let him get through most of the meal before asking a question that inevitably led to a quarrel. He could already feel the caustic stomach acids working—better chew some Tums. Another reason he wanted to move away. He had been diagnosed with a pre-ulcerous condition that had diminished in severity during his absence from home.

"Tobias," his mom called from the kitchen, "your dad just drove in. We'll eat in ten minutes."

Now is the time to muster up some maturity, Tobias thought. No need to argue back, if an argument started. He would just change the subject. He knew how his dad felt. Under the same circumstances, Tobias was sure he would feel the same way. His dad was not much for social dialogue. Straight to the point, no nonsense, black or white—that was Clark Henry. He would just have to accommodate his dad's idiosyncrasies and down more antacids until school started in August. He paused at the top of the stairs thinking about what he considered one of life's great mysteries; how his mom and dad got together in the first place.

"Tobias! Tobias, get your butt down here!" Clark Henry shouted.

"Comin'," he answered, smiling. Only two occasions would draw that kind of command from his dad: when he was angry or when he was happy. Tobias knew his dad had nothing to be angry about.

Suppertime went off without a hitch. No arguments, no lectures about ranch responsibilities, just easy talk.

"So, Dad, what about the sick cows?"

"No big deal, just prairie bloat. Ever since the Japanese moratorium on buying cattle from the US, the State sends an inspector out to examine sick cows before they can be shipped. I knew it was bloat, the hands knew it was bloat, but you have to quarantine them 'til the government runs tests on the cows and the feed."

"Is there a chance they could be infected with mad cow?"

"Hell no! We've got the best checks and balances system in the world." Clark had been staring under the corner of the table where Tobias was sitting. "Been want'n to ask you something, son."

Here it comes, Tobias thought. "What, Dad?"

"What kind of shoes are those?" Clark asked, scrunching his left eye and pointing toward Tobias's feet.

"Clogs."

"Clogs. What are clogs? How in the hell do you walk in 'em?"

"Oh, Dad, they're so comfortable. I bought you a pair."

"Son, I wouldn't wear something like that to the outhouse in pitch dark." Clark realized he had become the brunt of a joke. Tobias choked back tears and tried to swallow a bite of mashed potatoes, and Rosalind left the room.

"Okay, so ya'll got a good laugh on an old man." Clark saw the humor and covered a smile with the napkin he seldom used.

Rosalind returned shortly with three pieces of apple pie sitting on the mahogany serving tray Tobias had made in junior high woodshop. "Your favorite, right?" she asked.

"My favorite," Tobias confirmed.

"Son." Clark looked down at his empty plate. "I haven't been fair to you."

"What do you mean?"

"I've pushed you to take over the operation, and that wasn't right."

"Dad, if I'd been in your shoes I would probably do the same."

"Be that as it may, I just want you to know we're behind you a hundred percent." There was a pause following Clark's affirmation. No eye contact, only the sound of forks nervously scooting the dessert remnants around on the plate. Tobias knew how difficult it was for his dad to make such a statement. The moment seemed thick with emotion; he did not want to look directly at his dad for fear he would tear up. Fixing his eyes on his nearly empty plate, Tobias impaled the last bite and replied, "That's a weight off my shoulders. I never wanted to be a disappointment to you and Mom."

"I'm just sorry it took me so long to tell you," Clark said, voice shaking.

"As for me," Rosalind added, her own lips quivering, "you have never been a disappointment to us, not ever."

"So, tell us about this internship you're doing," Clark suggested, partly out of curiosity, but mostly to hide his feelings.

"It's part of the program at the university. Each student majoring in journalism must complete four hundred hours interning for a newspaper, magazine, radio, or TV station before graduation. During Christmas break I made arrangements to do mine at the *Buffalo Ledger*."

"And what does that mean?" his dad asked.

"Means I do grunt work for ten weeks. If I'm lucky maybe the editor will let me do a story or two. The whole experience is just to introduce the student to the operation of a news outlet."

* * *

Tobias finished his nightly bathroom ritual and started to set his alarm and realized it was Friday night. He could relax during the weekend and be ready Monday morning to start his internship. Tobias turned out his lamp and thought about the conversation with his folks. It had been a pleasure, far from what he had expected. Under the circumstances, spending the summer with his parents had shifted abruptly from something he was dreading to something he was now looking forward to. Sleep came quickly.

CHAPTER 5

Monday, May 29, 7:53 a.m.

Tobias Henry had never been in the *Buffalo Ledger* before, and he had only talked with Mr. Thompson, the editor, one time, to ask if he could do his internship there. As he stepped from his car, a wind gust caught his door, nearly jerking him off balance. The gel had kept his hair in place; his face, however, was covered in a fine layer of red dust, and his eyes were full of grit. *Welcome to the Oklahoma plains*, he reflected. He made his way to the front of the all-metal one-story building that housed the newspaper. The wind was relentless, forcing him to struggle with the door just to open it. He crossed the worn-out indoor-outdoor carpet to the customer counter and stood, startled at what he saw. Tobias expected to see several employees working feverishly to finish the news before press time. Instead, he saw an empty building, no one in sight. To his right he saw a stack of FedEx packages awaiting collection and two older model Xerox machines where locals could make copies for ten cents a page. Behind the counter and toward the rear of the building were two desks, one with a computer on it and the other with an IBM Selectric typewriter. In the middle of the building were two long and very old folding tables with what appeared to be copies of news stories arranged in some kind of order, probably by date published. The only light, other than that coming through the side windows, was from two fluorescent bulbs hanging over the folding tables. At the rear of the building he could see a door that appeared to be marked OFFICE. Next to the door hung a calendar announcing in bold four-inch numerals that the day was May 29, but there was no sign of life anywhere.

"Mr. Thompson," Tobias called out, stopping just short of shouting; he waited for what seemed like a long time, then called out again louder. A bald head emerged from behind the office door.

"Yes, can I help you?"

"Looking for Mr. Thompson."

"That would be me. What can I do for you?"

"I'm Tobias Henry. We talked by phone a few months ago concerning interning with you this summer."

"Ah yes, Judge Henry's son."

"Yes sir."

"Come on back."

Tobias had encountered the "Ah yes, Judge Henry's son" greeting on several occasions since his mother's appointment, and he never knew just what was to follow. Sometimes the greeting was friendly, sometimes cordial, and sometimes he could hear the disdain, but this time he was unsure. He scooted sideways around the folding tables to Thompson's office and entered, hoping his shocked expression was no longer apparent. Never had he seen a more cluttered room. Magazines and old newspapers stacked everywhere and barely enough space on the rolltop desk to manage a legal pad for writing.

Thompson shook Tobias's hand vigorously. "Sit down." Tobias took the handshake as a good sign.

"I've known your folks for years, no finer people around. I just hope you've got half their qualities."

The greeting was both comforting and intimidating. Tobias felt at ease because of Thompson's respect for his parents, but he realized there was an element of high expectation in the not-so-veiled remark. Small talk followed, mostly about his parents, the journalism school, and what his future plans were, which of course he didn't have a clue about. Nevertheless, Tobias tried to sound like he had forged some kind of occupational direction in his life. They both knew better.

"Young man," the editor shifted from friendly to professional, "I'm going to tell you what we do here. How we put the news together and how we get it out to the people. That doesn't take much knowledge and practically no skill." Thompson peered over the top of his $14 reading glasses, making sure the college kid was listening. Tobias nodded.

"Do you know what the hardest part of putting out a newspaper is, Tobias?"

"No sir."

"Accuracy."

"Yes sir, I'd think that would be a given."

"You'd think, but it isn't. I can pick up any paper, *The Oklahoman, The New York Times, Washington Post,* and show you spelling and grammar errors. Worst of all, I can show you lies and misrepresentations. Point I'm making is that truth and accuracy are the cornerstones of this paper, and I expect nothing less from you."

The only fitting response to Thompson's remarks

Tobias could think of was a simple "Yes sir."

"That desk in the back," Thompson pointed to the one with the typewriter, "that's yours. Use the Selectric; don't touch the computer. That belongs to Mrs. Baker, my assistant. She actually runs the place. She'd bury us both face down in the Cimarron River if we so much as touched her computer."

"That's okay, Mr. Thompson; I've got a laptop. Never used a typewriter."

"That's right; it is the twenty-first century, isn't it? Anyway, Baker will be in soon. You'll enjoy working with her. Grab some coffee and make yourself at home. Snoop all you want, get to know the place. I'm finishing a story on the Lavern house fire and need time to myself."

"Thanks, Mr. Thompson, and I appreciate having this opportunity to learn from you." The remark was out before Tobias realized how canned and truly pathetic it sounded. Thompson turned back toward Tobias, slid his glasses down farther on his nose. "Yeah, 'learn from me,' that remains to be seen," he said, sounding skeptical.

Tobias spent the next 30 minutes rummaging through his desk, finding nothing useful. He pushed stacks of yellowing documents aside, set his laptop down, flipped it open to Outlook Express, and checked his e-mail. Nothing.

Mrs. Baker returned from her morning errands. "Morning. You must be Tobias."

"Yes ma'am, and you're Mrs. Baker."

"That I am, and please, for the sake of everything that's holy, don't call me ma'am. I'm Judith." She reached across the stack of documents with an outstretched hand. Tobias stood and took it.

"I'm Tobias Henry..." Before he could complete his own introduction, Baker cut him short. "I know you. Been watching you grow up. Known your mom for ages. We serve together on the Governor's Native American Advisory Council. Made many trips with your mom to Oklahoma City, even one to DC. A fine woman she is." Baker pointed toward the editor's office. "He tell you to stay away from my computer?"

"He did and I will."

"Forget what he said. The warning is for him and he knows it. Dan wouldn't know the difference between a computer and a carburetor. I see you have a Dell laptop."

"Yeah, goes with me everywhere."

"Dan give you your first assignment or did he leave that for me?"

"He didn't say anything about an assignment. Guess he's working on a story about a house fire in Lavern. He said for me to snoop around."

"My suggestion is that you pull your chair over to those folding tables and begin reading back copies of the *Ledger*. Read every word, study the headlines, even the ads. Get a feel for the news and how it's presented in print. Later this afternoon we'll talk about your first assignment." Baker went back to her desk and sorted mail. Tobias chose a stack of the most recent *Buffalo Ledgers* and began reading. He was surprised to see how professional the stories sounded, not at all small town or unsophisticated, as he'd expected. The news was reported intelligently, it was easy to read, and it was thought provoking. He wondered how Dan Thompson, an intelligent and talented editor, ended up living and working on the high and desolate plains of western Oklahoma. And Judith Baker, obviously Native American, probably Cheyenne-Arapaho like his mother, attractive, he thought, even for a 40-year-old. He stared momentarily at Dan's assistant; he knew she was unmarried, according to his mom. The framed Stanford University diploma hanging above her desk confirmed she was well educated. She turned to see Tobias staring.

"You have a question?" she said, smiling.

Busted! Tobias felt his face flush, no way to recover gracefully. "No ma'am. Uh, just thinking, wondering if you're Indian?" He made something up and looked away, hoping the surprised look on his face would somehow vanish before he returned eye contact. It didn't.

"Three-quarters Cheyenne-Arapaho. Grandfather on Dad's side was a British immigrant."

"Oh. And family?" he asked.

"Two older brothers, one younger, and four younger sisters. You should know my sister Keona; she's about your age."

"Keona is your sister? Best girl's basketball player Buffalo ever had. Where is she now?"

"Oklahoma State on a basketball scholarship, finishing her senior year in pre-med. Wants to be an oncologist."

"I was in love with Keona until seventh grade. I thought she was the most beautiful girl in the world, like I said, until the seventh grade."

"So what happened in the seventh grade that changed your mind?"

"I hadn't seen her all summer. That was the first year I worked every day for Dad, cleaning cattle pens and painting stock tanks. Only made it to town once, and that was to help Dad's foreman load feed at the Co-op. School started and I had my eye out for Keona. I'd finally worked up the courage to talk to her."

"And?"

"She walked into math class, even more beautiful than I'd remembered, and she was four inches taller than me. Well, you can guess the rest."

"Yeah, guess a five-foot ten-inch seventh grader would be a bit intimidating. Did my sister ever know how you felt?"

"No, I never told her or anyone else. You're the first to hear it."

"Interesting how life takes its little twists and turns."

He nodded. There was silence while he thought about memories brought on by recollections long since forgotten.

The morning had flown by. Tobias had learned more than he had expected and was anxious to get started. He was actually enjoying himself. The anticipated dread of living with his folks had not materialized, and the first-day jitters were gone. He felt at home, relaxed and unburdened by school demands. The summer would be a good time to evaluate his future, get reacquainted with his hometown, the people, and especially his folks. Next year would be different. He would have to find a job, probably in a city out of state. Life would shift into high gear, and the pace would quicken. He looked forward to being on his own.

Tobias felt a light touch on his shoulder that startled him, bringing his daydream to a close. He looked up to see Judith handing him a yellow sticky note. He studied it; there were three names: Jefferson Thomas Smith (78), Samantha Mary Coker (89), and Nicolas Grantham (B). "Is this what I think it is?"

"Don't know. What do you think it is?"

"Could it be two deaths and a birth?"

"Bingo! You've just earned your first 'A.' You'll need to go to the funeral home and speak with the director about the obituaries and whether or not the family wants it printed in full. There is a charge for that. If they just want an announcement, that's complimentary. The same goes for the birth. If the parents want something special in the paper, there will be a charge. If they only want it announced, then that's free. Make sure you get the correct spelling, ages, and dates. If you make a mistake, Dan will have your head, and then he'll torture you," Judith said, smiling. "Do this well and he might give you a shot at writing an article."

The week was a blur. It passed quickly, and, according to Judith, he had mastered the *Transitions* section. No spelling or grammar errors, all dates were correct, and no complaints from bereaved family members or happy new parents. Dan called him into his office at five that Friday. "Any questions so far?"

"Judith said that once I got the *Transitions* down you might let me write an article. Is that a possibility?" he asked, barely hiding his enthusiasm.

"Judith told you that?" He raised his head, laid his glasses on the desk, pushed back from his desk, and grunted. The editor reached down and grabbed a pant cuff and lifted his left leg up and over his right knee, a maneuver required to cross his legs. He leaned back in his chair and laced his thumbs under his suspenders. A deliberate ritual, Tobias had learned while observing the editor, that implied deep consideration of an idea was to follow. "Well, young man, if Judith said it then we'd better follow through." He winked.

"So I can?"

"Yeah, don't you think it's time?"

"What kind of a story should I write?" Tobias quizzed excitedly.

"Now, boy, don't disappointment me. How many journalists do you think go to their editors and ask what kind of story they should write?"

"Yes sir, point taken. I'll think about it over the weekend and propose a subject on Monday."

"Good." The editor slid his glasses over his ears and returned to whatever it was that he was working on. Tobias took that to mean he was excused.

Judith was on her way out. "TGIF," she said as they passed.

Excited to tell someone, he caught her elbow. "Mr. Thompson gave me the go-ahead on my own article. Got to come up with something good by Monday."

The assistant smiled at his childlike enthusiasm, waved, and pushed against the front door. Then she hesitated and stepped back into the building. "Tobias, a thought for you to consider this weekend."

"You mean a subject?"

"Yes. Do you know Fred Gray, the rancher that lives about ten or fifteen miles southeast of town?"

"Heard his name before. I think my folks know him. Why?"

"You're an Indian, I'd guess a quarter. This would be a subject that would interest everyone and might even give you insight into your Indian heritage."

"I'm listening."

"For the last few years, archaeologists from the university have been working an excavation site on the Gray Ranch."

"What kind of excavation? Didn't even know Oklahoma had archaeologists, much less something worth digging up."

"That's what a lot of people think, and that's exactly why I'm suggesting you consider this. It's an ancient bison kill site."

"When you say bison, you mean as in buffalo?"

"Yes. They found extinct bison skulls and Clovis spear points. Last I heard they'd dated the discovery to about eleven thousand years ago."

Tobias was hooked. Ten minutes earlier he was thinking he'd have to spend the better part of the weekend coming up with a topic for his first article, and now the subject was crawling around through his brain like a mole searching for grubs.

"That's a great idea, Judith, thanks. Where could I get some information about the excavation?"

"That's your problem. I'm headed to Tulsa. Got two performances tomorrow."

"Performances, what performances?"

"Guest cellist with the symphony. I do it three or four times a season."

Tobias stood watching as Judith exited and disappeared around the side of the building. "Amazing, absolutely amazing!" he whispered.

By Monday morning Tobias had accumulated bits and pieces of information about the Gray Ranch dig site. His mom knew some of the details and so did an old high school buddy who had actually volunteered at the site one year. With a rudimentary story outline in hand, Tobias approached the editor first thing. Thompson was enthusiastic, congratulating him on the unique story subject, but noticeably disappointed when Tobias admitted it was Judith's suggestion.

"Well, Tobias, it would be better had it been your idea, but I guess nothing's original anymore. Let's see what you can do with the story. What do you do next?"

"Research. First the library, then the courthouse. There may be old records helpful to developing the story."

"Excellent. I'll be out of town the rest of today. When I get back, I'll want to see how you've fleshed the story out."

Judith was still out on her morning errands. Tobias scribbled a note saying where he would be for the next few hours and laid it on the seat of her chair. It was nearly nine. He would check the library first, then the courthouse.

CHAPTER 6

Monday, June 5, 10:14 a.m.

Rosalind Henry had occupied an office in the county courthouse for the last 12 years, eight as Assistant District Attorney and four as District Judge. Tobias stuck his head in his mother's office to say hello and, seeing she had someone with her, quickly apologized. "Sorry, I'll come back later." He turned to leave.

"Wait, I want you to meet the sheriff."

Tobias had heard about the sheriff. Bob Griffin, a friend, had tried to describe her. Griffin was well known for his embellishments; he had even acquired a special place in the Buffalo High School annual as the king of exaggerators, so most folks didn't take him seriously. Bob must have lost his technique for stretching the truth, Tobias thought, after getting a close-up look.

"Sheriff Crystal Stanton, this is my son, Tobias."

As he approached to shake her hand, Tobias prayed his facial expression would mask his thoughts. She stood and turned to greet him. The sheriff was his height, with broad shoulders that didn't detract from her feminine appearance. She was a blonde, natural or otherwise, he couldn't tell and didn't care. When she reached to shake hands, he caught sight of her sidearm. He knew enough about guns to know it was an automatic of some kind. The FBI emblem was inlaid in the wooden handles. She was drop-dead gorgeous, and he knew as he backed out the door, apologizing again for the interruption, that his face and demeanor had not hidden his thoughts. He was thoroughly embarrassed. He stumbled down the marble steps to the second floor, took a drink of room temperature water from a public fountain, gathered his post-adolescent composure, and walked into the county documents and records department. The huge room was quiet, no other people around that he could see. Banks of shelves eight feet high lined the walls and ran throughout the room. He approached the counter and could see someone in faded Wrangler's thumbing through a four-drawer file cabinet. "Hello." He announced his presence. He could see the Wrangler's turn.

"Tobias Henry?!"

"Audrey Spencer?!"

"This is a pleasant surprise, thought you were away at school."

"Yeah, just home for the summer, doing my internship at the *Ledger*."

"That's right, you're into journalism."

"What about you?"

"The same. Home for the summer, thinking about changing majors."

"From what to what?"

"Thought I wanted to be a nurse but got involved in campus politics, and now I'm not so sure. Maybe political science and eventually a law degree."

Audrey put the filing aside and came over to the counter. She smiled warmly, reached out, and patted his hand. "So what brings you up here today?"

"Need to do some research on an article I'm writing, and Mr. Thompson suggested I might find historical information relevant to the story here."

"What's the story about?"

"Evidently, archaeologists have been excavating a bison kill site on the Gray Ranch the past several summers. The site dates back thousands of years to what they call the Paleo-Indian era. These people were apparently some of the first on this continent."

"Sounds like the makings of a good story, but I've got a question."

"Hope I've got an answer."

"Your story is about a culture thousands of years old, right?"

"Right."

"What significance would the county historical documents have? They only date back to the 1870s, when Oklahoma was Indian Territory."

"My interest in the Gray Ranch is only as additional supporting information for the story. People who read the article will be interested in the area from two perspectives, ancient and current history."

"I see. Makes sense to me." Audrey looked perplexed. She fumbled through a large log book that had been lying on the counter and thumbed each page looking for something.

"What are you looking for?"

Audrey swirled the log around so that Tobias could see the contents. "This is a log that each person must sign when they research county records." She pointed to a name.

"Okay. John Smith of Smith Consulting, dated April

tenth of this year. So what?"

Audrey pointed to the next name.

"Ralph Peterson of Sooner Drilling, and it's dated the same day. Okay, what are you showing me? What's the significance of these two names?"

"Those two men and you make three people who've been interested in the history of the Gray Ranch recently."

"Is that unusual?"

"My mother's the county clerk, that's why I'm here; she gave me a part-time job until the fall semester. Mom said that sometime back a man came in and asked specifically for information about the Gray place."

"And your mother was curious? Why?"

"No, not yet. Mom said it's common for people working for oil and gas exploration companies to search land records to determine ownership and exact land location descriptions. What made her curious was that this guy asked to see historical information that is kept separate from land description logs. Mom says the historical information is of no use to exploration companies."

"I still don't see what you're driving at."

"It was the second request for the same information that really got Mom thinking. She mentioned that in her three years as county clerk, there had never been a non-relative ask to view the historical documents."

"Non-relative, what do you mean?"

"Descendents of the pioneers research the documents for genealogy purposes. You know, tracking their history."

"Duh! Guess that was a stupid question. What'd your mom do then?"

"Called Mr. Gray and told him."

"And?"

"That's it, that's all I know."

Tobias's enthusiasm was growing. Nervous feelings

swirled somewhere near his solar plexus, announcing growing anticipation. Was he on to something, or was this a case of an overactive imagination fueled by his need to write a good story, one that would please the editor? "Can you show me the records the two men looked at?"

"I don't know which ones they were, but Mom does and she'll be back any minute. Can you wait?"

"Can I wait? I'll pitch a tent if I need to. And while we're waiting, if you don't mind me asking, would you be interested in having dinner and attending a movie?"

"No, I don't mind you asking, and yes, that sounds fun." Audrey blushed and smiled awkwardly. She hadn't anticipated the invitation—as a matter of fact, it was a shock. In high school, Audrey considered Tobias out of her league. His mother was an assistant district attorney and his father a wealthy rancher. Her own mother was a cafeteria worker at the local grade school, struggling to pay rent and buy groceries.

"Tonight?" he asked.

"Tonight's fine. I get off at five and can be ready by six." Audrey pointed back over his shoulder. "You're in luck, here comes Mom now. Mom, you remember Tobias Henry, don't you?"

Instead of taking his outstretched hand, the county clerk embraced him. "Of course I remember Tobias. I have coffee with your mom almost every day; she's kept me abreast of your whereabouts. I even know you're doing a journalism internship at the *Ledger*. You know your mom is very proud of you."

"Yes ma'am. I'm just glad I don't have any sibs to compare with. Might not rank as high if I had." They laughed.

Audrey told her mother about Tobias's article. "Tobias would like to see the information the other two men looked at."

"Yeah, and Audrey told me you called Mr. Gray and informed him. What was his reaction?"

"Surprised at first. The longer we talked, the more alarmed he sounded."

"What'd he say?"

"Just asked their names, who they worked for, and asked me if they said why they were interested in his place. I told him they didn't say. That was it."

"Anything else?"

"Oh yes. He asked what documents they looked at. Now that I think about it, that's when he began to sound alarmed." Mrs. Spencer anticipated the next question. "All of the old historical information going back before the land run of 1893 is kept in journals simply identified as Book One, Book Two, and so on. You get the idea. Book Five was the one requested by Smith and Peterson; it's also the book with entries from known pioneers and settlers whose names begin with F, G, and H. Fred's grandparents are listed there."

"Can I see Book Five?" Tobias asked anxiously.

"Of course. Audrey, sign him in and show him where it is."

"Thanks, Mrs. Spencer."

"That's why we're here, to be helpful."

Audrey pointed toward the sign-in log. Tobias signed the book and printed *Buffalo Ledger* under the *representing who* category, then followed Audrey around bookshelves and past a sign that read HISTORICAL RECORDS AND DOCUMENTS. A second line instructed viewers to handle journals carefully. An hour later, he emerged from the stacks carrying Book 5.

"Find anything interesting?" Audrey asked.

"Lots of interesting entries. I could read all day, but don't really know what I'm looking for. There are no entries making reference to anything that might be archaeological."

"There's probably a perfectly rational explanation why two men came in on the same day and requested a copy of that page. And, by the way, I did a Google search of Smith Consulting and Sooner Drilling," Mrs. Spencer offered.

"What came up?" Tobias asked.

"Nada. Not a thing. Actually, lots of sites but nothing that would tie these two to the companies. I tell you that for what it's worth, may not mean anything, but it does add to the mystery."

"Yeah, it does, doesn't it? Can I have a copy of the page?"

"Sure. Audrey…"

"Already done," Audrey interrupted and handed the Xerox sheet to Tobias.

He laid the page from Book 5 out on the counter, smoothing it with his hand as if the effort would somehow draw out a hidden message. They studied the page together; Tobias asked for a magnifying glass. Mrs. Spencer opened her desk drawer, got one out, and handed it to him. He held the glass a few inches above the entry Jeremiah Gray had made and pointed to the margin. "What do you make of this?"

CHAPTER 7

Beverly Bethel shook her husband's shoulder. "Wake up," she mumbled, dozing off. The alternating on-again, off-again buzzing of the alarm continued to get louder. "Lee!" she said in a tone just one notch lower than a shout.

"What?" came the muffled and barely audible reply from somewhere under his pillow.

"Shut your alarm off. It's Monday."

Lee pulled the pillow off his head and slapped at the clock alarm button until the infernal noise stopped. "Okay, so what's special about Monday?" he whispered, sleep still beckoning. No answer. Beverly had returned to her dreams. Lee lay there, staring at what he could see of the ceiling and trying to recall his plans for that day. He remembered the call from Fred Gray. Words swirled through his awakening consciousness, and finally complete thoughts began to arrange themselves in patterns of memory he could understand. He sat up, scratched his head, and pushed his ruffled hair back. "Beverly."

She stirred. "What?"

"I've got to be on the road in forty-five minutes."

"I'll be ready when you're ready." Her voice trailed off somewhere under the sheet she had pulled over her head to block the lamp light.

Lee came out of the bathroom 20 minutes later and packed his shaving kit into his duffle bag. Beverly was up. He could see light from the end of the hallway, and the smell of coffee confirmed everything was on schedule. As he entered the kitchen, Beverly handed him the thermos. "Ready?" he asked.

"Just waiting on you, my dear."

The trip took ten minutes; Beverly pulled into the parking lot next to the Oklahoma Anthropological Society sign. Lee loaded his backpack and duffle bag into the university-owned truck and returned to the driver side of his wife's Subaru Forrester.

"You've got Gray's phone number?"

Beverly nodded. "You, my man, drive carefully." She turned her head for a kiss, and Lee obliged.

"I will. How about another evening at Morgan's when I get back on Friday?" He smiled and waved as she drove off.

Lee looked at his watch, 5:58 a.m. *Right on time,* he thought. From the university to the Gray Ranch was just over three hours; with pit stops he should be there by 10:00. He picked up the trip ticket attached to a clipboard and made the required entries: date, time, destination, and mileage. The use of a university-owned, properly designated vehicle was mandatory. It was policy that any employee of the university must be officially identifiable when in the field. This prevented many misunderstandings between archaeologists and the landowners. The truck bore the insignia of the university and the OAS. Visual identification by the locals was essential to maintaining a working relationship between the university and communities. There had been more than a few occasions when archaeologists had found themselves looking down the barrel of a deer rifle and explaining who they were and why they were on someone's land. The university always made a formal request of the landowner to be on his property. After the approval was signed, the university would make specific arrangements with the owner; however, it was common for the owner to forget to inform hired hands and neighbors. It was on these occasions when encounters occurred that required rudimentary skills in diplomatic maneuvering.

Lee finished the thermos of coffee as he exited Interstate 40 in Clinton, Oklahoma. He stopped for a refill and cinnamon roll, then headed north on 183. This route was a bit longer, but with fewer small towns to go through, in the long run he figured it took less time.

The long stretch of empty highway gave him time to think about Fred Gray. The man was either on to something big or maybe he was losing it. Either could be a possibility and both were equally concerning. What on God's green earth—or, in that part of the county, brown and red earth— could be so provocative that it would cause someone as tough as Fred Gray to act, or at least sound paranoid? Lee had never pegged the rancher as someone who would ever be alarmed about much. His other concern was the scheduled excavation at the bison kill site. Eight graduate students and around ten volunteers had signed up and made plans to assist in the two-week dig. Lee knew that everyone had made arrangements for the event, but with the possibility of something unknown altering the schedule, he knew a plan B had to be in place.

Lee drove north out of Woodward on 34 until he saw

the Cargill Salt Plant sign. He turned left a mile, then back north on a dirt road. The '97 Ford F-250 Lee was driving didn't have A/C, which didn't bother Lee. He thrived in hot weather, but when he turned west, the 20-mile per hour wind blew road dust in the open window with such force he had to roll the window up. Channel 5 had predicted 20 to 30 mile per hour winds from the south, with temperatures topping out at 95. It was early June, and the hot weather, he knew, was yet to come. Lee could see the Gray Ranch driveway ahead; Mrs. Gray prepared the best iced tea he'd ever tasted.

CHAPTER 8

Monday, June 5, 9:48 a.m.

Helen Gray finished slicing the last of the fresh peaches for the pie she'd planned for dessert. She bagged the skins so they could be added to her compost material and set the sack to the side. "Fred," she called into the den.

"Yeah, honey," he answered.

"Looks like Lee coming up the drive." Helen hadn't seen Fred this excited since their first child was born 46 years ago. She hoped this was a good sign. As Fred passed her on his way to greet Lee at the front door, he even had a smile on his face, something she hadn't seen in two or three months. Robert had been in the den with his father discussing cattle prices when Helen announced Lee's arrival, and he had followed him as far as the kitchen.

"Haven't seen that reaction in some time," Robert said to his mother, looking out the kitchen window and watching Lee exit his truck.

"I haven't, either. Did your dad say anything?"

"Nope, just said Lee was coming to discuss the dig site. Don't know what would get him all excited about that. Strange that he'd want me in on this discussion—never has before."

Helen took her apron off, wiped her hands with it, and laid it over a kitchen chair. She gave Robert a puzzled look. "You know, that seemed strange to me, too."

"What seemed strange?"

"Your dad asked me to be in on the talk."

Fred escorted Lee into the kitchen. Helen hugged him and Robert shook his hand.

"Before I forget it, Mrs. Gray, Beverly told me not to come home without your recipe for oatmeal raisin cookies."

"I'll copy it off tonight. Now, how about some tea?"

"Been thinking about your tea since six this morning."

"Sugar, right?"

"Lots of sugar, please."

Fred watched the friendly exchange and listened to the chitchat. It was all he could do to maintain reasonable composure. He had a story to tell—a story that had been developing since the first time his grandfather Jeremiah showed him the candlestick and told him the tale that went along with it. Finally, the day he'd been looking forward to for so long had come. All the people he wanted to share the story with were in the same room at the same time, and they were all talking nonsense. He had to get their attention and fast-forward the events that would follow.

"Excuse me," Fred said. Everyone turned. The expression on the rancher's face was all that was needed to get the trio's undivided attention.

Helen looked worried. "What, Fred?" she finally asked.

"If you would join me in the den." Fred swung his arm

in the direction of the hall. He pointed to the small round conference table near the corner of the pine-paneled den. A special bay window had been constructed for the corner that allowed sunlight to bathe most of the room in a warm glow throughout the day. The view was of the northwest pasture, which spread a half mile to the base of a cliff that rose 75 feet to a ridge lined with a cluster of wind-twisted juniper. On the table lay a manila folder; next to the folder stood a gold candlestick.

Fred slid a chair back for his wife and waited for her to sit, something he hadn't done in months. Helen glanced at Robert, who appeared as shocked as she was. When everyone was seated, Fred pulled the folder toward him but didn't open it. The anticipation swelled. The rancher was not especially skilled in lecturing. He hesitated, looked at the folder then the candlestick, avoiding personal eye contact while he thought of a way to put his story in an understandable sequence. He began. "Jeremiah and Hannah Gray were part of the land run of 1893, staking claim to the land this house is now on. Over the years, following the run, settlers decided farming and ranching in such wasteland was not for them, and they'd sell their holdings for next to nothing. My grandparents purchased a lot of this land, and that's how the ranch grew from a hundred and sixty acres to twenty thousand. Life was difficult, impossible for some, in the Cherokee Outlet portion of Oklahoma Territory. Problems between Indians and pioneers brought the cavalry to protect the settlers and wagon trains. Small towns were springing up and the railroad was being built. With all the growth came the usual criminal element. Wagon trains headed west were attacked by Indians and criminals. One in four died of disease before they were twenty. If one thing didn't get ya, something else would." Fred paused, collecting his thoughts, trying to imagine the hardships of that era.

"One day, as the story goes, my grandfather was freeing a calf that had gotten its hoof stuck between a rock outcropping and a cedar sapling. After the calf scampered off, Jeremiah noticed a cave that had been hidden by the outcropping and could only be seen from the one angle. He was curious, but it was late in the day and he didn't have the makings for a torch, so he marked the cave's location and went home. A month or so later, he returned to the cave earlier in the day, this time with a torch he'd made with a fresh cedar limb, an old bedsheet, and some kerosene. He was ready to explore."

Fred opened the file folder and took out three Xerox copies of the page from Book 5 and handed one to each person. "There are many entries on this page that relate to events important to the landowners specifically, and some related to the developing community in general." He gave them time to read the page. "Those old journals at the courthouse are a wealth of knowledge of how, when, where, and who pioneered this country before and after the government opened the land to settlers." Another pause while they continued to study the page.

"I'm assuming that you are focusing on this drawing in the margin next to an entry made by your grandfather?" Lee asked.

Fred nodded. "That scribbling, plus the story Grandfather Gray told me when I was about ten, got my curiosity up. As I studied the drawing, it became clear that it wasn't a map, but a picture of a location."

"Picture of what?" Robert asked.

"Turn the copy sideways. Look familiar?"

"Still looks like scribbling to me."

"See this rise and how it drops off to these three squiggly lines?"

"Yeah, so?" Robert sounded frustrated.

"The rise is the hill southwest of Little Bear Creek, these lines are the three tributaries, and where Jeremiah put the dot is high on the middle tributary. It's hard to see because of all the growth in the last hundred years."

Robert studied his page more closely. "And the dot's where the cave is?"

"Yes."

"But why would he make this drawing in a public record?" Helen asked.

"I believe Jeremiah went into town after purchasing land from a neighbor to officially document the purchase, just as the entry says there. Since he had pen in hand and paper to write on, he drew the location, knowing no one else would be able to interpret it. He wanted a record somewhere, and the only paper he had at home was a well-worn copy of the Bible, and he wouldn't have written anything in that Bible. That's my guess."

"So you think Jeremiah just wanted a place to record his discovery without spelling out what the discovery was, and the ledger provided him the opportunity?" Robert asked.

"That's what I think. Ya know, I've been all over that land for the past seventy-some years, and if I hadn't known every inch of those twenty thousand acres, I don't think I could find the location. That's what Jeremiah was counting on."

Lee studied his copy. "So you believe his intent was to return to the cave?"

"Without a doubt."

"Did he?" Lee asked.

"No. If I recall the story correctly, Jeremiah assumed the candlestick was loot from a wagon train robbery. Hundreds of families were moving lock, stock, and barrel from the east to California. The wagon trains hired their own security for protection, but even with hired guns they were sitting ducks for Indian war parties and bands of outlaws. The cavalry usually tracked the culprits down and either shot or hanged 'em, but by then it was too late for the settlers. Anyway, Jeremiah brought the candlestick back to the house and showed it to Grandma."

"And what'd she do?" Robert asked.

"Grandma Gray was levelheaded, always the voice of reason, smart. She told Jeremiah, in no uncertain terms, that he was to leave the loot alone, if in fact there was more, and never go back to the location."

Robert interrupted his dad. "Why'd she do that?"

"For good reason. In her mind, she believed if outlaws hid the loot in the cave and came back to get it and it wasn't there, they'd come lookin' for the landowner, assuming, on their part, the landowner found it and was benefiting from the outlaw's plunder. They both agreed to leave it alone for fear of harm coming to the family."

"Yes, I understand her reasoning," Helen said. "What happened then?"

"Nothing. Grandfather Gray told me the story another time or two. I couldn't have been more'n ten, eleven years old at the time. I think he told me the story so I'd help him look for it, but I was too young to understand, and he was too feeble to hike around those canyons. His mind started slippin' shortly after that, and he never brought it up again. I didn't give it much thought till 1956."

"1956? What happened then?" Robert asked.

Fred explained that his father sold some land to pay for school tuition, and the sale required an updated abstract with a legal land description.

"Since Dad hated paperwork and didn't like coming to town, he told me to do the record search. That's the first time I laid eyes on that drawing."

"Why'd you wait so long to search for the location?" Helen asked.

Fred reached over and laid his hand on Helen's arm. "You and the kids," he said, smiling.

"We're an excuse or a reason?"

"A reason. If you'll recall, that was about the time we started dating, then marriage. I was interested in you, not deciphering my grandfather's scribbling. Then kids came, and the ranch had to be tended to. Frankly, I forgot about it. When Robert took over the day-to-day operation of the ranch earlier this year, I had time to think for the first time in fifty years."

Helen smiled. "Sounds like a good reason. What'd you do then?"

"Had a copy made of that page and started looking for terrain similar to the drawing. I located the cave 'bout mid-March, gave the entrance a quick inspection, looking for snake dens. I wanted to do some exploring before snakes started crawling to sun. After three nights of below freezing temperatures, I thought it safe to enter the cave and look around. Dug around in bat manure off and on for the next week and luckily found no snakes, but didn't find anything else, either."

Helen and Robert were growing anxious, even impatient with the way Fred was telling the story. "Dad, would you get to the point?!" Fred pulled his chair closer to the table. The gesture drew the others into a close huddle, suggesting a secret was about to be revealed and concern someone was listening who shouldn't be. The phone rang. Robert answered, "Gray Ranch, Robert speaking."

Helen excused herself and went to the kitchen to make sandwiches. Lee and Fred listened to the one-sided conversation. Robert frowned and glanced at Fred then Lee.

"Tell me your name again? And you're an intern at the *Ledger*?" There was a pause while the person on the other end spoke.

"Yes, the excavation is scheduled in two weeks." Another pause. "Dr. Bethel is in charge."

Robert looked concerned, and his tone changed. "Who told you that?!"

The caller explained. Robert took notes and replied, "You'll need to talk with Dr. Bethel about that, but I don't see a problem with you coming to visit the site." Robert looked at Lee for a confirmation, and Lee nodded. "As for the journal page," Robert looked at his dad, "I don't know anything about that. He's not in the house now; you'll need to call back." Robert lied; he knew his dad would need time to think about the intern's request before answering questions.

"What was that about?" Fred asked.

"Says he's a journalism intern at the *Buffalo Ledger*. Wants to do a story on the dig. He asked if he could interview Lee."

"That's not a problem; publicity is good for the university. Lets people know what we're doing."

Fred interrupted. "What'd he say about the journal?"

"He asked what the significance of the page from the historical journals was. You heard what I told him."

"Yeah, I heard, but how'd he get that information? Damn it, this is get'n outta hand."

"What do you mean 'out of hand'?" Lee asked.

"This is my fault. I knew better, but it was too late. Remember, Lee, when I said someone was watching me?"

"Yeah, I remember it well. Was concerned."

Robert had listened to the exchange between his dad and Lee. "Whoa, whoa, whoa. Stop! What in the hell are you two talking about!?"

"We're off track, Robert. Gimme a minute to explain."

Helen entered the den pushing a serving cart loaded with food and iced tea. As she made her way to the table, she could feel the swirl of emotion between Fred and Robert.

"Okay, gentlemen," Helen said, trying to ease the tension. "Let's relax and enjoy lunch. We can continue after nourishment," she went on without giving the others an opportunity to speak. "Lee, I understand your wife is accompanying you this year on the excavation site."

"She actually wants to finish her dissertation, and she thought working a site would get her back on track."

"She's an archaeologist also?"

"Amateur only. She's getting her PhD in anthropology."

"Please let her know she's welcome to stay here at the house. I'd love to have another woman around to talk to."

"I will. She'll appreciate a shower and a soft bed. Beverly's an outdoor person, loves to hike, but at night she enjoys her creature comforts."

The food and casual conversation had its desired effect; Robert and his father were relaxed, but eager to continue.

CHAPTER 9

Helen cleared the conference table. Fred was even more anxious to finish the story. He cleared his throat, wiped his sweaty hands on the bandana he'd pulled from his pocket. "I knew something else had to be in that cave besides one lonely candlestick. I dug around for several days, didn't find a thing. I was about to give up. *One more day*, I thought. I stood outside the cave entrance looking around and noticed a mound of dirt about eighteen inches high near the opening of a smaller cave just left of the one I'd been work'n. I'd seen the opening but hadn't given it any thought. Instead of digging, I got a two-foot long piece of quarter-inch rebar out of the truck, crawled in, and started probing. I inserted the bar into the mound and struck something solid the first time. Instead of a shovel, I used one of Helen's garden tools and began scraping layers of dirt and bat manure away, and there it was."

"What?" Robert asked.

"That's what I'm gonna show you this afternoon. You'll all see it at the same time. I didn't do any more digging once I figured out what it was I struck with the probe."

"Why?"

Fred waved in Lee's direction. "Because of what I learned from Lee."

"And what'd you learn from me?" Lee cocked his head to one side and squinted, looking doubtful.

"I'd been on the bison kill site enough when you were teaching students. Let's see if I can quote you accurately: 'Proper excavation is absolutely necessary in order to preserve the immediate environment for identification purposes.' I knew what I'd found needed to be properly ID'd."

Lee smiled. "Thank God someone listened."

Fred looked at his watch. "We'd better head to the cave before we lose any more sunlight. I'll tell you more on the way. I loaded tools in the truck earlier, and there's bottled water in the ice chest."

Robert and Lee slid into the short backseats of the F-250 extended cab, Helen into the front passenger seat, and Fred got in behind the wheel. Bear tried to climb in through Fred's door. "No, Bear." Fred reached down and scratched the dog's ear. "You gotta stay here and protect the house." Bear gave a snort of disapproval and backed away from the truck.

Fred engaged the truck's four-wheel drive, shifted into drive, and headed southwest over a cattle guard into the pasture. "After I discovered what was in the cave in March, I took the candlestick with me to Oklahoma City to a man I discovered on the Internet. Robert had business at the stockyards, and while he was there, I met Paul Hansen. He buys and sells antiques and does appraisals. His Web site says he specializes in ancient artifacts and gold. He seemed knowledgeable, a down-to-earth kind of fella."

The rancher eased the truck over the side of a steep embankment into a draw not much wider than the truck, inching along until the draw opened up on a dry, rocky creek bed. He stopped and pointed. "See that tall cottonwood and the cedar grove?"

Everyone looked in the direction Fred was pointing. "I've been around that tree a hundred times," Robert said. "Is that it?"

"Yup." Fred put the truck back in drive, moving over the creek bottom and into sagebrush. The windows on the truck were down, and the scent of spring sage filled the cab. Helen closed her eyes and inhaled the aroma—next to fresh baked bread, it was her favorite smell.

"I'd never done business with an antique dealer. Guess I didn't know what to expect. I felt at ease when we talked. That's why I told him more'n I should. Anyway, Hansen examined the candlestick thoroughly. He pointed out some peculiarities."

"What kind?" Lee asked.

"Things in its design he said would help identify who made it and when. When Hansen finished his examination, he asked if it was a family heirloom and if there was a mate. I told him Grandfather's story, and soon as I did I realized two things."

"What two things?" Helen asked.

"That I'd given this stranger far too much information, and that he knew something about the candlestick he was keeping to himself. Now that I think about it, I even told him about the historical journal and drawing. Hansen said all the information I could share about it would ultimately help with the appraisal. What a fool I was."

"What happened then?" Lee asked.

"Hansen took several photographs, wrote down everything I said, wrapped the candlestick, and handed it back to me. He said to put it in a safe place, be careful with it, and he'd be in touch soon."

"That was two and a half months ago. What'd he mean by soon?" Helen asked.

"Don't know. I didn't want to call him until you three were told."

Fred brought the truck to a stop at the mouth of a narrow, shallow canyon. "We're still a quarter mile from the cave, but this is as far as we can go in the truck. Only way in is on foot."

They got out of the truck, opened the water bottles, and drank. The temperature was somewhere in the mid-90s, with no breeze to cool the sweat. Robert reached over, tapping his dad on the shoulder. "Looks like fresh ATV tracks coming down that slope and into the canyon in the direction of the cave."

"Any of our hands had the Ranger out lately?"

"No. As a matter of fact, it's got a flat."

Fred walked over to take a closer look at the imprint. "Ain't our tire tread." He followed the tire tracks with his eyes until they disappeared from sight. "Tracks can't be more'n two, three days old." The rancher lifted his work Stetson high enough above his head to wipe the sweat off his forehead and muttered words he didn't want Helen to hear.

"Let's see where the tracks lead us," Lee said, pushing a cedar branch out of his way. Helen had already started up the draw. The presence of an intruder added urgency to an already anxious situation. Their pace quickened without regard to the stifling heat that had settled down over them like a thermal blanket. Fred took a shortcut he'd found earlier and was now ahead of the other three. He summited the sandstone outcropping that guarded the cave and its contents. Fred could see someone had been there recently—broken tree branches, ATV tracks, footprints. The others joined him, but no one said anything. It was obvious Fred was fuming inside, blaming himself for the careless way he had shared information with Hansen.

CHAPTER 10

Tobias Henry put some finishing touches to the opening lines of his article and closed the document. It was 4:00 p.m. He'd have just enough time to drive home, shower, and be back in town for his date with Audrey. Life back in the small dusty cow town, population 2,500 according to the sign marking the city limits, had taken an unexpected turn. He'd expected an uneventful, boring summer complicated by the tension sure to surface between him and his parents. So far the opposite had been true.

Tobias had never been inside Audrey's home. The two had been friends in school, but nothing more. She was a cheerleader, a good student—from what he could remember—and athlete. Audrey lettered in basketball and hung out with the jocks. She was out of his league, he remembered thinking. As he turned onto the street where Audrey lived, he fought momentarily with his recollection of how inadequate he'd felt in high school, wishing again, for the millionth time, he could do it over.

He looked at his watch: 5:58. *Perfect timing*, he thought

as he rang the doorbell. Mrs. Spencer answered and invited him in. The house was small, tastefully decorated with a freshly updated kitchen that included new appliances. He could tell she was proud of her home.

"Welcome, Tobias, make yourself comfortable. Audrey should be out soon."

He sat down in a leather chair. The TV was on, and the evening news had just started. The breaking news at that moment was about a grass fire threatening fashionable homes near Oklahoma City. Tobias wondered if the fire would have been *breaking news* if the homes weren't fashionable. Mrs. Spencer returned from the hallway. "How about something to drink while you wait?"

"No thanks. You have a beautiful home. Looks like you've done some remodeling."

"Last winter, and let me tell you, I never want to go through that again."

"Problems?"

"One after another. Don't like to think about it. By the way, did you get a chance to talk to Mr. Gray?"

"Sort of. When I got back to the *Ledger*, I called, but he wasn't there. Talked with his son Robert."

"What did he say?"

"Not much. He was kind of evasive. Sounded irritated when I asked about the drawing."

"Don't you imagine, with all the attention that journal page has gotten lately, the Grays are getting suspicious?"

Audrey hurried into the living room, fumbling with her handbag. "I'm so sorry I've kept you waiting! The hair dryer decided to quit before I was finished." She slid her cell phone into a side attachment and kissed her mother. "We'll be back by midnight." Audrey turned to Tobias for confirmation; he nodded.

"Have a good time," Mrs. Spencer said as Tobias and

her daughter hurried down the steps.

Tobias guided his car the short distance to 183 south. He knew it was a 30-minute drive to the restaurant, and he'd rehearsed subjects to talk about, hoping to fill the awkward void that usually accompanied his dating disasters. "So, tell me again where you're going to school?" he asked as he fumbled with the radio dial.

The entire evening rushed by much too fast, as far as Tobias was concerned. He'd gotten to know Audrey; they had shared likes, dislikes, aspirations, and even a few secrets. They laughed at each other's perceived hang-ups and realized, after all, that their high school apprehensions were baseless.

"Look." Audrey pointed in the direction of her home as they approached. "Mom's still waiting up."

"Yeah, mine does too. Guess we'll always be children to our parents."

Tobias pulled into the drive and shut the engine and radio off. This was not a date, he told himself, only the rekindling of a friendship. That way he could relax and not be pressured to advance a romantic conclusion to the evening. Not that he didn't want to. He'd always thought Audrey was attractive, but her ability to make him feel comfortable and the soft, sweet way she related to him made her even more attractive that night. They sat silently, Audrey looking toward her mother's house. The living room light went out, and only the glow of the porch light remained.

"I've had a great time tonight," she said.

"I have, too. Maybe we can do this again sometime." He realized as soon as he uttered those words that his meaning sounded vague, even a little standoffish. Another example of his poor social skills, the result, he was sure, of spending most of his life on a ranch in the middle of nowhere. "What I meant to say was let's do this again soon." Before she could answer, he went on nervously. "How 'bout Saturday? We could ride horses at the ranch. You ride, don't you?"

"Yes, I love to ride, but we're visiting relatives in Amarillo. How about a rain check?"

"A rain check it is. I'll call you next week." At one level Tobias was disappointed, but at another he was relieved. She'd asked for a rain check, leaving the door open. This would give him time to think about his feelings toward her. He had his future to think about, and she had hers—could they both afford the distraction? As he walked her to the porch, he felt light-headed; his knees seemed weak, and he prayed they wouldn't buckle. Through the mix of emotions bouncing around inside him like a basketball in an F-4 tornado, he realized one important thing: this wasn't how the average person felt when renewing a friendship.

The intern arrived early the next morning, anxious to get started on the article Judith Baker had suggested. Two thoughts fought for his attention: the date with Audrey, and the strange scribbling in the margin of Book 5. He hurried by Baker's desk, hoping to avoid the casual morning small talk. He wasn't fast enough.

"Good morning, Tobias, how are you this morning?"

"Fine, Judith, and you?"

"Wonderful. Beautiful spring morning, great cup of coffee, nice people to work with. As the commercial says— it doesn't get any better than this."

Tobias sat down, flipped open his laptop, and was poised to type when he realized Judith was still talking.

"So, tell me about your date last night?"

He stared at the laptop keyboard, not wanting to make eye contact with Baker. He didn't want to encourage more questions. "Wasn't really a date. Audrey and I went to school together; we ran into each other at the courthouse and decided to catch up. That's it." He hoped his answer would end the dialogue.

"You know, I live two houses down from Audrey's mother, and I saw you two leave there around six last evening. I'm just a snoop, comes from working at a newspaper for so long." Baker turned back to her computer and began typing.

Tobias hoped he hadn't acted rude or impatient. He liked Judith and he didn't want to offend her, but there had been too many distractions already. He needed to get busy on his article. He pulled earphones out of his Lands' End laptop case and put them on but didn't turn the music on. The earphones would block distracting noises and allow him to concentrate. He began typing.

After you have read this article, step outside and take time to look at the ground beneath you and the plains, canyons, creeks and rivers that surround us. Imagine for just a moment that you are watching a herd of woolly mammoth grazing in the distance. You must be careful not to startle the huge animals and cause them to move farther away, making it that much more difficult to kill one in order to feed your tribe. There are no modern weapons or tools to help you accomplish the task before you, only stone implements to assist in the killing and butchering of this magnificent beast. You and your people have been following this herd for several days and have drawn only slightly closer. The small group of hunters that you are a part of must make a kill soon so the thirty or so members of your tribe will survive. Some of the elders and the very young are already suffering the effects of malnutrition... The intern continued to type, his thoughts unobstructed but knowing interruption could come at any time.

CHAPTER 11

Crystal Stanton's secretary, Maude Bingham, who also doubled as a daytime dispatcher and jailer, when on rare occasions the county had a female inmate, reached across the sheriff's desk and handed her a business card. The card revealed the usual information about the person waiting outside her door. Ralph Peterson, Landman, Sooner Exploration. There was no address or landline number, only a cell number. Sheriff Stanton was already suspicious before Peterson ever crossed the threshold. The lack of information on the business card raised the question she'd been trained to ask: What's he hiding? The sheriff looked at Maude. "What's this guy want?"

"All he said was it's important and personal."

"Okay, but in ten minutes stick your head in the door and tell me I'm late for an appointment."

Maude nodded, swung the door open, and invited Peterson in. Stanton motioned for him to have a chair. "What can I do for you, Mr. Peterson?" She was friendly but unmistakably in charge.

"We have an acquaintance in common." Peterson paused, waiting for a reply. Stanton didn't oblige, opting instead to let the visitor play his hand first.

"Does the name Gerald Webster sound familiar? Everyone calls him Jerry."

Stanton uncrossed her arms, hoping the intentional gesture would invite more information. "Yes, I know a Jerry Webster."

"Let's cut to the chase," he said.

"Agreed. I'm a busy woman. Now, as I asked before, what can I do for you?"

Peterson scooted to the edge of the wooden chair he was seated in to emphasize the importance of what he was about to say. "As you know, Jerry Webster is now the Assistant Director in Charge of the New York field office. My boss answers directly to him and is in charge of the Criminal Investigative Division. I'm FBI agent Carl Holt, working undercover as Ralph Peterson. I've been instructed to confide in you and you only, and here is the SAC's number for verification."

Stanton allowed herself a question. "Before I call anybody, I want more details of your undercover operation, specifically how the hell you ended up in my town!"

"I'll answer that but not here in your office. I don't want to draw attention to myself, so I suggest we end our conversation here. You can tell your deputy that I just wanted to bring attention to a possible cattle thief in the area, if she asks, and you can send me on my way. If I stay in your office long enough to explain the details of the operation, it might raise suspicion among your deputies, and I can't take that chance."

Stanton saw the logic in Holt's request. A long meeting behind closed doors would raise the deputy's curiosity and probably the curiosity of the entire courthouse. Stanton had been at the center of the small town rumor mill before and had successfully overcome the lies generated, she assumed, by her detractors. The previous sheriff had been in office ten years, and as each year passed, he and his deputies seemed more and more complacent, slow to respond to routine calls and, in some cases, abusive to jail inmates. After she was elected sheriff, all kinds of stories surfaced about her, none true, but nevertheless troublesome as she established her presence in the community. She was now into her third year, and her reputation couldn't be better. Stanton was not only viewed as a good law enforcement officer but a good community citizen.

"So what do you suggest, Mr. Peterson?"

"Is there somewhere we can speak privately?"

"Yes. I'll draw you a map." The sheriff pulled a legal pad from her lap drawer and began to draw. She tore off the page, scooted it across her desk to Peterson, and explained the directions. He studied the map then ripped it into several pieces and threw it in a waste can sitting to the left side of the sheriff's desk.

"Will three p.m. work for you?" Stanton asked.

"Perfect."

They stood, the meeting lasting just under ten minutes, and as Peterson turned to leave, Maude stepped in and reminded the sheriff of her appointment.

"Thanks for the heads-up, Mr. Peterson. I'll have a deputy check on that."

Maude heard the exchange, which was the sheriff's intention, and as soon as Peterson was out of sight, she turned to Stanton waiting to be briefed. "Well?"

"Well what, deputy?"

"What'd he want?"

"Peterson?"

"Yeah, Peterson."

"He's just trying to be a good citizen. Landman out of the city checking on survey information. Says he saw unusual activity on a ranch south of town, thought it might be cattle rustlers."

"Want me to send a deputy down there?"

"No, I've got some business that direction; I'll check it out myself."

The sheriff rifled through papers from her in-tray, hoping her casual, business-as-usual demeanor would satisfy Maude's curiosity. It did.

"Maude, I've got errands to run, then I'll check out Peterson's suspicion. I won't be back the rest of the day. Contact me if you need something."

Maude nodded and returned to her desk. Deputy Sheriff Maude Bingham had been at that same desk for 20 years, the only holdover from the previous sheriff. For the first time during those many years of dedicated service, she felt a part of the organization, an important part. No boss had ever given her the level of responsibility she now had, much less the pay. At 64, Bingham was the senior staff member, and Sheriff Stanton accorded her a level of respect she'd never felt before. Most of Maude's job was secretarial, and that's how she'd been treated; however, when Stanton took over, her first act was to promote Bingham to Deputy of Administration. This included dispatch scheduling and female incarceration oversight, jobs she was doing already and not being compensated for. Bingham didn't carry a weapon, but she wore the same deputy badge her peers did. She was proud of her position and thankful to the sheriff for elevating her title to reflect work she'd been doing for so long.

Maude thought about her first encounter with Crystal Stanton, just four years earlier. She'd gone into the local feed and hardware store, owned and operated by Crystal's parents, to buy some garden tools. As she was checking out, Crystal's mother, Margaret, asked her if she'd ever met her daughter. After the introduction, Margaret mentioned that Crystal might be returning to Buffalo to take over the family business. Maude remembered wondering why a beautiful, apparently single woman would want to live here. Maybe a messy divorce and she had nowhere else to go. She learned the complete story after Crystal was elected sheriff.

Crystal Stanton graduated with honors from the University of Wisconsin with a master's degree in criminology. She didn't have to look long for a job; as a matter of fact, she didn't have to look at all. Three months before she graduated, Crystal received a letter from the human resources division of the Federal Bureau of Investigation, inviting her to apply for the position of special agent. On a whim she applied, took the required exams, and at 23 became the youngest woman to graduate the academy in Quantico, Virginia. At 40 she'd concluded her tour of duty as a counterterrorism expert assigned to Luxembourg, Belgium. She returned to the U.S. and was assigned to Headquarters in Washington DC, a position she later regretted accepting. Stanton was used to working independently, a self-starter all her life, motivated by job satisfaction and not money or accolades from superiors. Headquarters, to her, was the epitome of confusion and government waste. After three years behind the walls of what field agents called the puzzle palace, she was discouraged, ready to leave. Stanton knew she was being groomed for a high-ranking job, possibly an assistant director position, but the bureaucracy was stifling. The longer she stayed, the more disheartened she became. She was ready to transfer, possibly to Homeland Security, when she received a phone call that changed everything.

Crystal's father was succumbing to Lou Gehrig's disease, and the burden of caring for him and running the store was too much for her mother to do alone. She was needed at home and was at rest with that decision.

Within 60 days of her mother's phone call, Crystal was living with her parents and operating the store. Six months later, her father died. The emotional and physical strain her mother had endured took its toll as well, and within a year, Margaret died from complications brought on by a stroke.

According to Maude's source, six months after Margaret Stanton died, a few concerned citizens approached Crystal suggesting she consider running for sheriff, and as they say, the rest is history.

Just then the phone rang; Maude shifted skillfully from her daydream state to all business. "Sheriff's Office, Deputy Bingham speaking," she answered with authority.

CHAPTER 12

Paul Hansen had been in the business of buying, selling, and appraising antiques a long time and thought he'd seen just about everything, but when the rancher brought the candlestick in for appraisal, he knew that assumption was wrong. From his cursory assessment, it was obvious the candlestick was very old, European in design. To think that the rancher said his grandfather found it on their ranch a hundred years ago only added to the mystery. Hansen knew of a few people who would, perhaps, be able to identify the artifact; he'd start with Monica Bouvier in New York City. She was well known within the circle of experts on ancient antiquities.

After two days of trying to track Bouvier down, he finally got through. Hansen sensed that she was all business and not inclined to engage in small talk. He got right to the point. "Ms. Bouvier, I have a photo of a gold candlestick and an interesting story that accompanies its discovery. Would you have time to look at the photo and give me your assessment?"

"I'll do the best I can. You realize, of course, Mr.

Hansen, appraising a photo is far from the professional standards we try to adhere to. No guarantees can be made; it'll be an educated guess at best."

"Yes, I completely understand. I'll send the photos and story via an e-mail attachment as soon as we conclude our conversation. And may I ask your fee?"

"I charge the standard fee of two hundred dollars for a single-piece appraisal. It will be at least a month before I can get back with you. Is that satisfactory?"

"Yes. The piece has been in the owner's family for a hundred years, so I can't imagine another thirty days would make a difference."

Hansen prepared the e-mail and attachment and clicked send. He made out a check in the amount specified, addressed the envelope, and dropped it in the outgoing mail stack. Hansen picked up the original photograph and studied it again, wishing Bouvier could appraise the piece more quickly. He had his own thoughts, but then he wasn't an expert in ancient artifacts. Hansen knew his gold, the antique stuff that circulated from one investor to another, but the candlestick had barely distinguishable markings that set it apart from what he normally dealt with.

Two weeks later Hansen received a phone call from Bouvier. Again, she was brief, businesslike, and to the point, her French accent barely perceptible but obviously her first language. "Mr. Hansen, I've concluded my assessment of the photo, and I will forward it in writing today. In the meantime, I'll tell you what I think."

Hansen grabbed a notepad and a pen, anxious to hear what this expert had to say.

"I believe the item to be of the purest gold, probably made sometime in the mid-1800s and the origin, I would guess without seeing it up close, to be southern France or Spain."

Hansen felt disappointment settling over him. Bouvier was right about the gold purity and right about its geographic origin, he thought, but her guess at the year it was crafted was off, maybe by as much as three hundred years. This was a mistake he didn't think an expert would make.

"And its value?" Hansen asked.

"If your measurements are correct, the quality is as high as I suspect from looking at photographs only, I would guess the candlestick would bring three thousand dollars, maybe more at a proper auction."

Hansen scribbled notes, hardly aware that Bouvier had paused.

"Mr. Hansen, are you still there?"

"Yes, I'm sorry, just taking some notes."

"I would be willing to offer the owner twenty-five hundred dollars, after authentication of course."

"Of course. I'll pass your appraisal on and your offer and will get back to you later."

Hansen hadn't anticipated the expert making such an error, if in fact it was an error. Maybe she was intentionally misleading him, but why? The more he thought about the conversation, the more he mistrusted her assessment. After Mr. Gray brought the candlestick in for an appraisal, Hansen did some research on his own, a customary tactic of his. He'd learned years earlier when asking for a second opinion that he should try to know the answer beforehand. In this case, the second opinion didn't line up with his research. Hansen was sure of one thing. Bouvier's appraisal was authentic enough to fool the average dealer and certainly authentic enough to fool an owner like Fred Gray.

He pulled a file from his desk labeled Gray Ranch and opened it, thumbing through the documents he had generated since his first encounter with the rancher a few weeks earlier. Hansen found the original story about how the candlestick had been found, the one he sent along with the photo to Bouvier. He felt a wave of anxiety move slowly throughout his body. He looked closely; there it was in bold type—FRED GRAY, BUFFALO, OK. His initial reaction was anger, anger at himself for being careless enough to include a client's personal information in a second opinion request, and anger with Bouvier for playing him like a drum. He clicked on his list of phone numbers and made two phone calls to area professors who might be able to refer him to an expert that was not a dealer—a person interested in the artifact for its historical value rather than its dollar value.

A few days later, Hansen received the call he'd been waiting for, from a friend who taught European history at a local university. His advice was to contact Dr. Diego de Cordona, Professor of Hispanic Culture at the Universidad Antonio de Nebrija (UAN) in Madrid, an expert in Spanish antiquities. This time Hansen sent only photos of the candlestick, along with a short note explaining how he got the professor's name. An hour later, Hansen received an e-mail reply from Dr. Cordona's assistant, acknowledging receipt of the photo and stating that he could expect a response from Cordona in several weeks. Hansen decided to wait for Dr. Cordona's response before contacting the rancher.

He typed in Bouvier's e-mail address—subject: Candlestick. *Ms. Bouvier, Contacted owner and he declined to sell. Thank you for your appraisal...Paul Hansen, Hansen Antiques and Appraisals Inc.*

Hansen hoped this would discourage Bouvier from any further contact with him, and especially with Fred Gray.

CHAPTER 13

T wo years earlier, FBI agent Carl Holt had been assigned to work with the CIA, ATF, and Homeland Security to disrupt and arrest a ring of thieves, forgers, counterfeiters, and con-men who were supplying known terrorist groups with financing. The ring had various business fronts such as coffee shops, antique, book, and appliance stores, car rental agencies, and flower shops around the globe. Businesses that could easily be dismantled and moved or abandoned at a moment's notice, all for the purpose of laundering and funneling money into the terrorists' war chest. Monica Bouvier was identified as one of the central figures within the criminal organization in the U.S.

Moroccan born, Bouvier moved as a child with her parents to Paris, then as a teenager to New York City where her father joined his brother in the men's clothing business. Although Monica's parents practiced a much more contemporary form of Muslim worship, Monica remained true to a more fundamentalist view. This separation in religious beliefs ultimately resulted in a serious rift between Monica and her family. The closeness the Bouviers once enjoyed suffered; calls came less frequently, and visits didn't occur at all. The parents were proud of their daughter's accomplishments and marveled at how rapidly she'd risen to her present leadership position but were saddened by the fact her success had apparently estranged their relationship.

Holt's assignment was to track Monica Bouvier's movements, and that included wiretaps. Evidence continued to mount in the federal case against the international criminal organization Bouvier was suspected to be a major part of, but the government was reluctant to make arrests until the net had been cast as far as possible.

The CIA had been tasked to monitor all of Bouvier's phone calls, text messaging, and e-mail. Many were routine, or at least made to sound routine, many were suspicious, and about one-third were coded messages. The counterterrorism division of the FBI believed the coded messages were for the purpose of activating a cell member or members to carry out orders previously issued by officials within the terrorist network.

In March, a call was intercepted from Paul Hansen to Bouvier, which the analyst flagged. The call was simply about an artifact, and the dealer, Hansen, wanting an appraisal from Bouvier. No coded message was detected; however, it was CIA protocol to follow the route the message took until positive assurance could be given that it was not a potential threat to national security. Shortly after this seemingly benign call regarding a candlestick was intercepted, another came through that raised the level of required follow-up to "report" status. The computer detected a coded message within the call, and the analyst was cued to follow up with a written document to be ultimately used with human intelligence in the investigative process. After a thorough analysis and cross-analysis, the document was forwarded to the Special Agent in Charge (SAC) and to the field agent, in this case, Carl Holt. Agent Holt read the deciphered message: ***Possible important find worth millions. Need further investigation for verification. Ref: Journal (Book 5), name: Jeremiah Gray. County cths. Leave now. Destination BufOK. Rancher Fred Gray. ABSOLUTE DISCRETION.***

This coded message was sent from Bouvier to a mercenary for hire from San Diego by the name of Elliot Heath. The FBI knew Heath well and had followed his activities for some time, which always seemed to be on the edge of criminal activity but nothing the Feds could hold him on, much less make a legitimate arrest. As far as the FBI knew, he'd never been mixed up with Muslim terrorists. A profiler had labeled him a polished con-man and a true sociopath. He could sell refrigerators to the Eskimos and talk a nun into marriage. Holt had heard that Heath could cut someone's throat without much provocation, leaving no evidence behind. He was intelligent, resourceful, cunning, and exceptionally confident at his trade, which made him a formidable foe. Elliot Heath was an ordinary-looking white man who could easily pass himself off as the neighborhood bank vice president or perhaps even a ranch hand.

CHAPTER 14

As far as Fred Gray could tell, whoever had been to the cave had not found the smaller opening. He was relieved. Motioning for the others to follow, Fred hurried down the embankment, pushing cedar limbs and thorny plum thicket branches aside as he made his way to the bottom of the small canyon where the mouth of the smaller cave was. Everyone's pace quickened. Robert called out to his father, who was ahead of the group, "Dad, slow down, you're not twenty-five!" No one, not even his mother heeded his plea. They were almost there.

Robert and Lee caught up with Fred and his wife just as the rancher was getting on his knees to crawl inside. Helen grabbed Fred by the shirt collar, issuing orders for him to slow down. He swung around and sat down. "Let's all take a breather," Helen cautioned.

"You're right. It's hot and I'm thirsty," Fred said.

Robert handed Fred his water bottle, and everyone sat down in the shade of the rocky overhang to catch their breath. Fred poured water on his head and sucked in as much of the hot afternoon air as his lungs would hold, then inhaled a second time. "You all right?" Helen asked.

"Fine, just getting some air."

Lee got to his feet. "I'm gonna take a look at the larger cave." He disappeared around the dirt embankment that separated the two caves and was back in less than a minute. "Looks like whoever was here worked that cave over pretty good. Didn't even make an effort to explore over here."

"Yup, fortunately for us, he made the same mistake I did."

Robert was on his knees, flashlight in hand, scouting for rattlesnakes around the opening of the smaller cave. "I don't see anything."

"Okay. There's just barely enough room for two inside the cave. Lee's the archaeologist, the expert, so I want him in there with me." He paused to draw in more air. "Dear, this is gonna take some time. Would you and Robert take the truck up on the ridge and watch for intruders? Hate to ask you, but that uneasy feeling I've had lately just got uneasier."

"What do you want us to do if we see someone?" Robert asked.

"That's another reason I want you on the ridge—you got cell reception there. If you see anyone, call the sheriff."

"Honey, don't you think we should call her anyway? With all that's goin' on, I'm concerned."

"Absolutely not! I don't want anyone to know about this till we see what's here."

Robert and his mother started for the truck. Fred and Lee entered the cave, which turned out to be nothing more than a channel made by water flow escaping from the main cave over eons of time. Fred set the high-powered light on a small ledge and pointed it toward the mound. The glow exposed where Fred had originally dug. He handed Lee the garden tool. "Prepare to be surprised!" Lee took the tool and began scraping soil away from the mound.

CHAPTER 15

Robert and his mother drove to the ridge and parked. There were no trees large enough to provide shade, and a stiff south breeze made sitting just bearable. Neither seemed aware of the heat, though, their thoughts immersed deep in the events of the day, wondering what was unfolding before their very eyes. From the ridge they could see five to ten miles in most directions. Grain elevators in the small, almost deserted town of Selman, and Buffalo, the county seat, were visible to the north and northwest. The Cimarron River to the northeast and following the river farther east, the Cargill salt plant. To the south a series of canyons and arroyos that appeared as fingers pointing in the direction of lower elevation, and finally to a dry creek bed that eventually dumped rain runoff into the river. The sight to city dwellers was desolate and foreboding, but to Robert and his mother it was home.

"It may not be the prettiest place on earth, but I love it here. With all that's going on in the world, this is where I want to be. It's so quiet and peaceful," Helen whispered prayerfully. She turned to her son. "I hope what your father's discovered doesn't change this."

"I agree, Mom, but you'll have to admit today's been pretty exciting."

"Yes it has, but excitement doesn't always bring happiness. Although it is good to know that our fear your dad was suffering from some mysterious illness wasn't true."

"Yeah, if he doesn't give himself a heart attack digging in that cave."

"I can't imagine how we'd keep him from doing what he's doing, though, do you?" Helen said.

"I've never seen Dad act like this."

"You mean excited?"

"Freaked-out is more like it."

"You shoulda seen him when you kids were born. He was a basket case. And every time you made a touch down in high school he was beside himself."

"All three of 'em, huh."

"Yes, all three. I have to confess it was more fun seeing his reaction than it was watching you make the touch down."

"Mom, I'm hurt."

"You're a big boy, you'll get over it."

Robert looked at his watch. "It's five-fifty. We'd better head back."

He started the truck, maneuvering down the embankment and into the creek bed; the ridge now provided shade from the sun. Two deer jumped across the creek in front of them and disappeared into a thicket of cedars growing along the bank. Robert brought the truck to a halt at the mouth of the ravine, marking the spot they'd have to walk from.

"If you don't mind, I'm going to wait for you here. I'm

too tired to make the trip to the cave and back."

"Good idea, Mom."

Robert hurried off down the creek bed and was soon out of sight. Helen leaned her seat back and rested; she was soon asleep. Robert forced his way through the brush and low-hanging cedar branches that led to the hidden cave, each step longer and faster until he rounded the embankment. His dad and Dr. Bethel were out of the cave, both men covered in dirt, sweat soaking through their clothes, neither man conscious of his appearance, but both acutely attentive to what sat between them. No one said anything while the three studied what was at their feet. Lee had taken a stiff paintbrush from his pocket and was dusting off the remaining dirt. "I don't know what's in this, but I can tell you it's no ordinary box."

"It's locked," Robert said, pulling on the latch. "So how did Jeremiah get the candlestick out?"

"There are two more chests like this one still inside. It'll take awhile to get 'em out. Looks like one's busted— maybe that's where it came from."

"Two more?" Robert was dumbfounded.

"We're losing light. Let's get this one back to the house," Fred said.

Robert reached down and took hold of the handles on each side, trying to lift the chest. He quickly set it back down. "How much you reckon that weighs?"

"I'd say between a hundred and thirty and a hundred and fifty pounds. It'll take the two of you to manhandle it back to the truck," Fred remarked as he led the way out of the ravine and began the descent down to the creek bed.

Helen woke up when she felt the truck dip as the chest was loaded into the bed. It took her a moment to gather her thoughts—she'd been soundly asleep. She looked at her watch and realized it had been an hour since she leaned the seat back and shut her eyes. Helen got out to see what had been loaded into the truck. She ran her hand over the chest, looking closely at the various carvings and the heavy latches. "What is this?" she asked.

"Don't know, but I don't think it's some pioneer's keepsake chest. Too well built. Fortified to keep people out," Lee answered, drawing on his education, trying to make sense of a mystery that had no archaeological parallel. He couldn't even make an educated guess. Had it been rock art, pottery, spear points, cliff dwellings, or remnants of ancient Indian cultures, he would feel comfortable hypothesizing, but not this. He wouldn't even speculate.

Robert drove, the others staring out the back window at their mystery cargo. The drive was slow; Robert avoided as many bumps as he could, hoping that a sudden jolt wouldn't disintegrate the old chest. As they neared the house, Fred suggested backing in so that the chest could be loaded directly onto the workbench. Bear greeted them as they got out. Lee and Robert lifted the chest out of the truck and set it on the table. Helen turned on the light above the table, exposing details they'd not seen earlier. Lee made a quick transition from the awe brought on by the day's surprises to the analytical scrutiny of a scientist. "I need a tape measure, pad and pencil." Helen returned quickly with the requested items. "While you're measuring, I'll fix sandwiches." She was gone again. No one noticed.

Lee took pictures from all angles while documenting measurements and drawing pictures of the chest. The top of the chest arched in typical trunk fashion, with the center higher than the edges, giving a dome appearance. From the base of the chest to the crest of the arch measured 18 inches high. The length was 30 inches and the depth measured 20 inches, and on a standard bathroom scale the chest and its contents weighed 127 pounds. The iron straps that held the chest secure were each three inches wide, and each strap had 12 rivets fastening the strap to the wood. Each edge and corner was reinforced with iron plates riveted solid to the chest as well. The latch was iron and molded to resemble a spear head; the lock itself weighed at least two pounds. Lee continued to clean the chest with the paintbrush, dusting away dirt from the top when he noticed an engraving. "What do you make of this?" he asked.

"Looks like a coat of arms to me," Helen said, squeezing in between Lee and Fred.

"Yeah, I think that's exactly what it is. Maybe if we can make out the design, it'll help us identify the original owner."

A large plastic tray stacked with sandwiches and a large bowl of sliced melon sat just an arm's length from the men. It was well presented, delicious-looking, and still untouched. It had, however, drawn Bear's attention, but before she pulled the first sandwich off the tray, Helen moved it out of her reach. The dog sat patiently while everyone devoured the food, periodically doing her woof-whine routine. One sandwich remained. Fred threw it to Bear, who caught it and quickly disappeared.

"Okay, Lee, you're the boss. What's the next step?" Fred asked, showing a mixture of excitement, impatience, and fatigue.

Lee hesitated, still studying the remarkable artifact that sat before them. He knew what the rancher wanted to hear. "Bottom line, Fred, it's your discovery. You found it on your property, and it's gone unclaimed at least a hundred years. We've measured and photographed the chest." He paused, eyes still fixed on the chest, caressing it gently, running his fingers along the ornate carvings that adorned the top and sides. "As I was saying, if it were mine, I'd open it!"

"That's what I hoped you'd say." Fred smiled, clapping his hands like a five-year-old on Christmas morning.

"Hold on, gentlemen. Don't you think we need some rest? It's one a.m. No telling how long it'll take to open it. Then we'll spend another few hours picking through the contents. It'll be sun-up and we'll be exhausted."

"Yeah, you're right as rain, Ma, but don't think I can sleep."

Helen pulled her reading glasses down halfway on the bridge of her nose, doubled her fists, and placed them in a deliberate move on her hips. "First of all, Fred Gray, I'm not your ma. You know better! You can at least clean up. You're covered in dirt and God only knows what else. Besides that, you stink. You can take a shower and try to sleep."

Lee and Robert retreated a few steps back from the workbench and watched, knowing who would win the dispute.

"Sorry, dear. I *could* use a shower and some rest." He pointed at the chest. "Been wait'n a long time for this. Guess a few more hours won't make a difference."

Robert left the garage and drove back to his house just over a mile south of his folks. He had moved from town into the original house after his folks moved into the new home Fred had been promising he'd build for 30 years.

Helen showed Lee to his quarters: a large bedroom with a full private bath attached, a small reading table, and an overstuffed leather chair complemented the room, giving it a warm, comfortable country appearance.

"You have a beautiful home, Mrs. Gray," Lee said as he set his backpack on the floor next to the king-size bed.

"Thank you, and for the last time, Lee, it's Helen."

"Sorry, just habit."

"You're forgiven. Now make yourself comfortable. Breakfast at six." She smiled, hesitated. "I'm glad you're here. Fred likes you and trusts your advice. Can't say that about most folks. For some reason he's suspicious of people and a bit cynical about life in general. Guess it's something brought on by the war, I don't really know. He never talks about it."

Lee showered, hoping it would relax him. It didn't. He looked over at the bedside clock for the tenth time: 2:38. He finally dozed off.

CHAPTER 16

Agent Holt followed the directions he'd memorized in the sheriff's office down a one-lane dusty country road in search of the location where he and Stanton were to meet. He drove into a draw between red dirt hills and could see a cattle guard and a sign sitting to one side that identified the location as Southland Royalty, Stanton #3 gas well. Holt eased over the cattle guard, hoping the rental car's clearance was high enough. The road followed a slight rise in the terrain to the northwest, disappearing behind a shallow canyon rim a quarter mile ahead. As he topped the rim, he could see a truck parked under a large tree near a creek bed. Holt drove slowly, trying to avoid washouts and thorny plum bushes he knew would play havoc with the car's finish. The windows were up and the A/C on, but somehow a thin cloud of dust had made its way into the car. Holt coughed, lifted his sunglasses, and tried wiping the accumulating dust particles from the corners of his eyes. As the cloud of dirt settled, Holt eased the window down, trying to see who the occupant of the half-ton Z-71 was. Just then the passenger side door opened and the sheriff stuck her head in. "Trouble finding the place?"

"None. You don't live out here, do you?"

"No, in town, but I love to come here for the peace and quiet."

"And dust!"

"Yup, some dust. Okay, G-man, what's this about?"

"Long story, I'll keep it short."

"I've got the time. Don't leave anything important out." The sheriff's words left no doubt that she was not in the mood for bureaucratic shuck-and-jive. "I want the details, all of 'em!"

Holt explained that he'd been assigned as a member to a task force of US government and international law enforcement experts specifically created for the purpose of bringing an international crime organization (ICO) to justice. "We know the ICO is tied indirectly to terrorists groups in Europe, North Africa, and Southeast Asia. The US arm of the organization funnels money to these groups, and we've followed the flow of dollars for the last two years, hoping it'd lead us to the leaders."

"Has it?"

"Don't know. I'm not high enough on the totem pole to be privy. All I know is that we want to spread the net far enough to catch the big dogs."

"Guess we'll never learn," Stanton said.

"Meaning?"

"Lots of crimes being committed, lots of people hurt. Tons of money going to support the bad guys, and we turn our heads waiting on the big capture. Makes good press, but everyone knows as soon as you disable the top dog, there's another worse than the one toppled ready to take his place."

"Amen. You sound bitter."

"Not at all. Perplexed maybe. Okay, so how does all that affect us peace-lovin' folk out here in the middle of nowhere?"

"I'm working undercover, following up on a coded message from a member of the ICO to a known mercenary from California by the name of Elliot Heath." Holt pulled a copy of the deciphered message from his briefcase and handed it to the sheriff, giving her time to read it.

"I'm really confused. I know Fred Gray. Why would anyone be interested in his ranch, and something worth millions? There's got to be a mistake here!"

Holt took the message back and returned it to the envelope marked S*ecret, for your eyes only.* "You may be right, maybe it's a mistake. My job is to be the eyes and ears on the street. That's what I'm here for."

"Right, go on."

"Fred Gray took something to a dealer in Oklahoma City for an appraisal. The dealer in turn contacted one of our suspects in New York City. Next thing we know, the suspect is contacting Heath through a coded message. We're just trying to connect the dots."

"What's your next move?"

"We know Heath boarded a commercial jet on April first in San Diego and flew to Portland, Oregon. An hour later, using an alias, he caught a flight to Miami arriving late that evening. He stayed overnight in the airport Marriott and left the next morning back to LA. Heath rented a car under another alias and drove to Barstow where he caught a flight to Wichita. Next morning, using the name Otis Thorpe, our elusive Elliot Heath bought a dark blue 2000 Ford F-150."

"Where to then?"

"Listen to this." Holt paused.

"I am."

"Our agent in Wichita was tasked to intercept Heath at the airport and follow him; on the way there, the agent was in a fender bender at a stoplight just a half mile from the arrival terminal."

"You lost him?"

"My guess is that the SAC didn't give the Wichita guys a full briefing."

"You mean they didn't explain the level of importance?"

"Exactly. This joint task force op is so secret they don't even give their own people enough details. If they'd leveled with the Wichita agents in the first place, they would have had a contingency plan."

"Yeah, we always had a back-up plan in mind should something go wrong. Hell, sometimes we had a third plan rehearsed in case the first two failed," Stanton said.

"Anyway, as soon as we learned they'd lost his trail, I caught the next flight into Oklahoma City."

Stanton interrupted. "Why Oklahoma City? I'd think Wichita would be the best place to pick up Heath's trail."

"We struggled with that question but finally decided that since we were confident he was headed to Buffalo, Oklahoma, we'd just pick his trail up there. The other reason I flew into to Oklahoma City was because I wanted to pay a visit to Paul Hansen."

"Who's Paul Hansen?"

"Appraiser Fred Gray visited who caught the attention of the computer monitoring our New York suspect's calls."

"You think this Hansen is part of the ICO?"

"Don't think so but wanted to pay him a visit anyway."

"And?"

"I browsed his store awhile and visited with him about his merchandise. Didn't want to ask too many questions, just wanted him to think I was shopper and nothing more.

Seemed like a nice guy."

"Anything on AFIS?"

"Navy, honorable discharge. One DUI twenty years ago. No other arrests, no bad credit, no lawsuits. Appears clean."

"Then what?"

"Been here ever since, posing as a landman for Sooner Exploration, watching Heath."

The sheriff gave Holt a stern, disapproving look. "Let me get this straight. There's been a man in my community who, according to the FBI, is dangerous and may be involved in some kind of criminal activity, and I'm just finding out about him today?!"

"Yes, that's right. I know it sounds bad, but let me explain."

"Please do and it'd better be good." Stanton was to her boiling point.

"First of all, I was under strict orders not to divulge any information to anyone, not even you. Secondly, we weren't a hundred percent sure it was Heath; we wanted a positive ID first. The capture of these thugs and the disruption of the ICO have top priority worldwide, and you know as well as I, it'd only take one person to unknowingly compromise the entire effort."

"And that's supposed to make me feel better?"

"Guess not, but I'm giving it to you straight. I'm just a worker-bee doing my job. Don't be pissed at me."

"Okay, but for the record I will express my disapproval at the way this was handled to Webster."

"Fair enough. There's more to the story. Should I go on?"

"Of course."

"Once I'd located Heath, I spent the next few days establishing my cover as a rep for Sooner Exploration. Got to know a few landowners and folks at the courthouse, and I watched Heath's activities. Fortunately he didn't move around much the first few days, just stayed holed up in his motel room."

"When was this taking place?" the sheriff asked.

"First part of April. Then on the fifth he answered an ad in the local paper for seasonal help at the Gray Ranch. He got the job, moved out of the motel into a small rental house three blocks south of your office. Twenty-four hours later I received a call from my boss, advising me that the CIA had intercepted another coded message from a pay phone in Lavern, Oklahoma to Monica Bouvier that simply read, *'I'm in. Follow up in forty-eight.'* The obvious interpretation of the decoded message, of course, is that he got hired and would contact Bouvier with details."

"I'm assuming this Bouvier is the suspect you mentioned earlier. Is she a major player in the ICO?"

"Affirmative. She's a savvy, successful antiquities dealer slash appraiser in New York. We know she's a significant part of the ICO, and she's the person Paul Hansen contacted regarding the item Fred Gray wanted appraised."

"And subsequently Bouvier is the one who contacted Heath?"

"Right. I drove to Lavern and found out two hired hands from the Gray Ranch had been to the feed store and purchased wire and steel posts for fencing. Heath must have made the call then."

"I know one of Gray's hired hands. Been around here for years, worked for Fred and Robert the last four or five."

Holt interrupted. "Yeah, we checked Curtis Russell out and so far don't think he's a part of this. We pulled prints off a beer bottle he'd trashed and ran a history on his Social Security number."

MARVIN WIEBENER

"What'd that turn up?"

"Desert Storm vet, guard at a private prison near Watonga, Oklahoma. Moved here six years ago, attends the First Baptist occasionally, and dates a waitress that works at the Percolator Café. Parents are dead. One sister living in Texas. Never married and one speeding ticket. Other than the girlfriend, no other known associates. No drugs, no bounced checks, but he likes his Bud Lite and watching football. My biggest concern for Russell is that Heath is an accomplished manipulator."

"Yeah, I see where you're going. Russell, a decent guy and a loner, could fall prey to someone like Heath."

"He could end up an accomplice and we can't warn him. He's got to act as natural as possible around Heath so we don't spook him."

"Not good." Stanton was not pleased with the arrangement. "It's like throwing Christians to the lions. We'll have to give this some thought. Any other details I need to know about Heath?"

"To my knowledge, he's used two aliases since arriving in Buffalo: John Smith and Otis Thorpe. Thorpe is the name he goes by as ranch hand and house renter. Smith is the name he used to get access to county records."

Holt could feel sweat running down his neck under the collar of his white tie-less dress shirt. He mopped at his head with a handkerchief, pushing his dull brown and gray hair away from his temples. He wanted to start the car and turn the A/C on but didn't want to appear puny in front of the sheriff, especially a woman sheriff. He endured, and marveled at Stanton's ability to look composed. How someone could be so attractive and formidable at the same time puzzled him.

"Tell me more about this find or discovery supposedly worth millions," Stanton requested. Holt took a deep breath and slid sideways toward the sheriff, trying to avoid rays of sun coming through the driver side open window; he stared straight ahead for a moment. "You know, Sheriff," he paused again, "no one has put a lot of thought into that part of the message from Bouvier to Heath. Our attention has been on the ICO and more recently on tracking Heath. Only thing we really know is the rancher took a candlestick in to Paul Hansen for an appraisal, and Hansen contacted Bouvier. That's when Heath, Hansen, and the rancher popped up on our radar screen." A bead of sweat ran down his forehead, between his eyes, and dripped off the end of his nose before he could catch it with his handkerchief. He knew Stanton saw it; he was embarrassed by his pathetic appearance. Holt started the car, raised the windows, and turned the A/C on high.

"And from what you've deduced, Hansen's connection with Bouvier is legit?" she asked.

"Yeah, our guess is Hansen just needed a second opinion. One thing's for sure, Sheriff."

"What's that?"

"I don't think there's a candlestick in the world worth millions, do you?" Holt didn't expect nor did he get an answer. "'Bout the second week in April, I followed Heath to the county clerk's office at the courthouse. Fifteen minutes after he left, I went in and gave the clerk my card, told her I was doing research on land owned by Fred Gray for survey purposes and needed to see the land description. I acted like I was studying the ledger, took some notes, then asked the clerk if I could see Book Five, also."

"The historical journal Bouvier referred to in the message to Heath?" she said.

"Right. The clerk said it was a coincidence that two people had asked for the same journal in the same day. I tried to act nonchalant by saying oil and gas exploration companies tried to check out all available documents before approaching landowners regarding leases."

"Did she buy it?"

"Don't think so. She could tell I didn't know my butt from a hole in the ground, but she complied. Even offered to make a copy of the same page Heath had requested. The clerk went on to say that exploration companies only wanted information relevant to a specific legal land description and weren't usually interested in the historical documents."

"What'd you say?"

"Just that I was new to the job and wanted to make sure I had everything I needed. I could tell she was suspicious. She handed me the copy and asked me to sign the register. That's where I saw that Heath had signed in as John Smith, Smith Consulting."

"That's original," Stanton remarked.

"That's Heath. Arrogant SOB. He's playing this scheme a little too loose this time."

Holt handed the copy of the page from Book 5 to the sheriff. "What do you make of this?" Stanton looked at the document, reading the entries as best she could without her glasses. "Interesting, but nothing that would provide an immediate clue other than the obvious reference to Jeremiah and Hannah Gray. I'm assuming they're Fred's grandparents."

"That'd be my guess. Now look at the mess of lines next to Gray's entry. What's that about?"

"Yeah, that's what I'm looking at. First glance you'd think a map, but then it could be a drawing. One thing for sure."

"Yeah?"

"It's intentional, too detailed for doodling. It represents something. Wish I had my glasses."

"I've studied it with a magnifying glass. Could be a cliff or embankment of some kind." Holt pointed. "These could be tributaries leading into a creek."

Stanton shook her head. "They could be anything. You can tell from the Xerox copy that the original page was stained." The sheriff laid the page on the seat between them. "It's getting late, and I need to check in with headquarters. Let me think about all this, and let's get together Saturday."

"That'd be the tenth, same time and place?"

"Yeah, and if anything unusual comes up I want to be notified. Here's my cell number."

The agent took the sheriff's card and slid it into his shirt pocket. He could feel the moisture from the perspiration soaking through. "One last thing," he said as Stanton was getting out of his car. She turned back to listen. "And?"

"CIA hasn't intercepted any more cell, text, or landline messages. As you know, that doesn't mean they're not communicating. They could be on to us."

The sheriff leaned back into the car far enough for Holt to be able to see her expression. "Right now the only thing I'm concerned about is the safety of the community and the Gray family." Stanton hesitated just for a second to watch Holt's reaction. There was something about this guy; she couldn't put her finger on it. She tried pushing another button. "When it comes down to where the rubber meets the road, Agent Holt, protecting lives trumps the FBI's investigation every time." Stanton stood holding the car door open, waiting for Holt's acknowledgement.

"Of course, I wouldn't expect anything less of you. It's your sworn oath."

Stanton thought he sounded sarcastic, but didn't want to drag the conversation out further. "See you Saturday," she said, closing the door.

CHAPTER 17

Paul Hansen had followed the same daily routine for as long as he could remember—a man of habit. The custom he'd fashioned for himself over the years worked well in his line of business. He could still see his father wagging his finger when he wanted to make a point, saying, "Always be faithful to your customers, be on time, be honest, and never back out of a promise." To Hansen, those words were the foundation of his success.

Hansen unlocked the back door of his store at 7:30 a.m., just as he'd done for most of the last 40 years. His part-time morning shift employee would arrive at 8:00 and begin her routine, which included dusting displays, cleaning the bathroom, and unlocking the front entrance at 9:00 sharp. Customers trickled in one or two at a time until mid-afternoon; 2:00 p.m. seemed to be the magic hour for buyers. Sales rarely exceeded $1,000 before 2:00 and after, rarely below $3,000. The slow mornings allowed the dealer an opportunity to do book work, make customer calls, and do appraisals.

Hansen turned on the light, illuminating the inventory of antiques waiting for appraisal. Some pieces were waiting to be shipped to buyers and others ready for display and sale. The building and contents were insured for $5 million, and on this day Hansen was nervous; his holdings actually exceeded that amount. He intended on spending the morning preparing items for shipment and then let FedEx worry about it. As he entered his office, he saw the number two flashing red on his answering machine. He took $100 in small bills and change and opened the cash register so that it would be ready when Alice opened the doors for business at 9:00. Hansen hurried back to his desk and took out his pen and writing pad, then punched the button on his answering machine to retrieve the messages. *Mr. Hansen, this is Monica Bouvier in New York. I was disappointed when I got your e-mail saying Mr. Gray wasn't interested in my offer. I thought it was a very fair offer. Please call me at your earliest convenience.*

Hansen smiled as he listened. He knew she had lowballed the appraisal, but he never expected her to call back.

The next message began; he sat closer to the machine, unable to hear the caller clearly. He could tell the person's English was a second language; he'd play the message again. This time he sensed the caller was anxious, which only complicated the man's broken English. Hansen pushed the replay button for a third time. *Mr. Hansen, I am Dr. Cordona from university in Madrid. I have looked at photo of candlestick and must talk with you soon. Madrid is six hours ahead of US Central Standard Time. Call my office or home anytime night or day. I will talk to you.*

Hansen scribbled the international phone number down, thinking the simple candlestick query was taking on a mysterious air, just as he guessed it would. He thought about calling the rancher, but there wasn't anything substantial yet to tell him. Best to wait until after the conversation with Cordona. Hansen finished writing the information down on the legal pad and repositioned his reading glasses so that he could see the number clearly. He dialed the international number, and on the third ring the phone was answered by a woman speaking Spanish. "Miss, I only speak English, do you understand?"

"Yes, I speak English. What can I do to help you?"

"My name is Paul Hansen and I'm returning…"

The woman cut Hansen off. "Mr. Hansen, yes, the professor is expecting your call. One moment please."

The piped in music was classical Spanish guitar, much better, Hansen thought, than the typical elevator music he was used to hearing while on hold in the US. Less than a minute into the piece, Dr. Cordona answered. The professor spoke very clear, precise English. "Mr. Hansen, thank you very much for returning my call." There was a short pause. Hansen could tell Cordona was out of breath, clearing his throat he continued. "I've examined the photos of the candlestick and would like to know more about its whereabouts. Who is in possession of it?" Another deep breath and another. Hansen hoped Cordona wasn't having a heart attack. "Please forgive me, Mr. Hansen. My office is on the fourth floor, and the elevator was too crowded. I ran all the way."

"No need to apologize, Dr. Cordona," Hansen said, thinking the professor must also believe the candlestick to be special.

"Have you seen the candlestick up close or only the photo?" the professor asked.

"Yes, I've seen it. I examined it carefully, but I'm not an expert. That's why I sent the photos to you." Hansen knew he must ration what information he divulged. "I do know who has possession, but, with all due respect, I feel obliged to maintain his anonymity."

"Oh, Mr. Hansen, I completely understand. I just needed to know if you possessed firsthand information or secondhand."

"Firsthand, Dr. Cordona, however, I wish to keep that confidential as well."

"Yes, of course. Let me think." The professor mumbled something in Spanish. Hansen could hear paper shuffling. "Ah yes, I found it. Are you still there?"

"Yes, Dr. Cordona, I'm still here."

"I'm sorry. Was looking for a phone number in the US. Mr. Hansen, you are familiar with the Smithsonian National Museum of Natural History in Washington DC?"

"Yes."

"I have a dear friend and colleague, Dr. Carlos Ramirez, there. If you and the person possessing the candlestick agree, I would like for him to examine it."

"I will have to visit with the owner; I'll get back with you then."

"I understand. Please, Mr. Hansen, convey to the possessor this is very important, and we will honor his decision either way."

Hansen sat back in his chair collecting his thoughts, processing the Bouvier message and his conversation with the professor in Madrid. Two things bothered him about his conversation with Cordona. Why did he refer to Gray as the possessor and not the owner? And Cordona's closing remark about honoring Gray's decision either way. Of course he'd have to honor Gray's decision. There was no other option. Maybe these were just language quirks, translation issues that meant nothing. Still, Hansen was puzzled. He heard the bell ring, announcing the first customer. Hansen opened his office door partway, scanning the store for Alice. He saw her approach the shopper. He eased the door shut, looked at his watch, sat down, and reached for the phone.

CHAPTER 18

Tuesday, June 6, 5:45 a.m.

Lee Bethel bolted upright, seeing headlights reflecting off the dresser mirror and hearing short honks coming from the vehicle passing by his bedroom window. He looked over at the clock; it was 5:45 a.m. Bethel swung his legs out of bed and planted them firmly on the floor, willing himself to remember where he was and, more importantly, why. He looked at the clock again and remembered breakfast with the Grays at 6:00. By the time he reached the kitchen table, it was a few minutes past, and the others were half through. Helen had been up since 5:00, Fred since 5:15, and Robert claimed he'd been awake since 4:00. Lee poured himself coffee as Helen ladled a scrambled egg mix of peppers and sausage on his plate. "Toast or biscuits?" she asked.

"Biscuits, please." He remembered how tasty they were the last time he was out. Lee buttered the first biscuit, scooped a forkful of eggs, and glanced across the table at the rancher and his son. Their expressions, which Lee assumed were involuntary, said it all. He shoveled the breakfast into his mouth as fast as he could without making a complete idiot of himself, wiped his mouth, and raised his cup to Helen. "Mind if I take this to the garage with me?"

"Please do. Here, let me freshen it." She looked at her husband and son. "Don't pay any attention to those two."

Lee smiled. "That's hard to do. Besides, I'm just as anxious."

Fred shuffled around on his chair, took another swig of coffee, and tried to act less anxious. "Sorry, Lee. Take your time."

"I'm ready!" Lee said with a mouth full of food. He stood and followed the others into the garage. The foursome gathered around the workbench, their hearts pounding. "After you all went to bed, I sprayed all the hinges, lock, and latch with penetrating oil," Fred said as he pried and poked around with a screwdriver. "Don't think it did a darn thing to loosen anything up."

"Too much rust, Dad. Oil only does so much."

Just then, there was a knock at the back door. "Curt and Otis. I forgot about the hands," Robert said.

"Give 'em assignments and don't let 'em come back here!" Fred ordered. "Don't even let on we're in the garage. Curt's a great kid, but he's the biggest gossip between here and Amarillo. If he doesn't know for sure what's goin' on, he'll make something up."

Robert was gone just short of five minutes. "That was fast," Helen said.

"As soon as they're outta sight, open the garage door; get some air in here." Fred was already mopping sweat off his head. Robert looked out the side window and watched as the two hands disappeared from sight. Then he punched the button to open the garage door.

Fred's eyes were on the chest as he pecked away at the rusty lock, growing frustrated with the plan of trying to preserve the chest in its original state. He tried to push the screwdriver between the lock and latch, but the rust held fast. "What'd you tell the hands?"

"Count calves, check fence between Palmer's and us, and clean up the excavation site. Thought I'd better work in why Lee's here. Didn't want 'em to get overly curious about his truck." Robert stared at the unopened chest, but his thoughts were on something else. Being his mother, Helen sensed her son's attention had been diverted.

"You've got something on your mind, Robert?"

"Just an odd feeling."

Fred and Lee weren't paying attention to the side conversation.

"What kind of feeling?"

"Nothing really, just a gut feeling that won't go away."

"About?"

"Get'n strange vibes every time I'm around Otis."

Fred laid his crowbar down and leaned against the bench. Lee continued working on the chest. "Didn't want to say anything, but I get the same feeling around him, too."

"He never says much, but I can tell, maybe *feel* is a better word, he's sizing me up," Robert said.

Fred picked up the crowbar and began prying. "He's not an experienced cowboy, but picks things up quick, works hard. What puzzles me is he seems too smart to be work'n this hard for the wages we pay."

"Exactly," Robert said as he refocused his attention on the task that lay before him.

The men were working intently on the chest, their attention drawn back to the discovery like metal shavings to a magnet. Nothing was more important to them than what was in the chest—nothing.

Helen had listened closely to the brief conversation. She wasn't a woman easily alarmed, but she, too, had her own suspicions about the new hired hand. She'd had them since the day Fred introduced Otis to her. He had a way about him, she thought, that was sophisticated, big city sophisticated. Otis Thorpe wasn't just your ordinary ranch hand. She hadn't made her feelings known to Fred because her husband was pleased with his work, but she kept an eye on him any time he was close to the house, not so much out of fear as curiosity. Helen stepped up close to the bench. "Why don't we ask the sheriff to check him out?"

"How, honey?" Fred continued chipping and prying.

"We could give her his tag number and his Social Security number; can't they do something with that information, like find out where he came from?"

"Don't know, but if it'd make you feel better, give her a call."

* * *

Fred stood up from his bent over position and stretched to dislodge the kinks in his 76-year-old body. At six feet, two inches barefooted, nearly six four in his boots, the rancher appeared lean and youthful—only his face and hands betrayed him. Years of working in the harsh weather had permanently tanned all exposed skin, and the wrinkles around his eyes testified to the squinting required to keep wind, dust, and sun out. He put both hands on the workbench and leaned in closer to the chest. "Okay, Professor, what's your suggestion?"

"I don't think we're going to get that lock open. My suggestion is to take a hacksaw to it."

"Hoped you'd say that." Fred turned to the peg board mounted on the wall just behind him and took the saw from its hook. He laid the blade against the shackle and looked at the others, who were nodding. The rust that had sealed all the moving parts had also softened the metal pieces, making the cutting task much easier. Just as the saw cut through, the phone rang. Fred looked across the bench at Helen. "Just let the answering machine get it."

"Might be one of the kids. Better answer it or they'll be worried." Helen stepped from the garage into the hall, reached around the corner into the kitchen for the wall phone. "Hello, Gray Ranch, Helen speaking."

"Mrs. Gray, this is Paul Hansen of Hansen Antiques and Appraisals in Oklahoma City calling for Mr. Gray."

"I'm sorry, he's not available now. May I take a message?" What she told Hansen wasn't a lie; she knew her husband wouldn't take a call right now. No use even asking.

"Yes, please tell Mr. Gray I've something important to discuss with him; it's about the candlestick he asked me to appraise. Tell him it's very important. I need to talk to him soon!"

Helen could tell there was disappointment in the caller's voice. "I'll have him call you as soon as he's available."

She returned to the garage and saw that the men had gotten the lock off and were prying on the latch with a small crowbar.

"Who was that?" Fred asked out of habit rather than a true interest in the caller. The three men were tugging, prying, and hammering, doing anything they could to dislodge the latch.

"Paul Hansen. He said it was very important that he talk with you soon!"

With a dull pop, the latch broke free from the chest. Fred forgot what his wife had said about the caller, and with crowbars they began prying on the lid. Little by little, chunks of iron broke away until the only thing securing the chest was the rust around the straps that held the lid shut. Robert shoved the crowbar between the lid and chest, this time with more force. The iron bands creaked, but they resisted the pry bar, as if the bands were doing everything they were designed to do to keep intruders out. Robert finally struck the bar with a hammer; the crack sounded like a wooden baseball bat hitting a fastball. The lid was unsealed at last. Fred had located a larger crowbar and had driven the flat end deep into the opening and was prying up. With each push, the lid would give way slightly. "Hand me a flashlight!" Fred said.

Robert opened the drawer under the workbench and took one out, handing it to his father.

"It's open about an inch; maybe I can see inside." Fred took the light and shined it into the gap. "Nothing!"

Robert crouched down next to his dad, trying to see. "What'd you mean nothing?"

"Can't see anything." Fred pointed. "There's a lip built into the chest the lid fits over when closed. It's too high, blocks the view from this angle."

The rancher inserted the end of the large crowbar between the lid and chest, striking it hard with a hammer. The lid moved—and the phone rang again.

Helen looked at the three men. "Don't open that chest until I get back!"

"Gray Ranch, Helen speaking," she answered, with a slight edge to her voice.

"Mrs. Gray, Tobias Henry here. How are you?"

The Grays and Henrys had been friends for years. Both families had been in the cattle business since statehood, attended the same church, even played rummy on occasion. Helen tried to disguise the impatience she was feeling. "We are fine. And you, your folks?" She looked down the hall at the chest and the three men hovered over it. They hadn't opened it yet.

"We're all okay. Mrs. Gray. Is your husband there?"

"He's not available..." Helen repeated the spiel she'd just given Hansen, hoping it would conclude the call. It didn't.

"I talked to your son Robert yesterday about interviewing Dr. Bethel concerning the excavation taking place on your ranch in two weeks."

"Yes, Tobias, Dr. Bethel is here but, I'm afraid, unavailable to take your call just now."

"Would you ask him to give me a call?"

"Of course, Tobias."

"Do you think he'll call today?"

"I'll tell him, that's all I can do." She glanced into the garage again. The men were looking at her, their message clear.

"I hate to be a pest, but the reason I need to talk to Dr. Bethel today is that I'm writing an article that will be published in the *Ledger*. It's part of my summer internship requirement, and there's a deadline in order to get it to the printer in time."

"Tobias, I'll do everything possible to have Dr. Bethel return your call."

"One more thing," Tobias said.

"Tobias, I'm very busy right this minute. Can it wait?"

"It's about a page from a historical journal that I found at the courthouse."

"Oh goodness! My biscuits are burning; you'll have to excuse me. I'll give Dr. Bethel your message" and she hung up. Helen hurried into the garage. "One of you needs to call Tobias Henry back today!"

Lee nodded. "I'll call him after lunch."

"Thanks, he'll appreciate it, and so will I," she said, shaking her head.

Fred looked at everyone. "No phone calls, no interruptions of any kind. We're gonna open this now." He picked up a crowbar.

CHAPTER 19

Tuesday, June 6, 11:00 a.m.

P aul Hansen looked at his watch again for the fourth time in as many minutes. Should he call Mr. Gray back or should he wait? Dr. Cordona sounded anxious, and the feeling was contagious. Hansen's phone rang, and he glanced at his watch. It was 11:00, and without looking at caller ID he answered.

"Mr. Hansen, this is Monica Bouvier. Is this a convenient time?"

No, it wasn't, Hansen thought, but too late, he should've looked at the ID.

"Yes, Ms. Bouvier, this is a good time. Sorry for not getting back with you sooner…" He continued with an excuse, but she cut him off.

"Mr. Hansen, I understand and apologize for taking your time. Let me get right to the point. I've had the photo of the candlestick appraised by another associate, and we're prepared to pay top dollar for it, once it's examined by our people."

"I'm waiting on a call from the owner right now. I'll pass this on to him."

"You've not heard my offer, Mr. Hansen. I think you'll be pleased."

"And what's the new offer?"

"I'm prepared to wire transfer to your bank the sum of two thousand dollars right now. We'll call that a finder's fee. For that amount, I will expect you to step aside as the rancher's agent and allow me to deal directly with him." Dead silence followed.

Hansen's thoughts were racing. He wasn't interested in a finder's fee—his only concern was for the rancher and his family heirloom. There was a mystery unfolding before his very eyes, and the end result was clearly unknowable. The mere thought of stepping aside and giving Bouvier a clear shot at the old man sent a chill down his back.

"Mr. Hansen, are you there?"

"Sorry. Yes, Ms. Bouvier, I'm still here."

"Mr. Hansen, I consider this a very handsome offer for no more than an hour or two of your time."

"It's a very generous offer, Ms. Bouvier; nevertheless, I'll need to talk to my client first."

Bouvier was as tough as she was intelligent, but her youth gave way to immature behavior without much provocation. She reacted. "Mr. Hansen!" Bouvier addressed him with a cold, crisp, angry tone. "Buyers are fickle, and a seller must strike while the iron is hot. While you're playing middleman, agent, or whatever you call yourself, the client could be losing out on a substantial sale!"

Hansen had done business with rude, arrogant, high-pressure salespeople all his life. He had learned long ago, the only way to respond was courteously. "With all due respect, Ms. Bouvier, I will still need to…" He heard a dial tone. She'd hung up.

Hansen reached under his desk and got his digital blood pressure monitor out, wrapped the cuff around his upper arm, and pressed the start button. While the cuff inflated, he sat back in his chair, closed his eyes, and breathed deeply. The monitor beeped: 150/90—he lay his head back against the chair and continued his relaxation technique. He heard a knock; it was Alice. "Mr. Hansen?" Her soft voice was barely audible.

"Yes, Alice, come in." Hansen looked at his watch. He'd slept.

"It's nearly noon, Mr. Hansen; may I take an early lunch?"

"Of course, I'll watch the front. Take as long as you need."

After the morning he'd had, Hansen wasn't in the mood to deal with customers, but Alice was the perfect employee, if there was such a person. Always on time, worked hard, cheerful, never called in with phony excuses why she couldn't work. She'd been with him five years, and when she asked for schedule adjustments, he granted them.

Hansen felt refreshed; he could tell his blood pressure was down, and the ringing in his ears had stopped. He picked up Fred Gray's phone number and went to the counter near the front of the store. There were no customers. It was 11:45. He picked up the phone that sat next to the antique brass cash register and called Gray's number again, but got voice mail. "Mr. Gray, this is Paul Hansen. Please call as soon as you can. It's important!" He hung up the phone. A customer came in.

CHAPTER 20

Tuesday, June 6, p.m.

Sheriff Stanton had just finished booking a suspected cattle thief into the county jail when her cell phone rang. "Sheriff Stanton," she answered.

"Sheriff, this is Holt. Can you talk?"

"Let me close the door. Okay, what's up?"

"At 1500 hours today, Eastern Standard Time, the communications analyst confirmed an intercepted international call between Paul Hansen and Dr. Cordona, a university professor in Madrid. We don't believe either of these men is part of the ICO, but the CIA red-flagged the call because it's in reference to the candlestick."

"What was the message?" Stanton asked.

Agent Holt explained the message, emphasizing this level of attention given a candlestick was extraordinary.

"Yeah, well, we know there's something special about the candlestick. What else?"

"It's the common thread."

"You mean the candlestick?"

"The one common denominator between this strange assortment of players," Holt confirmed.

"What's the FBI's plan?"

"They're dedicating more technical and human resources to the candlestick issue."

"What in the hell does that mean, Agent Holt? Can I expect the 82nd Airborne to drop in anytime?"

"Shit! Work with me on this, Sheriff. I'm trying to keep you up to speed. Stop jerking me around!"

After 20 years with the FBI, Stanton knew how things worked. The agency was the best in the world, hired the brightest and most capable people anywhere, and spent millions training them. When it came down to investigations and arrests, the FBI was head and shoulders above the rest. But, in their zeal to catch the bad guys, they sometimes overlooked all the good people who got stepped on or ignored in the process. Stanton realized she'd pushed Holt as far as she should for the time being. At one level she knew her disdain for Holt was merely because he represented the FBI, but at a more primal level, Stanton had a feeling in her gut that just wouldn't go away.

"Sorry, Holt, just a little on edge trying to figure all this out."

"Yeah, understand. Anyway, back to the plan. The boss thinks the candlestick is the key to some unknown major acquisition."

"Any guesses what the acquisition might be?"

"Not yet, but they got people working on that angle."

"Doesn't take a brain surgeon to figure out—when you consider all that's happening—we've got a dangerous situation brewing."

"I couldn't agree more, Sheriff. Hate to say it, but I think people's lives are in danger!"

"And your next move is what?"

"Task force meeting in DC tomorrow afternoon. I'll catch a military flight out of Vance Air Force Base tonight into Andrews, be back tomorrow night. I'll contact you as soon as I arrive."

"What about Heath while you're gone?"

"Already taken care of. The AIC is sending someone out to tail him for the next twenty-four hours or until I get back."

Stanton flipped her cell phone shut and returned it to the case attached to her belt. The sheriff's hand touched the weapon holstered near the phone case; instinctively she drew the 9mm automatic out, saw the safety was engaged, dropped the magazine out, and checked to make sure it was full. She mumbled, "Safety on, one in the chamber, mag full." The sheriff holstered her weapon and reached for a pen. For the next few minutes she wrote notes in her Daytimer, recording dates, times, and who she talked with. Stanton knew the situation surrounding the rancher and his family had grown potentially dangerous. There was only one *right* thing to do, and that was warn the Grays. Her responsibility would grow exponentially from that point on. She'd have to provide protection for them while simultaneously respecting the confidentiality of the ongoing operation to bring down the ICO. *Impossible,* no. *Complicated,* very, she thought. One thing was obvious; she couldn't wait around for something to happen. It was time to act. The sheriff took the phone book from her desk drawer and turned to the G's.

CHAPTER 21

Tuesday, June 6, Noon

Robert was on one side of the chest and Fred on the other, both with pry bars, pushing down, trying to force the lid up. Lee was lifting up on the lid with his right hand and pulling down on the chest with his left. Slowly the lid began to move—with every tug, metal and wood would crack and fall away. Lee let go of the chest and stepped back. "Robert, if you and Fred will stand behind the chest and pull up on the lid, I'll pull down on the chest, and I think it'll open."

Within seconds, using the maneuver, the chest was open. Out of habit, from years of carefully documenting every aspect of an archaeological discovery, Lee checked his watch; it was 12:17 p.m. No one spoke. The four gathered in close. They looked at each other, then back to the chest. Lee brushed away debris that had fallen into the chest when the lid was removed. He reached in, running his fingers over what appeared to be another wooden container.

The entire flat wooden surface, which lay an inch below the top of the chest, was adorned with ornately carved soldiers astride horses wearing blankets that displayed the same coat-of-arms design as on the lid. Lee looked closer. "This is not one piece of wood. You can see three nearly invisible seams that appear to divide whatever is in here into four sections."

Helen ran her fingers over the seams. "Yes, I can feel them. What are these notches?"

"My guess is they're for the purpose of getting this wood covering out," Lee said, studying the carvings. "At one time there was probably a specially designed tool that slid in and under the notch so that..." He paused, examining the notches closer. Lee looked at Fred, who appeared perplexed. "This chest contains four separate containers."

"Containers of what?!" Fred asked.

"Let's find out." Lee took two screwdrivers and inserted one in each notch. Using the sides of the chest as a fulcrum, he pried down on the handles. The container slid straight up until it was an inch above the chest edge. "Grab the box!" Lee instructed. "I'm losing my grip. This thing's heavy!"

Robert shoved the emerging container against the chest, securing it temporarily while Lee repositioned the screwdrivers deeper into the notches. Lee pried down again, lifting the container another inch. While he held both ends of the screwdrivers in place, Robert tried pulling it out, but it wouldn't budge. "It's in so tight, hard to get a grip and lift at the same time."

Lee let go, and the container slid back into the security of the chest. He picked up the largest crowbar and looked at Fred. "Do you mind?"

"Go for it!"

"Wait! I'm as anxious as you all, but don't you think we need a break, something to eat? Lee, you can make that phone call," Helen said.

Fred checked his watch. "It's nearly one o'clock. Quick break!" The others nodded.

By the time the men had washed up, Helen had a platter of sandwiches she'd prepared earlier sitting on the table. She pulled the Saran Wrap off—manners weren't a consideration. The men grabbed two each; the first was consumed by the time Helen returned to the table from throwing the Saran Wrap in the trash. There was no prayer, no discussion of any kind, and no one saw the disgusted glare on Helen's face. She shook her head, but no one noticed that, either. She reached for the one remaining sandwich, laid it on her plate, and bowed her head.

The phone rang for the fourth time that day, and Helen answered. She listened for a few seconds. "One moment, please." She handed the phone to Fred. "It's Mr. Hansen."

The rancher took the phone. "Yes Mr. Hansen, this is Fred Gray." A lengthy silence followed. Fred stared at his empty plate and listened intently. Everyone watched. He looked up and nodded at Lee, signaling him to listen. "I don't think it's a good time for Dr. Ramirez to come out right now—" Hansen interrupted. Fred continued to listen. "Hang on, Mr. Hansen; let me see if I got this straight." Looking at Lee he continued, "You're telling me a Dr. Carlos Ramirez from the Smithsonian in Washington DC wants to fly all the way to Oklahoma just to see a candlestick?!" Lee watched Fred, but couldn't make sense of the one-sided conversation. He shrugged. Fred went on. "I guess if someone that important wants to spend his time and money looking at an old candlestick, I ought to oblige, but he'll have to come here. I ain't comin' to the city." He nodded a few times and said good-bye.

"What was that all about?" Robert asked.

"Hansen wasn't happy with that New York woman's appraisal, said he didn't trust her. He then sent a photo to some expert in Spain named Cordoban or Cordova, something like that."

"And?" Helen said, taking the first bite of her sandwich.

"I guess this guy in Spain said the candlestick might have some historical importance."

Robert had rinsed his plate and put it in the dishwasher. He was standing in the hall looking toward the garage, then back toward his dad, wanting to hear what else Hansen had said, but more important to him was the mystery chest sitting just ten feet away. "Dad, can we finish discussing it out here?" He motioned toward the garage.

Lee stood. "May I use your phone? I'll call the reporter and get that over with."

Helen handed him the phone, along with Tobias's number. "A little background on the person you're going to talk to?" she asked.

"Please."

"Father's a rancher, runs a big feedlot operation. Mother's a district judge. They're good people. Tobias is their only child, and I guess, from what I've heard, they're disappointed he's not interested in being the fourth generation Henry running the ranch. He's back this summer doing a journalism internship at the local newspaper."

"Thanks. That gives me an idea of who I'm talking to." Lee called the number. Minutes later, Lee joined the others huddled around the chest.

"What'd the kid want?" Fred asked.

"Routine questions about the excavation planned in two weeks. I gave him the usual info and invited him out when the digging starts."

"D' ask about the page in Book Five?"

"Yes, he asked if I knew anything about a document that had caught the attention of some oil industry reps. I lied."

"He believe ya?"

"I don't know. He sounded satisfied."

"Good, don't need some reporter snooping around, even if he is the son of a friend."

Fred pushed the button that opened the garage door. A hot breeze rolled in, carrying dust and a small tumbleweed. Bear crawled out from underneath Robert's truck, which was parked in the drive, and walked lazily to Fred's side, nudging his knee with her nose to get his attention. He reached down and scratched her ears. The dog walked a circle or two under the workbench, lay down, and went back to sleep.

Fred held the crowbar in his hand and sized the chest up, looking for just the right place to begin the destruction. "As I was saying in the kitchen, Hansen doesn't trust the gal in New York. He says she's lied to him, been pushy, and even tried to buy him off."

"Buy him off? What's that mean?" Robert asked.

"Said she offered him two grand to get outta the middle, let her deal with me direct. Hansen said if I wanted to deal with her he'd understand, but he warned against doing business with her."

"What'd he say about the Spanish guy?"

"Just what I said earlier—that he was an expert—thought the candlestick has some kind of historical importance."

"And that's why he wants this guy from the Smithsonian to take a look," Lee said.

"Yeah, that guy is supposed to call us. Meantime let's get this open."

CHAPTER 22

Tuesday, June 6. Later the same afternoon

It took another hour, but the iron bands circumventing the chest were finally breached. Disturbed by the sawing and prying, Bear had retreated to the shade of a tree just out side the garage.

Lee cleared the remainder of the chest off the bench into a trash bag, saving every piece for possible reassembly in the future. Four wooden containers sat before them, each one with its own unique carvings. He adjusted the overhead light and took photos from every angle.

"One thing's for sure," Lee said as he examined each container with a magnifying glass. "These aren't some pioneer's stolen possessions as your grandparents thought. No matter what's inside these boxes—even if they're empty—they are works of art. I don't understand how, but I can almost guarantee they are much older than a mere hundred years or so."

Interested more in the contents than the containers,

even if they were works of art, Robert picked one up, turning it this way and that, looking for a way to open it. "You're saying we shouldn't bust these boxes up like we did the chest?"

"Not if we can help it," Lee said without looking up.

"They're heavy. Something's inside." Robert shook the box; nothing rattled or felt loose inside.

"There has to be a way to open it. Look for an indention, a dowel, a pin of some kind, anything different that might be used as a release." Lee ran his fingers over the joints. "Look at how tight the mortises and tenons are. They're so precise it's hard to see them."

Robert wrinkled his brow and glanced in Lee's direction. "The what and what?"

"The dovetail joints. They're so well fitted you can't hardly see them."

"Yeah, you're right," Fred said.

Helen set the box she was examining on end and was scraping dirt away from one corner when the phone rang for a fifth time that day. No one paid attention this time, not even Helen; she was too busy picking at a sliver of wood, about as round as a matchstick, she'd found protruding slightly from the top edge of the box. The call rolled to the answering machine. "Mom, Dad, it's Beth. Chuck has Thursday and Friday off, and the kids start summer Bible school on Monday. Thought we'd come spend the weekend. Give us a call when you get this and we'll talk. Love you."

Helen looked at Fred. "Could you hear that?"

"Yup." He now had the magnifying glass and was studying one of the boxes closely.

"Well?"

He laid the glass down. "Don't think it's a good time."

She could tell it hurt him to say it. Helen knew how

much he loved Beth. He even liked her husband, but the grandkids were his pride and joy. He never turned down an opportunity to see them. "What do you want me to tell her when I call back?"

"Anything. Tell 'em we'll come there in a week or two. Tell 'em to come when the archaeologist is here with his students. I don't care; it just can't be this weekend."

"I've never lied to our daughter and don't plan on starting. I'll think of something." Helen tugged on Lee's sleeve and pointed to the anomaly. "What do you think this is?"

The archaeologist borrowed the magnifying glass and focused on the small protruding piece of wood. Helen disappeared down the hall to call her daughter back, and as she reached for the phone, it rang. The caller ID indicated that it was a local call, but a number Helen didn't recognize. She hoped it wasn't the young intern. "Gray Ranch."

"Mrs. Gray, this is Crystal Stanton."

Helen knew Crystal well. The Grays had traded for years at the feed store owned by her folks. Crystal was a year younger than Robert, so whatever school functions the Grays attended, she was usually there as an observer or participant. She had been an outstanding basketball player and lettered three years in track as well. Her senior year, Crystal was named Academic All-American with a 4.0 grade point average and was offered scholarships to the best universities in the U.S. Crystal chose the University of Wisconsin because of its acclaimed psychology department. Her parents had been so proud, Helen remembered, when Crystal graduated at the top of her class in just three years with an undergraduate degree in psychology, and how disappointed they were when they learned she had chosen criminology for her graduate study.

They had hoped she would become a school counselor and return to Oklahoma.

"Crystal! What a pleasant surprise. How are you?"

"I'm fine, Mrs. Gray. I need to visit with you and Fred soon. When would be a good time for me to come out?"

Crystal sounded all business, not at all like herself. Helen's first thought was that a tragedy had occurred and authorities were notifying her through the sheriff's office, but what? "Has something happened, someone hurt?" Helen held her breath.

"No, nothing's happened. I just need to talk to the both of you as soon as possible."

Helen let her breath out and some of the apprehension along with it. She knew what Fred would want her to say. "We have a quest here today. What about tomorrow sometime?"

Crystal hadn't wanted to insist, the Grays being good friends and all, but on the other hand, she wouldn't allow herself to be dissuaded. "Mrs. Gray, I need to see you and Fred today, the sooner the better."

The apprehension Helen had just overcome was back. "Of course, Crystal, come out anytime."

"I'll be there in thirty minutes. If Robert's around, he should hear this also."

"He's here now."

"Good." The sheriff was already on her feet and hurrying out of her office. "Maude."

"Sheriff?" the deputy said.

"I'll be at the Gray Ranch the rest of the day."

"Want to tell me why? Not that you have to, of course, just need to put something in the log."

One of the first things Stanton did when she became sheriff was train her deputies to document everything. Times, events, people involved, even down to the type of weather. The previous sheriff had very few records and didn't require much documentation from his deputies. According to the district attorney, prosecutions were down for that very reason, and Stanton wasn't about to let a criminal slip away due to errors on the part of her deputies. The drawback, of course, was that in order for Deputy Bingham to fulfill the sheriff's requirements, Stanton also had to account for her whereabouts.

"Mr. Gray suspects cattle thieves are prowling around in that area."

"You could send one of the other deputies—"

Before Bingham could finish, the sheriff cut her off. "Thanks, Maude, but if you don't mind, I think I'll try to handle this on my own." Stanton passed her deputy's desk without making eye contact. She knew her reply was uncalled for and didn't want Maude to see the irritation on her face. She'd apologize later. Right now Stanton had to think of a plan that would accomplish several tasks without violating the confidentiality agreement she had made with Agent Holt. Somehow she would have to include her deputies in her plan and convey the seriousness of their responsibility without compromising the ICO sting operation that was in effect. How to do that without deceiving or outright lying to them wasn't clear yet. All her deputies were dedicated, reliable people, but at the same time young and inexperienced. To order them into a dangerous situation was part of her job, and for the deputies to act appropriately to those orders was a given, but this was different, much more complicated. Stanton knew she'd have to supervise every facet of her plan to protect the Grays.

* * *

Helen hurriedly returned to the garage. "Fred, we're going to have a visitor in about thirty minutes."

Her husband didn't look up; he continued to turn one of the boxes, looking for a way to open it. Lee and Robert were still working on the small piece of wood Helen had found sticking out of one side near the top of the container.

"Who's coming out?" Fred set the box down hard and pounded the bench with a clenched fist. His jaw tightened and his words hissed. "Why didn't you stop them?!"

"Whoa, Mr. Gray!" Helen held her hand up, palm facing her husband; the men stopped talking and looked up. "Sheriff Stanton said she needed to talk to us today, it was important. Didn't think it appropriate to say no. Besides, I don't think she would've taken no for an answer."

"She say why?" Robert asked.

"No, just that it was important and it needed to be today."

"My guess is she has news about that bunch of cattle thieves. She's probably out warning everybody," Fred said as he turned his attention back to the workbench. "Remember last year when I followed those guys I thought might be thieves."

"How could we forget? That was the day I thought that pretty sheriff was gonna kick your butt," Robert said, watching his mother's reaction. She laughed.

"Lee, you should've seen it. Pretty, blond, young enough to be his daughter, standing in the middle of our driveway, in front of God and several of us mortals, hands on her hips, chewing the big tough rancher out," Helen said.

"Tell me more?" Lee asked. Fred shook his head, frowning, trying to act uninterested in the conversation he'd opened the door to.

"Long story short, after checking the alleged thieves out

who Dad had been following, the sheriff confronted him right out here in the yard, told him in no uncertain terms he should tend to his ranching and she'd tend to the law breakers."

Bear had been lying under the bench, staying as close to Fred and Helen as possible, when suddenly she bolted out the garage door barking fiercely.

Fred stood upright. "That's Bear's warning someone's coming up the drive." He pointed to a shelf. "Grab that tarp and throw it over the bench."

"Too soon for the sheriff. I'll see who." Helen hurried into the house. She pulled back the curtain on the window above the kitchen sink. "Fred," she called down the hall toward the garage where the others were. "I was wrong, it's the sheriff."

Robert finished stuffing the remaining chest remnants under the tarp. He looked at Lee. "That was fast. On a good day it takes twenty minutes to drive from here to town. According to my watch it's been fifteen since Mom talked to her on the phone."

"Well, gentlemen, we're about to find out what's so important." Fred shut the overhead light off and pressed the button to close the garage door. As they walked single file into the kitchen, they could hear Helen at the front door. "Hello, Crystal, it's so good to see you." Helen smiled, opening the door wide. The sheriff hurried through the door with only a 'hello,' no smile, no friendly chitchat. Helen gestured to her right. "Let's go to the study. I'll let Fred know you're here."

CHAPTER 23

Tuesday, June 6, late p.m.

Fred shook the sheriff's hand and made a crack about chasing bad guys, a joke in reference to the comeuppance he'd received from her a few months earlier. Stanton smiled slightly, then it faded. She greeted Robert; they exchanged a prolonged glance, and then she turned toward Lee. Helen introduced them. "Dr. Lee Bethel, this is our sheriff, Crystal Stanton. Crystal, Dr. Bethel is a professor in the archaeology department at the university. He brings his students to the ranch each year to excavate." The two shook hands.

"Fred, Helen, I'll excuse myself," Lee said, walking toward the door.

"Wait; let's hear what this is about first." Fred looked at the sheriff.

Stanton shook her head. "I'd prefer just the family."

Lee left the study. The Grays and Stanton took seats around the table. "Now, what's this all about?" Fred asked.

"A candlestick." Stanton unzipped her leather folder, exposing a yellow legal pad full of notes.

Fred groaned. "I was afraid of that. Before we go any further, I suggest we get Dr. Bethel back in here."

"He knows about it?" the sheriff asked.

"Yeah, that's really why he's here."

Helen stood. "If you'll excuse me, I need to make a quick call, and I'll tell Lee to come back."

While Helen was gone, Stanton asked, "How did Dr. Bethel get in the middle of this?"

"I've known him five years. Good man, trustworthy. Besides family, I needed someone I could rely on to help solve this mystery. With his education and experience, I figured he'd be the best person to have around."

"Mystery, you say, huh. So you know something about what's going on?" the sheriff asked.

Stanton had closed her folder, as if she didn't want anyone to see what was written on the legal pad. She sat back in her chair cocking her head to the left, squinting, looking perplexed, and running her index finger over the knurled grip of her holstered weapon.

"Sheriff, I don't know a damn thing. Seems that as each hour passes, I know less and less. There's odd things happening and I don't have a clue."

Helen returned to the study, and Lee followed.

"Did you get Beth?" Fred asked.

"Yes, everything is fine. They can come next weekend."

"Good. Lee, I want you here; it's about the candlestick. Okay, Sheriff, the floor is yours."

Stanton wanted to explore Fred's use of the word *mystery* further, maybe later after she'd shared the reason for her visit. "As far as we know, Fred, this all started when you contacted a man by the name of Paul Hansen in

Oklahoma City for an appraisal of a gold candlestick."

"We? Who is we?" Fred asked, looking painfully frustrated.

"I'll get to that soon. First, I must have your assurance that what I tell you remains between the five of us. It's, well—we'll call it of great importance that no one, not a soul, hears what I'm about to tell you." The sheriff drew in a deep breath, held it while she paused, then slowly released the air as she re-opened her folder. She looked around the table and with deliberate, measured words said, "I believe all of you may be in danger!"

Helen shot a fearful glance in Fred's direction. Robert shifted nervously in his chair. Fred cleared his throat. "Oh for Pete's sake, what in the hell are you talking about?"

Stanton went through her notes, line by line, explaining all that she'd heard from Agent Holt.

Fred had heard enough. He couldn't just sit there without saying anything, looking dumbfounded like everyone else in the room. "Sheriff, I'm just a country boy. This candlestick crap is beyond me." He sat up straight, his tanned neck sporting a red glow. "Hell, I've heard of opening a can of worms before, but this takes the cake. I'm befuddled. How can a simple request turn into such a mess?" He looked over at Helen. The last thing he ever wanted to do was put his wife in danger. In all the years they'd been married, he had never done anything that would have intentionally resulted in harm to the most important person in his life. And now, he'd put her, his son, and probably Lee in jeopardy.

"I don't want to oversimplify this situation, Fred, but it's like any other problem you face," the sheriff said, hoping an illustration would help lessen the rancher's growing anxiety.

"What do you mean?"

"What do you do, Fred, when your cattle get out?"

"Round 'em up, put 'em back where they belong, and fix the fence. What's that got to do with this?"

"In other words, you come up with a plan and implement it, right?"

"Yeah, but—"

The sheriff stopped him. "Same process. That's why I'm here. Together we'll come up with a plan."

"We're listening."

Stanton flipped a few pages of the legal pad to a place where she'd written notes. She looked at Fred. "Where you live has some bad points and some good. Bad because you live several miles from town. At the same time, being remote is good because you can see someone coming from a ways off."

"Yeah, assuming you're watching twenty-four hours a day," Robert added.

"That's where the Sheriff's Office comes in. I'll post a deputy." Stanton looked out the bay window and pointed. "Probably up on that ridge. Looks like a good vantage point."

"The best. You can see miles in any direction from there," Fred said.

"Good. Looks like a grove of cedars, too. That'll provide some shade and camouflage for the deputies." The sheriff turned another page. "Got a question, Fred?"

"Hope I gotta answer."

"I'm just assuming you're like every other rancher round here and carry weapons."

"That assumption would be correct," Robert said.

"In that case I just want to warn you not to be hasty with the firearms. If you ever feel so threatened you reach for a gun, then call me first if at all possible. If you think your life is in imminent danger, then by all means take your best shot. Don't aim at the legs, thinking you'll only wound him, and don't try a head shot—you'll miss. Shoot the torso; you've got a bigger and more vulnerable target." For Stanton, the thought of shooting someone was at best disagreeable, but at the same time it was a reality she had to be ready to face everyday. She had wounded a man on one occasion; other than that, she'd only drawn her weapon during arrests. The man she shot—a known gun runner on the FBI's ten most wanted list—was fleeing the scene of a crime, gun in hand, when Stanton encountered him running out the back door of a warehouse. She remembered seeing him raise his weapon and point it directly at her. Instinctively she fired directly at his head from 15 feet away. The man fell hard. Stanton raced over and kicked the weapon out of his hand, sending it skidding under a Dumpster. It was then she saw her intended head shot had actually hit him in the shoulder. She was justified in killing the fugitive, but glad in some strange way she hadn't.

Helen, a strong woman, dabbed her eyes with a tissue. "I can't imagine ever pointing a gun at another human being," she said, her voice breaking slightly as she choked back emotion at the thought.

Robert sat up straight in his chair, adding as much height to his stature as possible. "I wouldn't hesitate a second if I thought we were in danger. Got a Ruger P95 under my truck seat and carry a Remington 338 in the gun rack," he said angrily.

Fred didn't say anything. He was afraid to. The memories were coming back—the cold, gray winter; dying men all around; unanswered prayer that somehow God would intervene and stop the war. He had taken a man's life, many, as a matter of fact and it wasn't anything he wanted to be faced with again. Fred excused himself. "Too much coffee, gotta go. Be back in a jiff."

That's strange, Helen thought as Fred left the table, *he hadn't had any coffee since early morning. Maybe just a figure of speech.* She turned to the sheriff. "Would you like something to drink?"

"Yes, please. Anything would be fine."

"I'll bring tea."

"What about Thorpe?" Robert asked.

"Holt is watching him."

"What about when he's out here on the ranch? You said he might be dangerous and he's been here several weeks. I've never seen this Holt fella you're talking about."

"Holt is a trained, experienced agent; he's probably been closer than you think. Holt thinks, and I agree, Thorpe is here to gather as much information as possible and then feed that info to Bouvier in New York. If he's as smart as Holt says he is, Thorpe will not want to draw attention to himself by doing something out of character."

"You mean like killing one or all of us?" He smiled; it was forced, but a smile nevertheless.

Stanton returned the smile. "And that's why I'm here, to provide another layer of protection."

"Yeah, I see your point, but to think I've been a few feet away from this guy everyday for the last two months…" Robert's words trailed off as his mother came through the door pushing the serving cart.

Fred finally returned from what seemed like a long head call. "Sorry." He slid into the chair next to Stanton. "Okay, Sheriff, what's next?"

"The FBI is unsure of what Heath, Thorpe as you know him, is looking for. As I said earlier, they've tied him to Bouvier, and her interest seems to be the candlestick. Holt says neither the FBI nor the CIA has yet to connect the dots. It's a mystery." As Stanton talked, she noticed the others glancing curiously at one another. There was a new kind of nervousness among the four people sitting with her around the table that she'd not noticed before. "Is there something you folks want to tell me?"

Fred got up from the table and went over to a built-in file cabinet and unlocked it. He took out the gold candlestick and returned to the table, handing it to the sheriff. It was wrapped in a soft, white cloth. The sheriff felt the weight. It was heavy for no bigger than it was. She was no expert, but it looked old. There were a few faint engravings around the top and the base; other than that, the candlestick didn't appear special to her.

The rancher gave Stanton a minute to look the candlestick over. "Whoever they are—Bouvier and her bunch—I believe they've connected the dots. They know what the candlestick represents."

"And how do you know this?" Stanton asked.

Fred looked at the others. "We'd better show her. She might be able to help solve this mystery."

"Show me what?"

"Follow me."

They entered the hall that led to the garage. No one said a word. The drone of the air conditioner as it worked to cool the house that hot afternoon was the only sound—a sound loud enough to mask the roar of the work truck as it drove in from the pasture.

Curt pulled the truck next to the garage where it customarily sat until it was in use by the hired hands the next workday. Fred stepped into the garage, pressed the button to raise the door, and switched on the light above the workbench. Otis Thorpe stepped out of the truck just as the automatic garage door began opening. It startled him at first until he realized what was making the noise. As the door rose, Otis stepped out of the sunlight into the shadow the gable roof over the three-car garage provided. Curt was now standing next to Otis, and what they witnessed took them both by surprise—but what Robert Gray did surprised them even more. Fred had taken the tarp off the dismantled chest for Stanton to see. The others looked at the containers, then at the sheriff, watching her reaction. Seconds went by. Just then, Robert noticed the accidental observers standing a few feet away; he whirled around, nearly knocking his mother down. Waving and shouting, he ordered the men out, but it was too late. They'd seen what was on the bench. The element of secrecy everyone was counting on was compromised. Heath now knew the information Bouvier had paid him to find out—there was more on the ranch than just the candlestick. A small matter of a text message to his employer and he could return to the sunny beaches of Southern California and those bikini-clad girls. He opened the door to his own truck, tossed his straw cowboy hat and leather gloves inside, and headed down the drive. Curt was a hundred yards or so behind him.

Robert was already regretting his outburst; he knew his behavior had sent a message more revealing than what the cowhands had seen with their own eyes. Lee and Fred stood on the driveway watching the two trucks leave the ranch. The sheriff was still studying the four containers and what was left of the chest.

"This changes everything," the rancher said.

Everyone had gathered back around the workbench. "Maybe not," Stanton said without looking up. "Same plan, just need to move faster."

"No telling what Thorpe's next move will be now that he knows we've found something here on the ranch. As for Curt, whatever he thought he saw will be all over town by morning."

"Damage control, that's the next move," The sheriff said. "But, I'm still in the dark. What am I looking at?"

Fred looked across the table at Dr. Bethel. "Lee, fill her in. I'm done played out."

Lee brought the sheriff up to date, beginning with the story of Fred's grandparents, Jeremiah and Hannah Gray. Stanton stood mesmerized by the story, listening but having difficulty believing what she was hearing. If she hadn't known the Gray family, she would have thought they were nuts.

Fred waited until Lee was finished with the story. "He left something out, Sheriff."

She diverted her attention from the workbench for the moment. "And what'd he leave out?"

"Uh, well, Sheriff, he left out the part about there being two more chests just like this one still in the cave."

Stanton was speechless; she shook her head, touched the containers, and looked from one person to the next. "I'll have to say, folks, this is the strangest day I've ever had, and that's saying something."

"Yeah, well, I suppose that goes for all of us," Helen added.

"What's your next move?" Stanton said, pointing at the containers.

"Open 'em," one of the men said. She didn't know who. Her eyes and attention were focused on the workbench.

CHAPTER 24

Tuesday, June 6, 6:30ish

Heath pulled into the driveway of his small rental house, turned the ignition off, and opened the glove compartment in his pickup truck, where he kept one of his cell phones. A cell phone he used only when contacting Bouvier. He looked around the neighborhood to see if there were any curious onlookers. There was no one other than the old lady three doors down sitting in her wicker rocker, like she did every evening, reading, her cat lounging lazily next to her feet. He wondered if she was happy.

Heath jotted something in a small spiral notebook—a simple message asking the recipient *how she liked the movie and if she enjoyed the rare wine served with her dinner.* Then he wrote a few numbers and letters under the sentence, making sure the message would translate correctly. It wasn't sophisticated, but it was an encryption system Bouvier had developed and was partial to. He studied the message again, then sent it. Relieved, knowing that if everything went according to plan he could be out of this godforsaken place by the weekend. Just a matter of sanitizing the house and tying up a loose end or two. He knew that the aliases he'd used, along with the false identification, were enough to throw any local law enforcement off his trail. He thought through his mental checklist, making sure every area was covered. Anonymity and caution were the two most important foundation elements of his successful career, Heath reminded himself. Other than using false ID, no other crimes had been committed. He knew the FBI had him in their crosshairs from time to time, due mostly to the people he hired out to and not crimes he had actually committed. The only other thing was to wait patiently for Bouvier's return message; in the meantime he would continue to be Otis Thorpe, ranch hand.

* * *

Curt Russell hated conflict; he'd do just about anything to avoid it. Growing up in a home that had been a battleground between his parents taught him to flee when voices got loud. He and his sister tried being mediators when his folks fought. They'd carry messages back and forth between mom and dad, usually adding their own spin to the message to make it sound more palatable by stripping the anger away. When their attempts at adolescent diplomacy failed, they'd leave the house and run to the nearby playground or to a friend's house and stay until their parents found where they were and ordered them home.

When Robert Gray turned on him and Otis in the garage, a flood of memories returned. Curt's immediate plan was to run away, at least take shelter in his own little house. Maybe dull the sharp recollections with a few beers. God, he wished Lisa, his live-in girlfriend, was home, but she wouldn't be back from her grandfather's funeral until late Sunday, and he didn't want to burden her with a silly phone call complaining about his boss yelling at him.

Curt drove to the convenience store and bought a six-pack of Bud Lite and a sub sandwich, filled his truck with fuel, and went home. It was just about time for the game to start— Curt's Texas Rangers versus the Red Sox. He didn't hold out much hope the Rangers would win, but just the same, it was a good way to forget what had happened a few hours earlier. Curt opened the first can of beer, settled back on the only piece of furniture in his small living room, a love seat large enough for two, and reached for the remote. He punched the on button and the ESPN code, and a few seconds later the first image appeared, an advertisement for a Honda ATV. The ad reminded him of something. Curt sat up, clicked the TV off, and thought about the rider and all-terrain vehicle he'd seen a few days earlier while cleaning brush out of a culvert across from the McGraw spread. The man wasn't actually on the Gray's property; besides that, his vehicle, a newer model Chevy three-quarter-ton truck and trailer, had one of those magnetic signs on the side that said something about surveying. He hadn't paid close enough attention to remember details; he wasn't even close enough to the man to get a good look at him.

He settled back in his seat and clicked the TV back on. Besides seeking refuge away from home so he didn't have to listen to his battling parents argue, Curt withdrew into his own very active imagination, and sometimes that imagination became populated with bad guys. Like a tape recorder playing in his conscious mind, he still could hear his sister warning him to not let his imagination run wild. He watched the Red Sox' pitcher strike out the first hitter, and took a long swallow from the cold beer. Curt kicked off his boots, scooted down low in his seat, and leaned his head back. He needed to forget the day's activities. His sister was right; his imagination was beginning to crowd reality out of his thoughts. "What was that on Gray's workbench? Why was the sheriff there? And why did Robert act so crazy?" he repeated aloud, staring at the TV but not seeing the second Ranger strike out. Now the surveyor was even a part of the scene. He could feel the situation growing out of proportion to what had really happened. Curt finished off the first beer and went to the refrigerator for another. He got two.

CHAPTER 25

Tuesday, June 6, early eve.

Dr. Bethel took over the actual process of opening the containers. His education and skill as a trained archaeologist were necessary for the documentation and preservation of whatever was about to be revealed—a theory and practice that hadn't necessarily worked with opening the chest. Nevertheless, it was a process the rancher insisted on, partly to aid in his own restraint, but mostly to control the unbridled enthusiasm of his son. Fred was afraid Robert would throw caution and common sense to the wind and, in his zeal to open the chest, cause damage to something irreplaceable. Fred needed someone with a level head to be in charge.

The containers were so beautifully carved that, even empty, they would be considered artifacts. Lee approached the challenge of opening the first container in a way similar to what one might expect from a heart surgeon. Every move was made with delicate precision until the lid loosened. No nails had been used to seal the container, only finely carved notches and grooves fastened together with a very small dowel. An adhesive of some sort had been applied between the container and its lid, but had deteriorated over time, leaving only a fine dust. Lee could see the containers had been coated with a varnish-like substance that had also deteriorated, but had preserved the boxes in almost perfect condition. He finally withdrew the dowel Helen had discovered earlier and tested the lid. It was loose. Lee began lifting the lid; everyone's eyes were on the container.

"I'm sorry," Lee said. "I've forgotten my manners." He shoved the box across the workbench in front of Helen.

"Me?" Helen pressed her hands against her cheeks. Eyes wide, she looked at Lee. "Are you sure?"

"It belongs to you and Fred; you should have the honors."

Timidly Helen put her hands on both sides of the container and slowly began to lift. The lid came off easily. Everyone leaned in for a closer look, and no one spoke. A few seconds later there was a collective gasp of air as Helen peeled back a cloth wrapping, exposing the contents of the first container. She looked at Lee. "Can I…" He was nodding in anticipation of her question. Helen reached in and took the Crucifix out and laid it beside the container. A heavy silence fell over the group. Fred reached down to touch it, then quickly drew his hand back, as if, somehow, what was before him had magical powers. Maybe even a curse. He kept those thoughts to himself.

The sheriff pulled the cloth and the Crucifix closer. "Pieces of the puzzle are beginning to fall into place," she said quietly.

"You think this is related to Bouvier?" Robert asked.

"Maybe. It's becoming clear why the FBI thinks you

may be in danger. If there's more of this in that cave and someone knows about it..."

Fred interrupted. "How could anyone know about this? We didn't even know."

"Don't have an answer, but it's obvious the candlestick was the clue that captured someone's attention. It's not a matter of anyone knowing about the treasure being here on your place, just that someone, in this case Bouvier, is aware of the history of something lost," the sheriff said.

"Sheriff's right," Lee said, examining the back of the Crucifix with the magnifying glass. "Something as magnificent as this must have history. A bill-of-lading archived somewhere or spelled out on a ship's manifest. Imagine, this cargo was destined for somewhere or someone specific, and it didn't make it, for whatever reason."

"Yeah, maybe stolen?" Robert asked.

"Stolen or just hidden for safekeeping," Lee said.

"The question, of course, is why didn't they come back for it?"

"Most likely a very simple answer, Sheriff, like they forgot where it was hidden or maybe they were killed. I buried a jar full of wheat-head pennies in my backyard when I was ten. Went back to dig 'em up a month later and couldn't find them. Lost forever, or until the present day owner decides to put in a garden and finds the jar."

Lee held the Crucifix up to the light. "My UN-educated guess is it's nearly pure gold. The delicate carvings are so exact one would think it was done with some kind of computer- guided tool." He pointed at the sculpted body of the crucified Christ. "I'm not a gemologist, but these have to be rubies, and those emeralds. I don't know what those stones are."

Robert was anxiously awaiting his turn to handle the

treasure. "So, Sheriff, you think Bouvier sent Heath to find out what else, if anything, was here?"

"That'd be my guess."

"And me and my big mouth confirmed it loud and clear."

"Don't think what you did made any difference. Seeing the containers out here in plain sight with the five of us crowded around was all the evidence he needed to confirm more was here. What you did was merely put a period at the end of a sentence."

Fred cleared a place on the counter next to the workbench in anticipation of more treasure to come. "Lee, let's open the next box. We'll find out what we have here, then make a plan." He was growing impatient with the talk. No one knew anything yet, just a lot of guessing and theorizing.

Knowing how the boxes had been sealed made opening the next one much easier. Inside and wrapped carefully were two gold goblets. Gemstones encircled the rim and base. Ornate carvings of horsemen decorated the body of each chalice. The contents of the third container were no less breathtaking: three jeweled necklaces, which Lee guessed weighed more than a pound each, along with an assortment of matching bracelets and rings. Everything carefully wrapped and placed in its own separate compartment within the container. The fourth revealed six gold serving saucers, each engraved saucer depicting something different: war ships, soldiers astride horses, a castle on one, an image of a man and woman on another. All were beautiful, magnificent pieces of art.

Robert touched each piece as it was handed to him, running a calloused finger over the engraved designs. His mind was cluttered with self-doubt for the way he'd behaved in front of the two hired hands, and engrossed in the thought he might be rich beyond his wildest imagination. He was born in Buffalo, raised on his folks' ranch, played the usual sports, and never aspired to be more than an average student. College was not a consideration, even after a three-year stint in the Army. Robert married once at the age of 27 to a hometown girl who wanted more than the solitary life of a rancher's wife. Their marriage lasted two years, no children. When he went to church, which wasn't often, his mother would always compliment him on his appearance. How he looked didn't matter to him, at least it hadn't in many years, but now with the possibility of fame and fortune within his reach, an attitude adjustment might be necessary.

Robert glanced quickly, hoping no one noticed, at Crystal Stanton. He felt embarrassed. Even in her standard uniform—a blue khaki shirt sporting an American flag on one shoulder, a Harper county sheriff's patch on the other, and a gold-colored badge embroidered above the left breast pocket—she looked beautiful. He moved around to the opposite side of the workbench from Crystal, putting some distance between them. It occurred to Robert that he hadn't brushed his teeth since the night before, and in all the excitement he couldn't remember if he'd even showered. His clothes were dirty and covered with white stains from the sweat that had saturated through his tan work shirt and dried. He ran his hand over his chin; it had been at least three days since he'd shaved. The sun was beginning to set, and the inside of the garage was growing darker, the only light coming from above the workbench. Robert took another step back, hoping the growing shadow would obscure his grubby appearance.

"I'm speechless!" Lee said. "Never would I have believed this if I hadn't seen it with my own eyes."

"Agreed. We're all speechless. Unbelievable, in the

truest sense of the word,"

Stanton mumbled as if she were talking only to herself. She jotted something down in her notebook and stuck the pen back in the leather loop designed for that purpose. She cleared her throat like someone preparing to make a speech or issue commands. "A mystery is unfolding before us." She emphasized each word, making deliberate eye contact with the others, taking control. "I expect this mystery to take on a life of its own any time now."

"Speak English, Sheriff. What do you mean by that?" Fred said.

"When you consider all the variables; the candlestick, Hansen's initial contact with Bouvier, FBI involvement, the ICO with ties to terrorists, the professor in Madrid and his alleged agent who is supposedly with the Smithsonian, your ranch hand Heath. Think about the mix, Fred. You've got a helluva brew cooking and no way to predict how it's going to turn out."

"Yeah, well, what's your suggestion?" Fred asked, arms folded defensively.

"Priority one, safety first. Keeping your family out of harm's way is my number one function here. The events to follow will have to evolve and play out on their own. Not much we can do to affect the outcome."

"And the treasure, what happens with it?" Robert asked.

Stanton shaded her eyes from the glare of the fluorescent light, trying to see where Robert was. "Don't know, but I suggest you think about what this is worth to you."

"You're not talk'n dollars and cents here, you mean…"

"Right. I mean is this worth risking your life over?"

Being the family patriarch, Fred Gray was not inclined to want help, much less ask for it. He'd been self-sufficient all his life and damn proud of that fact, but things were changing, changing fast, and, if the sheriff was right, on the verge of spinning out of his control. He hated the way it made him feel, a helplessness he had never experienced. Fred's resistant posture relaxed as the realization of his situation became clearer. His arms unfolded and he allowed them to drop slowly to his side. He had to think of his family first, no question about that. "Okay, Sheriff, what's your plan?"

"Secure the treasure. You say there are two more like this one still in the cave?"

"One's intact, the other broken open on one end. We think that's where the candlestick came from," Lee answered.

"Okay, I suggest that you leave those two in the cave. They're probably safer there than in a bank vault. Speaking of a bank vault, I wouldn't recommend taking what you've found so far into town."

"Way ahead of you on that one, Sheriff. If we traipsed into that bank carrying anything larger than a business envelope and asked to keep it in the vault, Marion Mitchell, the head teller, would blab it all over town. We'll take it to Oklahoma City; in the meantime, I've got a hiding place in the basement."

"Good. Now, we know Holt's in DC at a task force briefing and should be back tomorrow evening with updated information, maybe even some advice for us." Stanton looked at her watch. "Sorry, I mean he'll be back tonight. Didn't realize it's nearly one a.m." The sheriff explained her plan for providing protection to the family. She turned to Helen. "My cell signal is weak. May I use your phone?"

"Of course, in the kitchen."

Stanton called her second-shift deputy and directed him to come to the Gray Ranch. The deputy protested, suggesting instead that he remain at his present location, which was across the street from the Saddle-up Bar and Grill. The bar, notoriously known countywide as the Buffalo Knife and Gun Club, was preparing to close. It was 1:40 a.m., and the deputy didn't want to miss the action. The sheriff knew that post at that particular hour was a favorite among her deputies. More arrests were made there in two hours than anywhere else in the county, and the resulting fines paid the salary of at least one full-time deputy. Furthermore, it was a public service, one that couldn't be ignored. Routine arrests resulting in charges being filed ranged from DUI to disturbing the peace.

"I understand, Deputy Parker, but those are my orders. See you in thirty minutes. By the way, I assume Trooper Crossland is sitting next to you in his black and white?"

"Yes ma'am, he is."

"He has jurisdiction. I'm sure he can handle it, don't you?"

"Yes ma'am, I'm on my way. ETA twenty-five minutes." Parker looked out his open window. "Gotta go, sheriff's orders."

The trooper nodded and waved. Parker picked up his radio mic and clicked the transmit button. "Unit two to dispatch."

The radio squawked. "Dispatch."

"Unit two leaving Saddle-up, destination Gray Ranch, ETA twenty-five minutes. Copy?"

"Copy two," the dispatcher confirmed.

"Ten-four dispatch."

"Dispatch clear."

Parker concluded his routine check-in procedure and pulled the cruiser on to the highway headed south.

The sheriff met Parker where the county road and the Gray Ranch driveway intersected. They both shut their car lights off and got out. Stanton pointed northwest. "See that ridge that runs in a semicircle behind the house about a quarter mile?" The moon was almost full and cast enough light to see the terrain for a half mile in all directions.

"Yes ma'am."

"Deputy!" She faced him, and he turned sheepishly to face her.

"We've had this conversation before. Call me sheriff, you can even call me Crystal in private, but don't call me ma'am."

Parker nodded. It was a hard habit to break, though, something drilled into him by his mother, the proper way of addressing a woman older than he was. But, it was more than just etiquette—other feelings ran deeper. Feelings that triggered sensations he had to hide. At 28, Parker had never had a woman boss, much less a woman boss who could outshoot him at target practice, kick his butt in hand-to-hand combat, and the big one, a woman who could probably win most swimsuit contests she'd care to enter. Not that he'd seen her in a swimsuit and could make that judgment fairly, but an imagination he had, a fantasy, one of those thoughts he had to conceal. He wondered if the other deputies, with the exception of Maude, had the same feelings. One thing was for sure, a very distinct boundary existed between her and the deputies, a boundary they knew better than to try to cross.

She pointed again. "There's a road running up the east side of the ridge. Mr. Gray said you'd have no problem driving up there. Park close to that stand of cedars, and you'll be able to see miles in any direction, watch for anything suspicious. Any questions?"

"What do you consider suspicious?"

"Great question. Familiarize yourself with vehicles owned by the Grays, also with a white Ford pickup owned by the university and driven by Dr. Lee Bethel, a professor. It has a red insignia painted on both doors. In about four or five hours, you'll probably see two more pickup trucks arrive. They belong to the hired hands. Curtis Russell, you probably know him."

"Yeah, I know him and Lisa, his girlfriend. I know what he drives."

"The other hand drives a blue Ford 150, I'd guess a 2000 model. His name is Otis Thorpe. He's only been around six or eight weeks, don't know much about him. Keep an eye on him. Watch for any other movement on the ranch, other vehicles of any kind. If you see anything curious, call me. You're on a hill, cell phone should work. If it doesn't, radio dispatch and have them contact me. From this point on, refer to the ridge-top location as 'Alpha one post.' Understand?"

"Think so. This is all about cattle thieves, right?"

Stanton paused, searching for an answer that wouldn't be an outright lie. It was difficult. "Yeah, thieves. Beef prices are high. But, you know, we've been over this in training. Avoid tunnel-vision, you get to thinking only about cattle thieves, and you might miss something else. Right?"

"Yes, you're right, Sheriff. I'll keep an eye out for anything suspicious."

He said the right thing, Stanton thought, but his voice sounded unsure. The sheriff hoped she'd be more convincing later when she briefed the others.

Stanton watched as the deputy drove his cruiser carefully onto the ridge. The road wasn't much more than two parallel indentions in the hard-packed ground created by the ranch truck scattering feed to the livestock. The deputy parked between two of the largest cedars, and from where the sheriff stood the vehicle was hidden from view.

The sheriff checked her watch, noted the time on a log sheet attached to a clipboard lying on the front seat. She drove onto the county road and listened for Parker's post confirmation. A minute passed, and Stanton reached for her mic, frustrated her deputy had forgotten a simple procedure. Just as she was ready to depress the transmit button, the radio cracked. "Dispatch, this is Unit Two, do you copy?"

"Copy, Unit Two, go ahead."

"Unit Two, Post Alpha One, time 0238 hours. Copy?"

"Copy two, Post Alpha One, 0238 hours."

"Ten-four, dispatch. Two clear."

"Dispatch clear."

Stanton slid the mic back on its hook, thankful she didn't have to intervene and remind Parker of his error. She headed north, thinking about the last 48 hours. It had been years since she'd felt this insecure about anything. The situation confronting her demanded more than what she had to offer. As an FBI agent, faced with a similar set of circumstances, all she had to do was pick up the phone and ask for reinforcements, Intel, consultation, and it was provided, but this was different. All of a sudden Stanton felt furiously helpless, at the mercy of people and events outside her realm of authority—an intolerable sensation. Maybe her feelings were the result of fatigue; after all, she'd only had a couple of hours of sleep since her first encounter with Holt, and here it was nearly three in the morning. Stanton hurried back to town, driving by Thorpe's house on her way to her own. The pickup truck was in the drive, lights in the house were off. The house and neighborhood looked peaceful, quiet, and safe. At least that is how the neighborhood appeared, a subtle contradiction for sure. If the people in those homes only knew... But they don't, she thought, and for now their ignorance worked in her favor.

The sheriff made a slow pass through the empty streets of downtown, then headed home. With some luck she might manage to get a few hours sleep before shift change at the Gray Ranch at 8:00 a.m.

* * *

Helen was already asleep by the time Fred came to bed. Lee and Robert re-packed the treasure back into the containers and took it to the basement. As the men climbed the stairs Robert said, "A beer before we call it a day?"

"Sounds good, but I have to head home early. Your dad wants me here when the guy from the Smithsonian inspects the candle stick, and I didn't come prepared."

Robert got to the top of the stairs and turned. "I'm curious, Lee." He paused. "What's your assessment so far?"

"This discovery, Robert, is so far outside my expertise, I wouldn't even venture a guess. One thing's for sure."

"What's that?"

"There have been significant paleontological and archaeological discoveries here in the U.S., but this may well be the most significant historical discovery ever in North America."

"And the implications of that?"

"The sheriff nailed it—the situation's out of our hands. A life of its own is how she phrased it. You and your mom and dad are players in a game—a game, I'm afraid, that has rules we don't understand."

"Yeah, that's obvious. That's what scares me, Lee, not for myself but for Mom. I can tell it's already taking a toll." Robert walked to the refrigerator and got a beer. "Sure you don't want one of these?"

"Thanks anyway. Shower and sleep is all I want right now." Lee disappeared down the hallway. Robert twisted the bottle cap off, turned out the kitchen light, and stepped outside into the night air.

CHAPTER 26

Wednesday, June 7, 7:20 a.m.

Lee walked into the kitchen at 7:20. Helen was sliding a cookie sheet dotted with biscuit dough into the oven. "Ready for some ham and eggs?"

"If it isn't too much trouble." Lee was surprised to see how energetic she was.

"No trouble at all. Love to cook. How are you this morning?"

"Great. And you?"

"Couldn't be better. Got a good night's sleep and I'm raring to go."

"Fred and Robert, where are they?"

"Robert's still asleep; Fred's out back giving the hands their work assignments. He should be in for breakfast any minute. What are your plans, Lee?"

"I'm going home this morning. I have things to do at the university. With what's taking place here, I think we should arrange to have the summer excavation somewhere else."

Helen set Lee's breakfast in front of him and in the same move touched his arm. He looked up. "You are coming back, aren't you?" Her question was more of a gentle, persuasive plea.

"You couldn't keep me away." Lee didn't have to be told what his presence meant to Helen. She wanted him there for Fred's sake.

Fred came through the back door, hung his hat, and sat down at the table. "You finally decided to get up I see." He smiled.

"Smelled Helen's biscuits, that's all it took."

Helen poured coffee as Fred sliced his ham, mixing the pieces with his over-easy eggs. He peppered the conglomeration and reached for the salt. Helen grabbed it first. "It's salted enough," she said, her eyes fixed on his, daring him to object.

Fred drew his hand back, smiled, and winked at his wife. "Yes ma'am."

"So how were the hands this morning?" she asked.

"Curt was a little jumpy, could tell he was nervous. Thorpe was cool as a cucumber. Acted like nothing happened. I know that FBI fella…what's his name?"

"Holt," Helen said.

"Yeah, Holt. He's FBI, must know what he's talking about, but at the same time I don't see evil in Thorpe's eyes."

"And what does evil look like in someone's eyes?" Helen laid her fork down and cocked her head to the side, frowning.

"Sounds dumb, I know. I've even been suspicious of the way he watches us, like he's studying our moves, but…hell, I don't know, just a gut feeling."

"Well, I just hope you don't let that gut feeling blind you into trusting him."

"Not a chance. As a matter of fact, let's make sure the doors are all locked and the garage shut until all this is behind us. In the meantime, Robert or me will always be in or around the house." Fred looked toward the cabinet next to the kitchen sink. "Remember, you've always got Smith & Wesson ready to help if need be." Fred looked at Lee. "What time are you leaving? Better yet, when will you be back?"

"Leaving now. Was telling Helen, I got a lot to do at the university. Want to check up on this Carlos Ramirez."

"How?"

"Couple of friends of mine made it to the big time. Both have important jobs in DC. I'm hoping they can help. I should be back by Monday."

"Five days from now? Was hoping you'd be back sooner."

"If Ramirez calls and wants to come out before then, just call, I'll be here. My guess is he won't be here until next week. That'll give me time to move the dig to another location and talk to my connections in Washington."

Fred walked Lee to his truck. Bear joined them. "So, what ya think?"

Lee reached down and patted the dog. "Just glad you didn't persuade me to come out two weeks ago." He tossed his backpack and duffle bag into the truck bed. "I don't know how I would've finished the semester with all this on my mind." Lee stepped into the cab and started the engine. "You know this is going to change all our lives."

"Yup. Just hope it's for the better."

* * *

Ten minutes later, Lee turned off the county road onto State Highway 34. He drove south through Woodward, stopping for fuel and coffee. Lee checked his cell phone; the indicator was flashing *low-batt*. He plugged in the charger and checked the time: 9:12, June 7. He was ahead of schedule. Three hours to Oklahoma City. That would give him time to plan his next move. His biggest challenge—how to tell Beverly that she couldn't go to the ranch with him. Lee knew it wouldn't be easy. He'd already promised her she could stay at the ranch house and help with the bison kill site excavation. Beverly was looking forward to it, and Helen was excited that she'd have another woman around to talk to, but the situation had changed and it wouldn't be safe. He'd have to use his most persuasive tactics to convince his wife it wasn't possible for her to go with him. Beverly was levelheaded and sensible. She would understand.

Lee pulled the address Fred had given him out of his breast pocket and read it again. He was nearing Interstate 35. Instead of taking the south ramp toward home, Lee went north all the way to NW 63rd then west to May Avenue. Hansen Antiques and Appraisals, according to Fred's directions, was located just north of that intersection. Lee was looking forward to meeting the dealer to see if he could coax more information about the candlestick out of him. He had no intention of telling Hansen about the chest; he was there only to get information and not give it. Lee turned north on May and drove slowly, looking for the store, expecting to see a typical junk store. He imagined a small, cramped, dusty building full of old stuff falling far short of being true antiques. Beverly had dragged him into enough phony stores claiming to sell antiques that he'd formed an opinion about such establishments and their proprietors, and it wasn't good.

Just half a block ahead, Lee spotted the sign HANSEN ANTIQUES and APPRAISALS. He changed lanes quickly without using his signal. The maneuver earned him a shaking fist and an extended digit from a gray-haired woman driving a Cadillac Escalade. Lee waved back apologetically and made his turn into the parking lot. The store was large with a clean, well-marked parking lot and attractive front window displays designed to attract a more discriminating clientele. The exterior of the building was tastefully decorated, none of your typical gaudy signs screaming NO MONEY DOWN or GOING OUT OF BUSINESS SALE. Lee pulled into a parking place near the front door. There were only two other cars in the lot at that time.

As he entered the store, a soft ring from a bell just over the door announced his presence. Two well-dressed women, mid-forties he guessed, were examining a large antique maple conference table, trying to decide how it would complement their executive boardroom. He passed them on the way to the customer counter and overheard part of their conversation. "You know, Susan, sixty-five hundred dollars for a table like this is cheap."

Lee stood next to the counter admiring picture frames hanging on the wall. One was $1,200, another $3,000. "This guy's either an accomplished crook or a real antique dealer," he mumbled. Just then he saw a man walking in his direction who smiled and looked friendly. "Good morning." His greeting was cheerful, sincere. Lee made a mental note to adjust his preconceived idea of antiques and dealers. "Good morning." he tried to sound as friendly.

"What can I help you with?"

Lee reached to take Hansen's outstretched hand. "Lee Bethel, with the University of Oklahoma. We have a mutual acquaintance in common. Fred Gray." He paused, studying the proprietor's reaction. Fred had asked Lee to visit with Hansen on his way home. The rancher wanted another opinion about the man, an opinion he could trust. With the events unfolding as they were, he was becoming suspicious of everyone and needed another set of eyes to help him see things as they actually were.

"Oh yes, Mr. Gray has mentioned your name. You're an archaeologist working some kind of site on his land." Hansen motioned for Lee to take a chair next to the counter. The chair looked expensive, like a real antique. He hesitated.

"It's okay, please sit." Hansen smiled. "All my antiques are functional. If you can't sit on them, eat off the tables, or sleep on the beds, then what good are they?"

Lee nodded as he cautiously lowered himself into the plush chair. The women had moved on from discussing the conference table and were looking at matching bookcases, out of hearing range. Hansen was still standing in front of an empty chair when the phone rang. He laid a brochure he'd been reading, Lee assumed, on the table next to the chair and answered the phone. The brochure was well worn, folded and refolded a number of times. Although it was upside down, Lee could read the title. "What African-American Men Should Know About Heart Disease." The man looked like the picture of health, Lee thought, even distinguished-looking. Hansen was impeccably dressed in a black pin-striped suit, the trouser cuff breaking perfectly over the laces of his plain toed and very shiny shoes. Hansen hung the phone up. "Sorry, my assistant is at lunch." He sat down across from Lee and picked up the pamphlet, stuffing it in his coat pocket. "My dad was just diagnosed with coronary heart disease. The doc says I'm a prime candidate also, so I'm reading all I can about prevention."

"Sorry to hear that. Hope they caught it in time to do something for him."

"They said he could prolong his life if he'd start walking, stop smoking, lay off chicken fried steak, butter, and eggs."

"He's following orders, right?"

"No. He never will, but I am."

"Good for you," Lee said.

"Now, back to our mutual acquaintance. How is Mr. Gray doing?"

"Fine. I've been out there the last two days planning the university's annual excavation exercise. He told me the story about the candlestick. Says someone from the Smithsonian is coming to look at it." Lee's intention was to feed Hansen bits and pieces of information and see what resulted.

"When I first saw the candlestick and heard Mr. Gray's story, I knew it was a one of a kind discovery. I also knew it was beyond my capacity to appraise. He probably told you I sent photos and a story synopsis to an expert in New York."

"He did, said you weren't happy with the New York appraisal."

"No I wasn't. Did he tell you I sent photos to an expert in Spain?"

"Yes. Something about expecting a call from some guy with the Smithsonian."

"The appraisal was actually conducted by a Dr. Cardona, professor of some kind at a university in Madrid. He called me very excited about the photos."

"Did he say why he was excited?"

"No, just wanted me to ask Mr. Gray if he'd be willing to allow the Smithsonian expert to look at it in person."

Lee already knew what Hansen was telling him and more. He was satisfied that the dealer was legitimate; he even felt a bond developing between them, but Lee wasn't about to divulge what he knew. He'd heard what the sheriff said loud and clear. Trustworthy or not, Lee knew he couldn't say anything else to Hansen. "Well, it's certainly an intriguing little mystery, isn't it?"

"I'll say. It's got my curiosity and my blood pressure up. Will you be going back to the Gray Ranch soon?" Hansen said.

"Summer excavation starts in about ten days. I'll be there for a couple of weeks."

"Please tell Mr. Gray hello, and let me know what transpires after the Smithsonian expert examines the candlestick."

Lee agreed, and as he was leaving, he overheard one of the women telling Hansen they were ready to buy.

CHAPTER 27

Wednesday, June 7, 1:40 p.m.

Lee Bethel found the nearest freeway on-ramp headed south. Home was only 20 miles away, but it would take at least an hour to get there through heavy traffic and construction zones. He thought about his conversation with Hansen: he hadn't seen or heard anything that alarmed him. As far as he could tell, Hansen seemed honest, more concerned about Fred's welfare than making a buck. Lee decided he'd pass that opinion on to the rancher with a disclaimer; there was always the possibility of misjudging another person's objectives.

Lee thought about what he needed to do before returning to the ranch. Traffic had come to a standstill while a road crew moved an earthmover across the highway. The delay added frustration to the anxiousness he already felt. Problems were sure to arise between him and Beverly, he thought, when he told her she couldn't go. The situation at the ranch had changed considerably; surely she would understand why he had to put his foot down. The week before, when they had discussed her coming along, the only danger confronting them was sunburn. She'd just have to trust him.

Less than a mile to his exit, he could see the green and white sign over the ramp. Lee looked at his watch. It was 2:10. He'd made good time. Beverly was expecting him home between 3:30 and 4:00, so his early arrival would be a surprise. He smiled.

* * *

Shortly after Lee left the ranch, Fred received the expected call from Dr. Ramirez inquiring about the best time to visit. The men discussed the candlestick and a repeat of its history, and they agreed on Monday, June 12. Fred told Ramirez four other people would be present. Ramirez did not object.

Fred hung up the phone, sat down at the breakfast table, and took a sip of coffee.

"Well?" Helen was usually a patient woman, but not then. "What did he say?"

Fred studied his tin cup, the cup his grandfather had given him his first taste of coffee from, a cup Helen had tried to throw away many times, only to find it back in the cabinet the next day. "Wasn't so much what he said." He paused, thinking of the right words.

"What, then?" Robert asked.

"He asked me to describe the engravings. You heard what I told him. Could hardly see 'em. I got the impression he knows more than he's let'n on. He said he'd seen photos and could tell there was something engraved on the sides. He wanted to know if it looked like writing or just decorative squiggles. I said I didn't know."

Helen filled the empty coffee cups and sat down next to her husband. "Guess all we can do is wait patiently till Monday."

Robert finished his coffee and stood. "Frankly, my patience is wear'n thin."

"What are you going to do?" Helen asked.

"First I'm gonna make sure the hands are where they're supposed to be, then to the cave."

Fred leaned back in his chair. "I know we're all excited, but running over to the cave isn't the best idea. Check'n on the hands is okay as long as you don't act suspicious. Remember what the sheriff said."

"What do you suggest we do between now and next Monday?" Robert said, pacing nervously around the kitchen.

"Evidently, son, you didn't remember the sheriff's advice."

"Okay, okay, what advice?"

"Act natural. Don't do anything out of the ordinary. Don't do anything that'd attract attention. Just stick to our normal routine."

"You need something to keep you busy," Helen said.

"Like what?"

"Feed cattle," his dad said.

"Cattle don't need fed."

"Damn it, son, feed 'em anyway. Fix the barn door. Go to town, shoot some pool, do anything—just don't run all over the ranch acting nervous-like."

Robert knew his dad was right. The sheriff had a deputy posted on the ridge, and the FBI was keeping an eye on Thorpe. The Smith and Wesson .38 was loaded and on the top shelf of the kitchen cabinet, just where it always was. Fred and his son agreed one of them would be in or near the house at all times. Nothing else left to do but wait on the Smithsonian expert to examine the candlestick. "Check on the cows, see how Curt and Otis are doing, then fix the barn door," he repeated. "Guess that'll keep me busy today."

"Don't forget the walkie-talkie; we need to stay in touch all day. When one of us is out we need to check in at thirty-minute intervals," Fred said.

"What about Lee and the sheriff? Shouldn't you let them know when Dr. Ramirez is coming?" Helen asked.

"I'll do that right now." Fred finished his coffee and went to the den to make the calls.

CHAPTER 28

Wednesday, June 7, 7:00 a.m.

Crystal Stanton was a deep sleeper, and today was no exception. Over the years she had tried setting her clock-radio to an early morning talk show, but that didn't work. She tried waking to music, and that seemed to lull her into a deeper sleep. The only sound that was guaranteed to wake her was the obnoxious, pulsating, squawking alarm, with the volume turned up high. Stanton struggled to move, to orient herself. She could hear the alarm and knew it meant something, but she wasn't sure what. Finally she swung her legs off the bed and sat up, rubbing her eyes. Where was that noise coming from? Was it her cell phone, and where *was* her phone? *Under that pile of clothes*, she thought, still too groggy to look. Finally Stanton saw the radio and the red button on top labeled OFF. She pressed it.

Silence. Thank God for silence.

She sat massaging her scalp, which helped her remember where she was and, even more importantly, who she was. Stanton stirred the pile of clothes next to her bed with her foot, and finally located her cell phone. She picked it up and punched speed dial for Deputy Cox. He answered, "Deputy Cox." He knew from the caller ID who it was. "Morning, Sheriff."

"Anything to report?" she asked, trying to sound alert and in charge.

"Hired hands arrived just before 0700. Someone from inside the house came out and talked to 'em. The two hired hands subsequently entered a farm vehicle and drove to a pasture I'd guess about a mile west. I've been watching them; looks like they're working on a fence."

"Good, Deputy. Anything else?"

"One other thing, probably nothing to get excited about. I did make a note in the log, though."

"Making a note in the log, that's good, Deputy. Now, what was it that prompted you to make a note?" Her rule about being thorough and documenting everything proved to be a bit tedious at times. Young deputies tended to focus on the rule rather than on what the rule was made for.

"A dark-colored—couldn't tell from here if it's black, blue, or green; it's just dark—sedan, maybe a Ford, has driven by twice. Once, the driver stopped on the road where it crests the hill south of here."

"What did you see? Did the driver do anything?"

"From what I could tell, it looked like he was scanning the ranch with binoculars."

"What's your assessment, Deputy?"

"Don't think he's a hunter, it ain't hunting season, and don't think he's a cattle thief 'cause of the car he's driving, and it looked to me, from this distance, like he's wearing a suit. Probably just another oil company employee lookin' for a site to drill."

Stanton figured it was the FBI agent assigned

temporarily to tail Thorpe until Holt got back from the task force meeting. If she was right, and she hoped she was, then Holt had followed through with his commitment to furnish a fill-in during his absence. On the other hand, she'd be angry. Holt promised the temp would check in with her so she'd know who was tailing Thorpe and what he or she looked like. On top of that, it was just courteous to coordinate with local law enforcement when conducting an operation in someone else's jurisdiction. Stanton still needed to call Assistant Director Jerry Webster to verify Holt's story, and now she would have to call the area agent-in-charge and give him a piece of her mind on the surveillance screw-up.

"Anything else, Deputy?"

"Norton just got here, Sheriff. I'll brief him and head back to town unless you want me to check the dark car out."

"No, Cox, I don't want you to do anything with the dark car. Tell Norton to keep his eye on it, though, and tell him I'll be out later this morning."

Stanton flipped the phone shut, laid it on a table next to the stationary exercise bike, and clicked on the TV. She set the bike timer for 30 minutes and surfed the channels until she found news. By 8:30 Stanton was up on world events and wondering how the Gray Ranch discovery would be reported by those same talking heads and, ultimately, how national news coverage would affect her community. She knew notoriety came with a price, consequences even a fortune-teller couldn't predict. Some people would benefit from the discovery, and others would be harmed. It must be a law of physics, she thought, something more sophisticated than Murphy's Law, although she instinctively knew if something could go wrong, it would. All she could do was plan for the worst possible scenario and then hope against hope the situation turned out better than expected.

Before going to the ranch, Stanton drove slowly through town to the outskirts and turned around in the gravel parking lot of a pipeline servicing company. She stopped for fuel at the convenience store and struck up a short conversation about the weather with Ruth, the daytime clerk. She made another pass through town, driving even slower by the café and Turner's Barber Shop. The sheriff drove by all the locations that informally kept track of her whereabouts. When she first became sheriff, she learned quickly that everything she did was noticed, scrutinized, discussed over coffee, and evaluated. She was having supper at the Percolator Café one evening about a month after she was elected, and two local store owners invited themselves to join her. She didn't object. In the course of the conversation, and much to her surprise, although she didn't let on, Stanton learned the two men knew where she had been that day, what she had done, and the approximate time she had done it. And, it wasn't just these two—seemed many others knew as well. Rather than being concerned about her lack of privacy, Stanton used it to her advantage. On this particular day she wanted the citizens to be aware that the status quo was in place. It was just another average day in a small town in Oklahoma. Stanton knew it would not be that way for long, but today and for as many days to follow as possible, it was her responsibility to maintain the illusion.

The sheriff arrived on the ridge just before noon. She found Deputy Norton sitting in a lawn chair he'd brought from home. The cruiser was tucked between cedars and couldn't be seen from the road, just as she had instructed. Norton was busy with the binoculars, and to his left was an ice chest with water and two cans of Dr. Pepper, his log lying on top of the chest. They exchanged greetings, and the sheriff picked up the log to read it rather than distract the deputy from surveillance with requests for information she could just as easily obtain from the documentation. She saw that a white pickup truck had left the ranch at 0843. Stanton knew Bethel was going home so that he could make preparations to return when Carlos Ramirez came to view the candlestick. She had received a call that morning from Fred advising her of the date and approximate time of Ramirez's future visit. The sheriff returned the log to the ice chest. "See anything?"

"Just a ten-point mule deer about a half mile down that draw. Too bad it's not huntin' season."

"Where are the ranch hands?"

"Looks like they found a shady spot and are having lunch." The deputy stood and stretched, twisting his torso to the right and left, working the kinks out that resulted from holding binoculars to his eyes for hours. "Is there something about those two I need to be aware of?"

"Don't know; I want you to keep your eyes on everything. Just because they're hired hands don't mean that one or both aren't scoundrels." The sheriff reached for the binoculars. "Let me have those, and you take a break. Go have lunch, walk around, and rest your eyes. Be back by 1330."

"Thanks. Anything else you want me to do while I'm in town?"

"Yeah, drive through town a time or two, make yourself visible."

Stanton pulled the lawn chair over to a shady spot and sat down; she could already feel the sweat accumulating around her neck. She raised the binoculars and steadied them on the ranch house. Someone was working on the barn door. She adjusted the magnification. It was Robert.

Stanton wondered about him, his divorce, why he never remarried. Nice guy, she thought, but for some reason it seemed like he had avoided her the night before. She swung around and trained the binoculars on the two ranch hands. They were still eating.

Norton returned to post Alpha 1 at 1320. The sheriff made observation entries in the log and re-emphasized the importance of contacting her if he saw anything out of the ordinary taking place on or near the ranch. She drove down the hill and stopped at the ranch house to talk with Fred and Helen. Robert was still working on the barn.

"Our surveillance is in place, and the agent tailing Thorpe has been around. Holt is due in tonight. Hopefully we'll know more then," the sheriff said.

"We're following your advice, Sheriff. Acting as normal as possible under the circumstances," Helen said.

"It's tough, I know, but it's for the best. We don't want to draw any unnecessary attention if we can avoid it. I'll check in with you again later. Right now I need to spend time at headquarters." The sheriff stood to leave just as Robert came through the back door. He was friendlier, smiled more, not at all like he had been the day before. He greeted Stanton with a warm smile; she felt a blush rising from her neckline. She smiled back.

"Didn't realize you were here," Robert said.

"Just dropped by for a minute," Stanton said, fumbling nervously with the snap that secured her holstered weapon.

On the way back to town, Stanton thought about the very brief encounter she'd just had with Robert. His smile touched her in a way she hadn't felt in a long time. There had been boyfriends over the years, even some serious relationships, but inevitably she would be transferred or assigned to work undercover for an extended period. After a few heartbreaking separations, FBI agent Stanton conditioned herself to tread cautiously when it came to matters of love. Had she become too cautious?

Deputy Bingham was at her desk finishing an arrest report when the sheriff arrived. "What's going on, Sheriff?" Her question was more of a greeting than a true inquiry.

"Just following up on the cattle thief concern." Stanton opened the door to her office and hurried through it, hoping to avoid questions she wasn't ready to answer.

Bingham kept writing, appearing absorbed in completing the report, uninterested in what the sheriff had just said. "Seems to me like a waste of manpower having someone on, what'd you call it? Oh yeah, Alpha One post, twenty-four hours a day."

Stanton knew concealing the truth from her deputies couldn't last long. With the exception of Maude, all the deputies were young and for the most part inexperienced, but they weren't dumb. Maude was already suspicious. Stanton could tell from her voice and her behavior. It wouldn't be long until everyone was suspicious, and she couldn't afford to hide the truth. Asking the deputies to follow her into a dangerous situation was one thing; asking them to follow blindly was a good way to lose their confidence. Stanton knew for the safety of everyone, including her deputies, they needed to know what was going on. She would have to trust them to be discreet and honor the FBI's demand for secrecy. The sheriff started to close her door; the best response to Bingham's remark was no response. Stanton didn't want to back herself into a corner. There were some things she needed to do, some information to confirm before she briefed her deputies.

"Oh! I almost forgot," Bingham said, rushing to the partially closed door. "Brent called in about an hour ago, said he wouldn't be in."

Stanton opened the door partway. "Why?"

"Wife's sick. You know she's had a rough pregnancy, and the doctor told her to stay off her feet."

"Yeah, and the baby is due anytime, isn't it?"

"Anytime."

Stanton stood at the half-opened door thinking about how to rearrange the schedule in light of Brent's situation. "How about filling in for him? That is, if you have the time."

"You're asking me to cover a shift?"

Stanton noticed Bingham's reaction. The deputy stood taller, almost as if she had come to attention. Her eyes widened and a faint smile crept across her face.

"Yes. You're a deputy, aren't you?"

"I am and yes, I would like to cover for Brent."

The sheriff opened the door and invited Bingham in to be briefed.

"This is a surveillance post only. You are not to investigate or to intervene in anything you see happening on or near the Gray Ranch. If you are suspicious of anything or you have a question, you are to call me, understand?"

"I understand, Sheriff."

"Good. Norton will brief you when you relieve him." Stanton described how to get to post Alpha 1. "I have phone calls to make, and I don't want to be disturbed unless it's an emergency."

Bingham left the sheriff's office and closed the door behind her. She was thrilled to be actually doing police work, something she had always wanted to do, but didn't dare ask the former sheriff for fear of ridicule. He was that kind of jackass.

CHAPTER 29

Wednesday, June 7, mid-afternoon

Stanton unlocked her desk file drawer and pulled out a small red booklet that contained official and restricted phone numbers. The FBI agent in charge was officed in Enid, a city of just over 50,000 people, located a hundred miles east of Buffalo. According to her directory, Enid's largest employer was Vance Air Force Base, a training base for new pilots just out of Officer Candidate School. The sheriff found the agent's cell number and called it.

"Agent Pete Miles," he answered on the first tone.

"Agent Miles, this is Sheriff Stanton, Harper County. Is this a convenient time to talk?"

"Yes, Sheriff, what can I do for you?"

Stanton explained the reason for the call.

"I'm sorry the agent didn't check in with you. That's my fault. Had to pull an agent from Amarillo to cover Heath—he's new. I should've called you myself, won't happen again."

For some reason Agent Miles didn't sound earnest about the oversight. Almost cavalier about the whole thing, Stanton thought. Her frustration grew. "Has your agent reported in yet?" the sheriff asked, hoping to hear some sincerity, something to reassure her that Miles understood how important the field agent's task was.

"No, I told him just to keep an eye on this guy and report back if he did anything unusual."

Stanton's anger was almost to the boiling point. "Agent Miles, what do you know about Heath?" she asked calmly, striving to mask the growing fury.

"Not much. I was asked to put someone on him for twenty-four hours, and that's what I did."

She could detect frustration in Miles' voice. Maybe he didn't know about the ICO. His own agency may not have thought he had a need to know, leaving him in the dark, a feeling she'd had on more than one occasion.

"Your supervisor didn't give you background on Heath?"

"Supervisor, what supervisor? I got a call from Agent Holt. He simply asked for courtesy observation of this guy. Didn't say much, other than he was a person of interest with possible ties to some criminal organization."

"He didn't explain that Heath might be dangerous?"

"Hell no! How dangerous?"

Stanton knew she was on thin ice with the agent in charge. If the FBI intentionally left him out of the loop, it wasn't her place to pull him in. She paused. "I have a suggestion."

"I'm all ears."

"Call your headquarters and explain the situation about Holt asking you to provide a tail on Heath. Ask them to bring you up to speed. See what they say."

"I'm ahead of you on that one. It's the next thing I'm going to do."

"Don't tell anyone I suggested you call. Keep me out of this. One other thing. After you've talked to your supervisor, give me a call back."

* * *

Agent Carl Holt left the task force briefing in Washington at 2:00 p.m. eastern standard time and crossed the street to his hotel. He stopped at the registration desk and made arrangements to stay two more nights. The task force commander had extended the meeting another day. He told the members to expect a long session Thursday and to plan accordingly.

Holt walked across the hotel lobby to the gift shop and purchased a cellophane-wrapped package containing five letter-sized blank pages and five envelopes. With the stationery in hand, he entered the hotel bar. It was dimly lit, as he had expected. The agent allowed his eyes to refocus and found a booth away from other patrons. He could see the waitress approaching. "Afternoon, sir. What can I get you?" She sounded more business than flirty. Probably a Georgetown law student, he thought, checking out the typical skimpy barmaid short skirt and plunging neckline. She was attractive but her behavior abrupt. She did not invite conversation, and as far as Holt was concerned, she wasn't getting the usual tip reserved for those who stood close, smiled, and on occasion touched him.

"Vodka and seven with a twist."

"Would you like a menu?"

"Just the drink, dear."

She disappeared into the bar's dimness and returned with the drink in less than a minute. "Should we start a tab?"

"No. This will be all." He was anxious for her to leave.

The waitress laid the ticket on the table and extended the obligatory invitation to come back.

Holt rolled his eyes. "Thanks, I will." He waited until she disappeared and then pulled out the package of writing paper. The agent reached into his briefcase, took out a pair of latex gloves, and put them on. All field agents were required to carry gloves to be used while investigating crime scenes. He unwrapped the package and laid one piece of blank paper on the table, and with a pen he'd taken from his hotel room he began to print. *Have candlestick and more. Make offer by disposable cell phone to 580.760.4921 at 9 am 6/12.*

Holt addressed the envelope, slid it into his bag, and finished his drink. He tossed a five-dollar bill on the table to pay the $4.50 tab, left the bar, and returned to the gift shop. He had noticed the shop had a mailing service for the convenience of hotel guests. Holt paid the $14.40 to overnight it to New York and went back to his room.

After a much needed two-hour nap, Holt called Stanton to advise her of the change in plans. She was disappointed and sounded angry when he told her he wouldn't be back until Friday sometime. He updated her on the briefing, explaining the task force had the evidence necessary to make the arrests, but they needed time to get the various agencies in place.

"And what about the situation here?" the sheriff said.

He could hear the crisp tone in her voice. "Yeah, well, it's like I told you before, Sheriff, the powers that be…"

"Damn it, Agent Holt!" She cut him off hard. There was a pause. "I'm gett'n sick and tired of the same old bureaucratic shit." She'd heard the agency shuck and jive before, and she was in no mood for it. Stanton sucked in a lungful of air and hesitated, realizing that in some bizarre

way what she was getting from the agency was just a
mirror image of how she was dealing with her own
deputies. It made her think twice about what next to say.
"Okay, Holt, I know it's out of your hands. Just get the
meeting over and return as soon as possible." She knew it
was a waste of time to say anything about her conversation
with Agent Miles.

CHAPTER 30

Wednesday, June 7, 2:37 p.m.

L ee grabbed the backpack and duffel bag out of the bed of the truck, tossed them over his shoulder, and walked to the rear of the house. The back door had always been their preferred entrance; only guests used the front door. Beverly's vehicle was in the drive. He set his bags on the ground and fished through his pocket for the house key. Lee inserted it and immediately realized the door was unlocked. Securing the house, and cars for that matter, was an obsession of Beverly's, a fear she had brought into the marriage years before. When Beverly was ten, she came home from school and found her mother on the kitchen floor unconscious. Her mother had come face to face with a burglar and had barely survived the beating. The emotional consequences for Beverly's family were devastating. Her mother recovered physically from the ordeal, but it dramatically changed her lifestyle.

Lee turned the knob and stepped into the back porch.

He stood quietly and listened. There was no music. Beverly always had a favorite CD on, but he heard nothing. Under normal circumstances, Lee would not be alarmed, but in light of what he'd seen and heard the last two days, he was instantly on alert. Adrenaline was coursing through his body, and the hair on his arms bristled. He drew in a deep breath, let it out slowly, and then took another. Lee felt anxiety give way to reasoning. Now he could think. He hesitated to take a step inside, remembering how the kitchen floor creaked when walked on. Lee stood in heavy silence for what seemed like an eternity; then he caught sight of movement in an adjoining room. He looked at the kitchen floor and knew it would be futile to try and cross it without making noise. Lee had to be patient. Just then he saw a glimmer of light reflect off the muzzle of a gun. He could see it clearly now, a revolver, and the business end was pointed in his direction. From his vantage point, behind the door frame, he could see the pistol come into full view, then the hand and arm. The arm was adorned with the bracelet he'd bought Beverly for her last birthday. He was instantly relieved, almost to the point of collapse. "Honey, I'm home," Lee said softly.

"Lee?"

He stepped over the threshold into the kitchen. "It's me, hon."

"Thank god. I was so scared!" She laid her .38 on the kitchen cabinet and braced herself. She was trembling, her color drained and her eyes tearing. Beverly tried to speak, but the words were lost as she gulped air. Lee took her in his arms and pressed her head to his shoulder. He'd never seen her so frightened. They stood locked in each other's arms for a long time. "I wanted to surprise you by getting home early, but I never intended to scare you," Lee offered.

"It's okay, really. I just let my imagination run wild."

"Tell me what happened."

"I had just gotten home from the store and finished bringing the groceries in from the car when the phone rang. It was Mom; she needed to talk. One of her anxiety attacks."

"And that brought the memories back?"

"Yes! Seeing Mom lying on that floor, blood everywhere." Beverly paused, brushing tears and damp curls of red hair away from her eyes. "Anyway, Mom said she felt better, and she sounded better. I told her if she needed me I'd come down, but you know her."

"Yeah, she's tough, doesn't want help."

"Not so much that she's tough, she just doesn't want to interfere. As I was saying, after we hung up I just sat there feeling sad for Mom and angry at the SOB who did this to her. I looked over toward the side window and through the curtains saw the shadow of a very large man slip by. It startled me. Then I heard someone fumbling with the back door, and you didn't call out your usual greeting, so I guess I must've jumped to conclusions. I was scared to death."

"That large shadow was me with my backpack and duffel bag over my shoulder. When I got to the back door it was unlocked."

"I didn't get a chance to lock it before Mom called."

"Besides the door being unlocked, I couldn't hear music playing and I jumped to conclusions, too." Lee tried not to let on how frightened he had been. He held her tight. Finally she pushed him back and brushed the last of the tears away.

"Okay, now that we've got this homecoming thing out of the way, I want to hear what got Mr. Gray so excited."

"And I'm anxious to tell you."

* * *

Sheriff Stanton finished supper. It had taken a full hour, just as she had expected. There wasn't a public place in the county, especially the only café in town, where she could find privacy. Everyone had an opinion on law enforcement, specifically how to deal with criminals. The conversations were tiresome, in most cases boring, but Stanton had to listen. She knew it was necessary to maintain good community relations. Today was no different, and by the time she'd paid the tab and was climbing into her car, she couldn't remember what she'd eaten.

Stanton slid the mic off its clip and radioed dispatch. She wanted to know if Bingham had been checking in regularly. The sheriff wanted all communication documented, a real-time record of everything that was going on. In a sparsely populated and normally quiet county, a sheriff didn't need to worry much about formalities and protocol, but this situation wasn't normal and no time to be careless.

Dispatch confirmed routine contact with Deputy Bingham at 1600, 1700, and 1730 hours. Stanton decided to freshen up before checking on post Alpha 1 personally. She stopped by her house, hoping to catch the six o'clock news; she watched but didn't hear what the anchor was saying. Stanton was distracted. She couldn't get Holt out of her mind. There was something about his character that bugged her. She hadn't liked him from the beginning—her intuition was trying to tell her something, but what? She looked at her watch; it was time to check on Bingham. She would call Webster first thing in the morning.

The sheriff turned off the county road onto the ranch driveway, then veered northwest up to the ridge. She parked next to Bingham's cruiser behind the cedar grove. The deputy was standing next to Norton's lawn chair with her binoculars fixed on something to the southeast. Stanton reached under the seat and got her own binoculars out and joined Bingham. "What do you see?"

"Look at the road just south of where the creek runs under the road."

"I see, looks like the top of a truck."

"That's exactly what it is, Sheriff." Bingham hesitated, adjusting the glasses. "It's been parked there awhile; I haven't seen anyone get in or out."

"When did you notice it?"

"About forty-five minutes ago it came from up north going south real slow. He turned around at the section line and came back north and disappeared over the hill. Ten minutes later here he comes again, driving even slower as he passed the Gray's driveway."

"Could you tell how many were in the truck?"

"Nope. They went on down the road, turned around, and parked where they are now. Haven't seen any other movement. I was just getting ready to call you when you pulled in." Bingham was taking the assignment seriously; she demonstrated a command of her responsibilities that was missing, at least in part, in the other deputies. Age and experience were the most likely explanation for the way she conducted herself. Stanton was pleased, but then again she had a hunch Bingham knew there was more to post Alpha 1 than just watching for cattle rustlers.

"So, Deputy, what do you think?"

"My orders were to *do* not *think*, Sheriff." For the first time since Stanton arrived, she dropped the binoculars to her side and smiled. "Like you ordered, Sheriff, I was gonna call and ask you the same thing."

Stanton returned the smile. "You did good, Deputy. Now we need to figure out why that pickup truck is sitting there."

"Want me to go ask 'em what they're up to?" Bingham

was looking through the binoculars again.

"No, I'll do that. I want to get it checked out before we lose too much daylight."

The sheriff put her binoculars back in their case and picked up the watch log. Bingham had been thorough about her entries. Time and location of events were well recorded, good penmanship, words spelled correctly. Nothing like the mess of misspelled words and scant incident descriptions the other deputies were prone to.

"Hired hands left about 1810?" The sheriff read aloud from the log.

"Yeah. Now that you mention it," Bingham adjusted the magnification, "that pickup looks an awful lot like the one the hired hand drives."

Stanton laid the clipboard on the chair. "Which hired hand?"

"Too far away to tell; both trucks are dark."

"I'm going down to check it out, and if anything happens, do not, I repeat, do not leave this post unless I ask you to. You are to call dispatch, announce calmly that you have a ten-thirty-three, and give the location, Alpha One. Hopefully every Tom, Dick, and Mary with a scanner won't be racing out here to see what's going on. Everyone knows that thirty-three means emergency, but only the deputies and Crossland will know the location of Alpha One, understand?"

"I understand," Bingham said.

The sheriff didn't hear much conviction in the deputy's voice. She knew that Bingham would follow orders and call it in, but on the other hand she knew the deputy would do everything possible to come to her aid. "I mean it, Deputy, you stay on post. That's an order."

"I understand, Sheriff." Still no assurance. Bingham knew it would take off-duty deputies and the highway patrol 30 minutes to get to their location. If the sheriff got into trouble, there was no way she'd stay on that ridge. Bingham watched the sheriff as she followed the trail, avoiding cactus and sagebrush, toward the ranch driveway. Another half mile and the sheriff would be side by side with the pickup. Bingham laid the binoculars down and checked her weapon, making sure a round was in the chamber; she holstered the gun, started the car, and left the driver's door open. Bingham picked the binoculars up and refocused them on the sheriff, who was now less than a quarter mile away from her destination.

Stanton turned onto the county road and accelerated to the top of the hill that was blocking her view of the pickup. She reached the crest and slowed the cruiser to assess the situation from a safe distance. It was dusk. She could easily see the vehicle, the road and trees off to one side, but details were impossible to make out in the evening light that remained. She turned on her headlights and accelerated to a normal speed. Her only option was to approach the vehicle as she would under routine circumstances. Stanton's lights illuminated the outline of one occupant. She could see the driver was behind the wheel, tilted slightly to one side in favor of the slant caused by the vehicle being partially in the ditch. Whoever it was didn't move. The sheriff slowed slightly as she approached, and as she pulled alongside the pickup, she stopped and hit the button to lower the passenger side window. Stanton was no more than ten feet away from the other driver; she had her weapon in her right hand, but out of sight. Her heart was pounding; she could feel the sweat accumulating between her hand and the 9mm grip. "Hey." Stanton paused, waiting for a reaction. "Everything alright?" The driver turned in her direction. With what remaining daylight there was, she recognized him.

"No, I'm just thinking, Sheriff."

"Strange place to be thinking."

"Not really, Sheriff." Curt Russell slid over closer to the open passenger side window. "Been Mr. Gray's hired hand for nearly five years. Kinda like home out here, peaceful, quiet. A good place to think."

"Can't argue with that." Stanton wanted to keep the conversation going without sounding nosy. "I see something in your hand. You're not transporting an illegal beverage in an open container are you?"

"No, ma'am." He held up a Dr. Pepper can.

She'd just have to take his word that's what the can contained. "You sure you're alright?"

Curt didn't answer at first, just looked in the direction of the ranch house, then back at the sheriff, as if something was on his mind and he was trying to figure out how to say it. He slid back under the wheel and nodded. "Yeah, Sheriff, I'm good. Like I told ya, just thinking."

"Okay, but if there's anything I can do to help, don't hesitate to call me." Stanton knew the conversation was over, and it was obvious there was something serious on Russell's mind, most likely related to what he saw in the garage. She had at least opened the door to more dialogue when and if Curt felt comfortable in talking. Stanton pressed the talk button on the radio mic and pulled away from Curt's vehicle. "Unit one to unit five."

"Unit five, go ahead," Bingham answered immediately.

Stanton explained to the deputy what she had discovered and that she should keep an eye on the pickup, but not to be overly concerned.

The sheriff turned around and drove back to the ranch house. She had to deliver the news that Holt wouldn't be back until Friday evening and that Curt was parked down the road thinking.

Curt watched the sheriff drive up to the ranch house; it was late, too late to talk with Fred. Now the sheriff was there, probably to report that he was sitting by himself just down the road from the house. How stupid would that sound to the Grays? For some reason they were already upset with him, at least Robert was, and he assumed Fred was also. Was it because of what happened in the garage? He had seen something, and the sheriff was there, but it didn't make sense. All he saw were some boxes and a pile of wood. It must have been important for Robert to have acted the way he did. Curt thought about the surveyor he'd seen driving around on the ATV. He'd brushed it off at first, thinking the man had a legitimate reason for being there. After all, he was just riding up and down the county road. But why did the surveyor keep watching him with binoculars? It made him nervous. That's why he finished the job and got the hell out of there. He just had an eerie feeling. Next day he went back to that location and found where the ATV tracks had crossed the cattle guard onto Fred's land, then disappeared where the buffalo grass was thick enough to hide the tire marks. He hadn't said anything about the incident to anyone, but it was festering inside him, making old thoughts resurface. Curt could hear his sister's voice reminding him not to let his imagination get away with him. Curt thought a minute; then he remembered she'd call him paranoid, whatever that meant. She used to say, "It's like you think somebody is after you, but they're really not." He didn't know anything about being paranoid, and he didn't think anyone was after him, but something wasn't right and Curt just felt like Fred ought to know.

CHAPTER 31

Wednesday, June 7, late afternoon

Lee Bethel filled the washing machine with dirty clothes, and Beverly fixed a late lunch. They wanted to get a few necessary things done before he filled her in. Beverly was anxious to hear what had happened on the ranch. She could tell Lee was excited to explain, but not in the usual manner—there was something serious about his demeanor that puzzled her. Maybe it was just the aftershock of the incident when he had arrived home. That had to be it, she thought, but it still bothered her. Beverly held her hands out in front of her; they were still shaking.

They finished eating and put the dishes in the dishwasher. "Want a beer, honey?" Beverly asked.

"That'd be great. I'm gonna throw some stuff in the dryer."

Beverly poured two Lone Star beers in mugs from the freezer and met Lee in the den. "Okay, start from the beginning. Is the rancher alright?"

"He's fine." Lee took a sip of foam, then a long drink. He set the mug down on the desk, moving it about on the coaster like a child would a toy car. Beverly watched Lee, but he wasn't looking at her, and that made her even more anxious. He studied the mug as he twisted it this way and that. Lee took another drink and looked at Beverly, still hesitating.

Beverly had held her breath as long as she could without losing consciousness. "Well, talk to me. What's going on?!"

"It's such a convoluted story, I'm trying to figure out where to start."

"Like I said, from the beginning!"

"Yeah, easy for you to say. Beverly, I'm not sure where the beginning is." Lee paused again until he saw the painful expression on his wife's face. "Okay. What I'm about to tell you is incredible. I mean incredible in the truest sense of the word, and before I go on I must tell you that you can not share one word of this with anyone, not anyone!"

"Now you're beginning to scare me, Lee."

"Bear with me…" Lee explained everything down to the smallest detail. Beverly sat on the edge of her chair. The condensation from the frosted mug of beer, which she hadn't taken a sip of, had soaked her knee, but she hadn't noticed. She didn't know whether to accept her husband's tale as truth or a sick joke he was playing on her. She even had the fleeting thought that someone out on that ranch had somehow brainwashed Lee and the rancher. Maybe they were under some strange kind of hypnotic trance. She peered into his eyes, looking for a sign, a glimmer of sanity. "Are you kidding me, Lee? Is this some kind of joke?" She'd heard the story but wasn't any more satisfied with the ending than anyone else was. She didn't even know if it was true.

"No joke. I told you it was hard to believe."

"Well, hon, that's an understatement. I'm not sure I believe you yet."

"Don't blame you. It sounds crazy. If I hadn't seen it with my own eyes, I wouldn't believe a word of it." Lee stood. "Want another beer?"

Beverly looked down at the wet spot on her jeans. "No, didn't drink any of this one." She set the full mug on a coaster and stared at the clock. An hour and a half since they sat down. It seemed like five minutes ago, she thought. Lee returned from the kitchen with another Lone Star.

"Say for the moment I believe what you've just told me." Beverly sounded more like the mother of an errant ten-year-old trying to get to the bottom of her son's mischief than the wife of a university professor. "You've never lied to me that I know of. You appear to be cognizant of your surroundings and in touch with reality. I hope you're not under the spell of a witch." They both smiled. Lee caught the subtle mix of humor and seriousness in her statement, though.

Beverly sat back in her chair and said, "What on earth do you do next?"

"Have to make arrangements to move the summer excavation to another location. That'll take some time. Then get in touch with Ron and Jim. I'm hoping with their connections they can shed some light on who this Carlos Ramirez is. Unless something happens before then, I plan to return to the ranch on Monday morning." Lee knew his last remark would start the debate he wished could be avoided. He drew a breath and continued explaining his plans for the next few days.

Beverly interrupted. "And where do I fit in?"

"Beverly, this is potentially a very hazardous situation. You heard me say that Thorpe was considered dangerous.

I'm not about to expose you to that kind of situation."

"Well then, my dear husband, you can't go, either." Beverly's response was perfunctory.

"But, dear, don't you see what I'm saying?"

"Of course I see what you're saying. That's why you can't go," Beverly said, still sounding matter-of-fact, unemotional.

"But, dear..."

"But, dear, what?"

"For Pete's sake, Beverly, don't you get it?!"

"Yes, Lee, I get it, but your desire to protect me from bad guys, while a noble thought, works both ways. Yes, Lee, I get it, but I want to protect you, too, just as badly as you want to protect me. So I propose two options."

There had been a fleeting moment earlier that day when Lee actually believed he could convince his wife he should return to the ranch alone, because of the danger element, but he'd always known, deep down, it was a pipe dream. "Okay, what do you propose?"

"It's simple. We both go, or we both stay home." Beverly knelt down next to Lee's chair and took his hand. "Remember the endless conversations we had years ago about exploring exciting places together?"

"I remember. We were so naïve back then. Danger wasn't a part of the equation." Lee knew he'd lost the debate. She was coming along.

"It's late, and we've got a lot to do before Monday," she said.

CHAPTER 32

Thursday, June 8, 7:00 a.m.

Sheriff Stanton finished her third cup of coffee and hurried to her office. It was 8:00 a.m. on the east coast, and she wanted to be ready to place her call to Webster at 9:00 his time. Stanton also needed to review the shift schedule for post Alpha 1 in case adjustments in personnel had to be made. Parker's wife was due any time, and that would take him out of the rotation schedule for over a week. Bingham had volunteered to fill in, but that would leave her duties unattended. The situation at the Gray Ranch was taking its toll on Stanton and the department. The sheriff was thankful that nothing requiring law enforcement intervention was occurring in other areas within her jurisdiction. Harper County was 1,039 square miles, with around 4,000 residents scattered between five communities, 99 percent of whom were law- abiding citizens. But, she knew it took only one incident among those citizens to drain her resources. Stanton prayed the situation on the ranch would be resolved soon.

The sheriff reached for her phone, but just as she was about to make the first call, there was a knock on her door. "Come in." She returned the phone to its cradle.

Bingham opened the door and stuck her head in partway. "It's just me."

"What are you doing here? You worked late last night."

"So used to gett'n up early I woke up bright-eyed and bushy-tailed, so thought I'd come in and see what you needed me to do."

"What I need, Deputy Bingham, is for you to take care of yourself. Now go home, nap, take a long soaking bath, watch a movie, just do something restful."

"Don't need a bath, Sheriff, can't sleep. Frankly I'd rather be here where I'm needed."

It was obvious, Stanton thought, Bingham knows something's up. "Okay, but you have to promise you'll go home early, to rest, in case I need you tonight."

"Will do, Sheriff."

"Contact our two reserve deputies; we haven't used them in a while. See if they can give us a few days. Notify all the deputies that we'll have a meeting sometime later today."

"Can I tell them what it's about?"

"No, it's important, that's all you need to say."

"Anything else?"

"Yeah, check on Norton by phone; see how Alpha One is doing. Then check on Parker, see how his wife is doing. Now, I'm going to make an important phone call. You know the drill; don't let anyone in unless it's an emergency."

"You got it." Bingham closed the door.

Stanton re-opened her personal phone directory and thumbed through to the W's. She located Webster's name and his three personal numbers. Stanton called his office number first, and it rolled immediately to his voice mail. She tried his cell phone; he answered on the first ring. "Webster." Just as Stanton remembered, strong voice, full of authority.

"Mr. Assistant Director, this is Crys Stanton."

His voice mellowed, still strong but personal. "My god, Crys Stanton, how the hell are you? What's it been, four years?"

"Four and a half, and I'm doing fine."

"Heard you were a sheriff out there in the Wild West."

"Jerry, I want to visit with you more about old times, but right now it's business and I'm short on time."

"You've got my full attention, but first let me tell you I've missed working with you. You were one of the best and a huge loss to the agency. Having said that, I'm all ears."

"Thanks, guess I needed to hear that. Anyway, you have an agent by the name of Carl Holt out here on assignment; I need to know what's going on and how he fits in. And I need it in fifteen minutes or less."

"That's a tall order, Crys, but I'll give it a shot. There's a joint task force made up of the CIA, Homeland Security, FBI, and some lesser agencies like DEA that are working cooperatively, if you can believe that, to break up and arrest..."

Stanton interrupted. "Sorry for cutting you off. I'm aware of the ICO and that one of the suspects is a woman named Bouvier and that she has had contact with an appraiser in Oklahoma City. Your agent filled me in. My question is more about Holt and what his orders are."

"I'm not following you, Crys. What exactly do you mean?"

"Not sure, Jerry, just a gut feeling. At one level he seems legit, but at another he appears deceitful, untrustworthy. Could be just my suspicious nature."

"Well, Crys, I've only seen Holt on one or two occasions, briefings I think. His boss assured me that when we reviewed everyone for this task force, he was okay. Seems to me, now that I'm thinking about Holt, he might have been passed over for promotion and targeted for retirement sometime this year. First thing I'll do when we hang up is get in touch with his supervisor, then call you back. Might take some time."

"How much time?" Stanton didn't want to push her luck by pressing Webster for information, but lives might be at stake. It was important.

"Saturday. Give me until Saturday afternoon. What's your number?"

Stanton gave Webster her cell and office number, then thanked him.

Bingham knocked as soon as she saw the light go off on the sheriff's phone. "Sheriff, I can have everyone here at noon for a meeting. Will that work?"

"That'll work, Deputy. Oh, did you talk with the reserves?"

"They're ready to go. Asked if they should come armed. I told 'em no, but I'd need to check with you to make sure."

"You told them right. They'll be filing reports and answering phones. How's Parker's wife?"

"Doing okay, staying off her feet. Her mom's here for a couple of weeks. Parker says he can stay on the job until the baby comes."

"Good, we need all the help we can get." Stanton realized she hadn't meant to say those words out loud, but it was too late. Bingham gave her the what's-going-on look. Stanton ignored it and grabbed some reports out of her in-basket to read. The deputy would have to wait until noon. She'd find out with the rest.

CHAPTER 33

Thursday, June 8, early morning

Lee Bethel's alarm woke him at 5:00 a.m. He bolted upright in bed, turned on his bedside lamp, and put his glasses on. Beverly stirred. "Go back to sleep, hon, it's still early," he said.

"It's still dark out. What time is it?" she asked, her voice barely audible.

"Five. I've got to e-mail Jim and Ron. Then come up with a plan for Susan. Sleep. I'll wake you in a couple of hours."

Beverly didn't hear the last thing Lee said.

Lee touched the mouse and the screen came to life. He clicked on e-mail and saw he had ten unread messages. He quickly reviewed the names of the senders and the subjects, then deleted five messages that were forwards from friends. Lee deleted a joke he didn't have time to read and an e-mail from some religious zealot warning people not to buy products from Proctor and Gamble. He wondered how many decades the P&G claim would hang around. Lee copied a recipe for barbeque sauce his sister had sent and shot her a quick thank-you. The last two were from doctoral candidates who were probably complaining about his evaluation of their dissertation defense. He'd read those later.

Lee hurriedly typed in the addresses of two very close friends and former classmates at the University of Texas. Jim Scroggins taught ancient history and archaeology at a university in Annandale, Virginia, and Ron Walters worked for the U.S. Department of State in Washington, DC. Both men had connections and for the time being were the only people Lee could think of who might be able to help identify Carlos Ramirez. Lee explained in his message that he was to meet with the man and was trying to dig up some information about him beforehand, and that he'd done a Google search on the name using Ramirez's alleged employer, The Smithsonian, as part of the search criteria, but came up empty-handed. He signed off and clicked send.

Lee sent another e-mail to his boss Susan Randal at the university, asking if he could meet with her at ten. If he hadn't heard from her by then, he'd have to track her down. It was vital that he talk to her that day. There was so much to do, and he wanted to make sure he had her permission first. He had a thought; Lee leaned back in his chair and took a drink of his coffee, which had cooled to a drinkable temperature. He'd always lived by the rule that if something needed to be done, and it was important, then just do it. His dad said it was easier to ask for forgiveness than it was to ask for permission. Lee didn't know if that principle worked a hundred percent of the time. Probably didn't, but he'd put it to the test today.

By 9:00 a.m. Lee had completed an outline of what

~ 196 ~

needed to be done to reorganize the graduate students' summer excavation experience. He read over the document. It looked thorough to him, right down to everyone's phone number. Lee printed two copies of the outline and put them in his briefcase. He smelled breakfast cooking. He'd been so busy he hadn't heard Beverly get up. Lee checked his incoming e-mail and saw that Susan had replied, saying ten o'clock would be fine.

Lee glanced at the dash clock as he turned into the office parking lot. He had three minutes. His relationship with Susan was more a friendship than anything else, but he'd never take advantage of that fact. If he said ten, then ten it would be, not five after ten.

Lee hurried down the hall to Randal's office. Her door was open, and she was doing something on her laptop. "Good morning, Dr. Randal," Lee said, standing just outside her door.

Dr. Randal finished typing a sentence and moved the laptop to one side. "Come in, Dr. Bethel, and good morning to you. How's Beverly?"

Lee stepped through the open door, closing it behind him. "She's fine."

"I understand she's going to spend time with you at the dig this summer."

"Well, yes, sort of. That's what I wanted to talk to you about."

"You wanted to talk with me about Beverly?"

"No, no, I want to talk to you about the dig." Lee pulled the outline from his briefcase but held onto it while he explained. "First, I need to take two weeks annual leave starting today."

Randal scooted closer to her desk as her warm smile faded and her brow wrinkled. She looked worried. "Is everything alright?"

"Yes, everything is okay. I'll explain." Lee paused, thinking of a way to clarify a complex situation. He remembered Beverly's advice from an hour earlier: *Be straightforward, explain that you're under an oath and can't divulge details just yet,* she had said. "I'm going to ask you to trust me on this one."

"Lee, you look so serious. Are you sure you're alright?"

"Very sure. There are some things I can tell you and some I can not just yet." Lee paused again, thinking.

"Okay, this is killing me. Tell me what you can."

"Fred Gray, the man who owns the ranch where the summer dig was to be held, found something significant on his land. There is international interest in what he found, but the authorities who are aware of this have ordered everyone involved not to disclose anything about the discovery yet."

"Can you tell me what authority?"

"No, I can't. The Grays have asked me to be a part of the events that are unfolding, and I agreed." Lee paused, thinking his last statement sounded a bit overconfident. "I hope not prematurely. I know what I've told you doesn't give you much to base a decision on—that's where the trust comes in."

"Of course I trust you, and certainly you can have the time off, but it sounds dangerous. Are you sure you'll be alright?"

"I'm very sure," Lee said, but for the first time he questioned his confidence.

Lee handed a copy of his outline to Randal. "I've taken the liberty of preparing a step-by-step outline on what needs to be done to move the summer excavation site to another location."

Randal looked the outline over closely. "Looks like

you've thought of everything."

"Wes will take over my role, and my grad assistant will work with him. There are eight students signed up for the two-week dig and about ten volunteers. I've already sent e-mail messages to everyone on that list explaining the move, but I'll ask Marlene to make phone contacts to be sure they got the word."

Dr. Randal scribbled "Approved" on the outline and signed her name. "When will you be going back to the Grays?"

"Early Monday morning."

"You know, Lee, you've got my curiosity up. Wish I could join. Promise to keep me informed."

"I will."

"By the way, gotta hypothetical for you. What if I'd denied your request?" Susan slid back in her chair and smiled. "Guess that's not a fair question."

"Very *un*fair question. Do you really want an answer?"

"I'm curious, but you don't have to answer."

Lee picked up his briefcase and was halfway out the door when he stopped and turned. "I've got a hypothetical for you."

"And?"

"Would you accept my letter of resignation or reject it?"

"Get out!" She waved a dismissive hand. "And, Dr. Bethel, please stay safe."

CHAPTER 34

Thursday, June 8, noon

Deputy Maude Bingham followed the sheriff's orders precisely as given. She had intercepted all of Stanton's incoming calls and either dealt with the callers herself or took messages. Bingham hadn't allowed anyone in to see the sheriff. Most visitors were just drop-ins offering to buy Stanton coffee. They understood when Maude explained the sheriff was busy, but Carl Overton, the District 1 County Commissioner, was fuming and demanded to see her. Maude had had dealings with Carl before and knew he could fly off the handle at the drop of a hat; she kept her cool, though. When the commissioner saw he wasn't going to get special treatment, he stomped out cussing, warning Maude and anyone else within hearing range that he was going to the mayor and lodge a formal complaint about the lack of communication and respect. Bingham smiled and continued to file arrest reports.

Hearing the commotion, Stanton opened her door just

as Overton made his angry exit. Bingham looked in her direction and shrugged, and the sheriff winked. "He's never going to get used to the fact his brother-in-law isn't sheriff any longer, is he?"

"Oh, Sheriff, it's worse than that."

"What do you mean?"

"He's never gonna get used to the sheriff being female."

"I suppose. Anyway, thanks for running interference this morning. Got a lot done." The sheriff looked at her watch. "It's getting close to noon. When the guys get here have 'em grab an extra chair and come on in." She closed the door partway and returned to her desk, hoping that briefing her deputies wouldn't turn out to be a mistake.

By 2:00 p.m. Stanton had concluded the briefing and was on her way to the ranch. The meeting had gone well, she thought. Even though she didn't tell them what the true secret was, they understood the secret wasn't the issue. Their task was to provide protection to the rancher and his family, and that was to be their only function. The deputies took an oath, by a show of hands, they would not repeat to anyone, including close friends and family, anything they heard that day. Stanton explained in detail the legal consequences of violating an order issued by a government investigatory agency.

* * *

Dr. Bethel left his boss's office and drove to a nearby sporting goods store. Beverly had given him a list of items they'd need since they were to be away from home an extended period, including ammunition for her .38 and his .45. They both had conceal/carry licenses, primarily for protection when camping. Their favorite pastime was wilderness hiking. It wasn't unusual for them to be gone five or ten days at a time, and although neither of them had ever pointed their weapons at any living thing, they wanted to be prepared. Lee finished shopping and hurried home, excitement building, but with it came the ever present apprehension stirring inside, so pronounced at times it felt like a punch to his solar plexus.

"Honey, I'm home," Lee announced as he unlocked the door and stepped in.

"How'd it go?"

"Great! She said to tell you hi. Also said she's a member of your dissertation panel, and when you're ready to defend they'll be ready to hear you."

"Yeah, I know, maybe this fall. What all did you tell her?"

"Just enough to get permission."

After lunch Lee checked to see if he'd gotten a response from either of his friends back east. He was anxious, but after all it had only been a few hours since he sent his request. Lee knew it could take a day or two to get anything back, and maybe they'd come up empty-handed like he had. "Patience, patience, patience," he mumbled to himself. He sat down and reviewed his checklist again. Lee kicked his hiking boots off and leaned back in the recliner. Beverly had left the house earlier to pay some bills and do her own shopping; she wouldn't be home for at least an hour. Lee closed his eyes and listened to the soft whooshing of the overhead fan, a hypnotic rhythm that lulled him to sleep.

At 3:30 Lee awoke. A noise had startled him, some kind of tone, but groggy from a hard nap, he couldn't tell if it was the doorbell or his cell phone. He checked the front door, but no one was there, then his phone—the display indicated no calls. He rubbed his eyes and walked to the kitchen, opened the refrigerator, and got an energy drink. Lee needed the caffeine to help wake him up. He looked out the window to see if Beverly's car was in the drive, but it wasn't. Lee stood staring blankly at birds perched on the feeder that hung outside the kitchen window and finished his drink. It finally occurred to him that the sound he heard must have come from his computer, the tone announcing an incoming e-mail; he hurried back to his office. Sure enough, a message from Ron at the State Department in Washington, DC. It was short.

Got my butt chewed for attempting to ID this guy. Call me ASAP...RW

Lee clicked on "addresses," found Ron's cell phone number, and called him.

"Hey, Lee!" Walters recognized the Oklahoma area code. "What in the hell are you doing?" The question came with an unmistakable serious tone, unusual for Ron Walters.

"Uh, well, it's a long story, and I'll get into that, but what's going on there? You sound..."

Walters cut him off. "Scared. Is that the word you're looking for?"

"Now that you mention it, yeah, kinda scared?"

"Scared shitless would be the more technical term."

"So what happened?"

"Some State Department employees have secret clearances and some have top secret clearances; I'm one with the latter. Because of that clearance, which by the way is very fragile, I have access to information only God and the Pope know. That information includes confidential stuff on many government employees and their activities. Lee, I could end up on a long flight in an unmarked plane to Kabul if I'm not careful."

"Slow down, Ron, you're talking to an archeology

professor; speak a language I can understand."

"Do you know the word *rendition*?"

"Sort of. It's where a government sends people to another country for interrogation."

"Right—in other words, extradition outside the legal process. Anyway, this is the kind of situation where if the spooks don't like your answers, you win that all-expense-paid trip to some bizarre out-of-the-way location."

"Okay, so we're into some cloak and dagger stuff?" Lee asked.

"That's right. Now, here's what happened. To use some of the programs on my computer, I must have my supervisor's approval in writing. I explained to him about your request and got his permission to search. He didn't see harm in accessing information on an employee of a museum." Walters stopped talking long enough to sip coffee. Lee could hear the familiar slurping Ron was known for in graduate school. "Well, Lee, my boss was wrong, not just wrong, but damn wrong. Poor guy's gonna have disciplinary paper in his file because of it. I feel like shit warmed over, really, really bad. I should've known better."

"What did they do to you?"

"Nothing, that's why I feel so bad. They said I followed protocol and asked permission; in essence I didn't violate any rule. They just gave me a warning."

"Ron, I'm sorry this has happened to you and your boss. I would've never asked you to do something that might jeopardize your job."

"Hell, Lee, I know that. You know me—I'm probably blowing this all out of proportion. Don't worry about it."

"Can you tell me what happened?"

"I typed Ramirez's name into the query box, added Smithsonian to narrow the search."

Lee could hear him sipping coffee. "What happened?"

"Nothing."

"Nothing? What do you mean?"

"My computer is fast, but nothing came up. I sat there five or ten minutes, and when nothing came back I did some paperwork and flirted with Morgan, the college intern. Oh, Lee, you should see her; tall, tanned, and she's got these…"

"Ron, please, you can describe her later. Tell me what happened!"

"Yeah, right, I got sidetracked. About thirty minutes after I sent the query, two guys in dark suits came into my office and flashed Treasury Department badges."

"Treasury? What's this got to do with Treasury?"

"Lee, think Secret Service."

"Oh."

"Yeah, *oh* is right. They closed my door and questioned me for an hour about why I needed information about Ramirez."

"What did you tell them?"

"I may not be the sharpest knife in the drawer, but I ain't no dummy. I told 'em the truth. I said you contacted me to see if I could help find some information about Ramirez and that you had a meeting with him and wanted some ID on him."

"What happened then?"

"They asked the same questions five different ways, and when they were satisfied I was telling the truth they left."

"Then what?"

"I go to lunch and when I get back, there it is."

"There what is?"

"A file on my computer marked *confidential,* complete with a photo. Many pages were in a locked file I couldn't get access to, but some interesting pages were available. Do you have a fax?"

"Yes." Lee gave Walters the number.

"Now, Lee, tell me what's going on out there!"

"Sorry, Ron, I've been ordered not to say anything."

"Damn it, Lee, you're worse than my first wife, get me all worked up then says she's gotta headache."

"You'll be one of the first to know, I promise. I do appreciate your help, but got to go."

"I'd better be one of the first. Take care of yourself and give your lovely wife Betty a hug and kiss for me."

Lee started to correct him, but Ron had already hung up. He hadn't changed—still loud, sometimes obnoxious, always self-centered, but without exception the most intelligent human being he'd ever met.

A minute later Lee had four faxed pages of information on Dr. Carlos Ramirez. Beverly had returned from her shopping and stuck her head into the office. "Anything on Ramirez yet?"

"Just got it. Come in, we'll go over it together."

They sat silently and read. The first paragraph was a bio synopsis: Born in Argentina of Spanish immigrants in 1948. Graduated from a university in Buenos Aires with a degree in history, then came to the U.S. in 1964 on a scholastic scholarship and attended Yale, where he received a law degree. He studied at Oxford, then returned to the U.S. to attend Princeton, where he received his doctorate in international finance.

Beverly pointed to a date on the bio. "He did all that before he was thirty. Amazing."

"Amazing is right. Look at this." Beverly leaned in closer. "He has a consulting firm, but only three clients."

"Who are they?"

"The UN, CIA, and the Department of Defense. On the

second page it says that the service he provides is authenticating and appraising UHA."

"Sounds important, but what is it?"

"I've seen these initials before, but can't remember where." Lee closed his eyes and laid his head on his desk. "Yes! I remember. They stand for Undisclosed Historic Assets. When an artifact, let's say a statue of Zeus, is discovered in a New York museum, or in the possession of a private citizen outside the limits of the country of origin, it is referred to as a UHA. If the owner cannot verify that the artifact was purchased or obtained legally from the country of origin, that country can claim it and demand its return. Evidently, Dr. Ramirez performs the authentication portion of the process."

"But why those three agencies?" Beverly asked.

"When Saddam Hussein was dethroned, museums in Iraq were pillaged. Billions of dollars worth of antiquities from the Babylonian era were stolen. Those artifacts have been showing up for sale on the black market everywhere. Many of those items are in the hands of forgers; they make counterfeit duplicates and sell them as originals."

"Sounds like it's become a huge business."

"Yeah, with a lot of the profit funding worldwide terrorism. That's why, I'm guessing, Ramirez contracts with those three agencies specifically."

"So you believe this guy is legit."

Lee pointed to the photo. "I believe that if this guy shows up Monday, he's legit."

"It's almost six; let's get something to eat. We can read the rest later."

"How about a cheeseburger at Coach's?"

Beverly nodded. It was her favorite.

"Give me ten minutes. I need to call Fred and tell him what I've found out."

CHAPTER 35

Thursday, June 8, 6:30 p.m.

Elliot Heath left the ranch just after six. The day's work had been hard, the wind and heat brutal. He was in no mood to keep the charade going much longer. Heath fished the cell phone out of the truck's glove compartment and checked to see if he had received any messages; there were none. Maybe Bouvier hadn't received his message, he thought. Too risky to send another message this early. Heath knew the NSA and CIA computer eavesdropping programs used many variables to target certain communications traffic, and one of those variables was frequency, especially if the computer program detected an encrypted message. He decided to wait one more day. Friday was payday, and although he had no plans to cash his paycheck, it was important that he play his role believably through to the finish.

Heath parked in front of the Percolator Café. It was six-thirty and the restaurant closed at seven; he was just in

time. There were still a lot of people eating when he walked
in, a few town residents, but mostly oil field workers and
cowhands. He actually felt a spirit of kinship with the
crowd. Heath was wearing faded, torn blue jeans, an old
pair of worn-out steel-toed work boots he'd bought in a
consignment store especially for this assignment. The
fingers of his leather gloves sticking out of his back pocket
told everyone he did manual labor, physically hard work.
For some strange reason, Heath took pride in the way he
looked. He sat down on a stool at the counter next to an
acquaintance he'd met a few weeks earlier. "Hey, Joe, this
seat taken?"

"It's all yours, Otis."

"Hard day?"

"Hell of a hard day. That goddamned wind nearly
knocked me off the tower twice."

"Bet it was pushing thirty maybe forty mile an hour,"
Heath said.

They both looked the menu over. "What's good?" Joe
asked as the waitress brought water.

"Everything, Joe, it's all good."

"Gimme the special."

"Me too."

The waitress snapped her gum and waved her pencil
back and forth in front of Joe. "Sorry, too late. We sold out
about thirty minutes ago."

"Chicken-fried steak then." Joe looked up; she was
writing the order down.

She moved over in front of Heath. "You?"

"Same, please."

Heath finished dinner, slapped Joe on the back, and told
him to take care. He checked his phone again when he got
back to his truck. The display indicated he had one text

message. "About time, Ms. Bouvier," he murmured once he'd read it.

Heath had some loose ends that needed attention before leaving Buffalo for good. His plan was to go over his rental house thoroughly that night to make sure he left nothing that could identify him. Heath carried a small cleaning kit with him everywhere he went, consisting mainly of Clorox wipes. They were great for removing prints and any DNA left behind in the form of epithelial remnants and body fluids. The next day he would work at the ranch, collect his check, and take care of the last-minute details, then leave. Heath destroyed the map used to plan his evasive exit. If the Crown Vic he'd seen the last couple of days was truly the Feds, his plan would leave them in the dust, literally.

Heath's alarm woke him at four a.m. He started to reach for the switch on the bedside lamp, then stopped. In the haze of early morning he'd almost forgotten that his plan was to avoid turning the lights on. No sense in alerting someone watching that he was up yet. His usual wake-up time was five, and this would give him an extra hour to add the finishing touches to the house before leaving for good. Heath had shaved the night before; all he had left to do was wipe all surfaces down with the Clorox wipes, and remove the sheets, pillowcases from the bed, and cover over the recliner. He carefully removed the collection bag from the vacuum cleaner supplied by the landlord. Everything, including kitchen trash, was wrapped up tight inside the bedsheet and stuffed inside a gym bag. His clothing, which didn't amount to much, had been loaded into his truck one item at a time over the past two days. The only thing he had to carry out of the house was the gym bag, and if someone was watching, they'd know it was the same bag Elliot Heath, aka Otis Thorpe, carried with him every day. There was nothing unusual about Thorpe carrying a gym bag.

That was the point—to condition the observer, whoever that was, into overlooking its importance.

At five, Heath turned the kitchen and bathroom lights on, just like he did every morning. An hour and fifteen minutes later, he emerged from the house, carrying the bag, and drove to the convenience store for coffee and an egg biscuit. He arrived at the Gray Ranch right on time; Curt Russell pulled in next to Heath a minute later.

"Morning, Curt."

"Morning, Otis."

"Ready for another day of fun in the sun?" Heath said.

"I'm ready for this day to be over."

"Yeah, me too."

They both stood next to the ranch work truck, waiting for someone to come out and give them their assignments.

CHAPTER 36

Friday, June 9, 6:30 p.m.

Curtis Russell parked next to the red 500-gallon gas tank that sat on angle iron stilts six feet off the ground, and filled the ranch truck with fuel. Otis unloaded tools into the barn and checked the oil and coolant levels on the truck.

"Doing anything special this weekend?"

"Nope. My girlfriend gets back Sunday. Just watch baseball, maybe church. That's about it."

"So, you don't have plans for tonight?" Otis asked.

"Nope."

Otis added oil to the crankcase and checked the brake fluid. He watched as Curt walked to the kitchen door of the ranch house. He saw Mrs. Gray answer the door, but couldn't hear what they said. Otis shut the truck hood, wiped oil off his hands, and went to his own truck. Curt met him as he was getting in. "Here's your paycheck."

"Thanks, almost forgot."

Curt was getting into his own vehicle. He turned. "You that well off?"

Heath realized his mistake; it was the little things, the small slip-ups that would eventually expose him if he wasn't more careful. "Just joking." He watched Curt's reaction; it looked to him like he bought it.

* * *

Curt asked to see the rancher, but according to Helen he was helping Robert fix a water well in the south pasture. Curt was determined to talk to Fred sometime that day. He'd put it off too long and wanted to get it off his shoulders and out of his mind. Paranoid or not, there were too many things happening he felt unsettled about. It all seemed to be closing in on him, and he hadn't felt this bad in years. Every time he mustered enough courage to tell Fred, he'd get the feeling the rancher wouldn't believe him, maybe even ridicule or poke fun at him. Curt's heart pounded, his hands so sweaty they kept sliding off the steering wheel. He knew he was having one of those attacks; he tried to think of what the doc had called them but couldn't remember. Curt thought about his sister reminding him to take his medication, but he hated the way it made him feel. Besides, he'd been feeling okay without it. Maybe a few beers would help. It had worked before, but this time he'd know when to stop. He drove faster. Curt parked in his driveway at seven-fifteen and rushed into his house, setting the beer on the table. He paced nervously, trying to think whether he should call Mr. Gray or not. He tore a can of beer from the plastic ring and guzzled it, the excess dripping off his chin onto the floor. The second and third he nursed slowly and felt the comforting buzz that beer gave him on an empty stomach. His courage returning, he picked up the phone and called his boss.

"Hey, Mrs. Gray, is Mr. Gray there?"

"Yes, Curt, he's here. Are you alright?" Helen handed the phone to Fred and whispered, "I think he's been drinking, slurring words."

Fred took the phone. "This is Fred."

"Mr. Gray, I need to talk to you," Curt slurred.

"Go ahead, Curt."

"No, not over phone…in person. Tomorrow?"

"Yeah, tomorrow's fine. Can't you tell me what it's about?"

"No shir."

Helen got her husband's attention. "Ask him out for lunch."

Fred nodded. "Why don't you come for lunch, we can talk after we eat."

"Anybody el-sh there?"

"No, just the three of us. How about noon?"

Curt hung up his phone. He felt better. Maybe he could relax. He pulled another beer from the ring, turned the TV on, and sat down. Curt was exhausted and about to doze off when he heard a sharp knock at his front door. He set the half-empty can on the floor and pushed himself off the couch and stood. The room swayed. The knock came again. He could make out the silhouette of a man through the thin curtain that covered the front door window. He took two staggered steps and opened the door.

* * *

Heath was less than a quarter mile behind Curt, thinking about what he needed to do before leaving Buffalo that night. He had to arrange a series of events in order to make his evasive exit believable. No matter who was following him—assuming someone was—he had to shake them. There was no room for error, not even a small one. He was still angry with himself over the paycheck blunder.

Heath watched as Curt accelerated. The dust growing thick, he slowed his own truck down in order to see where he was going. By the time he reached the highway, Curt was nowhere to be seen. Heath stopped at the convenience store to fill up his truck and buy beer. He carried on a short conversation with another customer and joked with the cashier before he left the store. Heath had established his whereabouts at 7:20 p.m. for those who might be interested. He didn't need or want the beer; it was just another theatric prop. Ten minutes later he parked behind Curt's truck and got out with the six-pack of Bud Lite.

CHAPTER 37

Friday, June 9, evening

Elliot Heath left Curt's house around 8:00 p.m. The sun was beginning to set, but he knew it would be another hour before nightfall. For Heath's plan to work, it had to be dark. He could sip on a beer at the Saddle-up for an hour while he waited for the right moment to initiate the cat-and-mouse game that would free him of the suit in the Crown Vic.

Sheriff Stanton spent the better part of two hours with her deputy at Alpha 1. She watched Russell and Thorpe drive in from the pasture and service the truck in preparation for the next week. Deputy Parker noted the time both men left the ranch in the watch log and handed it to the sheriff. "You think one of those hands is tied in with the crime organization?"

"As I explained in the briefing yesterday, the FBI thinks that Elliot Heath is somehow working for the organization.

They don't think Russell is a part of it, but you can never tell. That's why we are watching both men carefully."

"Sure am curious what's so important about the Gray Ranch that some big city criminals are all in a pucker over it."

"I know, Deputy, wish I could tell you. Maybe the first of next week." Stanton put her binoculars in the case, slid it under her car seat, and started the engine. "Remember; call me if anything happens, even if it's just suspicion on your part."

"Will do, Sheriff."

"Oh, I almost forgot. If your wife has to go to the hospital, call dispatch. We'll have someone out here in twenty minutes to relieve you, even if I have to come myself."

"Thanks, Sheriff. Mother-in-law is with her, so I'm not too worried."

"Nevertheless, Deputy, call if you need to go home." Stanton put her car in reverse and backed away from the cluster of trees that provided shade from the evening sun. She checked her watch; it was after seven and still hot. Her cell phone rang, and Stanton answered. "Sheriff speaking."

"Sheriff, Holt here."

"Holt, I was beginning to wonder—"

The agent cut her off. "Just now got authorization for military flight into Vance. I'll arrive there about nine your time."

"That'll put you in Woodward about ten forty-five. Know where the Wal-Mart is?"

"On that main drag as you come into town on 412, right?"

"South side of the highway. I'll be in the parking lot near the home and garden center in my own truck."

"Gotta go, Sheriff. The flight chief's waving me aboard."

Stanton was relieved; she hadn't heard anything from Holt since Wednesday, and her patience was wearing thin. Information was power, and she was running low on that commodity. Hopefully, her briefing with Holt would provide a broader understanding of what was going on, particularly how it affected her community in general and the Grays specifically.

The sheriff hurried into her house. She'd been on the job since early that morning and didn't want to meet with anyone, not even Holt, feeling the way she did. A shower and a power nap would help.

Stanton was startled awake by the ring of her home phone. "Hello. Sheriff Stanton speaking." It took a few seconds before she fully understood what the caller was saying. "I'm sorry, guess we have a poor connection. Who'd you say you are?" Stanton could hear, but was still groggy from the nap.

"Sheriff!" The caller was talking loudly, pronouncing each syllable deliberately. "This is A-gent Mur-ray with the F-B-I. Can you hear me?"

"Yes, Agent Murray, I hear you. What can I do for you?"

"Special Agent Miles wanted me to call you and brief you on Elliot Heath."

"Okay, but where is Miles, and why isn't he calling me?"

"He's been in St. Louis since yesterday."

"Why's he in…oh, never mind. Tell me about Heath."

"The suspect eluded our surveillance detail at approximately 2130 hours. We are in the process of—"

"Whoa, Agent, slow down. Did I hear you say you lost him?" Stanton could tell he was young.

"Yes, ma'am, about twenty minutes ago."

I understand now why Miles didn't call, himself. A

remark she didn't intend on saying aloud.

"Ma'am?"

"Who was the idiot that lost him?"

"That idiot would be me, ma'am."

"Agent Murphy, right?"

"Murray, ma'am."

"Okay, Murray, start from the beginning and describe what happened."

"Yes, ma'am. I followed the suspect when he left the Saddle-up bar at approximately 2110. The suspect, driving a dark blue Ford F-150 pickup OK tag WDF-419, proceeded south on Highway 183 three miles. He exited 183 going east on a gravel road two miles, then turned south on a dirt road. The suspect sped up, causing dust to obscure the road. I slowed down, couldn't see. I continued south three miles until there was no dust in the air. I suspected the driver left the main road and turned into a pasture and hid."

"Where are you now, Murray?"

"I was in a low spot, couldn't get recep on my cell, so I drove to the top of a hill a mile from where I lost the suspect and called Special Agent Miles. He told me to call you."

"Stay at your location, Murray, until you hear from me. If you see Heath's vehicle come out of hiding, you are free to resume tailing him; otherwise, stay right there. Understand?"

"Yes, ma'am."

"Don't call me ma'am. Now, what's your cell number?"

Murray gave Stanton the number. She leaned back in her chair, closed her eyes, and tried meditation techniques that were supposed to help relax her. They didn't, never did, which had frustrated her instructor at the academy years earlier.

Sheriff Stanton instructed dispatch to notify Alpha 1 and the Oklahoma Highway Patrol to be on the lookout for the blue Ford F-150. Stanton explained she'd be on official business in Woodward until midnight or after and could be reached by cell phone only. She then drove the short distance to 183 and turned south.

* * *

Heath watched in his rearview mirror as the Crown Vic turned off 183 onto the gravel road. The hook was set. His pursuer was doing exactly as Heath had planned. He sped up, and within seconds, the storm of red dust engulfed the road for nearly a quarter mile. Heath could see the cattle guard off to his left just up ahead, his cue to shut the lights off. For the next hundred yards, he could barely see while his eyes adjusted to the darkness, but he'd practiced the maneuver on this exact stretch of road several times. He brought the pickup to a slow crawl and turned into the pasture and across the cattle guard, then followed a rocky creek bed to an embankment he estimated to be 15 feet high, just high enough to hide behind. The person tailing him was still temporarily delayed by the dust that now was beginning to settle. Heath watched as the car drove slowly past his location and on to the top of a hill, where it stopped. A few seconds later, the car turned around and drove back in the direction he'd come from. Slowly Heath eased out of the creek bed, eyes fully adjusted to the dim light of a half moon, and onto a path headed east across a pasture to the next section line. With his lights still off, Heath drove onto a road that took him south, then east to Highway 34. He stopped long enough to put the original Kansas license plate back on and headed north.

CHAPTER 38

Friday, June 9, 10:30 p.m.

The Wal-Mart parking lot was virtually empty when Sheriff Stanton arrived. The east side of the building was dark and deserted. Stacks of mulch, fertilizer, and an assortment of tree saplings in their ready-to-plant containers sat arranged in rows, waiting for the Saturday morning customer rush. Stanton parked her truck away from the nursery; she didn't want to draw the attention of local police, who might assume she was stealing. Of course, all she'd need to do was flash her badge; on the other hand, a sheriff from a neighboring county sitting alone in a dark and empty parking lot late at night would surely raise the curiosity of the cops, especially if it happened to be a boring night. Better to avoid that possibility altogether.

The sheriff hadn't been in the lot more than five minutes when she received a call from Holt telling her that he was still 20 minutes away. She took the opportunity to inform him Heath had evidently made a clean and clever getaway. Holt was furious, or so it seemed. He'd said all the appropriate things, dotted here and there with four-letter words, and promised to have the head of the agent responsible. Stanton listened to Holt's rant, but was not convinced of his sincerity. After the conversation with Holt, Stanton called Agent Murray. "Anything new I should know about?" the sheriff asked.

"Nothing new, Sheriff. I'm still on location where you told me to stay and haven't seen a flicker of light anywhere."

"Okay, Murray, this is what I want you to do. Call my dispatcher and ask him to notify the OHP and surrounding county sheriff departments to be looking for Heath. Describe the truck and of course give them the license plate."

"Should he be arrested if spotted?"

"No, we've nothing to charge him on. We just need to re-acquire his location so you can continue to follow him. My hunch, Agent Murray, is that Heath had a planned escape route through a pasture to a county road a mile east or west of your location. He's probably already on either 183 or 34, and if he is, he could be in Texas, Kansas, or still in Oklahoma somewhere."

"You're probably right, Sheriff. I'll contact dispatch and get back on the highway myself. When will you be back?"

"An hour or so." Stanton saw Holt's rental car pull into the parking lot. "Gotta go, Murray, but call me if anything develops." She snapped her phone shut.

Holt drove to a parking space near the front of the store and got out. Stanton had started her vehicle and eased up close to where the agent stood. He got in. "Good to see you, Sheriff."

She said nothing, just slipped the truck into drive and left the parking lot, heading west. "Thought it'd be better if we were on the move while we talked. Never can tell when someone I know might be shopping late and see me. I'd rather not have to explain why I was in the Wal-Mart parking lot with a stranger."

"Good idea, Sheriff. Don't want those small town busybodies to think you're out hook'n."

Out of the corner of her eye, under the glow of the amber streetlights, she caught a glimpse of Holt's sleazy grin. She reached down between her seat and the console where she kept a few tools of the law enforcement trade and ran her fingers over the top of the 26-inch telescopic steel baton. She pictured the damage she could inflict by striking Holt across the larynx. Just touching the baton relaxed her. Maybe she'd discovered a new relaxation technique; Stanton wondered how her yoga instructor could fit that into her teaching routine. The thought was humorous, and her anger mellowed. "Okay, Holt, what's going on in DC?" she asked, trying to soften the jagged edge of her growing disdain for the agent. Stanton knew she had to control her attitude around Holt. She couldn't afford to have him suspect she didn't trust him, or like him, for that matter. It was a role she had to play, and to play it effectively, Stanton had to bury her true feelings.

"Yeah, lots going on. First, is it okay if we dispense with the formal names and titles?"

"Sure, call me Crys." She felt the knot in her stomach tighten.

"Crys, I like that. Call me Carl."

"Carl it is." Stanton forced a smile, the constriction cinching tighter around her waist.

"Now, doesn't that feel better?"

Stanton didn't look at him; instead, she glanced left,

away from Holt, checking for oncoming traffic, and rolled her eyes.

"You were getting ready to tell me about the joint task force briefing." She found a dark street and turned onto it. Stanton thought it would be easier to hide her expressions where there weren't so many streetlights.

"Yeah, they're ready to tighten the noose. They have the evidence, and the indictment's under seal, along with warrants ready to be served. We're waiting on two of the biggest players to return from Cairo before closing in."

"Any idea on a time frame?"

"Sometime in the next five days is my guess."

"What about Heath, the Oklahoma City appraiser, and the candlestick?"

"The boss didn't spend much time on any of that. Don't think I ever heard him say a word about Heath. Just the loose connection between Bouvier and Hansen, and for the most part that was discounted; I believe his word was *superfluous*." Holt had difficulty with the pronunciation.

"Did you ask him specifically about Heath?" Stanton was losing patience.

"Yes. Said they'd picked up another message from him saying something more was there. But, because Bouvier was about to be arrested, the message was irrelevant."

"Irrelevant? That's all he said?"

"Yeah. I'm here to tell you the task force is focused on the ICO and the two terrorists from Egypt and nothing else. By the way, ever figure out why Heath left town?"

"No. The only thing that we're certain of is that he gave his tail the slip. We don't know where he is or what he's doing. As far as we know, he could be in a neighboring town attending a movie."

"If Heath is truly gone, then my mission here is through. They'll want me back east to help with the arrests."

"Your next move?" Stanton asked.

"I'll call my boss first thing in the morning for orders; probably do a cursory search of Heath's rental house. I understand he never leaves clues, but you never know—we might just get lucky."

Sheriff Stanton had already planned a search of Heath's residence, but she didn't let on. "That's a good idea, the search I mean. I'll help. What time?"

The sheriff pulled through the McDonald's parking lot so that she could turn around and head back toward Holt's car. The lot was well lighted, and she caught sight of his expression when she offered to help with the search. It looked to Stanton like he'd regretted sharing that bit of information. A few seconds later, after he'd had time to think, he said, "Good, the more the merrier." Again, no genuineness in his reply.

"What time?"

"Nine okay with you?"

"Yeah, nine is okay with me."

"By the way, Crys, what's your opinion about the candlestick? I mean, what's so special about it other than the fact it's gold?"

Stanton realized she wasn't the only person fishing for information. She knew Holt had access to all the intelligence. He'd already said that Heath's last message had indicated there was more. More of what was the information Holt was looking for. "That's been my question all along, Carl. Now I realize it's just that—a very old candlestick, probably a family heirloom old man Gray just wanted appraised." She downplayed the candlestick's significance in hopes Holt would find another subject to discuss until she dropped him off at his car. Her subtle maneuvering worked; Holt didn't pursue the candlestick issue. He had other things on his mind.

"How 'bout a nightcap, Crys?"

"It's been a long day, Carl, and it's late. Thanks but not tonight."

"Maybe tomorrow night?"

"As long as we're not sure about Heath and the safety of the Grays, I don't feel much like socializing." Stanton pulled alongside Holt's car and left the engine running.

"Guess I'll just have to be satisfied with seeing you at Heath's in the morning."

"Guess so. Nine. I'll be there."

Holt opened the door and got out. "Sure you're not interested in a drink?"

"See you tomorrow," she said and drove away, thankful Holt was out of her truck.

* * *

Agent Holt closed the door to Stanton's truck and watched her drive away. "Just another ball-busting bitch," he mumbled as he got into his own car. Holt gave the sheriff a ten-minute head start; then he headed northwest back to Buffalo. He passed the Saddle-up just before one a.m. There were at least ten vehicles, mostly pickups, still in the parking lot, and the OHP trooper was parked in the shadow of some trees 200 yards south of the bar. Holt knew the only other law officer on duty at that hour was a deputy sheriff providing protection on the Gray Ranch. He drove by Stanton's home to make sure she was there. Her truck was in the drive, and the only light visible came from a small window in the east end of the house, a bathroom, he assumed. Two minutes later, Holt shut his lights off and turned down the alley in back of Heath's rental house. He shut the engine off and sat looking around, making sure he hadn't attracted the attention of someone watching late-night TV. Other than an occasional barking dog, there was no activity, no lights on in any of the houses he could see from his vantage point, not even the flickering glow a TV might make on a window or closed curtain. Holt took a flashlight out of his black Lands End carrying case, got out of his car, and stuck the light in his back pocket. He made his way in the dark up to the back door; there was no vehicle in the drive. Holt put on his gloves and tried the door. It was unlocked. Opening it wide enough for him to slip in, he crouched low to the floor and turned on the flashlight. He could smell a faint Clorox odor, which didn't surprise him. Holt crawled from one room to the next on his hands and knees, shining the flashlight under furniture, in cracks and corners, anywhere something small could have inadvertently fallen. He wasn't a forensics expert, but with 25 years of investigatory experience under his belt, neither was he a greenhorn. No matter how smart the bad guys were, they always left something behind that might eventually lead to their capture. That concept had been drilled into his thinking for so many years, and, without exception, it was true. The cops just had to be smart enough and tenacious enough to stick with it when investigating a crime scene.

Agent Holt crawled into the kitchen, where he'd started 20 minutes earlier; there was just one more place to search. He opened the slender door next to the refrigerator, a closet probably used for a broom and a dust mop. It, too, was clean, but a piece of paper caught his eye. He pulled and it came free from being partially hidden by a wall stud. The paper was about the size of a credit card; Holt could tell it had been torn from something larger. One side was blank, but the other revealed a two-color pattern of dull green and light tan, with the letters "AX" visible. Under the letters was a partial number with only five numerals visible, followed by a "Q." He knew immediately it was the remnant of an airline ticket—whose ticket he didn't know for sure, but he had a hunch. Holt put the piece of paper in his pocket, took another look around the broom closet, and left the house as carefully as he had come. The scrap of paper wasn't much, but it was all he had, and it would have to do. Holt knew time was running out, and from here on, everything would have to fall into place perfectly for his plan to work. The agent got in behind the wheel and fished around in his bag for pen and paper. He wrote LAX, assuming it was a ticket from the Los Angeles airport, and copied the number and letter on a notepad. He started the car, shut the door quietly, then drove out of the alley in search of Russell's house.

* * *

Heath drove into Wichita, Kansas early Saturday morning and checked into the Stratford Inn located on the outskirts of the city near Interstate 35. He used the name Paul Davis and showed the desk clerk his Illinois driver's license and credit card to prove his identity.

Heath focused his tired eyes on the young man's name tag. "Larry, how about a room in back? I'm tired; don't want highway noise keeping me awake."

The clerk went back to his computer and typed in a code of some kind. "Yes sir. Would you prefer ground or second floor?"

"Second floor would be perfect." Heath was anxious to get some sleep.

The clerk handed him a card key and explained that the adjoining restaurant opened at six.

Heath unlocked his room, hung his suit in the closet, and tossed two bags on a chair next to the bed. He lay down without undressing and fell immediately to sleep.

Four hours later, the motel room alarm clock awakened him. The previous guest had neglected to shut it off, and by the time Heath found the off knob, he was wide awake. He was accustomed to getting up at this hour anyway, and he had the rest of the weekend to rest. By eight o'clock, Heath had cleaned up and eaten breakfast. He perused the free *USA Today* he'd found in front of his door and finished off his fourth cup of coffee. There were a few things he needed to do before returning to his room, where he planned to hole up, undisturbed, for the next 48 hours. By ten o'clock, Heath had purchased a new cell phone at a Radio Shack just down the street from the motel. The phone was purchased under a completely different name, and the one-year contract was paid for in cash. It would be used only one time. Heath filled the truck's gas tank, checked fluid levels, and aired one tire that was low. He bought a few ready-to-eat packaged meals, some bottled water, three cans of diet Coke, and a paperback mystery called *The Cold Dish.*

Heath returned to his room, satisfied that everything was in place for what he hoped would be his final mission. In the last 12 hours, he'd eluded what he suspected were federal agents, and made a successful transition from ranch hand Otis Thorpe to Paul Davis, Midwest representative for the Xerox Corporation, an identity he was well prepared to inhabit. Besides the driver's license and credit cards, he had a letter of introduction from the east coast Vice President of Sales and Marketing to verify his new persona. Like the cell phone purchase, though, the new identity was short term—an identity created specifically to usher Elliot Heath safely into another life completely different than the one he'd been living.

CHAPTER 39

Saturday, June 10, 8:50 a.m.

Sheriff Stanton pulled her car to the curb in front of Heath's house at 8:50 a.m. She was early, but so was Holt. The agent got out of his car and met Stanton as she made her way to the rear of her vehicle. "Morning, Sheriff." His voice sounded different to Stanton. It lacked the arrogance she'd noticed the night before.

"Good morning," she said as she opened the trunk of her car.

He looked at the small arsenal of weaponry. "Looks like you're loaded for bear."

"Well, you know, it's just hard to tell when you'll need it." She took a duffle bag out of the trunk and closed it before Holt could get a good look.

"What's in the bag?"

"Forensic equipment, cameras, stuff like that."

"The county furnish you with that?"

"No. It's all mine, paid for outta my pocket."

"You're really serious about this sheriff business."

"I guess it's my job." Stanton turned to Holt. "Before we set foot on that property," she nodded toward Heath's residence, "I want to be clear about who's in charge, what procedures we're to follow."

"Hey, Sheriff, this is your territory. I'm just here observing. Whatever protocol you follow is fine with me."

Stanton thought his response to her question odd. Any agent worth his salt would have insisted on following strict FBI standards; after all, this was a federal case. In most instances she'd be viewed as a law enforcement bystander and nothing more. It was a well-known fact that FBI agents were territorial and considered themselves to be above local cops from a training perspective. Although an arrogant attitude, for the most part it was true. The FBI had the most rigorous admissions standards and the best training of any other federal agency. Stanton considered the interaction that morning with Agent Holt out of character. The sheriff set the duffle bag on the hood of her car, took out a camera, and adjusted the lens. "Have you tried to enter yet?" She noticed that Holt looked surprised but quickly masked his expression. "No. No, just waiting for you."

"Okay, Carl, let's do a sweep of the outside first, then go in."

"I'm with you, Sheriff."

Stanton noticed Holt was not referring to her as Crys, and she was curious about what had happened since midnight to alter the closer relationship the agent had suggested. Maybe he'd sensed her mistrust or even the anger she'd felt toward him, or perhaps it was something totally different.

Holt walked to the rear of the small bungalow to survey the backyard. There was no garage or other detached buildings, only a yard of unattended Bermuda grass and a healthy growth of weeds. One lonely hackberry tree stood in the middle of the yard providing shade from mostly dead limbs. Stanton was taking photographs of the house and surrounding property; at the same time, she kept an eye on Holt. The sheriff had no idea why she was so vigilant around Holt—she just knew to follow her instincts, and that's what she was doing.

Stanton worked herself around back where the agent was. "Find anything?"

"Just a messy yard."

"I think we're done here. Let's go inside." Stanton and Holt donned latex gloves. The sheriff tried the back door and, finding it unlocked, stepped into the kitchen, and Holt followed. Both moved cautiously, trying not to touch or move anything. Stanton took photos, and then they moved into the combination dining area and front room. The rental house had come furnished with a breakfast table and two straight-back chairs, refrigerator and stove. There were two swivel rockers, a lamp and lamp table, as well as a TV in the front room and a double bed and small dresser in the bedroom.

Without looking at Holt, the sheriff said, "You take the kitchen and front room. I'll take the two bedrooms and bath."

Holt disappeared without acknowledging Stanton's order. Ten minutes later, she heard the agent sit down in one of the rockers, which squeaked. "That was fast," she mumbled. "Through already?" Stanton said aloud.

"Yeah. That kitchen isn't just clean, it's super clean."

"True. I'm not finding anything. You know as well as I that everybody leaves something behind, *everybody*. But not this guy There isn't a smudge anywhere. I'm done."

"Me too. I believe I'll call it a day. Maybe sleep. I'll tell the boss Heath's not around anymore, and she'll order me back east."

"Well, that's what you want, right?"

"Gett'n used to the wide open spaces, the slower pace. Who knows, might decide to retire somewhere close by."

Stanton cringed but said nothing, afraid any response might be interpreted as an invitation.

"What're you doing the rest of the day?" Holt asked.

"Now that we know Heath's gone, I'll reassign my deputies to regular duties and spend the rest of it doing paperwork."

"Ah, yes, paperwork. What'd we do without it."

Stanton returned the bag to her trunk. "In case you have to head east and I don't see you again, take care and let me know how the bust goes." She didn't really mean that, but she had to say something friendly that would work into a proper good-bye.

Holt stood watching the sheriff as she put away her gear and got in behind the wheel of her cruiser. He could tell she was in a hurry to leave; it was glaringly obvious she didn't like him, and that was okay—Holt wanted some distance between them, and acting like an asshole was a surefire way of accomplishing that task.

Stanton checked in with dispatch but didn't say anything about searching Heath's house. She was not totally convinced he was out of the area for good and didn't want to imply he was, for fear her deputies would let down their guard. The sheriff had warned her deputies not to underestimate Heath; she knew that advice applied to her, too.

Stanton had lied to Holt; she had no intention of pulling her deputies off Alpha 1 yet. There was still too much at stake. Just thinking about a rural ranch family sitting on top of something that might be worth millions, with sophisticated criminals knowing about it, gave her goose bumps. She turned her car north and headed toward the courthouse just as her cell phone rang. Stanton recognized the number on her caller ID and pulled to the curb. "Sheriff Stanton."

"Crys, Jerry here. Can you talk?"

Stanton pulled the notepad off the dashboard clip. "I can talk. What'd you find out on Holt?"

"Nothing concrete, only opinions at this point."

"I can work with opinions."

"I talked with his supervisor, and this is her perspective."

"So his boss is female?"

"Yeah, Latisha Johnson. You remember her?"

"Worked with her a few times. Excellent agent if I remember correctly."

"One of the best. Not as good as you, but close."

"Yeah, yeah, thanks, but I'm not coming back. Tell me about Holt."

"Seems Holt's job performance has been mediocre at best, and when Johnson became his boss, he spread it around that she got the job because she was female and black."

"I figured he had issues with the opposite sex."

"Especially if she's your boss, but there's more. Do not repeat to anyone what I'm about to tell you, okay?"

"Yes sir!"

"Did I sense correctly a bit of sarcasm in your answer, Sheriff Stanton?" Webster asked, amused.

"Maybe just a little bit, Mr. Deputy Director."

"Guess that's one of the things I miss most about you—always finding humor with appropriately timed sarcastic remarks."

"Guess that's one thing I don't miss about the agency. The bureaucrats, present company excluded, are humorless.

Anyway, what about Holt's secret?"

"Holt must have done something wrong in 2002. Whatever it was is in a sealed file that only the director has access to. Latisha knows that an agreement was reached between Holt, his supervisor at that time, and the director. She said the only thing she knows about the agreement is that Holt will remain at his present pay grade and will retire at the end of this year. His job description has been modified to read, *He will work for and at the pleasure of his immediate supervisor.*"

"Which means basically that he's a flunky and does relatively unimportant jobs?"

"That's how I read it, Crys."

"So how'd he get picked for this detail?"

"Johnson said they wanted him out of their hair while the task force closed in on the ICO, so they sent him as far away as possible to follow a lead that wasn't considered vital to the overall operation. We originally thought the dealer in Oklahoma City might be a part of the ICO, but we now know that's not true. When I heard the Oklahoma action included Harper County, I immediately thought of you and—"

Stanton interrupted. "And you guys thought I could babysit him?"

"Well, yeah, sort of. When you put it that way, it doesn't sound professional, but that's about right."

"Okay, I'm on board with the babysitting, but tell Johnson that I'm expecting to extract favors from the two of you."

"Good to hear you're not above extorting favors from former friends and colleagues."

"Well, Jerry," she said, laughing, "when you put it that way, it doesn't sound professional. Okay, jokes aside. You're telling me Holt's only assignment was to follow up on the connection with Hansen?"

"That's it."

"He wasn't supposed to follow a Bouvier operative by the name of Elliot Heath?"

"Heath, hmmm, yeah, I know about Heath but don't recall that being a specific assignment. Remember, Crys, I'm heavily involved in the big picture and not so much the specifics. Maybe that was a piece Johnson added later, I don't know. I'll ask her."

"No, Jerry, don't bother her with small details. You guys have enough on your mind. You've already helped a bunch."

"Crys, if you've got a minute, I have a question."

"Sure, what's the question?"

"I've got this ICO sting operation on my mind seems like night and day, but I have this feeling from talking with you there's something else going on. Obviously you have some questions about Holt. Matter of fact, you've got me concerned, too. What else is going on out there? Anything I should know about?"

There was a pause while Stanton considered the consequences if she told Webster about the treasure. He certainly had the right to know, but then again if he thought it so important to bring others into the picture, it could get out of hand. "Jerry, right now what's going on here is interesting to say the least, but I need to piece more of the puzzle together before I tell you. I can assure you of one thing."

"Okay, Sheriff, assure me."

"I'll call you before CNN breaks the story."

CHAPTER 40

Saturday, June 10, 10:43 a.m.

Agent Carl Holt left Heath's rental house as soon as the sheriff was out of sight. He drove straight to his apartment and went right to work, documenting the search and completing required forms. During performance review sessions with previous supervisors, Holt had always received high marks for his thorough report writing, something he took pride in and yet embellished from time to time in order to assure the higher-ups of his competence.

Holt finished the paperwork. One thing left to do before he rested. He searched around in his bag until he found the information he'd copied from the piece of airline ticket. Holt called the task force support group on intelligence and gave the analyst his badge number and his assigned code identifying him as a task force member. The analyst verified his identity.

"Yes sir, Agent Holt, what can I do for you?"

"I need verification of a document, probably an airline

ticket belonging to someone who either flew into or out of LA, sometime in April of this year. If it was a ticket, I need to know who it was issued to. Here's all I have, probably the rear end of a confirmation number." Holt gave the analyst the five numerals and the letter Q.

"How soon you need this, Agent Holt?"

"How soon can you get me the info?"

"Assuming your preliminary assessment is correct and it is a ticket issued in April and the numbers are correct, I can have the info for you by Sunday morning. If you need it faster, I'll have to have the request approved through your supervisor."

"No. Ah, Sunday is fine, that's just great. Give me a call back on my land line." Holt gave the analyst the number, closed his cell phone, and leaned back; he hadn't realized how tired he was until then. Holt glanced at the microwave oven clock; it was nearly 1:30 p.m. The oven reminded him he hadn't eaten since his two pieces of toast and banana six hours earlier. He was too tired to go out; the usual TV dinner would have to do until after he slept.

Holt tossed the empty plastic tray in the waste container, walked into the bedroom, and closed the dusty blinds. As he began to unbutton his shirt, he strained in the dim light to see his shape in the dresser mirror. The reflection was not complimentary. The lack of exercise and poor diet over the years had contributed to his soft appearance. Muscle tone, solid and defined at one time, was now only a distant memory. His pale skin and hairy shoulders and back reminded him of an albino ape. His flabby gut hung over his trouser top like froth escaping from an overflowing beer mug. Holt was disgusted with his pathetic appearance. He thought of his two failed marriages, thankful there were no children. He would have surely damaged them emotionally like he had his wives.

Holt shut his cell phone off—he wanted some uninterrupted rest—and lay back on the bed, staring at the nicotine-stained ceiling. Life for him was about to change, for the better he hoped.

* * *

Helen Gray put the finishing touches on dinner, slid a pie into the oven, and set the timer for 45 minutes. "Fred," she called into the den.

"Yeah, hon."

"Dinner's ready. Where you suppose Curt's at?"

Fred came into the kitchen and sat down. "Don't know, but it's not like him to be late."

"Why don't you call him, in case he forgot?"

"Don't think he'd forget. He sounded way too anxious."

"He also sounded tipsy." Helen hated the word *drunk*. She'd never been around anyone who was intoxicated. Fred and Robert would have a beer or two on a hot day or when they watched a football game, but she'd never seen either under the influence. To her, the word *drunk* conjured up images she'd only seen on TV; it was hard for her to visualize anyone she knew looking and acting as terrible as that.

"You mean drunk?" Fred knew how she felt about the word, but couldn't resist the chance to playfully torment his wife.

"No Fred! I don't mean drunk. Curt is a good boy. Just can't see him drinking too much."

"Yeah, he is a good boy, but good boys do some stupid things."

Helen knew better than to ask Fred if he'd ever drank too much or done anything stupid. After all, he'd been in the Army, and that's all she needed to know.

Fred called Curt's number, but there was no answer. "Probably on his way. Can we wait a few more minutes?"

"Yes, just can't guarantee the gravy won't be lumpy."

"Lumpy or not, your gravy's always great."

Fred read the rest of the paper he'd started earlier, and Helen busied herself making sure the gravy was stirred and everything stayed warm, but they were worried. They were fearful that somehow Curt had become the first victim of what the sheriff had warned them about—the danger, she said, that might be beyond their ability to control, but neither said anything about the way they felt. Knowing the FBI had their eye on Heath wasn't particularly helpful; the sheriff had explained that Heath was dangerous and cunning. The FBI had never been able to catch him in the act of committing crimes, she'd told them. Suddenly, the thin reassurances they'd heard from the sheriff seemed artificial at best.

"Honey, it's been twenty minutes. Don't you think we should try to call again?"

Fred put the paper away; Helen could see the worry on his face. "Yeah. If I don't get him this time, think I'll go to town and look." He called again. No answer.

"You need something to eat before you go. Let me fix a plate."

They both hurried through dinner without much thought of how it tasted. "I'll get Robert to stay with you," Fred said as he rose from the table.

"That's not necessary, hon."

Fred turned to her as he put his hat on, cocking it back so the wide brim wouldn't get in the way when he bent to kiss her. "I wish it wasn't necessary." He took her in his arms, holding her tighter than usual.

"You're worried," she said, patting the small of his back.

"Yeah, a little."

Robert drove in from the south pasture ten minutes later and met his dad coming out of the house. "What's going on?"

"Curt wanted to talk to me, so we invited him for dinner. He didn't show. I'm a little worried. You gonna be around awhile?"

"Yeah, you need me to do something?"

"I'm going to town and look for him. Like for you to hang around close to the house."

"Sure, Dad. You think something happened to him?"

"With everything that's going on around here, it wouldn't surprise me."

Fred left the house at 20 minutes after one, speeding along the country road, trying to think of all the legitimate reasons why Curt hadn't shown up for dinner. None were very reassuring, and his apprehension grew.

He met the sheriff where the dirt road and highway intersected. She pulled adjacent to his truck, the billowing dust settling, and pressed the button to lower her window. "Where you headed?"

"Town, looking for Curt. He was supposed to have dinner with us and didn't show. I'm a little worried. You headed to the ranch?"

"Yes, gonna check on my deputy, then bring you all up to date on what I learned from Holt."

"He finally get back?"

"Last night, late. You need help looking for Curt?"

"Don't think so. I'll look in the usual spots, check with some of his acquaintances. That's about all I can do."

"I'll be on the ridge. When I see you return, I'll join you at the house."

"Okay." Fred waved and turned onto the blacktop. A few minutes later, he turned down Curt's street, where he could see the house from two blocks away, the truck in the drive. Fred felt a rush of mixed feelings. Had Curt been gone and just returned home? He hoped that was the case. On the other hand, what if something terrible had happened? Fred pulled into the drive behind Curt's truck and got out. He went to the front door and knocked. The shade was pulled. Fred listened for sounds but couldn't hear anything. He knocked louder and waited, then tried the door. It was locked. Fred went back to Curt's vehicle and found the doors unlocked. He looked around inside, for what he wasn't sure, just any kind of clue. He closed the truck door and went to the first window on the east side of the house and tried to look in, but that shade was pulled, too. The next window, if he remembered correctly, was a bedroom. That shade was only partially down, but he couldn't see any movement.

He could see into the kitchen through the back door window. Part of the counter was visible, and Fred saw a six-pack of beer; no cans were missing from the plastic rings. That door was locked. He knocked—no answer. Fred thought about trying to pry the door open or even breaking the window, but resisted the temptation. What if Curt was in a deep sleep? Maybe he had a hangover and just didn't want to be disturbed? Breaking into someone's house was a drastic step Fred wasn't yet ready to take. The idea crossed his mind that Curt's girlfriend might know his whereabouts. All he really knew was that her first name was Lisa and she worked at the Percolator Café. He drove there, only to find out she was away attending a funeral. She was expected back to work early Monday morning, and according to Kathryn Thelen, the owner, she'd overheard her say she would be home Sunday evening sometime.

Fred left the café even more discouraged. He'd hoped Curt was with his girlfriend, but she'd been out of town since last week. The rancher made a slow pass through town, stopping at the city park long enough to see Curt wasn't there, either. Only thing Fred could think of to do was return home and take the sheriff up on her offer of help. Maybe Sheriff Stanton could justify breaking into Curt's house; surely there was a law that would permit law enforcement that latitude. Twenty-five minutes later, Fred drove into his ranch just as the sheriff arrived from checking on her deputy. "Find him?" she asked as they got out of their vehicles.

Fred shook his head. "No, no luck at all. Let's go in. Helen and Robert need to hear what I found out."

Helen fixed iced tea for everyone while Fred explained what he'd done to try and find Curt. "Almost broke in, but didn't."

"Why not?" Robert asked.

"How'd you feel if you were home sleep'n and someone came busting through your door?"

"Uh, well, I see your point, but what if he's sick or hurt?"

Fred turned to the sheriff. "Good question. What if he's in there hurt?"

"He ever say why he wanted to talk?" Stanton asked.

"No, just called late last night and asked if he could come out."

"How'd he sound? I mean, did he sound happy, sad, angry, what?"

"Sounded a little drunk, slurred words, but kinda urgent. Back to the original question: what if he's in the house hurt or sick?"

Stanton didn't answer right away, just sat thinking, tapping her index finger on the holster snap. She turned to Helen. "May I use your phone?"

"Yes, of course."

Stanton called her office, while the others listened. One of the reserve deputies answered. "Deputy, this is the sheriff." There was a short pause while the deputy acknowledged the sheriff and relayed two messages. "Thanks. Now, listen carefully. This is important." Another pause. Evidently, the person on the other end of the line was looking for something to write on. Stanton put her hand over the phone and whispered, "Got two reserve deputies. Wonderful guys, willing to do anything to help, but slow as molasses." She removed her hand from the mouthpiece. "Here's what I want you to do. Call whatever deputy is on the call-in rotation list—" The reserve interrupted her. "The list is posted on the left-hand side of the bulletin board on the wall in back of you." The sheriff smiled out of frustration. "Yes, that's the one. Now, call whoever is at the top of that list and tell them they are to go to this address." She waited until the deputy had it written down. "Would you please read that back to me?"

The sheriff told the reserve deputy to contact Trooper Crossland and ask him to provide backup for the deputy. "Tell them they are to use whatever means necessary to gain entrance to the house, but as with all such cases, remind them to knock on both the front and back door first." Another pause while the reserve repeated the entire order back to the sheriff. "The last thing, Deputy: have them call me the minute they finish looking through the house."

The sheriff hung up the phone and returned to her seat at the kitchen table. "It'll take the deputy some time to get over there, maybe thirty, forty minutes. We should know something then."

"You know, Sheriff." Fred stood and hung up his hat. "I think we're all hoping Curt isn't one of Heath's victims."

"I know, been thinking about that myself." Stanton

thought about where Agent Murray said Heath was an hour before he lost him. She decided to wait until after the search of Curt Russell's home to say anything about Heath's disappearance. "Anyway, it'll be a few minutes before I hear from the deputy. In the meantime, let me fill you in on Holt's meeting with the task force in DC."

CHAPTER 41

Saturday, June 10, 5:15 p.m.

Agent Holt checked the time. *Impossible,* he thought. Holt couldn't ever remember taking a three-hour nap; the longest had been two, and it had followed a 30-hour stakeout he did solo over a decade ago.

He felt sluggish and decided a cold shower would revive him, then a trip to a neighboring town with a restaurant that stayed open late, preferably one with a bar. Maybe even see a movie; he had nothing else to do until Monday morning. Holt strained to fasten the button on his jeans and then looked in the mirror again. Still not pleased with what he saw, his appearance had improved. The rest had helped. He tried to tuck his Polo shirt in but there wasn't room—that was okay. He'd read somewhere that tails out was the in thing right now. He reached for his keys, turned on his cell phone, and was heading out the door when the apartment phone rang. He answered, "Agent Holt."

"Yeah, Agent Holt, it's the analyst you talked with earlier."

"Didn't expect to hear from you until tomorrow."

"The project was easier than I expected. Just pulled all LAX incoming flights for the month of April—there was a ton of 'em. Ran the five digits and the letter Q against the airport arrivals database, and there was only one that ended with that combination of numbers and the letter Q. How lucky is that?"

"Not luck at all, I'd say. Looks more like professional expertise to me. You can be sure the task force bosses will hear about this," Holt lied. "Now what's the name on the ticket?"

"Ralph Simmons."

"I need another favor. Can you run that name for aliases? I know it's a common name—"

The analyst cut him off. "I'm ahead of you. There are fifteen aliases associated with Ralph Simmons."

"Any of 'em Heath?"

"Elliot?"

"Yeah, that's great. Thanks again for your help."

Holt hung up the phone and smiled, picked up his keys again, and headed for his car.

* * *

The sheriff looked at her watch; it had been 45 minutes since she'd talked with the reserve deputy. Plenty of time had lapsed to contact whichever deputy was on call and for a preliminary search of Curt's house. Stanton saw that Helen was becoming increasingly upset. She dabbed constantly at her eyes with her handkerchief, tried to busy herself cleaning the kitchen counter, and shot nervous glances at her husband. It seemed she was preparing herself emotionally for bad news. Finally the phone rang; Fred answered and then handed it to Stanton. "It's Deputy Norton."

"This is the sheriff."

Everyone watched Stanton as she sat listening intently to what the deputy said.

"Listen carefully, do not touch anything. I'll be there in twenty-five minutes." The sheriff stood and hung up the phone, then turned slowly toward the family. She heard Helen trying to hold back sobs. "I have bad news." Stanton returned to her seat next to Helen. "Curt is dead." The sheriff was shocked at the sound of her own words. They were raw, without feeling, and she immediately regretted her direct approach. Helen buried her face in Fred's chest, crying. He embraced her, turning his head away from Robert to hide his own tearing eyes. Robert's face turned an angry red; he slammed his clenched fist on the table and stormed out the back door. Stanton leaned in close to Helen, stroking her back, and said, "Helen, Fred, I'm so very sorry about Curt. I know he meant a lot to you."

They both nodded; neither looked at the sheriff.

"I must go, but I will let you know when I learn more." Stanton got to her feet and left. She needed to get to Curt's house quickly. Norton said it looked like suicide to him, but Stanton wasn't convinced. She needed to look the scene over carefully before making any comment regarding cause of death. She knew the Grays would jump to the conclusion that the cause of death was murder and the murderer was Heath. Although murder was a possibility, it would be a mistake to identify a person of interest prematurely.

The sheriff brought her car to a stop in back of the Crossland's OHP black-and-white. Norton's personal vehicle was in the drive behind Russell's pickup, and an ambulance was backed up to the front door. *So much for discretion*, she thought as she walked through the front door. Stanton was surprised to see that Norton had secured the immediate scene just the way she'd taught him. Once the deputy had determined Curt was in fact dead, he called the ambulance but wouldn't let the paramedics in until she arrived.

Norton was anxious; this was the first death he'd ever investigated that hadn't been an accident. "Well, Sheriff, suicide, right?"

"Certainly looks that way. You did good, Norton. Thanks for securing the scene."

Stanton walked over to a table and picked up Curt's billfold and looked through it, then handed it to Norton. "Take this back to headquarters, go through it thoroughly, and see if there's any information on next of kin. If there is, leave name, address, phone numbers, just whatever you find on my desk. Bag the rest and leave it on my desk also."

"Yes, Sheriff. Anything else you want me to do?"

"Follow me." Stanton gestured toward the front door. Norton followed her out to the porch where the other three were. "Gentlemen, this appears to be the scene of a suicide, and right now there's nothing more any of you can do here. I'll call the state medical examiner, and they'll take it from here. No need for an ambulance and no need for law enforcement intervention just yet. The only request I have is that you say nothing about this to anyone."

"Won't it get around anyway, Sheriff?" the trooper asked.

"Yes, it will. My guess is the Buffalo phone lines are already jammed with folks talking about us standing on this front porch right now, but no official word should come from any of you. When and only when a thorough study of the body and scene are complete will we issue a statement."

Five minutes later, everyone was gone, and Stanton returned to the room where Curt Russell's body was. She called dispatch. Bingham was covering. "Deputy Bingham, glad you're there."

"Yeah, figured you needed the help. Besides, ain't nothing on TV."

"You've heard?"

"Reserve deputy brought me up to speed when I relieved him. Too bad. Wonder what made him want to kill himself?"

"Don't know. Haven't found any kind of note yet. It's just one of those tragedies we may never understand. Anyway, Bingham, I need you to call the ME. Call me back and let me know how soon they'll be here."

Stanton walked over to where Curt's body was. Without touching anything, she made notes of how the body was positioned, the bullet entry point, which hand the gun was in, and its caliber and make. She counted the number of empty and unopened beer cans. Stanton looked through the remaining rooms for anything that might be a clue of any kind. She returned to her car and got the bag of forensic equipment out of the trunk. Stanton assembled the camera with the proper lens and snapped 40 photos. All the empty beer cans were collected in two large evidence bags. According to Agent Murray, Heath had stopped by Russell's house with a six-pack of beer just hours before he disappeared. Maybe Heath and Russell had had a friendly beer together before Curt died. The cans, assuming Heath drank one, would have DNA on them. That would be enough to arrest Heath on suspicion of murder and grounds for a nationwide APB.

Stanton took out a sterile vial and swabbed Curt's right hand—the one holding the gun—returned the swab to the container, and snapped the attached lid shut. She decided not to do any more until the ME had completed his preliminary and removed the body.

The sheriff called Bingham back. "Any news on when we can expect the ME?"

"Just hung up with her, said it'd be about three hours. You gonna stay there for three hours?"

"No choice. I'll have to."

"Want me to send someone to relieve you?"

"No. I'll be alright."

The sheriff walked through the house looking for anything she might have missed. Three hours was a long time to wait on the ME, but it would give her time to study the scene while the body remained in the original position when death occurred. Stanton was in the kitchen when she heard a knock coming from the front. She opened the door and stepped out, closing it behind her. The young man looked familiar, but she couldn't remember where she'd seen him. "Yes, may I help you?"

"Yes, ma'am, we met in my mother's office." He stuck his hand out. "Tobias Henry, with the *Ledger*."

"Yes, of course, Tobias, sorry. What can I do for you?"

"Got a call from Mr. Thompson saying he'd heard there had been a suicide at this address. He sent me over to look into it."

"Tobias, I'm going to ask you to bear with me on this one. True, someone is deceased inside this house, and I'm waiting on the ME, all standard procedures. I will not issue a statement until the ME has thoroughly examined the body."

Tobias was writing down everything the sheriff said in a spiral steno pad. "Later tonight or maybe tomorrow you'll know?"

"Tobias, it could be two weeks. We know the person didn't die of natural causes and that's it."

"If he didn't die of natural causes, then how'd he die?"

The intern stood poised with pen in hand, expecting the sheriff to tell him.

Stanton gave Tobias an understanding smile. "Tell you what, as soon as the ME releases the scene for me to do my investigation, and the next of kin has been notified, I will call you first."

That seemed to satisfy him for the moment, and he left. Stanton quickly surveyed the street from one end of the block to the other. She counted at least 25 people on porches and in their front yards looking in her direction.

At 9:30 p.m. the ME arrived, and by 11:00 she'd completed as much of her on-site examination as possible. "I'm done here, Sheriff. I'll take charge of the body and have it transported to Oklahoma City for autopsy."

Stanton had stayed out of the ME's way during the exam. She said nothing to the doctor about theories of how the death might have occurred, nor had she asked questions that might be perceived as leading or putting thoughts in the examiner's head. "Any guesses or prelims on cause of death?"

"You mean aside from the obvious?"

"Well, Doctor, in my business, one can never be too careful. I don't want to utter a word about how someone dies without confirmation."

"Yeah, I'm with you on that. With all the crime investigation shows around, the general public wants to know every detail. Something, unfortunately, we can't always give 'em." The ME finished putting her equipment away and stood up. She pointed at Curt Russell's body half sitting, half hunched over the love seat arm. Blood from the head wound had dried in three separate streams down his neck, saturating his white T-shirt all the way to his belt. "That's reality." She stood quietly, almost reverently next to Stanton for a minute and didn't say anything. "You asked about cause of death. Sheriff, it looks like a textbook case of suicide." The doctor paused. Stanton could tell the ME wanted to say more, but was careful not to prompt her.

The ME finally turned and faced Stanton. "I have some concerns."

"And they would be what?"

"I've examined ten suicides by gun in the last three years, and in every one of those cases I was absolutely sure it was suicide. This one I can't say that."

"How so?"

"For right now let's just say that I want my boss to do the autopsy. Whatever I say at this time would be purely speculation, and you can't initiate an investigation on that. I'll put a priority on this, though."

The examiner left, and within 30 minutes an official transport from the ME's office arrived to transfer Curt's body to Oklahoma City. Stanton strung caution tape around the house and placed forms at the front and back doors warning that the premises were off limits. She went back to the kitchen to shut the light out, and as she passed by the couch where Curt's body had been, she noticed something on the floor about where his boot had been. Stanton pulled another small evidence container from her bag of forensic equipment and placed the piece of paper inside. She locked the front door and returned to her car.

The sheriff sat there thinking about all that had happened that day. She was tired, running on adrenaline, and she couldn't remember what or even when she'd eaten last. Maybe there was something in the refrigerator at home; it was midnight and too late to get anything at the convenience store.

On the way home, Stanton passed the church her folks had attended most of their adult lives. *Tomorrow is Sunday*, she thought. Maybe she would go.

CHAPTER 42

Sunday, June 11, 9:00 a.m.

Sheriff Stanton awoke abruptly to the ringing of her house phone. She fumbled with the clock to see what time it was and reached for the phone, knocking it off the lamp table to the floor. It was the first morning she could ever remember regretting that she was the sheriff. "Hello."

"Morning, Sheriff. I wake you?"

"Yeah, as a matter of fact you did. Who is this?"

"Sorry, but thought you'd want to know I located a sister."

"Sister? What sister? And I still don't know who I'm talking to." Stanton was muddled, her morning state of mind a fog of confusion. She tried communicating coherently, but something was interfering, a sadness Stanton hadn't felt since her mother died. Then it became clear. She remembered Curt Russell, and her thoughts began to fall into place. "Norton? Is this Norton?"

"Yeah, Sheriff, this is Norton. Got Curt's sister's

address and phone number. Want me to call her?"

"No, I'll call her. What about parents?"

"Mom died five years ago from breast cancer, dad died of a heart attack about a year later, and no other siblings."

"Good work, Norton. Just give me the information and I'll make the call."

Stanton ignored the morning news and her exercise ritual. She downed a bagel and two cups of coffee in record time. Shower, a little makeup, and a pantsuit she hadn't worn in two years, and she'd be ready for church. She tried to remember how many times she'd attended since her mother died. Five, maybe six times in four years? It didn't really matter; she was going today. All she had to do for the next hour was make two calls and drive by Russell's house to make sure no one had tampered with it.

Stanton sat down at the kitchen table and called Fred Gray first. According to the rancher, Helen hadn't slept well until about 4:00 a.m. She was still asleep, and he guessed they'd skip church. Even if Fred woke her now, she wouldn't have time to get ready. Robert was out checking on cows.

Stanton explained that Curt's body had been transported to the ME's office in Oklahoma City and that cause of death appeared to be suicide.

"When will we know for sure?" Fred asked.

"Could take ten days, maybe more."

"Why so long?"

"After they do an autopsy, a lab will analyze various tissue, blood, and residue samples. That all takes time. I'll keep you posted. Is there anything I can do for you?"

"No, Sheriff, but I want you to know we appreciate all you're doing. I know you've put in several long days. All I can say is the next time you run for sheriff, you'll have our vote."

"Thanks. I'm just doing my job. And, Fred, you could do me a favor."

"Anything."

"Next time I run for sheriff, don't vote for me." They both laughed.

"Oh, Sheriff, almost forgot, did Curt have family?"

"One sister who lives in Borger, Texas. I'm getting ready to call her now. Do you want her name and number?"

"Yes please. We'll call her later today. Maybe we can work with her on burial expenses."

The sheriff dialed the number Norton had given her. After the third ring, a soft, tired female voice answered.

"This is Crys Stanton, sheriff of Harper County, Oklahoma. I'm calling for Angela Russell Case."

"Yes, that's me. What's wrong?"

"You're the sister of Curtis Russell, a resident of Harper County?"

"Yes. Is there something wrong with Curt? Where is he?" Her voice became shrill, cracking with apprehension.

Stanton explained that Curt had died of an apparent suicide. All the sheriff could hear were deep, breathless sobs. Curt's sister tried to ask questions, but emotion overcame her before she could utter a full sentence. The sheriff let her cry. Finally Angela spoke. "Sheriff Stanton, is that right?"

"Yes, that's right."

"I haven't seen Curt in two years, but I thought he was doing well. Was he still taking his medication?"

"What medication was he taking? I didn't see any prescription bottles in his house."

"I was afraid that would happen. He hated the way they made him feel, the pills I mean. The VA doctor in Oklahoma City examined him, said he had bipolar disease and that he must take his medications."

"What was his behavior like when he wasn't taking the pills?"

"The worst part was the depression. He'd get so depressed, so unhappy he'd forget to take it. The doctor had a social worker check on him to see that he took it, but when he moved to Buffalo, there wasn't anyone familiar with his situation. He was embarrassed and wouldn't go for more help. I came there two years ago and took him to a doctor in Woodward, and he gave him a new prescription. I called him twice a week to remind him. I thought he was doing better. He really liked working for that rancher, even said he had a new friend—"

"Do you remember the friend's name?"

"No, he never said, just that they worked together on the ranch. I do remember his girlfriend's name. It was Lisa, I think. How is she?"

"She's out of town and doesn't know yet."

"That poor girl. Sounded like they really loved each other. Curt said she was helping him with the meds."

Stanton told Curt's sister the rancher wanted to visit with her about arrangements. "He'll call soon. Curt's body will be with the ME for the next ten days. You and Mr. Gray can plan funeral arrangements in the meantime."

Angela didn't have any more questions and began to cry softly. Stanton told her that if she needed anything to call; otherwise she'd keep her posted. Crys Stanton was tough, but not that tough, and after they hung up she cried.

Crys dabbed some makeup under her eyes and refreshed her mascara. It was 10:40 a.m.—just enough time to drive by Curt's house and on to church. She had filed Angela's comment about Curt's friend away for future consideration. Evidently, Curt had thought enough about Heath to actually tell his sister that a friendship was emerging. She didn't think of it as peculiar, however; Stanton knew that one skill a true psychopath developed from childhood was the ability to befriend and convince people of their sincerity. That would fit with what Holt said about Heath.

Stanton drove by the secured house. The tape was in place, and the warning was posted on the front door. She drove down the alley and saw that the back door was still sealed and the warning prominently displayed. The sheriff had no reason to believe anyone in the small town would cross the tape just out of curiosity.

In the crowded parking lot of the United Methodist Church, Stanton found a space and shifted to park just as her radio crackled.

"Dispatch to Unit one."

Without a second thought, Stanton pulled the mic off the bracket and pressed the button. "Unit one, go ahead."

"Ten-twenty?"

"Church parking lot."

"Ten twenty-five headquarters."

"Ten-nine?"

"Ten twenty-five headquarters."

"Ten-four." Stanton drove straight to the courthouse and hurried inside. Bingham saw the sheriff and pressed the button releasing the magnetically locked door, allowing her boss in. "What's going on?" asked the sheriff.

Bingham pointed toward the partially closed office door and whispered, "You have a visitor." The sheriff hated surprises. She stopped abruptly in front of Deputy Bingham with a scowl on her face; she had really wanted to go to church. The scowl grew deeper, disfiguring her usually pretty face. Her appearance was almost comical, but Maude Bingham knew better than to laugh, even smile for that matter. "He flashed a badge, said he was Peter Miles, FBI."

"On Sunday?"

"On Sunday."

"Okay, but before I go in there, I have something important for you to do. Curt Russell's girlfriend is out of town and is expected back late this afternoon. As far as we know, she doesn't know about Curt—"

Bingham interrupted. "I know Lisa pretty well. She attends the same church I do. I'll bring the pastor and his wife up to speed, and they can break the news."

"Thanks, Maude, that'll be a great help to me. Now I'll see what this Fed wants."

CHAPTER 43

Sunday, June 11, 11:13 a.m.

When Sheriff Stanton stepped through the partially closed door to her office, the agent stood and offered his hand. "Sheriff, Special Agent Pete Miles." He presented his badge for verification.

She shook his hand and motioned for him to take a seat. "Sunday morning, this is a surprise." Stanton wasn't unfriendly, just more controlled than usual.

"I realize this is a little unusual, but let me explain."

"Please."

"First of all, let me apologize for not getting back with you as I promised." Miles paused, waiting for the sheriff's acknowledgement until he became uncomfortable. "As soon as I talked with you, I took your advice and called my boss. Long story short, within thirty minutes after discussing my concerns about being left out of the loop, I got a call from Gerald Webster. Understand the two of you worked together in the past."

"We did, a long time ago."

"He filled me in on your background. I had no idea you'd been with the agency."

"Would that have made a difference?"

"It shouldn't, but frankly, the truthful answer is yes."

The best way for anyone to get along with Crys Stanton was to be honest and to the point. Pete Miles was unknowingly doing just that.

"So what did you and Jerry talk about?"

Miles pulled his chair closer to Stanton's desk. "Webster asked me to come to St. Louis for a teleconference concerning a matter of national security. After the briefing, he asked me to work directly with you until the ICO was shut down. He said you'd brief me on how Buffalo, Oklahoma and the ICO operation are connected."

"I'm still not clear on what you mean by *working directly with me?*"

"I'm to stay in Buffalo, assist you with anything you need. The vast resources of the agency are at your disposal. I'm here to make sure that happens smoothly."

"Okay, Miles, tell me what you know, and I'll fill in the details."

"I know about the ICO and Bouvier and that Bouvier and someone by the name of Paul Hansen, who is here in Oklahoma City, have communicated about a candlestick. According to Webster—he wasn't clear about this—the candlestick is owned by a local rancher. The rancher took the candlestick to Hansen for an appraisal, and from that event a quasi connection between Bouvier and Hansen emerged. He said you'd have more information about that."

"Some, but here's where it gets complicated. What else do you know?"

"Webster says the FBI is no longer interested in

Hansen; guess he's an innocent player and nothing more."

"What do you know about Agent Holt?"

"He was sent to Oklahoma to follow up on the link between Bouvier and Hansen."

"What'd you find out about Heath?"

"Not much. Webster said he was a player, but not on the A-team."

"Did you ask why Holt considered him dangerous?"

"Sorry, didn't ask that specifically. When I mentioned his name, the subject was brought to a close quickly. I felt like I'd pressed the wrong button."

"Just seems strange an agent would be sent here on one mission and then he focuses most of his time on another task."

"I don't see it that way, Sheriff."

"Tell me, then, how you see it."

"Could be just a simple communication error. You know how confusing agency directives can get. By the time they filter down to the field, it's a miracle we get it right as often as we do."

"Yeah, you have a point there." Stanton didn't want to drag the conversation out; she could see Miles' natural reaction was to come to a fellow agent's defense, even if he'd never met Holt. Defending fellow field agents to non-FBI types was something she'd done a hundred times herself. Seeds of the come-to-the-rescue mentality were planted early at the academy when minds were fresh and attitudes malleable. Stanton knew she'd need evidence to get Miles to view Holt more suspiciously, and right now all she had was her gut feeling.

The sheriff brought Agent Miles up to date with what had happened over the past 24 hours, including her suspicion that Curt Russell might have been murdered.

"What do you base your suspicion on?" Miles asked.

"It's all circumstantial stuff. The night Russell died was the same night Heath eluded your agent, and Murray said before losing him he followed Heath to Russell's house."

"That's pretty convincing circumstantial evidence. Do you have anything else?"

"I swabbed Russell's hand, the one gripping the pistol, for residue, and I have the gun. I was going to ship them off to the Oklahoma State Bureau of Investigation for analysis first thing in the morning."

"You know how long that'll take, don't you?"

"Ten days if I'm lucky." Stanton looked up suddenly, and for the first time that morning she smiled. "What about the FBI lab in Dallas?" she said eagerly.

Miles shook his head. "Chain of evidence problems."

"Damn it, I forgot." She hadn't forgotten, though. Stanton swiveled her chair to the west and looked out the window, hoping Miles would pick up the hint.

"Sheriff, I'm here to help. Was anyone with you when you swabbed Russell's hand?"

"No."

"Have you written anything on the evidence tube?"

"No. Not yet."

"Give it to me."

"You sure?"

"Give it to me now before I get cold feet."

Stanton handed the evidence bag to him. "There's something else." She dug around until she found the bag containing the piece of paper and handed that to Miles.

"Don't have a clue what this is. Found it on the floor in front of where Russell's body was found. Might as well have the lab see what they can make of it."

Miles held it up to get a better look. "Maybe a piece of an airline ticket?"

"Now that you mention it." Stanton nodded.

"Don't want to get ahead of myself here, but you know this looks more and more like an old-fashioned MSM."

"Yeah, Agent Miles, I've had that feeling. Someone murders the victim and makes it appear like a suicide, but arranges the evidence to point at someone else. A murder made to look like a suicide made to look like a murder."

A sharp knock on the sheriff's door startled them both. "Come in," Stanton said.

Deputy Bingham stuck her head through the opening and told the sheriff that the situation with Russell's girlfriend had been taken care of. "The pastor and his wife are with her now. Lisa just got back and is taking it real hard. Some of her family is on the way here."

"Thank you, Maude, that helps me. One other thing. I'll want to visit with her before she leaves town, assuming her family will want to take her back to wherever she's from."

"I'll pass the word." Maude backed out and shut the door.

"It's about two; I haven't had anything since breakfast. You hungry, Agent Miles?"

"I could eat something, yes."

"Our choices are drive thirty miles one way—that'd be Woodward—or I could fix a ham sandwich at the house. What's your pleasure?"

"I'm with you."

"Let's have sandwiches. I need to get rid of the ham."

On the way to the sheriff's house, Stanton detoured and pointed out where Heath lived and also Russell's house. Then, by the ten-unit apartment complex where Agent Holt lived temporarily, she pointed. "Holt lives in apartment four, and that's his car."

"You know…" Agent Miles hesitated. "You know, I get the feeling you don't like Holt."

"Really."

"Yeah, there's something in your tone when you say his name."

"Before you leave in the morning for Dallas, let me arrange a quick meeting, maybe over breakfast, for the three of us. I'd like to see how he acts; see what he says when he finds out you're here to assist with the investigation."

"What do you think that'll prove?"

"Maybe nothing. I'll just introduce the two of you, ask him what his plans are now that Heath's gone. That's it. After he leaves I'd like your honest opinion, that's all."

"Like I said before, I'm here to help, but I think you might be blowing this out of proportion."

"We'll see." Stanton turned into her drive.

* * *

After making arrangements to meet early the next morning, Stanton dropped Miles off at the courthouse where he'd parked his car. She went back to her office and called Tobias Henry. The sheriff explained the circumstances of Curtis Russell's death and that the state medical examiner had conducted a routine investigation and was ordering an autopsy, the results of which would be available in ten to fourteen days. Preliminary evidence indicated that Russell had died of a self-inflicted gunshot to the right temple. Next of kin, a sister in Borger, Texas, had been notified.

"Thanks, Sheriff. I appreciate the information. Oh yes, one more question."

"Hope I can give you an answer."

"You ever find a note, you know, anything explaining why?"

"No. No note, nothing."

"Thanks again, Sheriff, and if anything comes up, please call."

Stanton agreed, although she had no intention of notifying some wet-behind-the-ears reporter intern of any new developments, even if he was the son of a judge.

The sheriff told the reserve deputy filling in for the regular shift dispatcher that she was going to check on Alpha 1.

CHAPTER 44

Monday, June 12, 7:00 a.m.

That Monday morning in Harper County started much like any other. Ranchers checking on their herds, townspeople gathering at the local café for coffee, news from around the world, and the latest spin on local gossip. The only thing different about this day was the topic of conversation; everyone was shocked to hear that Fred Gray's ranch hand had committed suicide. The shock spread as word got around that the young man—most people didn't know him—had dated Lisa, a waitress the regular Percolator customers knew well. Speculation centered on the misconception Lisa was breaking up with him, an idea someone had suggested more as a question than a statement of fact. But, as those things go, the concept seemed rational to a table of retired businessmen sitting within earshot, and from there what was once a mere question was now a fact. By noon it was well known from one end of town to the other that Curtis Russell had killed himself because of a broken heart. The thought of losing his girlfriend was more than he could stand, everyone assumed.

* * *

Sheriff Stanton stopped in front of room six at the local motel and honked. Pete Miles tested the motel door to make sure it was locked and got in next to the sheriff. "Right on time, Sheriff."

"On time, but empty-handed," she said.

"Problem?"

"According to the apartment manager, Holt got his deposit back last night and left early this morning, around seven. Must have left just before I called him."

"Holt probably got orders to return to New York, and he's on his way to catch a plane."

"Yeah, hope so."

"Well then, since the plans have changed, I'll head to Dallas with the gun and other evidence; see how much ass I gotta kiss to get this fast-tracked."

"That's a good idea. Got stuff to do at the office. Guess nothing else can be done until I hear from you." Stanton wanted to tell Miles about the treasure, and about the Smithsonian expert who was due in, but under the circumstances, with Curt's death and how that might alter the plans, she decided to delay that conversation.

Agent Miles looked at his watch. "You know, it will take seven hours to get to Dallas. Then another half day to process the evidence, and that's if we're lucky. Better not expect anything from me until late tomorrow or early Wednesday morning. Again, I want to emphasize, *if we're lucky.*"

"Hang on a minute." The sheriff scrolled through some

numbers, then punched one in and put the phone on speaker. It rang twice. "Hello."

"Reed, Sheriff Stanton here."

"Sheriff, haven't heard from you in three, four months."

"Yeah, been staying busy. You too—guess you've been flying all over?"

"About 250,000 miles since January, most of it for AN."

"Speaking of Angel Network—"

"Ya got a sick child in Buffalo?"

"No, Reed, an FBI agent that needs to get to Dallas."

"When?"

"Now!"

"Is he willing to ride in the cockpit with me?"

Miles nodded.

"Yeah, he'll ride tied to the wing if that's all the room you got."

"Tell him being an old Navy dude, I can tie a good knot."

"You just told him, got you on speaker. Reed, meet Pete Miles."

"Nice to meet ya, Miles. Kidding aside, I'm due in Amarillo in two hours. Got a kiddo that needs to be in Houston this afternoon for some kind of treatment. Can you all be here in thirty minutes?"

"We'll be there in twenty-five." Stanton shut the cell phone off. "We're in luck; Larry Reed is a former Navy pilot. He operates a large ranch on the Texas-Oklahoma border, mostly as a hobby. Twenty years ago, his folks went belly-up trying to raise cattle in the midst of a five-year drought. Six months before the bank was set to foreclose, some wildcatter hit gas on their land, a lot of it. Now there are five producing wells. His folks have a nice home in Woodward and travel. Larry plays rancher and flies sick kids to hospitals all around the southwest for treatment, free of charge."

"Where's the airport?"

"On his ranch. Got an airstrip and a nine-passenger King Air. It's about forty-five miles southwest of here near Slapout."

"Near what?"

"You heard me, Slapout. Take your car and follow me."

Miles got out of the sheriff's cruiser and into his own. He gave her the go sign, and Stanton pulled onto the highway. When they were safely out of the city limits, she punched a button labeled L/S for lights and siren. Stanton leveled her speed off at 90 and radioed dispatch, giving her destination and her estimated time of return.

Two hours later, Sheriff Stanton turned off the county road onto the Gray Ranch drive right behind Lee and Beverly Bethel. Stanton flashed her headlights and Lee pulled over.

* * *

Earlier that same morning, Agent Holt pulled his cell phone out of the holder and looked at the calling number. It was the sheriff. Holt didn't answer; he tossed the last bag into the trunk, got in behind the wheel, and left town. He knew exactly how long it would take to get to his destination. He had nearly two hours, and it took only 45 minutes to get there. Holt stopped in the first one-horse town he came to and bought an *Oklahoman*, the only paper on sale at the convenience store. He tossed everything but section A, found a roadside table under a tree five miles this side of his destination, and pulled under the shade. He didn't want to arrive too early, just get there a few minutes before and leave immediately after. Holt knew the shorter his stay, the less chance of some curious snoop being able to identify him. He read all the articles covering developments in the war on terrorism. It was 8:43.

Seven minutes later, Holt pulled to a stop in front of the only working payphone he'd found within a 60-mile radius of Buffalo. He got out of his car and stretched, looking around to see if he'd drawn anyone's attention. The payphone was located on the property of the only service station in the town of, he guessed, no more than five hundred people. There were two men working at the service station, one changing a flat on a farm truck and the other measuring the fuel level in the underground tanks. Holt looked nervously at his watch. Sweat was beading on his forearm, and he felt the first rush of acid pour into his stomach. He reached into one of the travel bags for his Tums and chewed three. The combination of anxiety and heat from the morning sun was all the stimulus his body needed to cause him to sweat. He looked around, spotted the service station's outside entrance to the men's bathroom, and hurried over. Holt pulled three paper towels out of the dispenser, dampened them, and mopped his forehead. The agent stared momentarily at his reflection in the cracked, grease-stained mirror over a sink that hadn't been cleaned recently. The toilet was no better, and the floor appeared to have flooded lately with whatever had plugged the stool. He turned to leave and caught a glimpse of *Jesus saves* written across the two condom dispensers hidden like some brain-teaser game among a surfeit of vulgar graffiti.

Holt reached the payphone just as it rang for the first time. He stood trembling, unable to answer it at first, thinking of the possible consequences, but it was too late—consequences or not, he had to take the next step. On the third ring, he answered in a muffled tone, trying to modify his voice. He knew that if any governmental agency targeted the conversation for review, a voice pattern analysis might expose him; he just hoped Bouvier had followed his instructions and used an untraceable phone to make the call.

A mechanically distorted voice responded. The words were clear, but the caller's gender was unidentifiable. The conversation was short, intentionally short to thwart tracing. The caller's instructions were clear, simple, and precise. There was no room for negotiations, just as Holt had expected. He hung up the phone, got back into his car, and took a deep breath. He was still trembling, but relieved. Holt turned the A/C on high and fumbled with the radio tuner, trying to find something besides the simpleminded country-and-western music that seemed to dominate the Oklahoma airwaves. A customer drove into the station, and the two attendants waited on her, a good distraction. Holt eased onto the highway and left town.

CHAPTER 45

Monday, June 12, 10:45 a.m.

"Good morning, Sheriff." Dr. Bethel opened his car door as she approached. "Want you to meet my wife." The sheriff reached through the open door and shook hands with Beverly. "Has anyone heard from Dr. Ramirez yet?" Bethel asked.

Stanton didn't know until that moment whether Bethel had been told of Curt's death.

"I don't know, just getting here myself. Lee, have you talked to Fred in the last twenty-four hours?"

Dr. Bethel could see there was something different about Stanton's demeanor. "No, why? What's going on?"

"Curt Russell, his hired hand, we found him dead."

"Dead! How? When?"

"We found him yesterday, at his home."

"Oh my God!" Lee looked at his wife. "How? Was it murder?"

"Looks like a self-inflicted gunshot."

"Suicide?!"

"That's the way it looks, but we're still investigating."

"How are the Grays?"

"He was like a son. Devastated, you can imagine."

Lee turned to his wife. "Let's go on to the house and express our sympathy. I'll tell Fred we'll come back when he's ready."

Beverly nodded.

"What about Heath?" Lee asked.

"Left town Saturday night and hasn't been seen since."

"I thought the FBI was following him."

"They were, but he gave them the slip."

"Doesn't that seem coincidental? I mean, he's supposed to be dangerous, and he evades the feds. The next day you find Curt dead. Isn't that a coincidence?"

"Of course it's suspicious, I'm trained to be suspicious, but it's useless to speculate. Right now we're waiting to get results back on a couple of things. We'll know more then."

Beverly was listening, but her heart was with the family she'd never met. "Lee, shouldn't we go express our condolences and be on our way, let the family grieve?"

"Yeah. Are you going up to the house, Sheriff?"

"Later. First I'll check on my deputy, give him a breather; then I'll be down."

* * *

Dr. Carlos Ramirez pulled into the convenience store and parked next to the fuel pumps. He checked his watch and looked at the map he'd printed off his PC. Fred Gray's ranch was about 15 miles southeast of Buffalo, accessible only by dirt and gravel roads. Ramirez had bypassed the ranch and come directly to Buffalo. He needed to get gas, and he wanted to get a look at the terrain. He took two

Xerox-copied maps—actually drawings—from his briefcase and laid them on the front seat next to a satellite picture of the area for comparison. Ramirez ran his finger along the Xerox drawings and tried to find topography that resembled the land featured in the sat-photo. He knew that if the candlestick turned out to be what Dr. Cardona thought it was, he'd need to charter a helicopter to fly the route and photograph the area around the Gray Ranch.

Ramirez folded the maps and put them back in the briefcase, then got out to gas his rental car. Another car drove in next to the pumps on the opposite side, and a young man got out. "From out of town?" he asked Ramirez.

"Yes. Are you from around here?" Ramirez wasn't looking to strike up a lengthy conversation, but a little local information would help him understand Buffalo from a social perspective, a very valuable tool in his appraisal business.

"Lifelong, if you don't count college. And you, where are you from?"

"I live in Annapolis. My office is in DC."

"Wow, long ways from home. What brings you to these parts?"

"Just some business with a local rancher."

"Don't mean to be nosy, but that wouldn't be Fred Gray, would it?"

Ramirez was shocked but didn't show it. "Why yes, do you know Mr. Gray?"

"If you're from around here, you know everyone. Does your visit have anything to do with the archaeological discovery out there?"

"What discovery is that?" Ramirez decided the best response would be in the form of a question. He didn't want to reveal any more about himself.

"That bison kill site they've been excavating out there

the last few years."

"Perhaps—it might have something to do with it. And what do you know about the archaeological site? By the way, what's your name?"

"Tobias Henry. And yours?"

"Carlos Ramirez."

"I'm doing my journalism internship this summer with the local newspaper, and I'm covering the story. Are you going out there today?"

"Just on my way."

"You aware of their ranch hand?"

"No. What about the ranch hand?"

"Found him dead yesterday. Sheriff says it was suicide. Guess the Grays are pretty torn up about it."

"Well, no, no, I didn't know. This changes things. I'm glad I ran into you; otherwise, I would've blundered in not knowing of their loss. This is obviously not a good time to visit." Ramirez picked up his cell phone. "I need to call and reschedule my visit, but no reception." He looked around for a payphone.

"There aren't any working payphones. You're welcome to use my cell." Tobias handed Ramirez his and gave him the number he'd memorized.

Fred answered, and Ramirez explained who he was and offered his sentiment concerning the death of the ranch hand. "When you feel like it, Mr. Gray, give me a call and we'll reschedule. I'll come back later and take a look at the candlestick. In the meantime, express my sympathies to your wife."

"Just a minute, Dr. Ramirez, let me collect my thoughts." Fred paused, trying to coax his mind into rational thought. He was tired, concerned about his wife. "Where are you, Dr. Ramirez?"

"Please, it's Carlos, and I'm in Buffalo."

"You've come all this way; it's silly for you to go back. I want you to come on out."

"Are you sure? I don't want to be an imposition to you and your wife."

"Nonsense. Do you have the directions?"

"Yes, I can find my way." Ramirez flipped the phone shut and handed it back.

Tobias had been standing less than five feet from Ramirez during the conversation and overheard two words from a one-sided conversation that caught his attention.

"Mr. Ramirez, I planned to go there anyway, interview the archaeologist about the kill site. You could follow me." The intern thought about the offer he'd just made and how easy it was to mislead the stranger, all for the sake of a story. He had no idea what a candlestick had to do with anything, but the fact that someone flew a thousand miles just to look at it gave him cause to think something else was going on at the ranch. Maybe somehow the excavation site, journal page, the candlestick, and even the suicide were tied together. The idea of passing up an opportunity to find out what was going on out there was too enticing.

"I don't want you to go to extra trouble on my account. I've got a map."

"No trouble at all, Mr. Ramirez, just follow me." Tobias called Judith at the *Ledger* to tell her he was following up on his story and wouldn't be in the rest of the day.

When they arrived at the ranch, Tobias parked under the shade of the cottonwoods just south of the oval drive, and Ramirez did the same. "This is a beautiful home. The Spanish architecture is incredible," Ramirez said.

"Yeah, guess ten years ago they had a Mexican ranch hand that happened to be a carpenter. When ranch work slowed, they'd work on this house. Took 'em four years to build."

"Just look at the stucco walls, tile roof, and that double door. I've never seen anything like it."

"Ranch hand's father carved those in Monterey, Mexico. Guess Robert and the hand drove all the way there and back to get 'em."

"Magnificent, just magnificent." Ramirez stood admiring the home. "Guess we'd better go in."

As they walked toward the house, Tobias said, "The sheriff is here; guess that's because of the suicide. Don't know whose SUV that is, never seen it before, and that truck over there belongs to their son, Robert. Looks like a houseful."

"Mr. Gray told me there would be others here the day I visited."

"Who?" Tobias asked.

"He didn't say."

Helen watched the two emerge from their vehicles. She called to her husband, who was in the den with the others. "Fred, Dr. Ramirez is here."

"I'll meet him at the front door." Fred got up and started toward the living room.

"Tobias Henry is with him," she said.

"What! He wasn't invited." Fred turned to see if anyone in the room would contradict him. They didn't.

Robert jumped to his feet. "I'll run him off!"

"Hold on, Robert," Stanton cautioned. "Let's be hospitable, see what he wants first."

"Good idea, Crys. If we run him off, that'll just make him more curious." Fred motioned for Robert to sit down, then went to the front door. A few minutes later, he and Helen led the two back to the den and made the introductions.

Lee and Beverly Bethel had arrived at the ranch just as Ramirez called Fred from the convenience store in Buffalo;

they'd been there a half hour. As soon as the introductions were completed, Fred had called the sheriff, who was on the ridge, and she came down to the house.

No one mentioned the candlestick; the only conversation was about Curt Russell and what a tragedy his death was. It was an uncomfortable and somber gathering, a mix of sorrow, frustration, empathy, and anger. Tobias was embarrassed. He felt awkward, not knowing what to say or do for that matter, but he sensed something was going on, something he couldn't quite put his finger on. He didn't want to leave.

For a while there was only a sad silence and occasionally Helen's faint, muffled sobs. Eventually Beverly came over and sat down next to Helen and took her hand. "You know, Helen, this must be very hard for you. We can do this another time. No need for all of us to interfere in your life right now."

Helen shook her head, sobbing, trying to speak. "No, I'm glad you all are here. Company is what I need. I need you to stay. Please don't go." Fred held her and she continued to cry.

"Would you like to rest?" Fred asked.

She nodded. "Yes, I think that would help."

"I'll be right back." Fred said, helping his wife down the hall toward the bedroom.

CHAPTER 46

Monday, June 12, 12:30 p.m.

Sheriff Stanton met Fred in the hallway as he was returning to the den. "About Tobias…"

"Yeah, what d'ya think?" he whispered.

"If we run him off he'll go to Thompson, and then *he'll* be in the picture. I think the best thing is to bring him in on all of it, get him to agree not to say a word until we give him the go-ahead."

"Okay, if you think that's best. Will you talk to him?"

"Yeah, I think I can get him to agree." Stanton went back to the den and motioned Tobias to follow her into the kitchen.

"What's up, Sheriff?"

She turned and looked the intern in the eye; she didn't blink, just held the stare for several seconds. Tobias finally looked down, and then away. A flush rose from his neck to his cheeks, and Stanton knew he was ready to listen and listen close. "Mr. Henry, you were not invited to this

~ 280 ~

meeting," she paused, "were you?"

"No. Ah, well, sorta…supposed to interview Dr. Bethel."

"That's next week."

"Well, I thought they were starting early."

"Tobias! Tobias, stop and think. You didn't have a clue Dr. Bethel was going to be here today, did you?"

"Well, I—"

"Did you?"

"No, I didn't. When I met Ramirez and he said he was coming out here, I figured something was up. That's all. Sorry."

"If you want any, and I mean *any* cooperation from the Grays, you'll have to be honest, not scheming." She added a twist. "What would your folks think?"

He thought about that, but not for long. "Okay, I'm sorry, won't happen again."

"Before I let you back in that den, you have to agree to some stipulations."

"Sure, I'll agree, but what are they?"

"Simple. What you hear and see today cannot, I repeat, *cannot* be shared with anyone, not your folks, not your friends, not your editor. Do you understand? Not even your priest."

"I'm Methodist."

"Well, it's good to see you haven't lost your sense of humor."

"Yes, I understand, but what good is a story unless I can report it?"

"You will report it and you'll be the first; you just have to be patient."

They joined the others in the den. Fred invited everyone to sit around the small conference table; he set the briefcase containing the candlestick next to him on the floor. "Dr. Ramirez—"

"Please, Mr. Gray, call me Carlos. The doctor is for my students. Sometimes I teach or lecture—it's for them, a credibility thing. To my friends and associates I prefer less formality."

"Good, and, Carlos, I'm Fred."

"Forgive my rude interruption. Please go on, Fred."

"The people you see around the room, with the exception of Tobias, are all aware of everything that's occurred since my first encounter with Paul Hansen."

"Yes, the dealer in Oklahoma City who contacted my friend Dr. Cardona."

"We'll educate Tobias as the afternoon progresses. Right now, your sole purpose in being here is to look at the candlestick and assess its worth and origin?"

"Origin only, Fred. Where the candlestick came from and how it got here are my only concerns. The value is a matter for others to decide and, as of now, is of no importance to Dr. Cardona." Dr. Ramirez discussed his background and who he'd worked with in the past. He did not mention any association with the UN, CIA, or the DOD. He explained where he was educated and his relationship with museums around the world, all to establish trust with those gathered in Fred Gray's den.

Lee hadn't yet shown Fred the information his friend in DC had faxed him, but it was clear the man representing himself as Dr. Ramirez was, in fact, the man in the photo.

Carlos continued. "After Dr. Cardona saw the photograph of the candlestick, he asked me to see if I could somehow view it up close. That's when I called you."

Fred set his briefcase on the table and opened it. He unwrapped the candlestick and placed it on the table in front of Ramirez. Using the cloth it had been wrapped in, Carlos picked it up and held it close to a floor lamp to get a better look. He laid it back down and fished in his bag for an eyepiece, a magnification lens used by jewelers. Carlos studied the base and the shaft closely, turning it over and over, all the time making humming sounds and nodding. Ramirez finally laid the candlestick on the cloth and leaned back in his chair. Everyone was eager to hear his assessment. "My friends," he began, and then hesitated, looking directly at Fred. "It is without a doubt authentic!"

CHAPTER 47

Monday, June 12, 3:46 p.m.

P aul Davis walked confidently through the glass doors into the Stratford Inn lobby and up to the desk clerk. "Andrea, didn't expect to see you here at this hour!"

"No kidding, Mr. Davis. Judy didn't show, so I'm working a double. How was your day?" Andrea Kaufman had been a desk clerk at the Inn longer than anyone and by default had become the supervisor. The promotion resulted in a two dollar an hour raise and the responsibility of filling in during absences, which occurred often. She was recently divorced from her husband of ten years and had no children. Andrea wasn't beautiful, but she had attractive qualities, one of them being a warm, friendly—almost seductive—smile. Her exotic dark eyes were intoxicating as they sparkled in unison with her pleasant expression.

"Just fine. Made a sale and renewed a couple contracts. Andrea, are there any messages, letters for me? Got a new phone and haven't figured out how to access messages yet."

"I know what you mean, still haven't mastered my remote." Andrea turned away from the counter long enough to retrieve an envelope. "You got a FedEx overnight about an hour ago." She handed it to Davis.

"Thank you." He turned and walked toward the stairway. The desk clerk watched him. She had no idea how old he was—maybe late forties, she thought. He was handsome, a bit above average height; his short, dark brown hair gave him a rugged appearance, not the typical businessman look she was used to, and he wasn't wearing a wedding ring.

Davis unlocked the door to his room and checked to see if the six-inch piece of white thread was still in place. He'd left the room shortly after housekeeping cleaned it, and, as was his routine, he placed the thread strategically so that, if disturbed, he would be warned of a possible intruder. A trick he'd learned watching an old James Bond movie. He hadn't expected an intruder, but knew it was when you least expected it that you needed to be on your toes the most. The Xerox executive took off his dark gray pin-striped suit coat and hung it carefully in the closet. After loosening his tie, he sat down in the only chair and opened the envelope. The note had no greeting, just two short sentences, typical Bouvier. It read: *Offer rancher 1 mil for stick and 4 boxes. Your share 100K as prearranged on delivery of verifiable items.*

Davis tore the note into several small pieces, put them back in the FedEx envelope, and laid it on the dresser. He'd discard it himself in the motel Dumpster and not take a chance of someone else finding the note and piecing it together.

In order to make Bouvier's offer sound legitimate, he'd need to present it in a convincing way. Davis thought about identifying himself as Otis Thorpe, explain to the rancher he'd been in his employment under false pretenses; he would apologize for the deception and hope for forgiveness. He also knew Fred was a man of honor and wouldn't appreciate being lied to, even if he was being offered a million dollars. Davis knew of no other way to entice the rancher other than being upfront with his explanation. He looked at his watch; just enough time to drive to another area code to make the phone call. Davis wanted to wait as long as possible to phone Mr. Gray, to be sure no one else was around. He knew Gray's wife would be there, but that couldn't be avoided, and he knew from past experience the rancher was the one to answer most of the late evening calls. His plan was to leave the 316 area code region and make the call from the 405 area in Oklahoma.

An hour later, Davis checked into a motel 30 miles south of the Kansas border under another fictitious name and paid for the room with cash. Davis checked to make sure the phone in his room was in working order. He turned on the TV and surfed to a news channel. The rotating time indicator at the bottom of the screen rolled to Central Standard Time.

Another 90 minutes.

* * *

Agent Miles grabbed the computer-generated document showing the test results of Sheriff Stanton's swab. No residue on the hand holding the gun, just as Stanton expected. He thanked the lab technician. "Here's my card. If you're ever in Oklahoma and need anything at all, call me. I appreciate your fast-tracking this."

"No problem, glad I could be of service."

Miles raced from the Federal Building and hailed a cab.

"Love Field," he said, sliding into the backseat and speed-dialing Stanton at the same time. The sheriff answered immediately. "Crys, I'm just leaving the lab for Love Field. Larry is waiting. I've got the GSR and fingerprint results, both negative." Stanton had excused herself from the group in the den; whatever the results, she didn't want to discuss it in front of the others. "Just as I thought. What's your ETA?" she asked.

"Between nine and ten."

"I'm at the ranch right now; can you come straight to my office when you get back?"

"Yes, I'll call as soon as we're on the ground and I'm headed your way."

The sheriff returned to the den. "I'm sorry for the interruption. Please, Carlos, go on."

CHAPTER 48

Monday, June 12, 4:10 p.m.

"Authentic?! What do you mean authentic?" Fred said, eager to hear the rest of what Ramirez had to say.

"What you see here is a piece of the treasure brought to this country by Francisco Vasquez de Coronado in 1540."

"Coronado the explorer, the one who discovered the Grand Canyon?" Beverly Bethel asked.

"Yes, that very same explorer."

Lee looked around the room. Everyone was in a state of shock—even Dr. Ramirez was moved by his own declaration, his voice incredulous, each word shrouded in disbelief.

Ramirez cleared his throat. "Let me tell you the history of Coronado. Some facts we're sure of, some legend we're not so sure of, and then there's myth. Personally, I never indulge in the study of the mythical claims; ninety-nine percent of the time it's a useless endeavor."

"What does the candlestick represent, Carlos? Legend or myth?" Lee asked.

"Possibly both. Here's why. We know Coronado came from Spain to Mexico with Antonio de Mendoza, the colony's first admiral, in 1535. It's a fact Mendoza heard stories about the Seven Cities of Cibolo, where streets were lined with gold and jewels. After hearing this, he sent Coronado to claim the wealth for Spain. This occurred in 1540."

"If I remember my history correctly, the Seven Cities of Cibolo actually was a Zuni Indian village. Coronado conquered the Zuni, but found no gold," Lee said.

"Yes, that's right. Coronado was disappointed, but not discouraged. From there he led his army of three hundred soldiers and about a thousand enslaved Indians east toward what is now Texas. We have factual evidence Coronado was headed to a place called Gran Quivera, now an historical site near Salina, Kansas. Again, he'd heard it was a place rich in gold and silver." Carlos paused, then pointed to Fred's PC. "Are you connected to the Internet?" he asked.

"Yes, just gotta turn her on. Why?"

"I can show you as I talk."

Robert scooted up to the computer and accessed the 'Net. "What Web site?"

"Try *Coronado's Journey through New Mexico, Texas, and Oklahoma* first. I think that site will give us a map to follow as I talk."

Within seconds, a site appeared, giving historical details of Coronado's exploits. Everyone moved their chairs in close for a better look.

Ramirez pointed. "This is the part that has been legend up until now. The only evidence of Coronado's lost gold is from two diaries recovered from the belongings of soldiers who accompanied Coronado on this trip into Kansas. According to entries in those diaries, Coronado was carrying a cache of gold objects, some encrusted with jewels."

"Was there a description of the gold objects in the diaries?" Lee asked.

"No, none that we're aware of. That's one of the reasons there are skeptics. The diary entries seem to be assumptions on the author's part. No one claims to have actually seen the gold, just crates or chests that supposedly held it."

The sheriff had only listened up to this point. "Carlos, what category do you ascribe to, the believers or skeptics?"

"Honestly, I've been a skeptic. There are those who believe in legends and myths just for the sake of believing in something, you know, kind of like believing in UFOs. I learned a long time ago not to follow that path. There are just too many authentic tales to follow and treasure to discover, but this candlestick may be grounds for me to rethink my position." A quiet fell over everyone but Carlos and the intern; neither knew what secret was about to be revealed.

"Let's stay with what we know as fact for now. According to a manifest that's part of the Coronado collection in a Madrid museum, Mendoza was given several chests packed with objects to be used for trade or bartering. It was currency Mendoza was to use only if something of much greater value was discovered. Imagine the explorers trading a beautifully handcrafted gold object studded with precious stones for an entire goldmine, for instance. The Spaniards considered themselves superior to anyone on earth, and the king actually believed God put gold in the world exclusively for him and the kingdom. Anyway, back to the manifest. Each item packed in those chests was stamped with the king's five-pointed crown, such as the one on the candlestick. It's barely distinguishable, but nevertheless it's there."

"Who else knows about this five-pointed crown engraving?" Stanton asked.

"You mean then or now?"

"Now," Bethel said. He knew where the sheriff was going with her question.

"I'd guess many would know. Any antiquities dealer who specialized in gold objects would know. Probably a hundred right here in the US, maybe hundreds more worldwide. It isn't a secret. There are forgeries."

"Can you tell a forgery from the real thing?" Robert said.

"Yes, that's my expertise. That's why I'm so awestruck by the candlestick. As I said earlier, it's authentic."

"So there are folks in, ah, let's say New York City who could identify this piece?" Stanton asked.

"Oh certainly, without a doubt." Ramirez paused, still looking at the computer screen. He pulled a pen from his shirt pocket and pointed. "Look at the map. You'll see that Coronado veered in a more easterly direction at this point toward what's now northwest Oklahoma. These maps are drawings done by cartographers on the expedition. They follow the geography, drawing hills, rivers, tributaries that they see from their perspective. When land is flat, canyons shallow, there aren't many obvious landmarks to navigate by, so if the mapmaker isn't skilled, it's easy for expeditions to get disoriented."

Lee pointed to the drawing with the border of Oklahoma and Kansas overlaid on the original map. "Look here, Coronado veered almost straight east at this point, and when he came back he veered west, picking up the original trail here. It's almost like he's trying to avoid something."

"Exactly. According to the diaries, Coronado's scouts discovered a large Indian encampment. The scouts said the Indians were unfriendly and would react violently if they thought the expedition was competing with them for the scarce food supply. Instead of going the direct route, which would've taken them northeast and near the Indians, they went east. Look where the expedition returned to a more northern direction."

Fred took a large map of Oklahoma out of his desk and laid it where everyone could see. The room grew still; the only person moving about was Tobias Henry. He'd look first at the computer screen, then the map. His nervousness was obvious. Dr. Ramirez was as excited, but his skepticism acted as a sieve, proportioning out anticipation in small controllable amounts. "The diaries say that Coronado decided to send an advance party of about thirty men from here, in the Texas panhandle, on to Gran Quivera and leave the rest of the army and slaves near this river where they'd have water and could hunt bison. Coronado believed the small detachment could move faster; we know this to be fact."

"What'd he do with the treasure?" Fred asked.

"Took it with him. He was afraid the officers left behind would abscond with it."

The journalism intern was practically in a panic. If music had been playing, it would have looked like he was dancing. "What happened next?!" he blurted.

"Diaries say Coronado became worried that if accosted by Indians they'd steal the treasure, so he hid it."

"Where?"

"No one knows. All we are certain of is that he didn't have it when he returned to Mexico. Look again at his return trip. The trail diverges here just north of the Kansas-Oklahoma border."

"That's odd. Why wouldn't he take the same trail back?" Lee said.

"Lost, or at least that's what we assume. Here's another strange thing about the diaries—they never mention the treasure again."

"Not at all?" Robert said.

"Nothing. Some of my associates believe Coronado kept the treasure for himself; others think he hid it and couldn't find it. Others believe, and I'm of this group, there were chests, but they weren't filled with gold. Maybe tapestries, carvings, and other trinkets to be used for barter, but not gold, at least not much gold."

"What about the candlestick? Wouldn't that be proof the treasure existed?"

"Not necessarily, Tobias. The candlestick could be the only thing gold amid the contents of those chests. That's how a legend is born, young man. Take some truth, mix in myth or mystery, or both, then pass it on from one generation to the next."

Tobias didn't want the excitement he was feeling to fade. He was onto something, but he couldn't understand why the others weren't as fascinated by Ramirez's story as he was. To him it was obvious that something had happened in or around the very county he lived in, possibly even the Gray Ranch. If he was going to be a journalist, he knew asking difficult questions was crucial to his success. Why the others hadn't asked the obvious question was puzzling. No one was saying anything, just sitting, looking at the computer screen and then the map. "Dr. Ramirez." He paused, thinking if no one else would ask, he would.

"Yes, Tobias."

"Is it possible that Coronado buried the treasure around here somewhere? To me, if the story about the gold is true, and one trail took him through this area, it just looks to me like he could have hidden it here just as easily as somewhere else!"

"Sure it's possible, but probable, no."

Sheriff Stanton stood before Tobias could ask another question. "It's getting late; I've got a meeting shortly. Are you staying overnight, Carlos?"

"Yes, I've got a room at the motel in town."

Helen returned from her rest in time to hear Tobias's question and knew instinctively Stanton was attempting, for the time being, to sidetrack his curiosity. "That's nonsense, Carlos, you'll stay with us. We'll call Barbara at the motel and explain you're staying with us. She'll cancel your reservation."

"Please, Helen, I appreciate the offer, but don't want to intrude. This has been a difficult time for you—"

Helen held her hand up. "Carlos, you and the Bethels are our guests, and we don't send guests to a motel if I've got anything to say about it."

"Then it would be my pleasure. I'll leave first thing in the morning. I'm flying to Istanbul on Wednesday."

"Another authentication?" Lee asked.

"As a matter of fact, yes. Someone has come up with a very old parchment scroll alleged to have been stolen from a museum in Baghdad."

"Sounds exciting," Beverly said.

"Not at all. I'm not looking forward to an eighteen-hour flight one way, ten or fifteen hours poring over a document, and then the flight back. I will, however, stop in Madrid and report what I've found here to Dr. Cardona. He's an old friend; we'll have dinner, tell stories. I'm looking forward to that."

During the conversation between Helen and Carlos, the sheriff made her way to the kitchen. She had motioned obscurely for Fred to follow. Once inside the kitchen, and away from the others, she said, "Fred, I have to get back to town, it's important, but I need to know your next move."

"I'm not following you. What d'ya mean?"

"Here it is, short and to the point. Looks like you've got your hands on Coronado's lost treasure. Have you stopped to think what that's going to mean for you and your family? Hell, Fred, for that matter, what's it going to mean for little old Buffalo?"

"Frankly, Sheriff, I haven't given it much thought since Curt's suicide."

"That's another matter." She paused, looking for the right words. "That call I got earlier, that's what it was about."

"About Curt?"

The sheriff nodded. "Yes, about Curt."

"What about him? You said it was suicide."

"That's what it looked like. My deputy and the OHP jumped to that conclusion, so that was the story. I'm convinced now it was murder."

"Murder! You think it was murder? Of course—Heath! That son of a bitch." Fred's eyes searched the sheriff's for confirmation.

"I don't know if it was Heath."

"Goddamn it, Crys, it had to be. You said Holt warned he was dangerous. This proves it?"

"Maybe. Bear with me, Fred; I've got a lot to do before I'm ready to say it was Heath. Anyway, in the meantime I need to know what you plan to do next."

"Regarding what?" Fred was beginning to feel the effects of sleep deprivation himself.

"Are you going to tell Carlos about the gold?"

Fred leaned against the kitchen counter, arms folded, looking out the back window at the darkness. He hadn't realized night had come.

"Yeah, alright, I'm gonna show him. This whole thing's gotten out of hand; I'm thinking it's best if we just get it over with."

"I agree. Since you're going to show him, I'll stay a few more minutes."

"Good. I'd like you to be here."

Fred stepped back into the den and asked everyone to follow him downstairs. The group collected around a pool table as Robert turned on all the basement lights; the dark room had suddenly become as bright as noon on a cloudless day. Beverly noticed the faint smell of burned incense, a sweet odor covering an unmistakable scent of mildew. She stepped up to the table, aware of what was under the tarp. Lee had described the treasure in detail to her, but being cognizant of something absent the enhancement only the senses can truly reveal left her unprepared.

Dr. Ramirez stood near the center of the table and Tobias next to him, Fred and Robert at each end, and the rest gathered anxiously around, eyeing the various shapes hidden under the blue plastic tarp. Fred picked up the corners of the covering and motioned for his son to do the same. Together they lifted the tarp off the table, unveiling the dismantled chest, four ornate boxes, and the treasure. The only sound other than the crackling the tarp made as Robert folded it was Tobias and Beverly gasping for air. Dr. Ramirez put a pair of white cotton gloves on and began studying each piece closely. Finally he took the glasses off and leaned on the table, breathing heavily.

"Are you alright?" Helen asked.

"Yes, I'm alright." Ramirez studied the Crucifix again. "This is it! It's Coronado's treasure. I can't believe what I'm looking at!" He turned to Fred. "Where did you find this?"

"In a cave."

"Here on your ranch?"

"Yes."

"Can I see it?"

"Of course, but...there's something else, something more."

"What do you mean more?"

"There's more."

"More what?"

"More treasure...two more chests like this one."

"Mr. and Mrs. Gray, do you have any idea what this means?"

"Trouble. So far, nothing but trouble." Fred started to say something about the treasure and the link to Curt's murder, but the sheriff caught his attention, shaking her head.

"This could possibly be Spain's most significant historical discovery in the last two centuries. How difficult will it be to recover the other two chests?" Ramirez asked.

"Not difficult at all. If we left by seven a.m., we could have them back to the house by noon."

"I'll call and reschedule my trip to Turkey; this has become my priority now. I can stay another day or two."

"And what if this is Coronado's treasure, what then?" Robert asked.

"That's a good question. Here's what I think will happen. My employer, Dr. Cardona, is the foremost expert on Spanish history as it applies to the New World: North, Central, and South America. He's obligated by contract to the Spanish government as a consultant on antiquities. When I inform him of what you've found, he will share that with the government."

"Yeah, then what?" Robert pressed.

"Most likely the government, through their ambassador to the UN, will petition the US to reacquire the treasure."

Anger and frustration were feelings difficult for Fred and his son to hide. Helen—always the mediator—was too tired to intervene; she looked at Lee, who acted swiftly.

"Fred, there is a reciprocal agreement between participating countries that provides for the safe return of all historical artifacts to the country of origin—"

Fred was willing to listen, but not Robert. He'd never heard of such a thing. Just as they'd possibly become rich beyond his wildest imagination, some city slicker comes onto their property and tells them what they found isn't really theirs. "Whoa, whoa, wait! Lee, I need to hear that again. You're telling me that what we found on our land may not belong to us? Lee, tell me I misunderstood."

"No, Robert, you didn't misunderstand. Let me explain. Years ago, around the first of the twentieth century, a lot of archaeological exploration was taking place, primarily by the British. Over the years, the explorers took artifacts from Italy, Greece, Israel, and Egypt and brought them to museums in the west. Naturally, when officials from those countries discovered that the explorers and museums were making a fortune from selling and displaying the artifacts, they were angry. They wanted them back. Eventually an agreement was reached, and from that agreement an international law was drafted. What Dr. Ramirez is saying is if this truly is the king's treasure, it *might* fall under that law."

"I don't think it's right," Robert said angrily. "Do you?"

"What I think is irrelevant, Robert."

"So what do we do?"

Stanton interrupted. "I have to leave, but whatever you decide to do, please do not forget that everyone in this room could still be in danger."

"Heath's gone, isn't he?" Helen asked.

"As far as we know, but that doesn't mean some other entity isn't maneuvering to take his place."

"You mean there may be others trying to get at the treasure?" Beverly asked.

"Any number of individuals, maybe groups of people. Look, I have to go. Just stay on your toes."

"Like how?" Tobias said.

"Watch for strangers, out of town vehicles, rental cars, and if you think someone is following you, drive to the courthouse or call 911. Above all, don't say anything about this to anyone, not friends or family. I'll leave a deputy on the ridge and be back tomorrow late morning. Now I really gotta go." She left hurriedly, anxious to hear more from Miles.

Tobias followed the sheriff out. "Sheriff Stanton, Sheriff, please, I've got questions."

"Yeah, I'll bet you do." Stanton stopped on the driveway in front of the house. "I do, too, Tobias, got more questions than I have answers." She moved toward her car.

"Can't you at least elaborate on the danger you referred to, and the other entities you said were interested in the treasure?"

"No, Tobias, I can't elaborate…maybe later. I told you I'd share facts when I had them, and I don't. Be patient." Stanton drove away. She thought about Tobias's questions. He was young and anxious to break a story, a big story. The sheriff had seen something else in his eyes, and there was a faint but noticeable tremble in his voice. She'd seen it before, a mix of curiosity and primal fear, the kind of alarm a person feels when swimming near a beach and something large and cold and alive brushes by. They were all floating free, like the swimmer, not knowing what danger might be lurking just under the surface.

CHAPTER 49

Monday, June 12, 9:00 p.m.

Sheriff Stanton arrived at headquarters at 9:06 p.m. On her way in, she'd heard from Agent Miles. He'd just landed and would be in Buffalo around nine-forty. Stanton stopped long enough to brief Bingham, who was filling in at the dispatch desk. "I'm expecting Agent Miles in the next few minutes; just have him come on in."

"Any news on Heath's whereabouts?"

"No. Maybe Miles can shed some light on that issue when he gets in."

"If you don't mind me asking, why did Miles go to Dallas?"

"Hand-carried some evidence to the FBI lab to speed the process. OSBI would've taken two weeks; he got it done in one afternoon."

"Why the rush?"

Stanton realized Bingham had no idea she was questioning Curt Russell's cause of death. "I'm not convinced it was suicide."

"Why am I not surprised? You think it's murder."

"We won't know anything till it's all pieced together."

Pete Miles knocked on the glass door just then. Bingham pressed the button, and the lock released. "Thanks, Deputy." He looked at Stanton and held out a manila envelope. "This what you've been waiting for?"

Stanton motioned for him to follow her into the office. She tore the flap of the envelope and pulled three pages out. "Yup, this is it."

"We verified the piece of paper was from an airline ticket issued to a Ralph Simmons, no prints."

"You check alias?"

"No."

"That's okay; my guess is that it'd eventually track back to Elliot Heath."

"If it did, wouldn't that prove Curt was murdered by Heath?"

"What that'd prove to me, Pete, is that someone was trying to set Heath up. You know this isn't rocket science. The suspect thought, for a reason unknown to us, that Curt needed to be silenced. We know Curt was trying to communicate with Fred Gray about something important. Whoever killed him used the murder-suicide twist to throw us off track long enough to get away."

"Sounds like you're trying to arrange the circumstances in favor of suspecting Holt."

"Not at all, Pete. Matter of fact, just the opposite. I'm trying to rule him out." Stanton laid the lab reports on her desk. "Problem is, he just won't go away."

"But, Crys, listen to what you're saying! Why does he need an alibi? He's an agent of the FBI sent here on a legitimate mission. He's one of the good guys." Miles could see her reasoning, but wasn't buying the good-guy-gone-bad theory yet.

"You know, Miles, you're right. At this point, I'll confess, it's just a gut feeling. But I'm not ready to say it was Heath, either. And speaking of him, any news on your end about his whereabouts?"

"None that I know of; last word I got was the efforts to locate him have been increased."

"How?"

"The FBI, local metropolitan law enforcement, and the highway patrol in Texas, Kansas, Colorado, Missouri, New Mexico, as well as Oklahoma have been notified. If he's as slick as everyone thinks, he'll dump his vehicle soon, and hopefully someone will spot it."

"If he's as slick as everyone thinks, I wouldn't count on anyone spotting him."

"Hope you're wrong, Crys." Miles thumbed through the lab report the sheriff laid on her desk, shaking his head. "I'm lost, Sheriff." He studied her face for a clue.

"Yeah, Pete, I bet you are. This isn't making sense, is it?"

"No. Seems like a big piece of this Oklahoma affair is missing. It's kinda like watching a movie without sound— you can see what's going on, but the crucial elements of the story are a mystery."

Stanton thought about the consequences of bringing the agent in on the discovery. "I'm going to show you something Webster doesn't know about. Not because he shouldn't know; it's a security issue."

"Something Webster doesn't know? I don't understand. How can there be a security issue and he's not in on it?"

"Sounds strange, I know, but given the set of circumstances I was facing until you came along, it seemed the prudent thing to do." Stanton took her digital camera out of the forensic equipment bag and scanned through recently taken photos. She plugged in her portable developer and inserted the card. In five minutes she had four photos that she laid out in front of Miles. He looked disbelieving as he studied each photo. "What in the hell is this?!"

Stanton smiled. "Yeah, thought that'd get your attention."

The sheriff's phone rang, and she punched speaker. "Bingham, what's up?"

"Mr. Gray on line one."

CHAPTER 50

Monday, June 12, 10:00 p.m.

Davis clicked off the TV; it was almost 10:00 p.m. and time to call Fred Gray. He'd thought about his original plan and decided against being upfront and honest with the rancher. Anonymity had served him well in the past; there was no reason to change his approach now. All he had to do was disguise his voice, and that was easy for someone who could speak three languages. In the early '90s he'd perfected an Irish accent while smuggling guns to the IRA, an event that almost cost him his life. If not for a quick thinking MI5 agent, he would have been Belfast dog food.

Davis reached for the bedside phone and called the rancher. "Mr. Gray, sorry for the late hour."

"Who is this?" Fred answered in a muffled but unmistakably cross voice. He was in no mood for a late night phone call from a stranger. Helen was showering in the adjoining bathroom, and Fred didn't want anything to upset her. Hearing the phone ring at such an hour would've only added more apprehension to her fragile emotional state.

"Mr. Gray, my name is William O'Shay. I've got something important to discuss with you if you'll grant me the time."

Fred listened. The shower was still running, and he knew it would be several more minutes before Helen came out of the bathroom. "What's so important it can't wait till tomorrow?" he said angrily.

"One million dollars, Mr. Gray!"

* * *

Stanton punched the line-one button on her phone. "This is the sheriff. What's going on, Fred?"

"Got an interesting phone call about fifteen minutes ago and thought you should know."

Stanton looked over at Miles poring over the photos. "Fred, I have an FBI agent with me; is it okay for him to hear what you're about to tell me?"

"Holt?"

"No. Holt's gone; I think he's back east. This is Special Agent Peter Miles from the Enid office. He's here to help."

"If it's okay with you, then it's okay with me."

"I'm going to put you on speaker. Can you talk louder?"

"Not much, don't want Helen to hear. She just went to bed. I'm back in the den, and she doesn't know about the call."

"Okay. Who called?"

"Said his name was William O'Shay, had an English or maybe Irish accent—hell, I can't tell the difference."

"O'Shay, spelled O-S-h-a-y?"

"Yeah, that's right."

"We'll run the name. What'd he want?"

"Said he was acting as an agent for a dealer in New York City. He said the dealer had heard I was in possession of rare Spanish antiquities and wanted to make an offer sight unseen."

Stanton pointed to the photos as Fred spoke. Miles sat shaking his head in disbelief.

"What was the offer?"

"One million."

"What'd you tell him?"

"No."

"And?" Stanton prompted.

"He said the offer was good until noon Central Time tomorrow. I asked him who the dealer was; he said he wasn't at liberty to say."

"How was the exchange to be made?"

"He said at one o'clock CST, my account would be credited with the money. I didn't even have to give him my bank account number. He said that would be done confidentially between banks. Then, Wednesday morning, a person from Houston would show up at my door to take possession of the purchased items."

"What else did he say?"

"Said he'd call at one o'clock tomorrow to find out what I'd decided. I told him no need; I'd made my decision and wasn't selling. I figure if the dealer is offering one million sight unseen then it must be worth twice that. I didn't tell him it might not even be mine to sell."

"My guess is the dealer already knows the law Ramirez told us about, and that's why it's a rush deal. If the dealer can get his hands on it and sell the pieces off to individual private overseas collectors before Spain can petition the UN for recovery, it'll be too late."

"Wouldn't the dealer be in trouble for selling the artifacts?" Fred asked.

"Not necessarily. My understanding is the country of origin, in this case Spain, must petition through the UN before the international law can be invoked."

"So wouldn't that same situation apply to me? Since Spain hasn't signed a petition yet, couldn't I sell it?"

"I'm not an attorney, Fred. If you're thinking of doing that, better get you one with a background in international law and let them advise you."

"I was just asking. I'm not selling it, especially if I'd have to hire an attorney to do it."

"Didn't think so. Think you all will be back to the house by noon tomorrow?"

"Yup, if we get going by seven."

"I'll be out; I'll bring Pete with me, if that's okay."

"Sure, see ya then."

Stanton hung up the phone and looked at Miles.

"As I was saying, what in the hell is going on?!"

"Pete, just look at all that treasure!"

"I am! What you think I've been doing the last twenty minutes? I'm in shock." The agent laid the photos on Stanton's desk and wiped the sweat from his palms on his dress slacks. "Really, Stanton, I need to know what's going on."

"All that treasure you see there came from inside those four carved boxes. The boxes were contained in a chest." She pointed to a photo of wood fragments. "That's what's left of the chest." Stanton paused while Miles studied the photos closer. "Pete, there are two more chests just like that one still buried in a cave on Fred Gray's place." It was late, but Stanton didn't want to keep Miles in the dark any longer. He'd already been a big help and deserved to know everything.

CHAPTER 51

Monday, June 12, 10:37 p.m.

On his way back to Wichita, Davis sent a text message to his employer informing her that the offer had been refused. As he crossed a river bridge, he tossed the new cell phone into the water. A calm came over him; it was as though the act of throwing the phone away symbolized a release from his surreptitious lifestyle. True, he thought, counting the days.

Davis drove by the Stratford Inn at 12:10 a.m. to see if anyone was around who might see him come in at the late hour. The only light besides the motel sign was in the lobby, and there was no one inside but the desk clerk, a young man Davis had never seen. Instead of turning into the Inn, Davis drove to the nearest all-night convenience store at the next intersection and filled his car with gas. He bought the latest issue of *Sports Illustrated* and returned to the motel, parking in back away from streetlights. He sat in the dark several minutes watching for movement of any kind. When he thought it safe, he made his way through a rear door and up the steps to the second floor. As he approached his room, Davis hesitated. Something wasn't right. He eased up to his room door and flattened himself against the wall, out of peephole range. The thread he'd placed near the upper right-hand corner wasn't there. Davis looked down and could see it lying on the floor. Someone was either in his room or had been there sometime since he'd left just a few hours earlier. The only illumination in the hallway were security lights at either end; the main lights shut off automatically at midnight. Davis's eyes were beginning to adjust to the dimness. He could see light coming from underneath his door and heard sounds from inside. It sounded like a conversation; the voices grew louder, then a gunshot. His TV was on; he remembered turning it off when he left. The person or persons inside weren't trying very hard to hide their presence, he thought. Davis crouched down and took his P-32 out of the ankle holster and released the safety. He slid close to the door, reached out with his left hand, and knocked. Within a few seconds the door opened, safety chain in place.

"Yes?"

Davis heard a feminine voice answer the knock. He hid the gun behind his back and stepped closer, looking through the partially opened door.

"Andrea?"

CHAPTER 52

Tuesday, June 13, 7:43 a.m.

"I have to go, Andrea," he said.

"When will you be back?"

"At least a month, hard to tell, maybe two. The company is expanding in Cleveland; I'll be there for some time," Davis lied.

"When you get settled, I could...that is, if you want, I could come there." She knew her humiliating offer was in vain. The drapes in the room were still drawn, the only light coming from the bathroom. Davis was shaving and couldn't see Andrea's eyes tearing.

"Yeah, that's a good idea. I've got your number; I'll call in a couple weeks."

Davis zipped the last bag shut and sat down on the bed next to her and reached to turn on the lamp. She gently stopped him. This good-bye needed to be said in the dark.

"Paul." She touched his cheek. "Believe it or not, I've never done this before—"

"You don't have to explain, Andrea."

"But I do. There's just something about you that's different from the other men I've met. I know it sounds cliché, but, Paul, it's true, please believe me."

He leaned down and kissed her. He felt the same, but this was neither the time nor the place for a love relationship to blossom. "I do believe you, Andrea, but I have to catch a flight." He was afraid to say more, afraid he'd say something he would regret, make a commitment he couldn't fulfill. Davis picked up his bags, opened the door, and hesitated. Andrea drew in a breath, hoping. She pulled the bedsheet to her eyes and dabbed the tears. He was gone.

* * *

Elliot Heath left the Stratford Inn at 8:30; the airport was only 30 minutes from the motel. It was important, in case he was being followed, to make it appear as though he was catching a flight out of town. He checked in his rental car and asked the attendant where the Delta counter was; of course he had no intention of taking a plane. He was simply creating another illusion in case someone was tailing him. Heath decided his actual point of departure would be Kansas City. Oklahoma City would be too risky, especially since the phone call he made to the rancher was from the 405 area code, which was the same as the Oklahoma International airport.

Heath walked to the first rental agency out of sight of the attendant he'd just done business with. With keys to a Ford Focus, rented under another alias, he bought a large diet drink to go and walked directly to the nearest men's bathroom. He found an empty stall, locked the door, and poured the drink in the bowl. Heath cut his Paul Davis driver's license and car rental papers under that name into several pieces, stuffed the remnants into the drink cup, replaced the plastic lid, and discarded it in the nearest receptacle.

Twenty minutes later, Heath located Interstate Highway 35 north; he'd be in Kansas City by early afternoon. Nice town, KC, he thought. Too bad he wouldn't have time to enjoy it. He had things to do, important, dangerous things. He thought of Andrea—a one-night stand, or was there more to it? One thing for sure, he couldn't let her be a distraction now.

* * *

It was nearly 7:30; the four men had finished breakfast and were on their way to the cave. Beverly offered to stay with Helen and help her with household chores that'd been neglected.

Deputy Cox watched the crew-cab truck leave the ranch house, cross a cattle guard into a thousand-acre pasture of short grass, cactus, and occasionally a large growth of sand plum bushes. The truck moved slowly, disappearing periodically into a draw, then reappearing only to disappear again until there was no sign of its whereabouts. Cox focused his binoculars on a landmark near where the truck last slipped from his view. He wanted to make sure he could at least isolate the area where the truck was last seen, should the sheriff ask. The deputy jotted a note in the watch log, wondering if that was the location of the *secret* Sheriff Stanton wouldn't yet reveal. All he knew was there were four men and a dog in the truck, which vanished into a shallow canyon a mile or so to the southwest of where he was standing. Cox hadn't seen movement on the ranch of any kind, short of cattle grazing their way from a grassy hill to the shade of several cottonwoods. At 11:53 he saw a glint of sunshine reflecting off the truck windshield as it emerged from where it disappeared four hours earlier. The deputy sat down on the lawn chair, wiping the sweat that was dripping from his chin onto the watch log, and entered the time the truck returned to the ranch house. He watched as the garage door opened and the truck backed in. The door shut.

Helen and Beverly stepped into the garage carrying two pitchers of iced tea. As the men poured their drinks, the women studied the two chests. "Did you break this one getting it out of the cave?" Helen asked.

"No, it was pretty well busted up when we got to it," Fred said.

"You think maybe your grandfather?"

"Don't think so, honey, it was pretty well hidden. My hunch is some of Coronado's men tried unsuccessfully to get it open; maybe they got caught. Don't know. That's where the candlestick came from, though."

The others were busy dismantling the broken chest. Fred moved around the workbench to where Helen was standing. He put his arm around her and kissed her forehead. "How are you feeling?"

"The rest helped, and thank God for Beverly. She really helped me. No offense, Mr. Gray, but it was nice having a woman to talk to."

Fred smiled and held her tighter. "No offense taken. Can't imagine what it's like listening all the time to complaints about cattle prices and drought."

"It's not that. Those things affect me, too. It's just nice to...oh, I don't know, just nice to talk to people with a different perspective on life."

* * *

By mid-afternoon, the rest of Coronado's treasure had been freed from the containers and taken to the basement. All the pieces were arrayed on the green surface of the pool table. For the next several minutes Lee and Carlos took photos of the collective treasure and each piece individually. Lee asked everyone to gather on one side of the table. "I want a photo of everybody." He looked over at the rancher and his wife. "When you're ready, this story and the photos will make a best-seller, and the better we document it, the more attractive the story will be."

Fred and Helen reluctantly moved to the center of the group forming in back of the display table. "I think we're only interested in getting this over with. We want our lives back to normal. No books. We don't want our privacy disrupted anymore."

"I understand, Fred, but the truth of the matter is that you, the treasure, and your ranch are about to become famous, and there's no stopping that inevitability."

"I agree. I've had some experience with unwanted notoriety. It's better if you control the inevitable," Carlos said.

"I'm not following you."

"Someone is going to write a book about the treasure, and it's conceivable there may be a movie and TV adaptations, documentaries. I'll guarantee you when this hits the news, *National Geographic* will be all over it."

Fred was not a man to mince words; however, he had rules about swearing. The first rule was *never swear in front of a woman or children,* but in his anger he forgot. "That's just plain bullshit!"

"Fred!" Helen said sternly.

"Sorry, but this has gone too far. I'm just sick and tired of being told it's outta my control. I've got half a notion to box all this up and take it back to the cave."

Robert understood everything his father said, and to a degree he even agreed, but the thought of money persuaded him to side with Lee and Carlos. "Hang on, Dad, let 'em explain. I think I see where they're going with this."

"Okay, go on."

"You can be in control, Fred, but there are things you have to do to assure you're the boss."

"And?"

"Find a writer to co-author the book; it'll be an instant best-seller, and more importantly the book will be in your words. I'll turn all my photos over to you. They're yours, not mine to sell, and that way you can use them in the book. If you don't write the book then someone else will, and it'll be in their words and they'll get the royalties," Lee said.

"I suppose the next thing you'll be telling me is that I should get a good lawyer."

"Yes. The right lawyer, with the right background, absolutely."

"But won't that cost an arm and a leg?"

"Yes it will, but using your own analogy, if you don't, you could end up losing both arms and legs."

Fred smiled. "So how do I find a good writer out here in the middle of nowhere?"

"When we get back to Norman, I'll contact a professor in the English department; he'll know. I can also talk to a friend of mine at the law school about an attorney that might specialize in this kind of work. I won't tell what this is about; I'll present them with a hypothetical scenario. Now, if you all will stand straight and smile, I'll take a picture." Lee motioned for Carlos to join the group.

"I hope you understand, but I must refuse. It's better that I remain inconspicuous. As a matter of fact, since we're on the subject, I must ask that if you refer to me in any fashion, say that I'm a contractor for the Spanish government."

"You sure? You could become famous."

"That's exactly what I want to avoid." Carlos walked over to Lee. "Let me take the photograph and you stand next to your beautiful wife." He took several shots from different angles and handed the camera back to Lee. Carlos closed his laptop and slid it and his camera into a leather shoulder bag. "I must leave, but first I want to thank all of you for allowing me to share in this most important discovery."

"What will you do now?" Helen asked.

"Istanbul is my next destination. I'll stop in Madrid and report this discovery to Dr. Cordona; in turn, he'll report it to the government. On your behalf I will not divulge any identifying information in my report. It will simply be my verification of the discovery, an inventory of what was found, and photos. Once the Spanish government decides what they will do, then I will be obligated to give them your names and location."

"How long will that take?" Robert asked.

"There's no way of telling. They could file a petition with the UN that day. Most likely the process will take a few weeks."

Fred and Lee walked with Carlos out to his car. "One last thought before I leave." He opened the car door and put his bags inside. "Your sheriff appears extremely competent."

"Very. Former FBI. She spent years doing something in counterterrorism."

"Make sure she's in on everything you do."

"She has been. Why?"

"Fred, you must understand, this is bigger than you can imagine. I'm not one to throw adjectives around, but this discovery rises to the level of astounding. Consequently life could get more frantic and much more dangerous than it is right now. You have wise people around you; let them help. Filter every decision through them, and don't do anything in a hurry."

Dr. Ramirez got behind the wheel. "Take care, and when I get back to the States I'll call you."

Fred watched him drive away. "I don't know, Lee," he murmured.

"What?"

"Listening to Carlos…I just don't know if I feel better or worse."

CHAPTER 53

Tuesday, June 13, 9:00 a.m. EST

Monica Bouvier got her first taste of USA bashing as a teenager in Paris. The French tolerated U.S. citizens because of the tourist trade—some, who could remember, even admired the U.S., grateful they weren't forced to speak German. French Muslims, particularly the younger ones, hated America. Many were indoctrinated to hate anyone not a Muslim. It was simple to the fanatical groups: you either were a devout believer or you weren't. Islamism became Bouvier's goal in life; everything she did was Allah's will, and the end always justified the means when it came to fulfilling the local Mullah's wishes.

Bouvier stopped by her favorite coffee shop that morning on her way to work. She purchased the *Times* and a large cup of Turkish coffee and walked over to the only empty chair. "Excuse me." One person looked up from his newspaper, obviously perturbed by the interruption. "Is that seat taken?" The man shook his head and continued reading. She laid her paper down and took a sip of coffee. With a pen in hand, she began scrolling through messages she'd received since turning her cell phone off early the night before. Bouvier read Heath's message and tried to call him using the new number, but there was no answer. She typed out a quick text message ordering him to call ASAP. This opportunity to get her hands on the lost Coronado treasure was too good to be true. She had customers in the U.S., France, and Italy, all prepared to pay top dollar for something of this magnitude. Bouvier knew she could quadruple her investment overnight. Her group needed funds badly, and she wasn't about to let some country hick get in her way. Frankly she'd never heard of Oklahoma until Hansen sent her the photos and the story of some rancher finding a candlestick in a cave. If he was stupid enough to pass up a million dollars, then she had no alternative but to make him an offer he couldn't refuse. Plan A had failed, but Plan B was in operation. She'd just have to be patient.

* * *

Tobias Henry left the editor's office that Tuesday morning thankful he was still in one piece. He'd been so absorbed with the Gray Ranch situation, he had forgotten to submit the birth and death announcements in time for publication that week. It was all he could do to sit still and take his reprimand without saying a word about Coronado's gold. He had never in his life felt so compelled to say something, but there was entirely too much at stake for him to take that chance.

Tobias sat down at his desk, opened his laptop, and typed in *Explorer Coronado*; several sites appeared. For the rest of the afternoon he took notes. When the sheriff gave him the go-ahead, Tobias knew he had to be ready to write his story; if he didn't, someone else would. It was pure luck that he'd stumbled on it in the first place, and there was no way he was going to let this opportunity slip through his fingers.

* * *

Meanwhile, Sheriff Stanton and Agent Miles stopped by Curt Russell's house to look around. Miles hadn't seen where the alleged suicide took place, and Stanton wanted another set of eyes to look it over. The sheriff brought photos of Curt's body in just the position she had found him on Saturday.

"Did your deputy move the body before you got here?" he asked.

"That was the first question I asked when I walked through the door. He said he hadn't moved or touched anything but the front doorknob."

"You believe him?"

"No reason not to. State trooper was there. He tells the same story."

"In that case, here's why I agree with your murder theory. Aside from no GSR, look at the body position. The bullet impact normally pushes the head slightly to the left, and the pistol recoil would force the hand holding the weapon in the opposite direction. Whoever put the gun in his hand didn't account for that phenomenon. That's not enough by itself to say it was murder."

"No, but it helps." Stanton thought the same thing, but wanted Miles to mention it without any prompting. Like he said, it wasn't a big thing, but added to the rest of the evidence, it was significant.

"Ready to meet the Grays and see the treasure?"

"That I am. Lost sleep last night thinking about it." He studied Stanton's face for a clue. "It's unbelievable—still trying to figure out if I'm being played for a sucker."

"Yeah, well if you are, then so am I."

Miles watched the countryside float by as Stanton drove. "Webster told me you came here to help your mom when your dad was sick?"

"Yeah, then Mom died shortly after he died."

"Why'd you stay? Frankly, I don't understand why you'd want to settle out here. There's nothing here, no shopping mall, no theaters, your only restaurant closes at seven, no museums. I just don't get it."

Stanton turned onto the gravel drive and pointed toward the ridge in back of the ranch house. "That's where my deputies have been posted since last week. Great vantage point—you can see five miles in most directions." Stanton stopped on the circle drive in front of the house. "I'll introduce you around, and we'll take a look at the treasure. Remember, Pete, they were close to their hired hand. Helen's showing it the most."

"What about Mr. Gray? You said they have an adult son living here. What about him?"

"He actually lives in the old house just down the road, name's Robert. Robert runs the ranch; Fred and Helen are mostly retired. I can tell you, with some assurance, if Fred and his son thought Curt was murdered and knew who killed him, they'd hunt him down."

"So they're not grieving yet."

"No, not yet, just blaming themselves. Somehow they think they're responsible for his suicide."

Helen met them at the door before Stanton had a chance to knock. "Come in, come in, saw you from the kitchen window. Dr. Ramirez just left; the others are in the den."

Helen was smiling and as hospitable as usual, but

Stanton saw through the façade. "Helen, I don't want to bother you, just wanted to introduce another FBI agent who's been assigned to help us."

"Now, Crys, it's no bother, you're always welcome." Helen looked around Stanton's shoulder at Miles. "And this is the other agent?"

"Yes, Helen." Stanton turned. "Pete Miles, this is Helen Gray."

The two shook hands, and Helen pointed down the hall. "You two go on to the den. I'll be in after I've folded towels." Helen forced a pleasant expression and hurried into a bedroom. They heard a soft sob as she closed the door behind her.

The sheriff looked at Miles. "See."

"Yeah, she's really torn up."

Stanton and Miles entered the den, and the sheriff introduced Miles. "Fred, is it alright if I show Agent Miles the treasure?"

"Of course. You mind if I don't go? Been up and down those stairs so many times lately, my legs are worn out."

"We'll take a quick look then go," Stanton said.

Fred looked at Miles and chuckled. "That ain't gonna happen."

"You mean the quick look?"

"You can't take a quick look. You'll be there an hour at least. Then, if you're like me, you'll want to see it again and again."

Everyone went to the basement but Fred. He leaned his head back against the soft leather of his recliner, closed his eyes, and slipped into a shallow rest. O'Shay's Irish accent played over and over in his mind. The deadline had passed three hours earlier; had he done the right thing?

Helen folded the last towel. She was exhausted, ready for another nap, but she knew dinner needed preparing.

There were guests, and Helen wasn't going to neglect them. She dabbed on a bit of rouge, hoping color, even artificial, would lift her spirits. Just then the phone rang. Helen knew everyone was in the basement where there was no extension; she sat down on the bed and answered. "Gray Ranch, Helen speaking."

The phone woke Fred, but by the time he'd gotten out of his chair to answer it, the ringing stopped. He was relieved; someone else could deal with whatever the call was about. Fred turned back to his chair and flopped down, hoping he could return to the restful state he was in before the phone rang, but that was not to be.

Fred was the first to hear Helen screaming his name, something she'd never done before. He'd heard her yell his name when he was down near the corrals, but never scream. He bolted out of his chair, ran through the kitchen and down the hall, past the living room. Fred's heavy, quick steps over the kitchen floor got Robert's attention. He had never heard or seen his father run in the house; it had to be an emergency. Without saying anything to the others, Robert climbed the steps two at a time and disappeared down the hall to his parents' bedroom just as his mother was handing the phone to Fred.

"What's the matter?" Robert asked his mother.

Helen was crying hysterically. All she could do was shake her head as she buried her face in a pillow.

The others came up from the basement and were standing in the living room, awkwardly waiting for someone to tell them what happened. No one said anything; finally Robert emerged from the master bedroom and hurried toward them. Robert stood for a moment drawing in shallow breaths. There were tears in his eyes, but not from sadness. Everyone could tell he was in a rage. His voice trembled, each word uttered in cold, angry bursts. "My sister..." Robert halted, each breath taking all his energy. "My sister...my sister's daughter disappeared. She's gone, no one's seen her."

"Sit down, Robert, take your time." The sheriff led him to a chair. Stanton pulled another chair up close to Robert and sat down. "Now, slowly, where does your sister live?"

"Kansas City."

"What's her name?"

CHAPTER 54

Tuesday, June 13, 4:46 p.m.

Beth Gray graduated from a state university in nearby Alva with a degree in elementary education. Her lifelong desire was to teach, but not in her hometown or anywhere in western Oklahoma for that matter. A college friend coaxed her to Kansas City, Kansas, where teachers were needed and the pay was decent. Beth was the youngest of three siblings, but in many ways more independent than her older brothers. Fred and Helen hoped Beth would return to Buffalo and teach, but she had other plans.

Charles Gorman, a fellow teacher, and Beth were married in 1989. Lindsey was the first of their two children and at ten years old seemed more mature to her grandparents, perhaps 13 or 14 by their standards. Lindsey was independent like her mother, and Beth, everyone said, like her father. That's not to say Lindsey was disobedient. She wasn't. She was a good student, a leader, the teachers said during conferences, not afraid to take chances or to try something new.

* * *

"Beth…her name's Beth."

"Her last name?" Stanton asked.

"Gorman, Beth Gorman. Husband is Charles, we call him Chuck. He's a teacher like Beth." Robert raised himself from a slouched position and sat up straight. He looked around the room at everyone. "Chuck called, said Lindsey, their ten-year-old, has been missing over an hour. Guess she was swimming at a friend's house just two doors down. The friend went into her house for some reason, and when she came out Lindsey was gone."

"What time was that?" Miles asked.

"Around three. The neighbor girl thought Lindsey went home. At three-thirty the girl's mother asked where Lindsey was and she said home. She called Beth to make sure Lindsey had gotten there, but she hadn't."

"She call police?" Stanton said.

"Yeah, they came right away. Chuck said they're interviewing neighbors now."

"What about an Amber Alert?"

"Just getting ready to do that. It'll be carried over a four-state area at five."

"Any witnesses?"

"Don't know; guess that's why they're interviewing neighbors. I need to get back and see how Mom's doing." Robert disappeared down the hall.

"Pete, call the Wichita office, see if there's any news on Heath."

"You're thinking what I'm thinking."

"Just trying to consider all the possibilities."

Agent Miles called FBI headquarters in Wichita. After a few minutes of being passed around, Miles was talking with someone he knew on a first-name basis. "And when were you people going to let me know?!"

Everyone could see the agent was upset. Miles listened for a few minutes without saying anything. "Let me be perfectly clear, Tom. This situation is of the utmost importance. It may have resulted in the possible disappearance of a ten-year-old Kansas City girl." Miles listened again. "As soon as you know anything, I mean anything, call me." He angrily snapped his phone shut and looked at Stanton. "Agents in Wichita found a truck in a parking garage downtown matching the description of the one Heath drove. The license plate is different, checks out to an alias. They're trying to run that down now. Also had someone watching the truck since they discovered it yesterday around noon."

"Let me guess, no one's been around it." Stanton said.

"Right. They're going to try and lift some prints and talk to car rental agencies within walking distance."

"Okay, Miles, let's try to play this out with what we know." Stanton sat back down and ran her fingers through her shoulder-length blond hair. She leaned back; her right arm fell naturally to the holster strap securing her weapon, and unconsciously she fidgeted with the snap. "This is what's happening inside the KC police department right now, or at least this is what I'd be doing. Keep in mind the Kansas authorities know nothing about the ICO, Bouvier, Heath, or the treasure; therefore, they're treating this as either a runaway or more likely an abduction by a pedophile."

"Standard procedure," Miles added.

"Robert said they're issuing an Amber Alert. Next thing they'll do is start searching the sex-offender registry for perps living in the area. The cops will be visiting them, if they can find 'em, in the next hour."

"Yeah, all standard operating procedure in every city in the U.S."

"And probably a huge waste of time and resources, because they don't know what we know," Stanton said, shaking her head.

Miles nodded and opened his cell phone. Within a few seconds, he was talking with his boss in St. Louis, who had been a part of the teleconference between Miles and Webster just days earlier.

Stanton listened while Miles explained to his boss about the treasure, and the possibility it could be the motive if, in fact, Lindsey had been kidnapped. "What'd he say?" she asked.

"Said he'd get with the agent in charge of the KC office and tell her to cooperate with the police. He knows the police chief there, said he'd contact him and bring him up to speed."

"Okay, that should redirect some of the resources, assuming our theory is right. Anything else?" Stanton asked.

"Yeah, he asked if Beth Gorman knows about the treasure. I assumed they did. What about it?"

The Bethels listened to Stanton and Miles, reluctant to interfere in the conversation. The focus of attention had abruptly changed from treasure hunting to the rescue of an innocent little girl. There was nothing they could do but stay out of the way. Stanton turned to Lee and asked, "Do you know if the Grays' daughter is aware of the treasure?"

"I don't think so. After you said there was danger involved and the task force operation was highly confidential, I think everyone took heed. Maybe we should ask," Lee said.

"We'd better find out for sure."

Wanting to help in some way, Lee said, "Do you want me to ask?"

"Yeah, if you don't mind."

Lee walked down the hall to the bedroom where the Grays were. He knocked softly. Robert stepped into the hall and closed the door behind him. "How are your folks doing?" Lee asked, knowing immediately how unanswerable the question was.

"Not good, Lee. Dad's gonna take Mom to the doctor in town. She's in shock; we don't know what else to do."

"I'm so sorry, wish there was something we could do." A heavy silence followed, both men at a loss for words. "There is a question the sheriff has. It's about the treasure."

"About the treasure?" Robert looked angry.

"What I meant to say was does your sister know about it?"

"No. Why? Does the sheriff think there's a connection?"

"I think the cops just want to consider all the possibilities."

"My God, in all the turmoil I never even thought of that. Of course, it'd make sense, wouldn't it?"

"If that's the motive, Robert, then Miles believes the KC cops need to be informed."

"Gimme a chance to talk with Dad for a second, then I'll call Chuck." Robert went back into his parents' room. Lee waited in the hall. Five minutes later, Robert and his father came out of the bedroom together. "What's the sheriff going to do?" Fred asked quietly.

"I don't know, but Agent Miles has called his superiors in St. Louis. The question came up. Let's talk to Stanton." Lee motioned toward the living room.

"Sheriff, Agent Miles, that's got to be it!" the rancher

said anxiously. "They want the treasure. The phone call last night offering me one million sight unseen, I should've seen it coming."

"It's just a theory at this point, Fred, and we'll check it out. But, if the theory is correct, then either you or your daughter will be receiving a phone call demanding ransom," the sheriff said.

"Dad, while you take Mom to the doctor, I'll call Chuck and fill him in."

Robert turned to Stanton. "But what do I say?"

"Tell him briefly about the treasure your dad discovered. Let him know there is a suspect—and possibly more than one—the FBI is aware of, and they are trying to locate that person or persons as we speak. Explain that the treasure might be the ransom, and he should expect a phone call with demands," Stanton said.

"So what does Chuck say if they demand the treasure?"

"Ask the caller for instructions and tell him it will be delivered."

Robert picked up the house phone and called his brother-in-law.

"Hello!"

Robert cringed, hearing the raw desperation in Chuck's voice. He knew he'd need to be especially patient with his brother-in-law and to expect the unexpected. How does one explain something so complicated to a man whose daughter had just gone missing?

"Chuck, this is Robert. I need you to listen closely to what I'm about to say." Robert looked at Stanton for reassurance, and she nodded. Everyone listened while he explained what had recently transpired at the ranch.

"I know, it's going to be difficult to explain all this to Beth. Hell, Chuck, I'm not sure I even understand what's going on." Several brief interruptions occurred during the conversation; Robert repeated some of the details more than once.

"Dad's taking Mom in to see the doctor. If she feels like it, we'll be up in the next day or two."

Robert finally hung up the phone. "I can't imagine what they're going through." He couldn't look at anyone; Robert just sat looking at the phone, feeling empathy he'd never experienced before.

"For what it's worth, you did a good job of explaining to your brother-in-law. Now all we can do is wait and let law enforcement handle it from here," Stanton said.

"Chuck says the Amber Alert has been issued, and all local TV stations are running it. He said the cops told him the FBI is involved, too."

"Good, that's fast. Usually takes hours for two different agencies to hammer out the jurisdiction and communication issues." Miles was relieved. So far the FBI hadn't performed up to its usual standards; hopefully the agency was now back on track.

"While you were on the phone, Robert, I got a follow-up call from Wichita. Seems a man fitting Heath's description rented a car from an agency located near the parking garage where Heath's truck was found. That car was checked back in at the rental agency's airport branch around ten-thirty this morning by a Paul Davis. According to the agency clerk on duty, he fit Heath's description. Our guy's checked all the airlines that had departing flights today, and no one had a Paul Davis on board."

"That's not surprising. I mean, I wouldn't use a well-worn alias. What about a picture of Heath? Anything come up with a photo attached?"

"Nothing, Crys, but we do have a sketch artist working with the witness from the rental agency…"

Robert interrupted. "We have a fax machine, Agent

Miles. If you want to have them fax it over, I can take a look. I've been around him more than anyone else."

"Great idea." Agent Miles called the Wichita office, and within half an hour Robert was studying the drawing.

"Well, does it look like him?" Stanton asked.

"Yeah, it resembles him. Only problem I see is that he looks like thousands of other guys."

"Did he have any distinguishable features that'd set him apart?" Miles asked.

"What d'ya mean?"

"Big nose, crooked nose, big ears, scars, eye color, receding hairline, facial hair, short neck, long neck, did he have tattoos anywhere you could see?"

"Not that I remember. The drawing looks like him."

"Okay." Miles studied the drawing. "We'll confirm it, and Wichita can forward it on to Kansas City." Agent Miles opened his cell phone and was ready to call when the Grays' landline rang. Robert reached to answer it, but Miles caught his arm. "Let me answer."

Robert nodded and stepped away from the phone.

"Gray Ranch, Robert speaking." Pete Miles listened intently to the caller. "Yes please." A short pause followed; then Miles asked, "Are you alright?" Seconds later, the agent hung up the phone and looked at Robert. "That was the kidnapper. He described the bathing suit she has on and allowed her to say she was okay. Her voice sounded strong."

Robert was anxious to call his sister with the news. "What does he want?"

"As we expected, he wants the treasure. His words were 'The candlestick and the four boxes.' Evidently he's not aware of the other two chests."

"Yeah, the only thing Heath saw the day I ran him and Curt off was the four boxes. I can't help thinking if I'd kept my mouth shut, none of this would be happening."

"Doubt that made any difference. I believe the plan was already in motion. Think about it, Robert," Stanton said, hoping her words might soothe some of the anguish he was feeling.

"I have been thinking about it; that's why I feel so helpless."

"I don't want to trivialize the emotion you're feeling right now, but at the same time you can't afford the luxury of wasting time beating yourself up over something you have no control over."

Robert knew the sheriff was right. "What do you suggest?"

"Call your sister. They need to know she's alive; they need to know we're devising a plan to deliver the ransom. Encourage your sister; she needs to know people are working hard to get Lindsey back."

CHAPTER 55

Tuesday, June 13, 6:48 p.m.

Robert picked up the phone to call his sister just as
Agent Miles speed-dialed Tom in the Wichita
office. Miles told the agent in charge about the ransom call,
but didn't say anything about what the kidnapper was
demanding. He thought the longer the treasure could
remain a secret the better; for the present time, all Tom
needed to know was that there was a ransom demand and
the Grays were prepared to pay it. "Anything new on
Heath's vehicle?" Miles asked.

"Just after we talked last, our folks found that Paul
Davis had rented another car at the airport. We got the
make, color, and license plate. An APB has been issued."

"Did you stress caution on the APB?"

"Yeah, we'll update it, though. We'll tell 'em there may
be a female kidnap victim with him."

"Good, Tom. Would you also notify St. Louis? I'll call
Webster; they all want hourly updates."

"Will do. What are your plans?" Tom asked.

"We're going to follow the perp's instructions right down to the last detail. I'll call you with the details later."

* * *

Pete Miles placed the next call to Deputy Director Jerry Webster, and as soon as Webster answered, Miles pressed a button and laid the phone on the coffee table in front of the others. "Got you on speaker, Deputy Director. The sheriff's here, along with close associates of Mr. Gray, Lee and Beverly Bethel. Mr. Gray's son Robert is here but on the phone with his sister right now."

"Yeah, fill me in, just got word there's been a kidnapping that might be related to what's going on in Oklahoma."

"That's right; the rancher has a daughter, son-in-law, and two grandchildren living in the Kansas City area. Just hours ago Fred Gray's granddaughter, Lindsey Gorman, was kidnapped. The perp called here and demanded a ransom."

"How long ago? Did you confirm the girl was okay?" Webster asked.

"Twenty minutes, and yes, Lindsey's okay."

"How much ransom?"

"Jerry, this is Crys."

"Hey, Crys, this Oklahoma thing just gets bigger and bigger. What's the story?"

"Remember when I said something really big was happening?"

"You told me I'd hear before CNN broke the story."

"Yes, well, the situation has become more complicated, and you need to know now. Here it is in a nutshell…"

Stanton explained what had taken place in the past 72 hours.

"Well, folks, any adjective I'd use to express my feeling would only be a gross understatement. I'm at a loss. What can I do to help?"

"Don't know of anything you can do here, but if it's not too much trouble, I'd like to know what Carl Holt is doing, where he's at."

"I'm meeting with his supervisor first thing in the morning. You know we're about to close in on the ICO. We've got the search, seizure, and arrest warrants ready to serve."

"Jerry, we need to know when," Stanton said.

"This is Tuesday night. I'd say early Thursday morning at the earliest, Friday the latest. Why?"

"If our theory is right and the ransom isn't in the hands of the kidnapper before you close down the ICO, then Lindsey is no longer needed as a bargaining chip. We both know what usually happens then."

"I see your point, Crys. What are the details of the exchange?" Webster asked.

"Deputy Director, this is Agent Miles again. I took the call. The details are simple and straightforward. The Grays are to take the treasure out of the wooden containers and place them in a large unmarked cardboard box that's to be sealed tightly with packing tape. The name Charles Myer, an alias I'm sure, and a phony address are to be printed on each side of the box and then delivered to a commercial mail drop in KC by noon tomorrow. The perp says as soon as he is confident no one is watching the mail drop site and that no one's following him, he'll call the rancher and tell him where his granddaughter is."

"Does he know the FBI is involved?" Webster asked.

"He knows the police are because he said he saw the Amber Alert. Didn't say a word about the FBI."

"I suggest that you not underestimate this guy. Just

because he's a kidnapper doesn't necessarily mean he's stupid. What's your next step?"

"We've packed the box according to instructions, and we added a tracking device."

"What's your backup plan?"

"You mean in case he suspects a GPS device is in the box?"

"Yes."

"We'll have eyes on him, too."

"According to my watch, you've got fourteen hours to get the box to KC. Is that doable?"

"Yes, but I have to leave within the hour."

When the conference call ended, Miles turned to the sheriff and detailed his plan for delivering the ransom.

Beverly Bethel had kept her mouth shut up to this point. She knew it wasn't her place to stick her nose into discussions with the third highest ranking FBI official in the U.S., but nevertheless she'd developed the ability, over the years, to think through problems, and that's exactly what she'd done while listening to Miles and Webster. "May I offer a suggestion?" As soon as Beverly said it, she glanced at her husband; she knew him well, and her usual defense was just to ignore his perturbed expression. If she acknowledged his anguished look, it was certain Lee would argue, and there wasn't time for debate.

"Certainly," Stanton said.

"From what I gather, you think the kidnapper is a man by the name of Heath and that he's working for this Bouvier character the FBI is about to arrest."

Lee took the very short pause to caution his wife. "Yeah, honey, I think they've got their plan in place; let's let them do it without interference."

"This won't take long, Lee. As I was saying, if Heath is half as smart as everyone thinks, he'll spot you. No offense,

Agent Miles, but you just have that government appearance: clean-cut, athletic, all business. And Heath has seen the sheriff, so she can't deliver the box."

"Honey, please, there's no one else, and we're wasting valuable time."

"Bear with me. Looks to me like this exchange needs to be done in a way that Heath thinks minimizes his risk of exposure."

"That's right, Beverly. What's your suggestion?" Miles asked.

"You're assuming this person will be watching the mail drop location from the time it opens in the morning until at least noon, right?"

"Yes."

"If he sees anyone who raises his suspicion he's being watched, more than it already is, won't that only delay getting Lindsey back?"

"Possibly, but what's our alternative?" Stanton said.

Lee knew what his wife was about to say, and from a logical point of view she was right, but every precautionary neuron in his body was positioning to object.

"I suggest you allow me to deliver the ransom," Beverly said.

"No, no, absolutely not, that's entirely out of the question! You're not trained; you don't know what you're doing!"

"Honey, think about it for a second. I won't be in any danger. All I have to do is carry the box into the store, walk out, and drive away. The bad guy won't recognize me. I'll just be a face in the crowd. He won't even know it's his box until he comes in the store and asks for it."

Stanton and Miles looked at Lee. They both knew Beverly's plan would provide an element of deception neither of them could, but they didn't want to encourage disharmony between husband and wife. Stanton looked at her watch and glanced nervously at Miles. They both understood Lee's fear and reluctance to agree to a plan that could place his wife in harm's way. Contrary to Beverly's certainty that she'd be in no danger, there was never a guarantee of that, and everybody in the room knew it.

"You know, Lee, she's got a point, but I can't ask a civilian to participate in such an operation, no matter how safe it seems."

Beverly took her husband's hand. "Lee, if this was just about the treasure, I wouldn't do it, but it's about a little girl who needs all the help she can get—"

Lee interrupted. "Okay, okay, I see your point. One stipulation."

"What?"

"I'm going with you."

"You didn't think I wanted to do this alone, did you?" Beverly said, smiling.

Agent Miles was all business. "Okay, let me confirm what I think I heard. Beverly, you said that you would be willing to take the ransom to the store in Kansas City?"

"That's right, I will."

"Dr. Bethel, you said you wanted to go with her, is that right?"

"Yes. She's not going without me."

"Okay then, you must leave now. I will follow thirty minutes behind you in case you have car trouble, flat tire, whatever. At a preplanned location near KC, you will stop and change vehicles. We'll have a nondescript car with Kansas plates you'll use to make the delivery. When you've made the delivery, you will, and I emphasize *will,* leave KC and return to Oklahoma. Any questions?"

"How will we know where to change vehicles?" Lee asked.

"I'll call you when it's been worked out. Anything else?" Miles paused. "If not, you need to go. One more thing. I suggest you let Lee out of the car several blocks from the drop site. We must assume the kidnapper will be watching the store closely."

"Do you think he'll pick the box up tomorrow?"

"No. At least *I* wouldn't. Most likely he will watch the location for a day or two."

* * *

There was no moon that night to cast light on the flat, desolate prairie landscape. All Beverly could see was the two-lane road directly in front of them. Lee wanted to drive the first leg of their trip to Kansas City, which was okay with Beverly; all she wanted to do was sleep. Lee turned the radio off and slipped into his own thoughts of Lindsey, wondering how a child dealt with the intense fear of being separated from her parents. He realized there wasn't a reasonable answer or at least one that made sense to him.

Agent Miles left the ranch 30 minutes later and followed the same route east the Bethels had taken. As he neared Interstate Highway 35 north, which would take him north into Kansas, he received a call from the Wichita office. "Special Agent Miles, this is Agent Samuels in Wichita."

"Where's Tom?"

"Sir, Tom went home at midnight. He said if you wanted to talk to him directly, you could call his home. I have his number."

"No, Samuels, he needs his beauty sleep. You have something for me?"

"Yes sir. Arrangements are made for the car swap; here is the location."

"Hang on, let me turn my dash light on. Okay, what's the location?"

Samuels gave Miles the address and advised him that according to the Kansas Department of Public Safety surveillance video, the car, believed to be rented to Heath, passed through the Turnpike at Emporia headed northeast.

"Time?"

"Ten twenty-six this morning. Correction, sir, I didn't mean this morning—"

Miles stopped his explanation. "Yeah, Samuels, I know what you meant. This late hour has us all a little confused."

"Yes sir."

"Samuels, if he drove the speed limit from that point at ten twenty-six, how long would it take him to get to Kansas City?"

"If he didn't stop, I'd say an hour and a half, maybe a little longer depending on traffic."

"So from Emporia at ten twenty-six, he could've gotten to the Gorman residence by one or one-thirty yesterday afternoon?"

"Yes sir."

CHAPTER 56

Tuesday, June 13, 12:20 p.m.

Elliot Heath pulled to the curb on a quiet residential street two blocks from a corner convenience store. The store was crowded at that time of day, just as he'd hoped. Busy people always provided a thicker cover for what he needed to do. The cab he'd called pulled in next to an overflowing Dumpster. "You the one needing a cab?"

"Yeah, need to get to the airport in a hurry. My rental car broke down, and I've got a plane to catch."

"No problem, mister; you got the fastest cabbie in Kansas City."

"How long does it take to get from here to the airport?"

"Average person 'bout fifteen minutes, average KC cabbie about twenty minutes—they like to keep that meter runnin'."

"How about you, how long will it take?"

"Ten minutes."

Heath paid the driver and went directly to a car rental

agency. An hour later he checked into a rather sleazy-looking motel that had somehow gotten lost in the sprawl of an industrial district. The only guests, he suspected, were laborers assigned temporarily to one of the nearby industries, or the stop-and-go patrons who valued their privacy as much as he did. Heath set his duffle bag on his lap and unzipped a well-hidden pocket that only he knew existed. The pocket was not much bigger than a credit card and less than a half inch deep, just large enough to conceal a slim cell phone. The phone had no markings, no brand name, no numbers or letters on the keypad. Heath opened the phone, extended the three-inch antenna, and carefully pressed three blank buttons. It was imperative that he press the right buttons in the right sequence. If he didn't, the phone would automatically deactivate, rendering it useless. Heath heard the customary two short beeps and the same young, almost sultry female automated voice answer, "Martha's Flowers and Gifts, may I help you?" A pause followed, then one solitary tone similar to the high note on a xylophone.

Heath said, "Four-three-two-eight-four."

"Please repeat," the automated voice replied.

"Four-three-two-eight-four."

"Thank you, and will that be red or white roses?"

"Red."

The open phone line went dead. Heath folded the phone shut. In less than five minutes, the phone beeped and he answered, "Four-three-two-eight-four." Heath said nothing else, just listened. Again he folded the phone shut and leaned back, thinking about what he'd just heard. The voice on the other end of the call said the FBI had tracked him to Kansas City. Heath smiled, thinking he was either getting too old for the job, or maybe the Feds were just getting smarter. Whatever the reason, Heath knew it was time to think about doing something else. He thought about Andrea.

Heath had been counting on a little rest, then concluding his business, but as luck would have it, another job add-on derailed those plans. For the second time in a week, his responsibilities had increased. Maybe it was his imagination, but to him it seemed like the risks were growing substantially. When he was young, hazardous work was a motivator; the adrenaline rush added excitement to his life, but now it only brought dread. He looked at his watch. Not even time for a nap, and if the voice on the line was only half right, he could count on being awake at least another 24 hours.

CHAPTER 57

Tuesday, June 13, 3:40 p.m.

"**D**ude, listen to me—you're an idiot. This guy is using you. Sounds more like a drug deal than anything else!"

"Look, you weren't there. The guy's legit. He's in a bind and couldn't be in two places at once. He's just a businessman I ran into, and he needed help, that's all."

"Okay, so tell me the story again."

"The guy's name is Robert Frazier; he's a businessman from Denver. He had a shipment of training manuals that got on the wrong flight, and they ended up in Dallas. The airline sent them overnight to the Mail Box store in Prairie Village. All I have to do is rent a car, pick the manuals up, and drive the car to his hotel. I'll leave the key with the desk clerk under Frazier's name."

"And that's it?"

"Yeah, that's it. All you have to do is drive the five miles to the hotel and pick me up."

"And for that you'll give me fifty bucks?"

"Yeah."

"How much is he paying you?"

"Three hundred, and after I pay you, that'll leave just enough to pay for my books this semester, all for two hours' work."

"Okay, but if that's drugs in the box, I'll deny ever knowing you. And what's that?" The young man pointed to a small black plastic box his friend was holding.

"Frazier said that everything his company ships has a tracking device. That's how they knew the manuals were in Dallas, but when the airline shipped 'em to KC, it automatically caused the sensor to reset. I'm supposed to tape this to the box. He said that'll cause the home office system to reengage and show the proper location."

"Yeah, well, I guess that sounds right."

"Okay, so I'll call you Thursday when I get to the hotel—should be between twelve and one."

"Don't forget my fifty bucks."

CHAPTER 58

Wednesday, June 14

It was 6:12 a.m. when Beverly spotted the first exit into Olathe, Kansas. She nudged her husband. "Wake up, honey, we're getting close."

Lee stirred and opened his eyes. "Getting close to what?"

"Olathe, where we change cars."

"Oh yeah, the Cracker Barrel. I see the sign," he said.

The east parking lot at the restaurant was filling up fast. Beverly found a spot and parked. "You see anyone around that looks FBIish?"

Lee stepped out of the car and stretched. "No, not yet."

"You sure this is the place?" Beverly asked.

"Yeah, honey, the right town, right exit, right restaurant, right parking lot. Our contact is probably on his way." He got back in the car. "I'll go in and get us some coffee while we're waiting." Just then there was a sharp rap on the driver's side window that startled them both.

Beverly jerked her head around and saw an older man wearing faded jeans and a dark blue University of Kansas T-shirt. She carefully lowered her window halfway. "Yes sir, can I help you?"

"Sorry, didn't mean to startle you." He paused. Beverly didn't say anything, nor did she lower her window further. The man pointed toward a car one row behind where Beverly had parked. "I could use some help. Got a flat tire and can't get the spare out. Arthritis—it's always worse in the morning."

Beverly turned to Lee. "You want to help him, and I'll get the coffee?"

"Sure. I can help and watch for the FBI at the same time." Lee got out of the car and followed the man to the rear of his five-year-old Mercury Marquise. The trunk was already open. Lee leaned in and began unfastening the spare.

"Lee Bethel?" the man asked.

Lee stood facing the old man. "Yes," he said, surprised.

"No need to get the spare. I'll pull my car next to yours, and you can unload the box into my trunk. You give me your keys, I'll give you mine, and we can be on our merry way."

"Okay, but who are you?"

"Just an old retired special agent who contracts from time to time with the agency to do low-risk operations like this one."

Beverly came out of the restaurant carrying their coffee, just in time to see her SUV leave the parking lot. Lee motioned to her. "The old man was our contact," he said.

"Yeah, I'd guessed that when I saw him drive away in my car."

"We've got some time; want to get breakfast?"

"I'm starved, but we need to make it quick. We're not

familiar with KC, and I'd like to get a look at the store before I actually drop the box off," she said.

"Bring the city map; we can study it while we're eating."

* * *

Lee watched his wife cross the busy intersection. Her mission had been danger-free, but nevertheless, he was happy to see his wife was safe. As she stepped up on the curb in front of the corner coffee shop where she'd left her husband 30 minutes earlier, she caught a glimpse of him through the window. She could see he was relieved. He stood as she neared his table. "Everything go as planned?" Lee whispered.

"Yeah, nothing to it. Now what?"

"You realize we've only had three hours sleep in the last twenty-eight?"

"Not really. Seems all I can think about is Lindsey and her family."

"Me too, but I'm beat. I don't think either of us should try to drive back until we get some rest," he said.

"Let's find a motel and get some sleep." Beverly was deep into a thought. She sat stirring her coffee, staring into the swirl of white cream and black coffee as it blended. She looked up. "Agent Miles was adamant about us going back to Oklahoma, wasn't he?"

"Sure, he wants us out of danger."

"Makes sense. We don't want to interfere, do we?"

"Of course not. Honey, we've done all we can do," he said, knowing his wife was already hatching a plan. "Look, let's not think about what we're going to do until we've rested."

"Right. In the meantime, why don't you call Miles, tell

him we've made the drop and that we're going to get some rest before we head back," she said.

"Okay, but, honey, I can read you like an open book. You've got something going on in that pretty head. Come on, what are you thinking?"

"Do you want to go back to Oklahoma?"

Lee could tell the remark was just that, a remark. It wasn't a real question and what usually followed—when Beverly behaved this way—was an about-face, doing something contrary to the original plan.

He said, "I'll put it this way. I don't want to interfere with the rescue efforts, but I've got all this adrenaline coursing through me. I want to do something, I just don't know what."

"Call Miles, let him know I've made the drop. Let's see what he says."

Beverly watched Lee's expression as he explained to Miles the drop had been made successfully. The reply on the other end of the conversation was short. Lee shut his phone. "Miles is in rescue mode, not much for talking."

"What'd he say?"

"We were right; he wants us out of town ASAP. He's willing to let us stay overnight and rest, trade vehicles, but he put the emphasis on going back to Oklahoma."

"He say anything about Heath?"

"They believe he entered the KC city limits between noon and one yesterday, but that's all."

CHAPTER 59

Wednesday, June 14, 8:07 a.m.

Earlier that same morning, Sheriff Stanton advised Bingham she was on her way to the Gray Ranch and would be there most of the day. "Anything going on at headquarters I should know about?"

"Few people gettin' kinda curious about Curt, lotsa rumors about why he killed himself. And some folks wondering what's going on at the Gray Ranch. Don't know how long we can keep tell'n 'em we're watch'n out for cattle thieves."

"I don't doubt it; I'm surprised it's taken this long. Anything else?"

"Just one."

"Well?"

"Mayor came in a few minutes ago."

"Yeah, what'd he want?"

"Wants to talk to you about our friend the ex-county commissioner."

"Probably wants me to chew you out for the rude way you treated the commissioner," Stanton said, laughing.

"That'd be my guess."

"Well, Deputy, just consider yourself chewed out."

"You want me to contact him and say you'll call him later?"

"Yeah, and leave me a note stuck to my phone so I don't forget. And Bingham."

"Still here, Sheriff."

"For right now I need you to keep a lid on the rumor mill. A lot has happened in the last eighteen hours you're not aware of, so keep the cattle thief story going. It's at least partially true. I'll be back later today and bring you and the others up to speed."

Stanton headed for the ranch, knowing the town was a pot ready to boil over. It wouldn't be long, she suspected, until some folks were putting two and two together and coming up with five, but her main objective now was to be a link between the Grays and the rescue efforts taking place in Kansas City. Having a granddaughter kidnapped was bad enough, but having to wade through the excruciatingly painful, yet necessary, law enforcement process only increased the emotional toll. Maybe she could help.

Three miles south of town, Stanton got a cell phone call. She pulled to the side of the road to answer. It was Jerry Webster. "Crys, can you talk?"

"Yeah, just headed to the Gray Ranch."

"How are they?"

"Mr. Gray took his wife in to see the doctor last night. Guess he gave her a sedative of some kind."

"Did they tell anyone about their granddaughter's disappearance?"

"No, just that she was distraught because of their hired hand's suicide."

"What are they going to do?"

"I talked to their son earlier; he said they'd probably go to Kansas City to be with his sister and family depending on how his mother was today."

"What are you going to do?"

"Thought I'd just lend moral support and try to interpret procedures, be a link, so to speak, between them and Miles."

"Great idea. I'm sure they'll appreciate it. The other reason I called was to fill you in on Holt."

"I'm listening."

"He reported back to his assigned work location in Baltimore late Monday. According to Johnson, and without her knowledge, he promptly put in for ten days of emergency leave. He said his mother was ill and her condition was grave."

"Anyone check his story out, Jerry?"

"No, Crys, personnel isn't in the business of checking to see if an agent's excuse is legit or not. You know that."

"Yeah, I know that, but his mother's condition, it's too coincidental."

"I asked you this before, and you've never given me a straight answer."

"What?"

"Besides being an asshole, to use your word, what's he done to incur your suspicion?"

"I haven't given you a straight answer because I just don't know; it's a gut feeling. I just feel like he's somehow mixed up in all this." Stanton paused, waiting for Webster to object or say something defensive, but nothing. "There, I've said it, and no, I don't have evidence."

"Okay, Crys. Hell, I trust your intuition as much as you do. I'll have someone follow up, see if his mom's sick and see exactly where he is. Good enough?"

"Yeah, and one other thing."

"Sure, Crys, whatever you want."

"Can you hurry?"

"Damn, Crys, I wish some of my agents were as ballsy."

She laughed. "That just comes from working with you all those years."

"Hey, Crys, before we hang up, there's another matter I'm having our Intel people look into." There was a short pause. "Crys, gotta go. The director is calling, but in a nutshell, they're checking Heath out for you. I'll call you later."

Webster didn't say good-bye; he just cut the conversation off, but that's what you do when the Director of the FBI calls. You certainly don't tell him you've got someone on the line and you'll call back later. Stanton was curious, though. She hadn't asked Webster about Heath, so why would he ask intelligence to run background on him? A bad guy's a bad guy—all law enforcement needed was probable cause to arrest. As for Heath, the only issue now was to locate him before something tragic happened to Lindsey.

* * *

Deputy Cox entered the time Sheriff Stanton arrived at the ranch in the watch log. He moved the lawn chair to the left, trying to stay in what little shade the scrubby cedar offered. It wasn't even nine and the temperature was already approaching 95 degrees. He pushed his straw hat back on his head and focused the binoculars on the rancher's dog chasing a jackrabbit across the pasture below the ridge he was perched on. The dog soon gave up, lapped at a small pool of stagnant water preserved somehow between rocks in an otherwise dry creek bed. She found a shady spot and sat down. Cox wasn't looking forward to another day watching buzzards circle and an occasional car coming in and out of the ranch.

Stanton spent the morning trying to help Mr. and Mrs. Gray understand law enforcement's search protocol. She talked with Agent Miles and the Kansas City detective in charge of Lindsey's rescue effort, passing the details along as they came in. Finally Helen said she was feeling stronger and wanted to be with her daughter. "Crys, you've done so much for us, but I can't sit here when I know Beth and Chuck need family support. We're going to Kansas City."

"I can't imagine how much stress you're under. Frankly if I were you, I'd want to be there, too." Stanton turned to Robert. "Are you going?"

"No, since we don't have any cowhands, I got to stay and look after the ranch."

"I'll stay in touch with Miles, and if something comes up I'll call you. In the meantime I'm going to pull my deputy off the ridge."

* * *

"Unit three, do you copy?"

Deputy Cox picked up the handheld radio and answered, "Ten-four."

"Unit three, meet me at the ranch house."

"Ten-four. Unit three clear." Cox folded the lawn chair and put it and the ice chest in the trunk, just in case he wouldn't be returning to his post. He hurried down the sloping ridgeline trail, trying to avoid the deep ruts made by years of cattle following the same path from one pasture to another. Cox drove up to the front of the ranch house where the sheriff was standing. "What's going on, Sheriff?"

"I'm relieving you from the Alpha One post. You can return to your normal routine."

"What about the Grays?"

"They're going to Kansas City. You might as well hear this from me so you'll get the true story and not the gossip version I'm sure is about to spread."

"We still ain't supposed to say anything, right?"

"Yes, Deputy. I'm telling all the deputies today, but you and the others are still duty bound not to talk about what I'm going to tell you."

Stanton explained to Cox that the Grays' granddaughter had been kidnapped. The only detail she didn't divulge was the treasure, and, of course, since there were still a number of loose ends yet to tie up, she didn't tell Cox she thought Curt Russell's suicide was actually murder.

CHAPTER 60

Thursday, June 15, 12:10 p.m.

Tobias Henry ignored his growling stomach. It was noon, and the first draft had to be on the editor's desk by 2:00 p.m. Lunch would come later. The original story shouldn't have taken more than a couple days, but new developments changed everything, developments that he couldn't share with his boss, a predicament he'd never expected. Tobias knew Thompson would eventually understand why the Paleo-Indian story was late, and why he'd forgotten to submit the *Transitions* column on time. In the meantime, though, he would just have to take his lumps. If Mr. Thompson and Judith were beginning to think him incompetent, that was a risk he had to take. In a few days they'd change their minds. Tobias knocked and stepped through the door. "Mr. Thompson."

The editor nodded, but was focused on something else. Tobias felt intimidated. Thompson was angry, and his manner clearly communicated that to the intern. "Mr.

Thompson, sorry this is late, it just took—"

Thompson looked up. "It just took what, Tobias? Work?!"

"I...I underestimated the time it would take to research it."

Thompson didn't appear to be listening. Tobias laid the draft on the editor's desk and exited the office feeling summarily dismissed. He left the building without saying anything to Judith and walked to the restaurant, his thoughts on Coronado's treasure. He expected the sheriff to call at anytime, giving him the okay to release the story, and he had to be ready. He had to be first. Tobias knew a story like this wouldn't just "break" in a publishing sense, it would explode. There were journalists, he was sure, who would kill for the opportunity to be the first to write this story. Regardless of what his boss thought of him right now, Tobias had to have his ducks in a row. The story could not be written after the sheriff called; it had to be written and ready to go immediately. He rushed back to the *Ledger* and to his desk, and there, lying on top of his laptop, was the article he'd just given the editor an hour earlier. The article was covered in red marks and not just the standard journalism correction squiggles. There were angry notes pointing out his general writing ineptitude. Thompson asked, in one note, what mail-order journalism school he was getting his education from. Tobias put the article aside and opened his laptop. He didn't look up, and he especially didn't glance in Thompson's direction. He clicked on My Documents, opened the one titled "Gray Ranch," and began to type.

The phone rang. "*Ledger*, Judith speaking." She listened and turned toward Tobias. He was looking at her over the top of the monitor, his usual cheery expression gone. "Yes, Sheriff, he's here. One moment please." She placed the call on hold. "Sheriff on line one, Tobias."

He glanced in the editor's direction; Thompson was watching him. "Sheriff, this is Tobias Henry."

The sheriff didn't sound like herself; something in her voice gave it an austere, ominous quality. "I know you aren't able to talk privately, so just listen. I'll do the talking, understand?"

"Yes, I understand."

"The Gray Ranch situation has taken a turn for the worse; it's a life-and-death matter."

An awkward silence followed. Tobias was unsure if the sheriff was expecting a response or if he should just keep still. He didn't have to wait long. "I want to make it perfectly clear that you are still obligated to remain quiet about what you know already as well as what I'm about to tell you."

"I understand, Sheriff."

Stanton kept the call short. Tobias hung up the phone slowly, the sheriff's last words echoing audibly. He had never understood just how praying for someone ever helped, but she'd asked him to; he could at least try.

Tobias sat staring at his laptop a full minute before he noticed that the editor was standing next to him.

"Was that the sheriff?" Thompson asked firmly.

"Yes sir."

"Well?!" He stood peering down over the top of his reading glasses, fingers flexing in a way that made Tobias think he was about to be grabbed or, worse, choked.

"Is there something I need to know about?"

"No sir. I'd just asked her about cattle thefts in the area, that's all."

Thompson reached up and slowly removed his glasses, a gesture Tobias was sure meant the editor didn't believe a word of what he was saying.

"That's all she said, you're sure?"

"Yes sir."

"Then tell me, why are your hands trembling?"

Tobias watched as Judith hurried out the front door, hoping to escape the inevitable scene that was about to occur. He searched for an exit, too, but there was no way out. His hands were trembling and sweating profusely as he crafted another lie. "I guess, sir, I was embarrassed by the draft. I'll do it over." He could tell Thompson wanted to say more but was trying to regain his composure. Instead of saying anything, the editor turned and left the building. Tobias was relieved. He closed his eyes and leaned back, taking deep breaths. He couldn't remember inhaling or exhaling over the last few minutes. The oxygen revived him, and he began to type.

* * *

Sheriff Stanton watched as Fred and Helen drove away from the ranch on their way to Kansas City. "Hope your dad's up to that long drive."

"You and me both. He's a tough old man, but you can only take so much. I'm more concerned about Mom; if something happens to Lindsey it'll kill her."

"Well, I gotta get back. Planning to meet with my deputies this afternoon. They need to know more."

"Gonna tell 'em about the gold?"

"No, not yet. First things first. Getting Lindsey back should be the only thing on everyone's mind right now. If one of my deputies spilled the beans concerning the gold, the town would be in an uproar, outta control. That's something I'd like to postpone as long as possible."

On her way back to town, Stanton tried to piece together the investigation of Russell's death. She wouldn't have the coroner's report for another few days, a key element in the matter. Until then, Stanton was sure of only three things: Curt didn't kill himself, she had two suspects, and the really big thing—no proof.

Stanton drove into her reserved space at the courthouse. She could see that the others had arrived for the briefing.

CHAPTER 61

Thursday, June 15, 7:00 a.m.

Lee woke up as the first narrow strands of sunlight beamed between the drawn drapes. Beverly was still asleep. He got out of bed, closed the bathroom door softly behind him, and pressed the button to start the coffeemaker. By the time he'd finished his routine, Beverly had already ordered room service breakfast. She'd just hung the phone up when he came out. "Who was that?" he asked.

"Called the Mail Box to see what time they opened."

"And?" he said, layering scrambled eggs and bacon between two pieces of wheat toast.

"Nine. We've got an hour."

"While you're doll'n up, I'll get us packed."

The Bethels had met the retired agent and traded vehicles the night before. They'd also decided to do some sleuthing on their own. Lee made it clear to Beverly that they would not interfere in any way with the search. Their intent was to observe only, and that from a safe distance.

Since they knew what the box looked like, it made sense they could identify it when the kidnapper carried it out of the store. Beverly just wanted to see what the guy looked like and maybe later, during his trial, she could be a key witness. Neither wanted the aggravation of appearing in court, but they wanted to do something, no matter how small, to help the Grays.

"Find a parking place here," Beverly said. "We've got a clear view of the store from anywhere along this street."

Lee paralleled into a spot a block away and turned the ignition off. Beverly pulled a small set of binoculars from the glove compartment and trained them on the store.

"Be careful with those!" Lee said. "The kidnapper could be anywhere around here, maybe watching us. If he thinks we're part of a stake-out he won't pick the box up."

"Yeah, you're right, and that's what concerns me." Beverly sighed.

"Having second thoughts?"

"I want to help, but what if we actually cause harm to Lindsey? I couldn't bear it."

"I had the same thought; this is police business. We know the FBI is doing everything they can to get her back alive. We just need to back off."

"Lee, let's get out of here now. The more we talk, the more I see my idea was a terrible mistake."

Lee started the engine and slowly pulled away from the curb. He turned to see if there were any cars coming. "Damn it, there's a string of slow-moving traffic a half mile long coming our way."

"Hold on," Beverly said.

"I am. Can't do anything but hold on until these cars get by."

"No, Lee, that's not what I mean. Look!"

"Look at what?"

"That tan car." She was pointing frantically toward the store. "The one with its trunk open."

"I see. What about it?"

"That guy just loaded our box in the trunk. He's getting in. Follow him!" she shouted.

"I can't—too many cars in my exit lane."

"We're in a SUV; intimidate someone!"

"Here we go." Lee accelerated, forcing a Mercedes to stop abruptly. "Which way?"

"Straight. Okay, now he's in the left-hand turn lane at the next light. Can you ease over into that lane?"

"Yeah, but we'll lose him at the light; it'll turn red before we get there."

"Maybe not."

The left-hand turn arrow flashed green, and the long line of cars began to inch forward. "Come on, come on, move!" Lee demanded angrily as he watched the light turn yellow. The truck in front of him sped through the yellow light. Beverly was straining against her seat restraints. "Go! Go!"

Lee maneuvered quickly around an oncoming car already in the center of the intersection, barely avoiding a head-on crash. "Don't look at the guy!" Beverly screamed. "Just drive! He's not a happy camper. He's gesturing."

"Yeah, wouldn't you?"

Beverly didn't answer; she was focused on the tan car a half block ahead. "He's about four cars in front of us."

"I can see. That's a late model Chevy Malibu just like the blue one Susan bought last year. Can you see the tag?"

"No, but he's got his right turn signal on. Looks like he's headed for the interstate."

"What interstate?"

"Seventy, he's taking seventy east."

They followed the Malibu until it drove into the parking lot of the Hilton hotel at the intersection of I-70 and I-435.

Lee parked on the upper tier of the well-landscaped lot between two rows of Bradford pear trees less than 50 yards from the hotel's front entrance. Beverly took the binoculars out again; this time Lee didn't object. "What's he doing?"

"Just sitting."

"Can you see the license plate?"

"Yeah, it's Kansas GMB four-two-six."

"Okay, got it. Did you see anyone follow us in?"

Beverly was searching the lot through the binoculars. "You mean FBI or cops?"

"Yeah."

"Nobody followed us in, and no one has come into the lot in the five minutes we've been here."

"FBI's relying on their tracking device. Electronics are so sophisticated now these guys can follow you by satellite. They can pinpoint your location within feet."

Beverly unfastened her seat belt and turned to her left. "The guy's out of his car and walking to the entrance. Lee, he's just a kid. Looks more like a senior high honor student than a bad guy."

"Guess they come in all sizes and shapes—"

Beverly interrupted. "He's coming back out. Now he's just standing under the canopy. Looks like he's waiting on someone." Just then a red Pontiac Grand Am pulled up. "He's getting in that red car. Here, take this tag number down," she said, trying to focus the binoculars on the moving vehicle.

"Should we follow the red car or stay here?" Lee asked.

"We think the treasure is in the trunk of the tan car. I'd say stay here and watch it."

"You know that might not even be the right box."

"I've been thinking about that ever since we took it upon ourselves to violate several traffic laws, not to mention the wrecks we almost caused," Beverly said.

"Think I'll call Agent Miles and do some fishing."

"Fishing?"

"Yeah, maybe he'll tell me if the right box has left the store yet." Lee had Miles' number on speed dial. The agent answered, his voice quivering and abrupt.

"Agent Miles, Lee Beth—"

Miles cut him off. "Yeah, Lee, got caller ID, what do you want?"

"We're still in town, wanted to know if there's anything we can do to help."

"No! I thought I made myself clear yesterday—you need to go home. Now, I need to go. We got a problem."

Lee knew by the sound of Miles' voice that something had gone wrong, and he suspected that to pursue it would only bring the wrath of the agent down on him hard, but he needed to know. "What kind of a problem?"

"Shit, Lee, don't you understand I'm trying to save a little girl's life? And the longer I chitchat with you, the less likely I am to accomplish that. Now, we've temporarily lost the box! I need to find it! I'm hanging up."

"Wait!" Lee shouted, but it was too late. Miles had disconnected.

"What was that all about? I could hear him shouting."

"They lost the box."

"Oh my god, how?"

"Don't know, but I'm gonna try and find out." Lee dialed the agent again, but there was no answer. He waited a few seconds and dialed again; still no answer. Lee tried twice more, and finally Miles answered. "Bethel!" he screamed. "Do you know what the penalty is for impeding an investigation?!"

"Please, Agent Miles, just give me thirty seconds."

"You've got fifteen, now talk!" Miles yelled.

"We think we saw the box loaded into a car at the

store." Lee hoped the three-second statement would buy him more time.

"You what?!" Miles yelled even louder.

"We saw a young man in his early twenties load the box in the trunk of a tan late model Malibu, and we followed him."

The yelling mellowed to an angry, but controlled voice. "You followed him where?"

"The parking lot of the Hilton hotel, junction of I-70 and I-435. The kid parked the Malibu, and fifteen minutes later a red Pontiac picked him up and they headed back west."

A long pause followed. Lee could hear Miles issuing orders to get someone to their location immediately.

"You didn't by any chance get tag numbers, did you?"

"Yes, here they are." Lee read the numbers off to Agent Miles.

The agent repeated the numbers back, and without thanking Lee, he said, "Listen to me very closely. I want you to stay right there. Do not move until my people are there, understand?"

"Yes. I understand."

"When the agent arrives, I want you to point the Malibu out to him and then I want you to get the hell out of town. You are on the very edge of being charged with a serious felony." Miles regained some of his composure. "Dr. Bethel, the FBI appreciates what you've done, and I know the Gray family will want to thank you as well, but it's time to let the professionals handle it from here. You do understand, Dr. Bethel, don't you?"

"Yes, Agent Miles, but I can't—"

"Son of a bitch!" Miles screamed. His composure evaporated like a raindrop on a July day in Phoenix. "Idiot! Wasn't I clear enough about the penalty?!"

"Yes, perfectly, but what I was saying before you interrupted is that a man has gotten into the Malibu and is driving away... Agent Miles...Agent Miles, do you hear me?" Lee looked at the phone display screen. "Oh damn, Beverly; tell me you have our battery charger in your purse." They looked anxiously at each other. She didn't have to say anything; the answer was in her eyes. "Lee, start the car!"

The Bethels were no longer sleuths on a mission to identify Lindsey's kidnapper. They'd become a reluctant and unprepared link to her rescue. Lee watched the tan Malibu back out of the parking space and head for the parking lot exit. Beverly adjusted the binoculars. "Follow him, Lee, before he gets away!"

"Just wanted to give him some space. Don't want to appear overly anxious."

"If you wait much longer, he'll be out of sight. He's turned onto the eastbound I-70 on-ramp."

Lee drove out of the lot and was on the interstate thirty seconds behind the Malibu. Traffic was thin and moving just over the posted freeway speed limit. Lee moved to the middle of the three-lane highway and eased by slower moving cars. "I think I'm beginning to fully understand the meaning of panic," he said.

Beverly lowered the binoculars. "What are you talking about?"

"I'll summarize." He paused long enough to maneuver back into the far right lane. "We're in pursuit of a kidnapper, the FBI has threatened us with felony obstruction charges, our cell phone is dead, neither one of us knows a thing about Kansas City, and a ten-year-old girl's life is at stake. Have I left anything out?"

"Yeah, look at the gas gauge," she said, pointing at the dashboard.

"Oh shit, Beverly, we're in the red. How far will it go when the needle hits red?"

"Don't know, I've never tested it. Hey!" Beverly shouted. "He's exiting; sign says I-470 south; now he's veering onto another highway."

"What highway? I don't see him anymore!"

"Just drive, I'll keep an eye on him. Road sign says Michael E. Webster Memorial Parkway. Now he's turning off the Parkway onto a side road. Get ready to exit right. Sign where he turned off says Blue Spring Lake."

Lee exited, coming to a stop sign at the bottom of the ramp. They could see the Malibu disappear around a curve not more than a few hundred yards ahead. "We're running out of main road. I don't think we should follow any closer. If he sees anyone behind him on that country road, he's sure to get suspicious."

"Agreed, but what do we do?" Beverly asked.

Lee pointed across the intersection at a dilapidated combination convenience store and bait shop. "I'm going to drop you off there. You can phone Miles. I'll drive slowly down this road and see if I can spot the Malibu."

"It's not much of a road, barely wide enough for two cars to pass. Be my guess it doesn't go far," she said, studying the area with the binoculars. "Be careful or else."

"Yeah, I know. Like you always say, if I get myself hurt you'll kill me. But, you have nothing to fear. I'm about as nervous as I want to be, and I don't mind admitting it."

"Me too. When you spot the car, get the hell out of there. I'll call Miles and he'll be here in minutes, and they can take over."

Lee stopped in front of the store and let Beverly out. She kissed his cheek and pointed an index finger in his face. "Don't do anything stupid!"

He nodded and drove away. She turned and entered the

store through a door propped open with a twelve-pack of cheap beer. There were no customers, no lights, and no clerk behind the counter. She looked anxiously around for a pay phone as the realization settled over her that Miles's number was locked inside their dead cell phone, which, unfortunately, was lying on the console of her SUV. "Shit, shit, shit, what else could go wrong," she mumbled aloud.

"Can I help you, miss?"

Beverly heard the raspy voice but couldn't tell where it came from. "Yes, please. Do you have a pay phone?" She didn't have Miles's number, but the local FBI office would be listed prominently in the phone book, and she could just call them.

"Nope. Goddamned teenage punks ripped the last three right off the outside wall."

Beverly whirled around, searching for a face to put the voice with. A man or woman, it wasn't clear and it didn't matter—she just needed help. "Could you tell me where the nearest pay phone is?!" She tried sounding calm.

"Nearest to my recollection would be that Wal-Mart store over on Westbrook. Sometimes it's a workin' and sometimes it ain't." The woman got to her feet, slowly coming into Beverly's view from behind the beer and pop display case, all three hundred pounds of her. A cigarette dangled from her toothless mouth. "Scuse my rudeness, missy, but the only cool place in the store is behind that frigerated case, so I jest sits there till a customer needs help." What was left of the woman's flaming red hair stuck to her face in sweat-soaked ringlets, exaggerating her already obese facial features. Both forearms were adorned with indistinguishable tattoos that had faded and stretched over time. Beverly was feeling desperate. She stifled the tears that were beginning to form. "Ma'am, I really need some help! My husband is just down this road a ways, and he could be in serious trouble."

The woman moved toward Beverly. "What kinda trouble?"

Beverly instinctively moved back. "I'm sorry; I don't have time to explain." The first tears ran down her cheeks. "I must call the authorities. Can you help me?"

"Sure, missy, want to use my cell?"

"Oh yes, please, I'll pay you. Do you have a phone book?"

The woman dug around under the checkout counter for what seemed like an eternity. "Here 'tis, five years old." She handed it to Beverly like a jeweler hands a customer an expensive necklace to examine.

Beverly grabbed the book and thumbed quickly through the first few pages until she located the local emergency numbers, including the FBI. The woman wiped the sweat off her phone with a soiled grease rag and handed it to Beverly. She punched in the number, and a male voice answered, "Federal Bureau of Investigation, how may I direct your call?"

"Agent Pete Miles and please hurry!"

"I'm sorry, ma'am, there's no one by that name in the Kansas City district."

"Yes, I know, I think he may be assigned to the Enid, Oklahoma office, but he's working a kidnapping case here in KC."

"I'll give you the number of that district office, and they'll be able to help you."

Beverly's patience had dissolved several minutes earlier. "Damn it, now listen very carefully!"

Before she could explain, the man cut her off, cautioning her that if she continued to be rude he'd terminate the call. "Now, ma'am, do you want the Enid number or not?"

Visions of her mother lying in her own blood flashed through her consciousness. She recalled phoning 911 and the agonizing hours in the hospital waiting room while her mother was in surgery. Later, after her mother was home and recuperating, all she could think about was finding the bastard who had assaulted her. Beverly didn't want justice, she didn't just want her mom's assailant imprisoned, she wanted revenge, and that's the way she was beginning to feel about the son of a bitch on the other end of the line.

"Yes, please, may I have the Enid number and your name as well?" she said as clearly as possible through clenched jaws.

"That number is 580-555-2000." He paused.

"Thank you, and your name please?"

"I'm sorry; we're not allowed to give out personal information over the phone." And with that the line went dead.

Beverly turned to the store clerk, who was now standing over the ice cream case scooping cool air from the freezer and patting her neck. With every upward swing of her arm, cigarette ashes and drops of sweat would cascade down over the ice cream bars. Beverly ignored the sight. "May I make a long-distance call with your cell phone?"

"Nope. Sorry. Don't have LD; don't know nobody outside the city."

Beverly handed the useless phone back to the clerk, sat down on a stool next to the counter, and stared at the clerk's cigarette ashes drifting like polluted snowflakes into the ice cream chest. She thought about buying a soft drink, something for quick energy, and then remembered her purse was in the SUV along with their dead phone. Beverly pointed out the north window. "Where does that road go?"

"The lake."

"The lake. And how far's that?"

"Not far."

Beverly knew it wouldn't pay to get angry with the clerk. The woman was obviously limited and probably struggling at the top end of her intellectual capabilities. "How far would you say it is, maybe a block, a mile, approximately?"

"Mile would be a fair guess."

"What's down there?"

"Boat ramp, four maybe five cabins, some playground equipment."

"Who owns the cabins?"

"No clue, missy." The woman tossed the cigarette butt on the floor and stepped on it with her bare foot. Beverly flinched. "You know, missy, if your husband's in trouble, maybe you should call the cops. They patrol this area."

The idea had already crossed her mind, but the kidnapper said no cops. Miles even indicated the perp seemed to know every step law enforcement took; she just couldn't take the risk yet. Beverly stood and walked to the door. She had a plan. It might very well be the wrong plan, but there were no other options she could think of.

CHAPTER 62

Thursday, June 15, 4:10 p.m.

The deputies and Trooper Crossland stood when Stanton walked into the conference room. The sheriff walked over to a large and very old portable chalkboard; she started to write but stopped and just stood with her back to the others for what seemed like a long time to the small audience. The deputies shifted nervously in their chairs, glancing at one another and not knowing what their boss's quiet hesitation was about. She finally turned, her expression affirming and certain. "Deputies and Trooper Crossland, I want all of you to know how much I've appreciated what you've done the last few days. You've worked under some odd circumstances without once questioning my intent; you have worked overtime, and, for the most part, I've kept you in the dark." Stanton looked at the eager faces waiting anxiously. "I've worked with different law enforcement agencies around the world, but I don't think I've ever worked with a finer group of people."

A collective sigh of appreciation hummed over the room. Heads nodded, affirming she'd done the right thing. It was just what everyone needed to hear.

Stanton turned back to the board. "A few days ago I explained the Grays were in danger." She wrote "Grays in danger" on the board. "I said they were in danger because of something found on the ranch." She wrote that on the board, too. The sheriff chronicled the incidents one by one that had occurred during the past week, including the kidnapping of Fred and Helen's granddaughter in Kansas City.

"Although I don't think anyone in Harper County is in danger any longer, we must remain vigilant. Don't let your guard down. Report anything out of the ordinary."

Deputy Bingham raised her hand.

"Maude." Stanton acknowledged her.

"When do you think you can let us know what was found on the ranch and who specifically is after it?"

"Soon, maybe tomorrow. Rest assured, the minute I feel comfortable passing that information on, I will. It's all very complicated right now." Stanton looked at her watch. "It's getting late. Sorry I kept you longer than usual. Any other questions?"

"One more thing," Bingham said. "It's not a question, but if you don't mind, I'd like to suggest we bow our heads and say a prayer for the Grays."

A few minutes later they all filed out of the conference room. Bingham stayed behind to erase the board, and Stanton returned to her office. She picked up the note reminding her to call the mayor. After four rings, Stanton started to hang up the phone. "Hello-hel-lo, Mayor speaking."

Stanton could tell he was out of breath. "Bill, this is Stanton. You okay?"

"Yes, just outta breath. Was down the hall when the phone rang."

"Sorry for not getting back to you sooner," she said.

"No problem, Sheriff, it's really not important, but when you're mayor you gotta try and please as many constituents as possible. You understand?"

"Yeah, Bill, I understand. So, who you trying to please?" Stanton already knew the answer.

"I hate even bringing this up, but—"

"Bill, hang on a second." She cut him off and put the call on hold. The reserve deputy answering phones stood in her doorway motioning frantically.

"There's an Agent Miles on line one, says it's an emergency!"

Stanton pressed the button taking the mayor off hold. "Sorry, Mr. Mayor, but I have an emergency. I'll call back." She pressed the blinking button. "Pete, it's Crys. What's going on?"

"Not good, Crys, our pursuit fell apart. I need to know if you've heard from the Bethels."

"No, nothing. What happened?"

"In a nutshell, whoever picked the ransom up fastened a jamming device to the box. Anyway, we lost the signal. Our people on the ground lost them in traffic. Hell, Crys, it was like a Chinese fire drill around here. Everyone doing something but what they were supposed to."

"How'd the Bethels get involved?"

"I don't really know for sure, but twenty minutes after we lost the perp Lee calls and tells me he's sitting in some hotel parking lot looking at the vehicle used in the pick-up. He tells me that a young man got out of the car and eventually into another."

"He give a description?"

"Yeah, right down to color, make, model, and tag

number. We tracked it down and questioned the two occupants."

"Who were they?"

"Two knuckleheaded college kids trying to make a buck by helping an unfortunate businessman that'd lost his training manuals."

"You buy their stories?"

"A hundred percent. They both cried like babies during interrogation; one even wet his pants."

"The Bethels, Pete, you were telling me about them."

"I told Lee to remain in the parking lot until we could get some agents over there. He said he couldn't 'cause someone had just gotten into the car and was driving away. That's when his phone went dead."

"Nothing since then?"

"Not a word. Now I got to go."

CHAPTER 63

Thursday, June 15, late afternoon

Without saying anything else to the store clerk, Beverly ran out the door and hurried east along the road in search of her husband. As she topped a small rise, she saw their car parked alongside the road less than a half mile ahead. She quickened her pace, staying to the right of the road and as close to the trees as possible for cover. Beverly could see as she approached the car that it was empty. The driver side window was down, the dead cell phone still on the console, and there were no keys in the ignition. She looked ahead toward the lake and spotted the cabins a short distance from where she was standing. Beverly searched the trees and thick underbrush on both sides of the road, looking for a sign of her husband. She listened but could only hear the wind that had picked up since she left the convenience store. Beverly looked back in the direction she'd just come, hoping to see a police car, but the road was deserted. She spotted what appeared to be a deer path leading into the forest and followed it, thinking if Lee had taken the path she could see his boot print. The path took a southerly direction for a short distance, then turned east toward the campground. The trees provided perfect seclusion, but if Lee had been on the trail before her, it was impossible to tell. There just wasn't enough light for her to see any distinguishing marks on the ground. The trail was circuitous; nevertheless, within a few minutes Beverly found herself at the edge of the tree line looking directly across the grassy clearing at the cabins. The pines were casting a long shadow as the sun began to set. She looked at her watch; in another hour it would be dark enough for her to cross the clearing without being seen. From her vantage point, Beverly could see the tail end of the tan Malibu under a carport attached to the second cabin. In front of the fourth cabin, the one nearest the lake, she could see a beige late-model mid-size car. The other two cabins were apparently unoccupied. Playground equipment sat idle and there were no fishermen on the pier; gulls circled the cove undisturbed, looking for their last meal of the day. Beverly leaned against a tree, thinking about her next move, worried it could very well be disastrous. She scanned the clearing perimeter again in search of her husband but nothing, no movement of any kind, only wind and gray clouds moving northeast.

Lee watched as his wife hurried across the road into the trees. He'd called out to her, but she didn't hear his muffled yell. He didn't want to shout louder for fear of attracting the attention of the person in the cabin. Lee was on the opposite side of the road and a good hundred yards from his wife when he first spotted her, and by the time he'd returned to their car, she had vanished into the woods. He followed the same deer path until he could see the clearing and his wife leaning against a large oak. As he approached, Lee stepped on a dry twig, and the snapping sound startled her. She swung around gasping, "Lee, you scared the life out of me. Where've you been?"

"The other side of the road keeping an eye on the cabin." He could see she was frightened. He took her in his arms until she stopped trembling. "Are you okay?" he asked.

"Not really. I've been worried about you, and...and thinking about what to do next."

"Hey, we're alright. We'll stay right here and wait. FBI should be arriving any minute." Lee had no sooner said that when the first lightning bolt struck close, followed by an ear-shattering clap of thunder. A soft rain began pelting the canopy of overhead tree leaves. Several storm downdrafts, one after the other, swayed trees and splintered large branches, causing them to drop dangerously close to the pair. The rain came in torrents, interfering with their attempts to communicate. Lee shouted, "Let's get back to the car. It's outta gas, but we can get out of the rain!" He took Beverly by the arm and pulled her along the muddy path. She was finally able to grab the collar of his shirt with her other arm and jerked his head around. "Stop!" she screamed over the din.

"What?"

Beverly pulled his face down close to hers. "The FBI isn't coming!"

The storm was loud, the forest floor was as dark as a moonless night, and conditions were chaotic. Lee was sure he'd misunderstood. He searched for her eyes but couldn't see them; all he could do was feel her face cupped in his hands. "What did you say?!"

"FBI's not coming. No one's coming. It's all up to us. Did you hear me?"

Lee heard but didn't believe it. "What do you mean?!"

"No time to explain. If Lindsey is in that cabin, it's up to us to save her," Beverly yelled at the top of her voice, and before Lee could say anything she asked, "Who's in the other car?"

"Don't know. It passed me minutes after I ran out of gas."

"Man or woman? Was there more than one?"

"Looked like a man. Why?"

"Maybe he's in cahoots with the kidnapper, we don't know. But if he's just renting a cabin for the weekend, he might have a cell phone we can use."

The storm front and most of the noise had moved on to the northeast, leaving in its wake a steady downpour that reduced visibility to less than a half block.

"Okay, sounds like our best chance. You stay here and I'll go check him out," Lee said.

"I'm going, too."

Before Lee could object, Beverly was already dashing across the clearing toward cabin four. They took shelter under the carport, and Beverly wrung the water out of her hair. "I don't think there's anyone here," Lee said, peeking through a window. "I don't see any lights."

"Did you look in the car when you ran by it?"

"Yeah, there wasn't anyone in it."

"Guess that answers my question about whether he's in on the kidnapping or not."

"That means we might have two bad guys to contend with," Lee said.

"Now what?"

"It's still raining hard; they won't see me prowling around. I'll see if I can spot Lindsey." Lee disappeared into the driving rain, and two minutes later he was back.

"What'd you see?"

"Lindsey. She's okay. Looks like she's playing a video game. I could see the back of a man standing in the kitchen doorway. He has a gun."

"What are we going to do?" Beverly asked.

"We have to lure him out."

"Then what?"

"Clobber him with an oar I found in his carport."

"How do we get him out of the cabin?"

"Been thinking about that. If we make noise, he'll just hunker down and won't come out."

"So how do we do it?"

"Set fire to his car."

"Yeah, that ought to get his attention, but what are you going to use to start it?"

Lee pulled a small metal waterproof match container from his rain-soaked pocket and pressed it into Beverly's hand. "Remember this?"

"Your birthday, eight or nine years ago."

"Ten to be exact, and I've never gone anywhere without it." Lee slipped the container back into his pocket. "When he sees the fire, he'll run to the carport. You'll be waiting on the other side of the house, and as soon as he gets to the car I'll hit him with the oar. You go in, get Lindsey, and run as fast as you can to the tree line."

"What about the Toyota driver, what if there are two guys?"

"There's no one else in that cabin."

"He could've been in the bathroom."

"No, I could see in there. There was just the one guy. Are you okay?"

"Yeah." Beverly put a shivering hand on her husband. "I was just running my Murphy's Law checklist."

"No matter what our strategy is, honey, you and I know it won't go as planned, but I don't see any other way of doing this."

Beverly pulled her husband close, holding him tight. He realized her embrace was much more than an expression of affection; the feeling was deeper, touching his soul in ways he'd never experienced before. They stood wrapped in each other's arms knowing something could go seriously wrong, unable to justify avoiding what had to be done.

"Beverly," he whispered loudly to be heard over the storm. "I love you!"

"Me too, I love you, too."

"Ready?"

"Ready."

"We'll run to the carport. Stay with me. I'll have to find something that'll burn, something that's dry. Then when I'm ready to start the fire, you can go around in back of the cabin and wait for him to come out."

"Okay, let's go!"

Although the spring storm made for miserable conditions, the driving rain worked in the Bethels' favor. It would be nearly impossible for anyone to see them make their dash to cabin two. They crouched next to the Malibu. "See anything that'll burn?" Lee asked.

"It's so dark, can't see much." She tapped Lee's shoulder. He turned and knelt close to her. "What?"

"There on the other side of the car, I see beach towels hanging there."

Lee took one off the makeshift clothesline. "Yeah, and they're dry. This'll work." He grabbed two more and rolled them into a tight ball.

"They'll burn too fast, need some wood to pile on top the towels."

"Right. I saw some fireplace kindling in the corner." Lee crawled on hands and knees to where he'd seen the wood; he unfolded one of the towels and laid pieces of the driest wood on it. A distant lightning bolt scattered a flickering glow inside the carport, and Lee ducked, hoping the kidnapper wasn't looking out the window at precisely the same time. He remained frozen against the Malibu's front tire for several seconds praying they hadn't been discovered. The only sound he heard was the thunderous pounding of the rain. Another bolt showered more light; Lee grabbed the towel and crawled around the car to where Beverly was. "This ought to do it. Matches, dry towels, and some dry wood," he said as he took her hand. "Let's get this over with. I'm beginning to hallucinate."

"What d'ya mean?"

"That last lightning bolt, I thought I saw…"

"What? What'd you see?"

"I swear I saw the light flash off someone's eyes."

"Where?"

"The corner, behind a stack of lawn chairs."

"I don't see anything."

"It's pitch-black in here. Wait till another lightning strike." Just then the sky erupted in light from strikes so far away, the thunder took several seconds to reach them.

"I didn't see anything."

"Neither did I." Lee sounded disappointed. "Like I said—hallucinations."

"Where're you going to set the fire?"

"Inside. There's more stuff inside the car that'll burn."

Lee had a lot on his mind, too much for any one person to keep organized. The immensity of what he was about to do was overwhelming. He was certain that saving Lindsey was the only right thing to do, but on the other hand, he didn't want any harm to come to his wife. The warring dilemma occupied every thought; reasoning was losing ground, giving way to a serious miscalculation. Lee bundled the wood and towels together, stuck the waterproof match container between his teeth, and pulled the Malibu's door handle.

CHAPTER 64

Thursday, June 15, 6:00 p.m.

Tobias closed his laptop and gathered his research together, shoving everything into his shoulder bag. It was nearly six and Judith was preparing to close. Neither had said a word to each other since Mr. Thompson had stormed out hours earlier. She didn't want to interfere with what Tobias was working on, and after seeing how angry the editor was, Judith knew the intern needed his time to regroup.

"See you tomorrow, Judith."

"Hey, Tobias, about today."

"Wasn't one of my better ones."

"Don't be too hard on yourself or Thompson. He's just passionate about the paper. Give him a chance, you'll learn a lot."

"Yeah, well, it's my fault." Tobias stopped himself from saying more; he was on the verge of justifying why he appeared incompetent. He knew Judith would understand if he shared what he knew about the Grays. He was confident she'd keep the secret, but then if he told her and violated the sheriff's trust, he could just add one more blemish to his decaying character.

Tobias planned to spend the night repairing the Paleo-Indian article, which would at least get him through the *Ledger's* front door in the morning and hopefully restore some of the credibility he'd lost with Thompson. Friday he'd hide somewhere and prepare a story outline about the treasure and the Gray's granddaughter. All he'd have to do, once Stanton gave him the okay, would be to fill in the details and drop it on Thompson's desk. He could hardly wait to see the editor's eyes.

CHAPTER 65

Thursday, June 15, 8:38 p.m.

L ee lifted the door handle and discovered it was locked, but that was now the least of their problems. "Shit!" Lee blurted, with the metal matchbox still between his teeth. He dropped the towel and grabbed Beverly by the wrist. The car alarm he'd activated started the horn honking and lights flashing. Lee pushed Beverly to the rear of the car, hoping they could hide before the kidnapper had time to check on the alarm, but it was too late. As they rounded the back of the Malibu, a figure emerged from the cabin door, pointing a gun directly at them. "Stop!" the man ordered.

The Bethels froze.

"Inside!" he demanded.

With hands in the air, Lee and Beverly made their way into the cabin. As they entered, the kidnapper shoved Lee hard to one side and grabbed Beverly by her wet hair, pulling her back against his chest. "Turn and face your wife slowly," the man said.

The first thing Lee saw was a gun pressing menacingly against her right temple. He couldn't see their captor's face; he'd squatted low behind Beverly, obscuring his identity. Lindsey was sitting just to his left, but he couldn't see her face.

"Are you alright, Lindsey?" Lee asked.

Before the little girl could say anything, the kidnapper yelled, "Shut up! From now on, I do the talking, you understand?!" He pressed the gun barrel hard against Beverly's head, and she winced from the pain.

"Yes, I understand. Please don't hurt—"

The man shrieked angrily, "Goddamn it, I said shut up! You utter another word without being asked, and I will hurt her!"

Lee nodded, a mixture of fear and helplessness coursing through his body like high-voltage electricity. He was on fire, ready to strike but shackled by the ambivalence of what would happen if he made the wrong choice. He stood motionless, waiting for the kidnapper's next command.

The man moved toward the open front door holding Beverly's hair firmly as he stepped back. "Face the west wall," he yelled.

Lee did as he was told.

Slowly he let go of her hair long enough to retrieve a pair of handcuffs from a small lamp table and tossed them on the floor near a bunk bed. He switched on a flashlight that had been lying next to the lamp. "See those cuffs?"

"Yes," Lee answered.

"I'm shutting the overhead light off. I'll point to the cuffs with the flashlight. You are to cuff yourself with one end and run the other through that metal brace on the bed. Cuff your wife to that end. Understand?"

"Yes." Lee got down on the floor and did as he was told.

The man shoved Beverly toward her husband and Lee cuffed her. Holding the gun to Beverly's head, the kidnapper checked the cuffs to make sure they were fastened tight. He moved back and sat down at the table next to Lindsey. "Now, who in the hell are you people?" he demanded, pointing the light directly in their faces.

"I'm Lee Bethel and this is Beverly, my wife. We're the ones who brought the ransom to Kansas City."

"Who else is with you? And don't lie to me."

"No one."

"That's bullshit!" He jumped out of his chair and stuck the gun barrel in Beverly's face. "What'd I say about lying to me?"

"It's the truth. Please, I'll explain." Lee told the man everything that had occurred since they began following the Malibu earlier that day.

The gunman shifted the beam of light from Lee to Lindsey's face. She'd drawn her knees up against her chest and was sobbing. "You people caused a hell of a lot more harm than good. I suppose you thought you'd be heroes, win a medal or something, but all you succeeded in doing was to cause more problems. I was prepared to leave the girl here, but not now. She's coming with me."

"Please don't take her! Leave her here, you've got the ransom," Beverly said, knowing what the kidnapper said might turn out to be true, knowing she wouldn't be able to live with herself if anything happened to the little girl.

The kidnapper wasn't listening; he grabbed Lindsey by the arm and pulled her toward the door. Another far-off lightning bolt flashed, illuminating the doorway; the kidnapper had his back to the door, struggling with Lindsey, who was flailing hysterically trying to break free from the abductor's grip. In the second it took for the glow of the lightning to appear and then vanish, Lee thought he saw the silhouette of a man on the front porch. Another hallucination or a miracle? He held his breath, praying for the latter and hoping his terrified mind wasn't conjuring up another illusion. Just then the overhead light went on, and there, standing on the threshold, was a man holding a gun pointed directly at the abductor's head.

"Let her go, and drop your gun!" the man shouted.

Instead of complying, the kidnapper pressed his gun against Lindsey's head. "I'm walking out this door with the girl. Try anything, and I mean anything, and I'll kill her!"

"Kill her and you're a dead man!"

The two stood facing each other for what seemed like an eternity to the Bethels. Lindsey had stopped struggling; her eyes were wide and full of terror.

"Here's a deal you can't refuse," the man said.

"Yeah?"

"Point your weapon at me and let the girl go. I'll allow you safe passage to your car."

"What makes you think I'd fall for that bullshit? As soon as I let her go, you'll shoot. You think I'm a fool, asshole?"

"No, I don't think you're a fool. As a matter of fact, you have the upper hand in this deal."

"So how can I be sure you won't shoot me?"

"All I want is the girl. I don't give a damn about you. If I shoot you, there'll be a second or two before you die, assuming my shot's lethal, and in those seconds you'll return fire, killing me, assuming your shot's lethal. And as much as I'd like to blow your head off, I don't want to die doing it." A long and tense pause followed. No one moved. Then the abductor began inching his way around the Formica breakfast table toward the door; his gun inches from Lindsey's head. "I'll agree, but one small modification."

"And what's that?" the man said, moving his body to barricade the exit.

"The girl's going with me to the porch. When I'm safely there, I'll let her go. She'll stand in front of the door until I drive away. If she moves or you step outside, I'll unload this clip in her direction, and you can be sure one of those rounds will be lethal. Understand?"

"Yes, I understand."

"Good, now put your cell phone in that sack. Get theirs, too." He nodded toward the Bethels.

"We don't have ours with us. It's in our car back up the road, has a dead battery."

"Yeah, I remember your story. Thank God for dead batteries, right?" The kidnapper sneered. "Now your car keys." The man put his keys in the bag. "Hand the bag to the girl." Lindsey's trembling hand reached out and took the bag. Wrapping his arm tightly around Lindsey's neck, the kidnapper moved to the porch and released her slowly. She stood perfectly still, not even blinking, staring straight ahead into the eyes of the man inside the cabin who may have just saved her life. Lindsey watched for a signal from her liberator, and he was waiting to hear the sound of the kidnapper's car driving away. Nearly a minute passed; then everyone heard a thud—like a car door slamming—then another thud. No one moved, waiting to hear the engine start, but nothing.

CHAPTER 66

Thursday, June 15, 9:06 p.m.

Agent Miles paced back and forth in the makeshift command center, waiting to hear from anyone about Lindsey. He'd given up on a well-defined rescue strategy in favor of luck. Nothing had gone his way, and running down leads seemed to be going nowhere fast. No one had heard from the Bethels, and the family hadn't received the promised call from the kidnapper telling them where to find Lindsey, a call he doubted would ever come, but there was always hope.

"Agent Miles, you have a call on line two from Sheriff Stanton."

He hurried over to the desk and picked up the phone. "Heard anything from the Bethels?" he asked.

"No. That's why I called you. Obviously you haven't, either."

"Not a word from anybody. We're tracking down leads, but coming up with nothing."

"I've got a theory, Pete."

"All due respect, Crys, theories won't get the girl back."

"Yes, I know, but listen to me. Okay?"

"Nothing else to do." There was frustration in the agent's voice, but deeper still was the unmistakable tone of sadness.

"I know you don't have time to listen to details, so I'll be brief. Pete, think deep cover."

"Okay. I'm thinking deep cover, now what?" He sounded more irritated than eager to hear any more of Stanton's theory.

"In order for the joint task force to have the kind of evidence needed to bust the ICO, there had to be a person or persons on the inside, don't you agree?"

"Of course, Crys, tell me something I don't know."

"I believe the Oklahoma piece of the ICO sting operation wasn't considered high priority—Webster even admitted that in a roundabout way."

"So?"

"Think about it, Pete. Very few investigative resources were provided on this end, and that left us vulnerable. You weren't even informed a fellow agent was in your district working a case right under your nose."

"Crys, you and I both know that's not unusual."

"Maybe. If that was the only thing concerning me, I'd say it wasn't a critical point, but there's more. According to Fred Gray, there were signs of an intruder around the cave where the treasure was found. Boot prints and ATV tread marks all over the place. My theory is Curt Russell saw the trespasser, and that's what got him killed."

"The evidence points to Heath, that's obvious."

"No, it doesn't, and here's why. The only nearby towns that sell and rent ATVs are Enid, Woodward, and Seiling. I had Bingham call all three dealerships and inquire about rentals for the week preceding June fifth, the day Fred took the first chest out of the cave."

"And?"

"At ten a.m. on June second, an ATV and trailer were rented from the Woodward dealership and returned the next morning. According to the dealer's records, the man's name was Cliff Grissom, a geological surveyor for an exploration company out of Midland, Texas."

"I suppose you've already checked Mr. Grissom out?"

"Bingham called every surveying company in Midland and Odessa, but no one had heard of Grissom."

"Prints?"

"Can't get 'em; the ATV's been rented twice since then. Pete, the point I want to make is Otis Thorpe, AKA Heath, was somewhere on the ranch between the hours of noon and five that day. So we know he wasn't the one who rented the ATV."

"All that tells me is Heath had an accomplice. What you've got, Crys, is still just speculation, nothing to hang your hat on."

"You may be right; on the other hand, if I'm right you could be wasting your time."

"Spell it out, Crys. Just what are you thinking?"

"I think Agent Holt has made a deal with the devil!" A long silent pause followed. Stanton wasn't sure Miles was still on the line. There was no breathing or any other background noises for that matter. "Pete, you still there?"

"Yeah, Crys." His response was noticeably agitated. "What do you suggest we do with this information, Sheriff?"

Stanton could hear the angry sarcasm in the agent's question. She brushed off the impulse to justify her remark in favor of getting her point across as quickly as possible.

"If I were you I'd put all the resources you can muster on tracking down Agent Holt."

"And what if you're wrong?"

"Then I'm wrong and the consequences are tragic."

"That could be the mother of all understatements."

"What if I'm right?" she asked calmly.

"Tell me more about this deep-cover theory. I suppose you're going to tell me Dr. Bethel is some top-secret, undercover operative, or better yet, maybe his wife." His voice was now more placating than sarcastic, but nonetheless troubled.

"It's more speculation, Pete, bear with me—" As she started to explain, Stanton heard several cell phones ringing in the background; there was some kind of verbal commotion she was unable to make sense of.

"Crys, I gotta go. Something about Lindsey coming in!" The line went dead.

CHAPTER 67

Thursday, June 15, 9:22 p.m.

Lee maneuvered around on the floor to get a better look at the new face. The man stood pointing the gun toward the ceiling, his finger still on the trigger waiting.

"What do you think's happening?" Lee whispered.

The man shook his head, but didn't say anything.

"Who are you?" Lee asked.

Beverly tugged the arm she shared the handcuff with. "Shhh!" She frowned.

The tense situation was taking its toll on Lindsey. She hadn't moved, just as the kidnapper instructed, but the combination of fear and the cool, damp breeze left over from the storm was enough to cause her body to shake.

An uneasy quiet settled in, and frogs began their ritualistic post-storm croaking, but no sound of an engine starting. Beverly looked toward the door to see if she could get a glimpse of Lindsey, but the angle wasn't right. Instead she saw a shadow move between the illumination cast by the security lights and the cabin doorway. She feared the kidnapper had returned.

Relief came from an unexpected source. "Missy?! Hey, missy?! You in there?"

Beverly recognized the raspy voice immediately. "Yes, I'm in here."

At the same time, Lindsey turned her head slowly to see who was standing just to the right directly between her and the kidnapper. A very large woman came swaying from side to side toward her; for some reason, Lindsey's fear began to ebb. She didn't know why she felt safe—she just did.

The man inside the cabin maintained his defensive posture, lowering his gun slightly, making sure it wasn't pointed at Lindsey. The woman stepped through the cabin door holding Lindsey under her right arm and carrying an oar in her left hand.

"What the hell's goin' on in here?" the woman demanded.

"Did you see anyone out there?" the man insisted with his weapon still pointing directly at her head.

She either didn't notice the 9 millimeter or didn't give a damn. "Oh hell, yeah. Bastard came running at me with a gun."

"What'd you do?"

"Knocked the holy shit outta him with this oar." She paused, staring directly at the barrel of the gun pointed at her. "Kinda like I'm gonna do wit' you if ya don't put that down."

He holstered the weapon. "Who are you?"

"She's from the convenience store, she's okay," Beverly said. "I'm sorry I don't remember your name, but thank god you're here. The little girl, her name's Lindsey; she was kidnapped by the man you hit."

"What about the kidnapper?" Lee asked. "Is he unconscious?"

"Hell, I dunno, may be dead. Don't take kindly to some shit-head stickin' a gun in my face." She realized that Lindsey was still huddled close to her crying. "Miss Lindsey, evertings gonna be okay. Don't you pay no 'tention to my foul mouth—jest an old woman that don't know no better."

Lindsey wrapped her arms as far around the woman's waist as she could and sobbed.

"Ma'am, please tell us your name?" Beverly asked as tears of relief dropped, blending into her already soaked blouse.

"Mary Logsten. That's my maiden name. Was Mary Johnson, but divorced that son-of-a-bitch husband. 'Bout the tenth time he came home drunk and lit in ta me, I busted him up pretty bad. Called the cops, and they found meth in the saddlebags of his Harley. He's doin' eight to fifteen in Leavenworth for transport'n the meth from Kansas City, Kansas to Kansas City, Missouri."

The man stuck out his hand. "Mary, we are glad you came along. You may have saved a life and captured a kidnapper all at the same time. Now I'm going outside to check on the bad guy and get the keys to the cuffs." He was back in a short time, dragging a bloodied and unconscious kidnapper behind him. After freeing the Bethels, he cuffed Mary's groaning captive.

Beverly got up off the floor and found a blanket to wrap Lindsey in. "We need to get her medical attention before we do anything else," she said.

The man found his cell phone in the bag with everyone's keys and tossed it to her.

"Mary, do you know the finding address of this campground?"

"Tell 'em Blue Spring Lake road off Webster Memorial Parkway."

Beverly called 911. "Ambulance is on the way," she announced. "Lee, do you remember Agent Miles' cell number?"

"Yeah." He repeated the number as Beverly punched it in.

Everyone listened as Beverly explained that Lindsey was physically alright and that the ambulance was on its way. She repeated the location directions twice, closed the phone, and handed it back to the only unidentified person in the room. "Miles said they'd be here in fifteen minutes."

The man handed the cuff key to Lee. "That's my exit cue."

"What?!" Lee said.

"Gotta go and can't explain."

"But your name, I don't know your name. You saved us—"

The man held his hand up. "I really don't have time, please. Just one favor."

"Sure, anything."

"Tell the Grays I'm sorry about Curt. He was a nice guy, and I really enjoyed working with him. Tell the sheriff Curt's death wasn't suicide." He pointed at the man on the floor. "Tell her the murderer was captured by Mary Logsten."

"You're Heath, aren't you?"

The man hurried through the door. Lee and Beverly watched him run across the clearing, get into the Toyota, and disappear down the lake road. The Bethels turned back to Lindsey, Mary's comforting arms still around her. She'd stopped crying.

"Mary, what prompted you to come down here?" Beverly sat down on the bunk bed next to Lindsey.

"You was actin' strange, missy, you weren't makin no sense. Said your husband was in trouble, and I heard on the radio a storm was brewin' so I locked up and drove down here. Figured you might need some help."

"Well, Mary, you figured right. I don't know how to thank you."

The ambulance arrived first. By the time the paramedics were inside the cabin, an armored S.W.A.T. vehicle, followed by local police, sheriff deputies, and finally two unmarked cars filled with FBI agents surrounded the cabin.

S.W.A.T. personnel entered first, ordering everyone to lie face down on the floor. Mary was the only person reluctant to follow orders. Police yelled commands, but Mary simply raised her hands. "I can't, got arthritis in my knees. If I do I won't be able ta get up. So shoot me or shut up."

Lindsey was lying on the floor between the paramedics. She sprang to her feet and dashed over to Mary, crying, "Please don't shoot her, she saved my life!"

The S.W.A.T. commander motioned for the team to lower their weapons. He stepped outside and gave the all-clear signal. Agent Miles hurried in. "Is everyone alright?"

"Everyone's fine," Lee said.

Miles nervously fumbled with his cell phone; with shaking hands he called Stanton. "Crys, this is Miles. We have Lindsey. She's safe and on her way to the hospital. Everyone else is okay!"

"Thank God, thank God! Have you notified Lindsey's family?"

"No, you've been the lead law-enforcement officer on this since the beginning. You should do it."

"Are you sure? You're the one that rescued her."

"Oh no, Crys, I'm not. Who the hero really is may take

some time to determine, but one thing's for sure, it wasn't me. Now, please call the family."

"My pleasure." The sheriff reviewed the facts that had just been passed on to her from Miles. She'd asked him to repeat the information twice to make sure she could relay them accurately. Crys took a moment to regain her composure; it was 10:21 p.m. She took several deep breaths and called the Gorman residence in Kansas City. A familiar voice answered.

"Fred, this is Crys Stanton, and I have wonderful news!"

CHAPTER 68

Thursday, June 15, 11:40 p.m.

Tobias pulled out his lap drawer and fished around looking for his eyedrops. He squeezed the solution into each eye and leaned back, allowing the moisture to soothe the burning. It was late and he hadn't taken a break, but the Paleo-Indian article rewrite was just about finished and he wasn't about to stop now. He positioned his fingers above the keyboard and began to type, just as his cell phone rang.

"Tobias, this is Sheriff Stanton. Sorry for the late call but thought you should know."

"Know what?" He grabbed a pen and notepad.

"Good news. Lindsey Gorman, the Grays' granddaughter, has been rescued, and she's in good shape."

"Thank God! Where? How?"

"First things first. The reason I'm calling so late is that I suspect bright and early tomorrow morning, the media will be all over this story. Most likely they'll focus on the kidnapping and rescue."

"Yeah, then they'll start pushing for the story behind the story. That's how I've been instructed anyway."

"That's my point; the family is going into seclusion for the next few days. They know that the story is going to get out one way or another, and they'd prefer you'd write it. Can you do that?"

"As a matter of fact, I was going to do the outline tonight."

"Good. Got your pencil ready?"

"Always."

Stanton explained what she knew about the rescue, and that Lindsey was being hospitalized overnight for observation. "The family just arrived at the hospital and is reuniting with Lindsey now. The kidnapper was captured and sustained some serious injuries in the process of being subdued; he's been hospitalized, too."

"Do they have the kidnapper's name yet? Was it that Heath fella?"

"Should have that within the hour. One last thing, Tobias."

"What's that, sheriff?"

"When the story breaks, I'm going to get too many phone calls as it is, so when writing the article, say your info came from an unnamed family spokesperson. That way when the newshounds call, I can sidestep questions I don't want to answer."

"Is it alright if I tell Mr. Thompson who the unnamed person is? If I don't, he'll never believe any of this."

"Sure, just ask him to keep my name out of any conversations he has with the media."

Tobias finished correcting the original article and laid it aside. According to the time display on his computer screen, it was 12:53 a.m. He had just seven hours to get the article of a lifetime written and on his editor's desk. He looked over the ten pages of handwritten notes he'd taken in the last three days and began to type.

CHAPTER 69

Friday, June 16, 1:20 a.m.

C rys Stanton switched her clock alarm to the off position and settled back in a stack of pillows with the book she hadn't opened in several days. By the third page, she couldn't keep her eyes open; she was feeling relaxed for the first time in a week. She marked her page, laid the book on the nightstand, and turned out the light.

"I can't believe this!" Crys mumbled angrily, tossing clothes around the room searching for her ringing cell phone. "Hello!" she yelled.

"You're not in bed, are you?" It was Pete Miles.

"No, of course not. What now?"

Miles heard the sarcasm, but he knew Stanton would want to hear what he'd found out no matter what time of day or night it was. "I called Webster to tell him about Lindsey and that the suspect was in custody."

"And?"

"He was happy. He said the task force had served the

warrants and made nineteen arrests."

"Anyone hurt?"

"No. Suspects are in isolation and, as usual, demanding lawyers."

"Yeah, well, you and I both know the only thing they're going to get is an all-expense paid trip to never-never-land."

"A well-deserved vacation I'm sure. Anyway, what I really called you about is to tell you who the kidnapper is."

"Holt?"

"Yup, Holt. How'd you figure it out?"

"Criminal profiling one-oh-one. He came across as insincere; mad at the world, a little narcissistic, and very shallow. He's been divorced twice, and he likes to work alone. Holt tries to act like a good guy, but that's all it is, an act. There's not a genuine bone in his body. Bet there's a list of character flaws inside that sealed envelope in his personnel file. I'm surprised he made it through the initial psych evals."

"Doesn't say much about the FBI's employee screening process, does it?"

"Psychopathic personalities sneak into all professions. That's the skill they develop along the way."

"What about Heath?"

"I was trying to tell you earlier. Remember? You cut me off, for good reason, of course," Stanton reminded him.

"You wanted me to think deep cover."

"Right. My guess is Heath has spent most of his career as a deep-cover operative for one of the agencies involved in the ICO sting operation."

"If you're right, we'll never know."

"No, we won't. Those people are a different breed. They usually don't have family, and marriages, should they dare, don't last. Most successful agents spend their entire careers being someone else. I couldn't do that."

"Hey, Crys, it's late, just wanted to pass the culprit's name on. Get some sleep. I'll call you later."

"Thanks. You get some rest, too."

* * *

The family arrived at the hospital minutes after the ambulance brought Lindsey in. A steady stream of physicians and nurses moved efficiently in and out of her emergency room cubicle. High-ranking officials from the FBI, Kansas City police, and the sheriff's department gathered in a small waiting room and were sharing information concerning the individual parts they played in the rescue.

Lindsey was finally moved to a private hospital room. The physicians had determined there were no signs of physical or sexual abuse, but they wanted the entire family to visit with the psychiatrist before Lindsey could be discharged later that afternoon. Law enforcement agreed to let her rest a few days before asking for a statement.

Beth stood next to the bed stroking Lindsey's hair as she slept. Fred put his arm around his daughter, neither able to stem the flow of tears. "I'm going to take your mother back to the house so she can rest," he whispered.

Beth nodded. A nurse offered Helen a wheelchair so she wouldn't have to walk the distance from Lindsey's room to the parking lot. "Yes, thank you, that'll help." She smiled.

* * *

Lee, Beverly, and Mary Logsten spent the better part of the night answering questions. Stenos from the FBI and the police department took notes and typed out statements on laptops. Crime scene technicians swarmed the cabin collecting evidence, and at 5:00 a.m. the lead forensic investigator handed Agent Miles a document. "If you'll sign these two forms, we'll be on our way."

Miles looked them over and signed each one. "I want copies before you leave here, and I want your signature on both my copies."

The investigator nodded, and directed the steno to make another set. He signed them and handed the copies to Miles. After the remaining authorities left the cabin, Agent Miles sat down at the table. Lee, Beverly, and Mary sat wrapped in insulated blankets and wearing dry scrubs left by the ambulance crew. "Are you three alright?" Miles asked.

"Just tired," Lee said. "Finally dry and warm," He added.

Beverly and Mary nodded. Miles handed the two forms he'd just signed to Lee. "When you get back to the ranch, have Robert put this in a safe place."

Lee looked at it. "An inventory of the treasure?"

"Yes. The FBI is confiscating the treasure for evidence. No telling when they'll get it back. I checked it out myself; everything's there. Tell Robert to make sure it's all accounted for when it's returned."

"Will do. Now, if you don't mind, we need to get gas for our car and find a room."

"No, I don't mind. I'll help you get the gas, but before you go I must tell you." Miles leaned forward and ran both hands across the top of his burred head. "Dr. and Mrs. Bethel, I don't want to make a big deal of this, but you do understand if this situation would've turned out different and Lindsey was somehow harmed, you two would be facing charges." He paused, watching for an expression assuring him they recognized the importance of what he was saying. All he saw were the blank stares of two very exhausted people. "On the other hand, if it hadn't been for the three of you, I don't think we'd have Lindsey back safe." The blank stares remained, but they smiled, more for gratuitous purposes than genuine appreciation for the compliment. "Can I buy you breakfast?" Miles offered, realizing that talking had run its productive course.

"That would be great," Beverly said.

CHAPTER 70

Friday, June 16, 7:45 a.m.

Tobias arrived early, hoping the editor would be at his desk. Time was critical; if corrections needed to be made, they'd have to be done early to beat the printing deadline. The building was unlocked, and a light was on in Thompson's office, but he wasn't there. The intern laid both articles on the editor's desk with the corrected Paleo-Indian article on top and returned to his desk. A few minutes later, Thompson emerged from the bathroom and went straight to his office. Tobias watched as he moved the articles to one side of his desk and began reviewing paperwork Judith had left in his in-box the day before. Finally Thompson picked up the first article and read it. He rose from his desk and made his way around tables and stacks of old newspapers to the back of the building where Tobias sat.

"Much better. I've made a change here and there, but for the most part it's ready to publish." Thompson tossed the article on the intern's laptop and walked away.

"Mr. Thompson."

The editor kept walking toward his office. "What?"

"Have you had a chance to read the other article?"

Thompson seemed to ignore the question; he walked into his office, picked up his briefcase, and headed toward the front door.

"Sir."

"No! I haven't had time to read it," he barked. "I'll read it this weekend," Thompson said, pushing the front door open and stepping out of the building.

Tobias's heart pounded; he knew Thompson had to be stopped. "Mr. Thompson!"

The editor stuck his head back inside. "Mr. Henry, another word out of you and you're history. I'm running late and don't have time to play nursemaid to some wannabe journalist."

"Wait!" Tobias slalomed through the building to the editor's desk, grabbing the article and rushing out the front door just as Thompson was getting into his car. "Just read the headline, then fire me. I'll clean out my desk and be out of your hair in five minutes."

Thompson took the article, folded back the blank cover sheet, and read aloud. "LOCAL RANCHER'S GRANDDAUGHTER KIDNAPPED *Coronado's Gold Demanded as Ransom.*" He turned to the first page, then the second. Two minutes later he'd read the entire article. Thompson looked up at the intern standing next to the open car door. "If one word of this is inaccurate in the slightest way, I'll devote my life to making sure you never write another word as a journalist! Now, who is your unnamed source?"

"Sheriff Stanton."

"Follow me." Thompson got out of his car and went

back inside to his office. He didn't offer Tobias a chair. The editor picked up the phone and called the sheriff. "Sheriff, this is Dan Thompson at the *Ledger*. Got a couple questions." Five minutes later, he hung up the phone and looked at Tobias. "Is Judith in yet?"

"Yes sir, just came in."

"Get her and tell her to bring her pad. She'll be taking notes."

"Yes sir."

Judith hurried into Thompson's office followed by Tobias. "What's going on, Dan?"

"Sorry, I don't have time to explain the story. We've got too much work to do and not much time to do it."

"What do you want me to do?"

"I'm going to make some minor changes to this article, and then I want you to take it to the printer in Woodward. I've just talked to him, and he said if we could get it there by noon it'd be ready for evening distribution. Stay at the printers until it's done; bring two thousand copies back with you. You can read it while you wait. While I'm proofreading, I want you and Tobias to prepare ads and other area news, some state and national stuff to complete the paper for this special addition."

Judith left the office and began pulling articles together.

"Tobias, I want you to write a story synopsis, no more than four hundred words. Cite the *Ledger* as the source and your name as the reporter. Have it to me by three for review, and at four you will e-mail it to all the major news outlets." He paused, thinking about the ramifications of such a story hitting world news. Thompson peered over his reading glasses at Tobias. "Do you have any idea what it's going to be like around here later this afternoon?"

"No sir, no clue."

"Well, young man, we're about to find out."

THE MARGIN

Judith left for the printer at 11:30 a.m. with the corrected article she still hadn't had time to read. The editor made two phone calls and left the building a few minutes behind Judith. "Tobias, I'm having lunch with the mayor and Sheriff Stanton." He looked at his watch. "I should be back by two." Thompson hurried out the front door and down the street toward the café. The sheriff was already there and had found a table that afforded some privacy in a room generally reserved for service club meetings. The mayor arrived, making his way slowly through the main dining area, shaking hands and chitchatting with the lunch crowd. Thompson walked out to where the mayor was engaged in a discussion about subsidized farming and interrupted. "Mr. Mayor, the sheriff and I are waiting."

The three sat down and ordered; as the waitress turned to leave, Stanton asked her to close the door.

Bill Irvine was his usual cheerful self, totally unaware of what had taken place in his hometown. "You two look like you've just seen a ghost. What's going on?"

"No, Mr. Mayor, what you see on my face is apprehension," Stanton said.

"About what?" The mayor's perpetual ear-to-ear grin faded.

Thompson held up a copy of Tobias's article. "About what we're going to do when this hits the national news at six tonight." He handed it to the mayor.

The waitress brought their meals; Irvine's grew cold while he read. He finally laid the article on the table. "Is this a joke?!"

Stanton shook her head. "Not at all."

"How could all this happen without me knowing about it?"

"Don't feel too bad. I just found out this morning myself. My own intern knew what was going on but didn't share a word."

"At my direction," Stanton said. "The success of the rescue operation and the breakup of the ICO depended on secrecy. Neither of you had a need to know; it would've been counterproductive."

The mayor's face took on a crimson glow as his friendliness gave way to anger. "And who do you think you are, deciding who had a need to know and what would be or would not be counterproductive?"

Stanton had dealt with political territoriality before; it was just one of the consequences of choosing law enforcement as a career. Politicians and bureaucrats knew their strength resulted from the information they possessed, and not to be privy to that power source made them look weak. "Mr. Mayor, it's not that I don't want to debate the issue with you, but this isn't the time or the place. I suggest we devote what little time we have to how we'll manage the media and spectators the next few days."

"You're right, Sheriff. It's my guess we'll have satellite trucks from all the major networks and no telling how many curiosity seekers," Thompson said, hoping the mayor would cool off. He knew Stanton would make short work of the politician, and in the process, the mayor would embarrass himself, adding insult to his already injured ego. "I'll distribute a special edition containing this article late this afternoon. We're also releasing a synopsis of the story to the networks."

"What will happen then?" Irvine asked, his normal color returning.

"Your office, mine and the sheriff's will be inundated with calls."

"What do we tell people?"

"I've had some experience with this kind of media attention." The sheriff turned to face the mayor, a gesture she hoped would make him feel important. "We should plan a news conference for sometime tomorrow. When someone calls for details, just refer them to the news conference."

"Who should preside over the conference?" the mayor asked.

"You. Dan and I will assist. Maybe Robert can address questions about Lindsey."

The mayor had recovered from his momentary lapse of common sense. "I need to alert the hospital and the fire chief."

"Don't forget service providers. They'll want to stock up on groceries, gas, and the Perc will need extra supplies," Dan said just as the waitress came in to refill their water glasses. "Is Kathryn here today?"

"Yeah, she's in the office."

"Ask her to join us please."

"What about traffic control?" Dan turned to the sheriff.

"Each sheriff from surrounding counties will send a deputy if we request. OHP will reassign three troopers; they'll operate around the clock for the next four days. That might be overkill, but I'd rather have too many than not enough." Stanton stood and tossed a two-dollar tip on the table. "I'll go put some notes together for the news conference. Let's meet an hour before so we can compare what we're going to say."

Irvine nodded, and a partial smile returned at the thought of being on national news. "I'll hang around and tell Kathryn she's about to get busy."

* * *

Thompson sat at his desk trying to imagine what the next few days would be like and how notoriety would affect the town. Some good, some bad, he thought as he watched Judith rush through the front door with the first of 20 tightly bound stacks of the special edition. He looked at his watch and stepped out of his office looking for the intern. Tobias stood when he saw the editor approaching.

"Got the corrections made?" Thompson asked.

"Just finished."

"It's three forty-five. Send it!"

The intern looked the e-mail over one more time; then he hit send. "It's done. Now what?"

"Help Judith unload the papers. I have three high schoolers coming to distribute them house to house. You take one stack to the Perc, grab yourself something to eat, and get back here. We're going to be on the phones until midnight." Thompson walked back to his office, flipped off the overhead light, slumped into his chair, and leaned back. The ring of his desk phone startled him awake. He looked around hoping Judith or Tobias would answer, but they weren't in the building. Dan answered, "Buffalo Ledger."

"This is Lisa Rowe with the American News Distribution Center in Atlanta calling to confirm a story picked up by our organization a few minutes ago."

CHAPTER 71

Friday, June 16, 5:00 p.m.

"**M**om!"

"Tobias, where are you?"

"At the *Ledger*. Is Dad in yet?"

"Not yet, why?"

"Make sure you watch the national news tonight."

"Why? What's going on?"

"I can't talk right now, we're busy. Just watch."

"Are you coming home for dinner?"

"No. Should be home sometime after midnight. We're really busy!"

"Can't you give me a hint about what's going on?"

"The phones are ringing, Mom, gotta go. Just watch the news."

He'd no sooner hung the phone up when Judith turned, pointing at the phone. "Got a reporter from Perth on line two."

"Perth, never heard of it. What state's Perth in?" he

asked, reaching for the phone.

"You know, one of our more southern states. I believe it's called Australia."

* * *

"I don't know what's going on; he just said watch the news."

"What channel?"

"Didn't say." Rosalind Henry pulled the hot rolls out of the oven and set the pan on a cooling rack. "Just find a major network; it's almost six."

Tobias's dad sat down in his recliner perturbed by his son's mysterious phone call. Nothing in the Henry household, aside from an emergency, interfered with supper. It wasn't just his wife's great cooking—supper was a time to relax, talk about the day. The rule had always been no TV until the last person left the table.

Rosalind joined her husband just as the news was coming on. The broadcaster was not reading from a prompter. Instead, he was looking at a news story scrolling across a computer monitor buried in the news desk out of the viewers' sight. "ABC News has just confirmed an amazing story out of Buffalo, Oklahoma."

The news crew flashed a map of Oklahoma on the screen, with an arrow pointing to Buffalo's geographical location as the news anchor talked. "The details are sketchy at this moment, but apparently, according to a local newspaper reporter, Tobias Henry, a local rancher's granddaughter living in the Kansas City, Kansas area was kidnapped and held for ransom." The anchor hesitated, studying the scrolling news release closely. "This is hard to believe, but according to our affiliate in Oklahoma City, the ransom consisted of Spanish treasure lost by Coronado over four hundred years ago. The editor of the local newspaper in Buffalo says there will be a news conference concerning the granddaughter's rescue telecast from Kansas City and another news conference concerning the ransom to follow later from Oklahoma. You can be sure ABC will keep you abreast of this breaking news. Stay tuned. We'll be right back with news about the war on terrorism following this break."

Clark Henry was not a man to show his feelings outwardly. He had them, just like everyone, but they had been well concealed until now. "Rosalind!" He pointed at the TV screen, searching for words. "Rosalind, did you hear that? What rancher? Who has a granddaughter in Kansas City? And Coronado's lost treasure, what's that all about?"

"That's got to be Fred and Helen Gray. You remember their daughter Beth lives there!" Rosalind reached for the phone "I'll call Crys. Maybe she knows something about this."

* * *

Within an hour after the evening news broadcast, every room at the two motels had been reserved for a week, some indefinitely by reporters and news crews from around the nation. Calls poured into the *Ledger*, and Judith, who was in charge of traffic control, routed them to Dan and Tobias. By midnight they had answered calls from not only the U.S., Mexico, and Canada but from countries on every continent with the exception of Antarctica.

"That's it, Judith!" Thompson yelled from his office. "No more, just let it ring."

"I won't object to that." Judith added up the hash marks she'd made each time a call came in. "Two hundred and thirty-eight phone calls," she announced.

"Go home and get some rest. What we've experienced tonight is only a prelude to what's coming. Be back in here by nine."

"What'll happen tomorrow?" Tobias asked.

"Don't know, but you can bet it'll be a three-ring circus around here, and I'm afraid the *Ledger* will be center ring."

* * *

Thompson was right. By the next morning, satellite trucks and rental cars were everywhere. Some telecast crews, used to being on the road without creature comforts, pitched tents in the city park. Unfortunately, it was Saturday, a typical weekend day off for most people, and instead of planning some form of restful activity, many decided to see what Buffalo, Oklahoma looked like. Cars from Oklahoma, Kansas, Colorado, Texas, and New Mexico paraded back and forth through downtown. Many asked directions to the Gray Ranch, but fortunately for the family, no one who knew where they lived gave directions. Some sightseers parked near the courthouse, hoping to get a look at the sheriff, who had attracted the attention of several male correspondents.

A few days, later the small-town inhabitants had adjusted to the notoriety. Life was slowly recuperating from the chaos, and most of the media had gone. A late spring shower moved through the county, settling the dust and freshening the air. It was the same town and the same people, but a change had occurred, a subtle change— neither bad nor good—just a change that somehow would eventually alter individual perceptions of life and perhaps even someone's destiny.

CHAPTER 72

Tuesday, June 27, 10:23 a.m.

"**S**heriff, you have a call on your line from the ME."

"Thanks, Maude." The sheriff knew what the ME was going to say, but she couldn't move forward with an investigation until the official report was completed.

"Stanton here."

"Hey, sheriff, have things settled down for you?"

"Some. Most of the media's gone; I think we're getting back to normal, whatever that is."

"I can tell you Buffalo is the talk of Oklahoma City. Everywhere I go, folks are yakkin' about it."

"I'm just ready for a break. Excitement's over, and I'm tired, been thinking about Jamaica. Ever been there?"

"You kidding? With three little ones at home, I'm lucky to make it to Six Flags."

"Anyway, what ya got for me?"

"Your vic's cause of death is no mystery: a thirty-eight

slug from the gun found at the scene. The mystery is as you suspected."

"No GSR."

"Right, sheriff, nada."

"Anything else?"

"Not a thing. Every forensic scientist around would agree it wasn't suicide, but you and I both know if that's what you're basing your case on, it may not be enough."

"My suspect is going away for a long time, and there's no statute of limitation on murder, so I've got time. Something will surface sooner or later. In the meantime, Curt's sister and girlfriend can take some comfort in the fact he didn't kill himself."

"I guess that might make me feel a little better to know it wasn't suicide, hard to tell. Either way, it's a damn shame. Sheriff, I gotta run. Good luck on your evidence search, and let me know how Jamaica was."

"Will do, and thanks."

No sooner had Stanton hung up when Bingham buzzed in on the intercom. "Agent Miles on line one."

"Pete, what's happening in your world?"

"Good news! FBI has authorized the release of the treasure; they'll even transport it to a location of Mr. Gray's choosing tomorrow."

"What happened?"

"Don't know. Just out of the blue, Webster called and said to release it. You know, Crys, this is highly unusual."

"Yeah, but I think I know what's going on."

"Clue me in."

"Apparently, the treasure won't be around much longer."

"What do you mean?"

"The Grays got a letter from the U.S. ambassador to the UN saying that Spain had exercised their right to reclaim the treasure."

"You're kidding!"

"Nope. According to Fred's attorney, there's nothing they can do."

"Wow, that's a kick in the head. How they taking it?"

"You know, Pete, they're just glad Lindsey is okay. I think they just want to get back to their retirement."

"I still think it's a rip-off. The treasure has been there four hundred years. The Grays have owned the land for over a hundred, and if it wasn't for Fred it'd still be lost. I don't see the justice in this. Hell, Crys, it looks more like Spain stealing from the Grays."

"Yeah, well, unfortunately, it isn't up to us. Guess someone from the Spanish government is supposed to be here in a few days to pick it up."

"I see now why the higher-ups ordered the evidence released. Somebody higher up than our higher-ups pushed the right buttons."

"Seems like that's the way things work sometimes."

"Got to go, Crys. It's my twelfth wedding anniversary today, and I don't have a gift picked out."

"Yeah, you'd better get to the store, and congratulations. By the way, thanks for helping out. Can't imagine what this would've been like without you."

"Same to you, sheriff. Maybe we can work together again sometime."

Sheriff Stanton pressed the intercom button and instructed Bingham she wasn't taking any more calls that weren't emergencies.

"Going home?" Maude asked.

"Think I'll drive out to my place and just sit in the shade of one of those old cottonwoods the rest of the afternoon."

"Take me with ya?"

"Nope, somebody has to be in charge."

CHAPTER 73

One week later

F red Gray invited Lee and Beverly out to meet the Spanish representative who would be claiming the treasure on behalf of his government. The representative was to be accompanied by Dr. Ramirez, and he had specifically requested that the Bethels be invited. The sheriff coordinated law enforcement supervision of the actual treasure transfer with the Air Police from Vance Air Force Base.

A national news service contracted with Dan Thompson and Tobias to provide print news of the transfer and still photos for magazine publications. No other reporters or TV news people would be allowed on the ranch during the Spanish representative's visit.

* * *

Bear finished off the remainder of Fred's coffee and

laid her nose on his knee, a signal for him to scratch her ears. "Be glad when this day's done, Bear. Know why?" Bear fixed her brown eyes on Fred. "'Cause maybe this'll all be over. I just want our life back."

The dog gave an understanding snort.

Helen stuck her head out the back door. "Fred, just talked with Crys."

"Oh, what's going on now?"

Helen understood the frustration in her husband's voice. "Change in plans."

"I wonder if anyone gives a damn about our schedule," he said.

"Crys says the Spanish representative isn't just any old envoy; he's the ambassador from Spain himself. He's asked if we'll show him where the treasure was found. He also wants to hear the story behind the candlestick."

"Whatever will get these people off our backs, let's just get it over with. When will they be here?"

"She said two military vehicles from Vance Air Force Base are at the bank now with the authorization to pick the treasure up. The ambassador, Dr. Ramirez, and a U.S. official are in a military helicopter sitting on the front lawn of the courthouse waiting on our decision."

"We sure don't want to keep the ambassador waiting now, would we."

"Fred Gray, I'm ready for all this to be over just as much as you, but you need to change your attitude. I won't have you brooding like some child while we have guests in the house."

Fred knew when his wife slammed the door that hard it was for a reason. She had felt everything he had in the last three weeks, and in many ways she'd experienced the painful moments more profoundly, yet her view of life remained optimistic. For her sake, he could at least act like a gentleman while the guests were there.

The rancher returned to the kitchen. Helen was working hard preparing lunch for everyone. "You're right as usual," he said.

She smiled. "Want to help?"

"That's why I'm here."

"Set the table, and use the china and silver."

"Yes, ma'am. How many?"

"Crys, Robert, the Bethels, Dan Thompson and Tobias, Dr. Ramirez, the ambassador, the U.S. rep, and the helicopter pilot, plus you and me."

"That's twelve by my count. Right?"

"Right."

Robert was showering after fixing fence all morning; Lee and Beverly were just pulling into the drive, and Fred could hear the whapping noise of an approaching helicopter.

The ambassador was a gracious person, a small ranch owner himself. Fred was pleasantly surprised to learn he was a knowledgeable cattleman and horse breeder. The two got along very well.

"Mr. and Mrs. Gray, I've heard about the personal tragedies you and your family have endured the past few weeks. My condolences at the loss of your ranch hand. And I'm deeply sorry for what your family went through during your granddaughter's kidnapping ordeal. I can't imagine how terrible that was for all of you."

"We're thankful she's doing so well, and of course we're thankful for Sheriff Stanton and the Bethels. Without them and all they did, I just don't know how we would've survived," Helen said, brushing back tears with her napkin.

* * *

Later Robert and his father escorted the ambassador out to the cave. Fred repeated his grandfather's candlestick story and how he located the cave using the drawing he'd found in the margin of an old courthouse journal. Lee and Beverly spent the time discussing a set of documents Carlos Ramirez had been contracted to authenticate. "And who'd you say you were contracting with?" Lee asked.

"I didn't, and furthermore if I told you, I'd have to kill you," Ramirez said, smiling. "Anyway, just wanted your opinion. I may be in touch with you folks later if you don't mind."

The pilot had returned to the helicopter and was performing the routine flight check necessary before takeoff.

The three returned from the cave, and the ambassador said good-bye to the Bethels, Robert, and Sheriff Stanton. He turned to Carlos and the U.S. dignitary. "I'll be ready to leave in about twenty minutes. I need to meet privately with Mr. and Mrs. Gray." He turned and followed the rancher into the house.

The ambassador sat down at the kitchen table across from Fred and Helen. He laid his briefcase on the table and opened it. "Again, I want to thank you for the wonderful lunch and your Oklahoma hospitality. On behalf of my government, please accept our appreciation for allowing Spain to recover Coronado's treasure."

"You're most welcome, and please come back for a visit when you can," Helen said, fearing her husband would not properly acknowledge the ambassador's graciousness.

"There are just a few details I must take care of before leaving." He took some documents out of his briefcase and arranged them in order on the table. "First of all, here is a document that simply says that you are returning the treasure listed in the inventory to Spain and that you've not been coerced in any manner. I need both your signatures here and here." He pointed to red location arrows.

Fred's experience with the ambassador that day was much better than he ever expected; however, it was quickly weakening as he watched the skillful insertion of accumulating paperwork and bureaucratic nonsense into a process that, up to then, had been remarkably pleasant. He looked at his wife and decided not to embarrass her by making one of his anti-government intrusion comments. Fred signed the document and slid it to Helen.

"This is a copy of the international law concerning lost and stolen antiquities signed by the U.S. Ambassador to the UN for your files. Thirdly is a letter from the president of Spain, thanking you for returning the treasure. He also wants you to have the candlestick as a memento of Spain's appreciation." The ambassador took the candlestick from his briefcase and handed it to Fred.

Helen could see that her husband was not in the right mood to express his appreciation. "Thank you, Mr. Ambassador, we'll always cherish it, especially now that we know the full story behind it."

The ambassador handed an envelope to Helen. "This is for your family. When Lindsey is up to the trip, our president invites all of you to visit Spain at our expense."

"Oh, Fred, isn't that wonderful? Lindsey and her parents will be so thrilled."

Fred managed an appreciative smile.

The ambassador took one more envelope out of his briefcase. This one looked important, with a red wax seal and the Grays' names written in calligraphy across the face. "The last item." He turned the envelope so that Fred and Helen could see it clearly. He repeated, "The last item." He hesitated again. "Would you like to know what our appraisal of the treasure is?"

"Yes, of course, I think everyone wants to know that," Helen said.

"Antiquities experts all agree that an appraisal is nearly impossible. They say—whatever the market will bear. Of course, there will be no market because it will never be for sale. However, several estimates were made based on an implied market. Dr. Cardona, the most reliable expert on Spanish antiquities, has set the value at fifty million U.S. dollars."

Helen gasped. "Oh my word, I never would've imagined."

Fred sat wide-eyed, staring at the ambassador. "Are you sure?!"

"The only reason we appraised the treasure, Mr. and Mrs. Gray, was so that our government could honor your benevolence with a reward."

"But, Mr. Ambassador, you've allowed us to keep the candlestick, and the expense-paid trip for our family. That's so much," Helen said.

"On behalf of the president of Spain, we would like you to accept this with our heartfelt thanks." The ambassador scooted the envelope toward Fred and got to his feet. "Now, I have a flight to catch."

"We'll see you off," Fred said without opening the envelope.

"Please, stay inside. The wash from the helicopter blades will cause quite a dust storm. Look at what's in the envelope, and when you are ready to tour Spain, let me know."

Fred and Helen watched from inside the house as the helicopter lifted off and headed east. They both sat back down at the table, anxious to see what was in the envelope. Fred opened the flap that was held fast by the wax seal and pulled a check out far enough for them to see the amount.

CHAPTER 74

Wednesday, July 5, 10:00 a.m.

The Grays' attorney was as shocked at the amount as Fred and Helen. "Who knows about this, Fred?" he asked.

"No one, not even Robert. We were so flabbergasted, neither of us knew what to do, and that's why we're here. We need help."

The attorney studied the documents closely. "Did the ambassador tell you that this reward is tax free?"

"No, he didn't say a word about that," Helen said.

"Says right here in paragraph four that the reciprocating countries would not penalize rewards and finders fees through taxation. So, assuming the check doesn't bounce, the money is all yours to do with as you wish," the attorney said, smiling, and added, "like paying your attorney."

"I 'spec after all this is said and done, you'll get your hands on some of it," Fred said.

Helen wasn't sure how to read her husband's mood.

One thing was for certain, Fred hated doing business with attorneys almost as much as he hated doing business with government bureaucrats. As far as she knew, this attorney was the only one Fred had ever trusted, and maybe the silliness she observed between them was just a game. She shuffled nervously, waiting for her husband to clear the air.

The attorney frowned. "You'd better be on your toes, Fred. You know us lawyers—we'd like to get our hands on most of it." Both men laughed.

Helen sighed, shaking her head. "Men. It's a wonder you ever get any business accomplished." She took a small notebook from her purse.

"So, Mr. and Mrs. Gray, besides my hefty fee, what are you going to do with this money?"

Helen read from the notes she and Fred had prepared. "First of all, we want to pay the outstanding debt Robert owes his brother and sister for the ranch. He's been making quarterly payments for the past five years and still owes fifty thousand to each. Secondly, we want to give two hundred and fifty thousand dollars to Mary Logsten, the lady that helped save our granddaughter. We understand she has a six-year-old daughter, and we'd like to establish an education account for her when she's ready for college."

"How much?" the attorney asked.

"By the time she's eighteen, with living expenses included, we think it'll cost fifteen thousand dollars a semester. That amount times eight semesters would equal a hundred and twenty thousand dollars."

"Anything else?"

"Two hundred thousand dollars to the hospital for equipment and building upgrades. The same amount for the new courthouse voters just approved, and the same to be split evenly between the sheriff's office and fire department."

The attorney continued to jot notes on his legal pad. "Next?"

"Four hundred thousand dollars for county public schools, and ten percent of the total amount divided equally between the five churches in town."

"Okay, Mr. and Mrs. Gray, by my calculation we've reduced the total amount by nearly two million. Is there anything else?"

"Yes, we want to give the Bethels one million."

The lawyer pulled a law book off a shelf and studied it. "I'll need to look into that. Dr. Bethel may have ethical problems if he accepted a gift while carrying out duties as a representative of the university. He would be subject to a huge state and federal tax bite even if there isn't an ethical issue." He read further, and then called a colleague in Oklahoma City who worked for the attorney general.

"That was a friend of mine from law school; he says that if Dr. Bethel could clearly demonstrate he was not conducting business on behalf of the university, he might be able to skirt the ethics issue, but not the taxation."

"We want them to have something, one way or another. And I don't want the government to get their grubby hands on any of what we want those two to have. As far as I'm concerned, they saved our granddaughter!"

"I understand, Fred. We'll figure something out. Maybe an endowment to the university."

"What?" Fred's face wrinkled to a scowl.

"One million to the university for the establishment of an endowed chair in the name of Dr. and Mrs. Bethel."

"And how in the hell is that supposed to help the Bethels?"

"In ways you can't imagine. I'll make a list; you can look it over and see what you both think. You'll be surprised."

Fred continued to brood over their lack of control concerning the distribution of the reward. Helen put the notebook back in her purse and snapped it shut. "There's one more thing."

"Yes?"

"We'd like to do all this anonymously. Is that possible?" she asked.

"Yes, it's possible, but are you certain?"

"Oh yes, our family has had all the notoriety it can stand."

"Then anonymous it will be. And the rest goes into a trust to be distributed evenly among your heirs at the death of the surviving spouse." He finished writing the last instructions and laid the legal pad on the desk. "By the way, how are Beth and her family doing?"

"Remarkably well. Lindsey is in therapy, but the doctor says that since there was no physical or sexual abuse, she should recover completely. She's having nightmares, and she's reluctant to be out of sight of her parents, but they say that's normal and will diminish with therapy over time."

"That's good to hear. I know you all will be glad when all this is over."

Fred shifted nervously in his chair, moving from one side to the other like someone sitting on a bag of marbles.

"Take it easy, Fred; we've been off the clock for five minutes."

The rancher flushed, and Helen rolled her eyes.

"And, Robert—you know, he and I are the same age; we played high school sports together. We were actually pretty good friends, but I never see him."

"He's just like his dad, a little antisocial. He's more comfortable working cattle and fixing fence than socializing, although he did work up the courage to ask Crys Stanton to go with him to church Sunday."

"No kidding? They'd make a good-looking couple."

Fred stood and shook hands with the attorney. "Got to go. No hired hands, so it's all up to Robert, me, and the missus to keep the cows outta mischief. Let me know when you got this legal stuff ready, and we'll come back so you can gouge more money out of us," he said, laughing.

CHAPTER 75

One month later

The summer in Buffalo was passing quickly, faster, it seemed, than most. People were still in awe of all that had transpired, catapulting the town on the high dusty plain of Western Oklahoma into the world spotlight. All the events had been chronicled nicely within five articles appearing weekly in the countywide newspaper. Each of the articles written by Tobias Henry and Dan Thompson were already nominated for journalism awards from coast to coast. Readers were captivated by tales of ancient civilizations, Spanish explorers, and lost treasure, not to mention a brush with international terrorism.

* * *

Lee returned to the university and was conducting a short course on site-dating principles, and Beverly began analyzing research data so that she could conclude her dissertation by the following spring semester. It was Friday afternoon, and they both were looking forward to their date night.

"Well, here we are again," Beverly said, gently stirring her amaretto sour with her finger.

"Yeah, again. You know, there was a time this summer I wasn't sure we'd ever see another date night."

"It was scary, but don't you feel more alive? Not that I'd want to go through that again, but really, that kind of experience makes life more vivid. Honestly, Lee, I feel closer to you than I ever have."

"And you think that's 'cause we almost got killed?!"

"No, well...maybe partly. Sometimes it takes an eye-opening experience to make you appreciate what you have."

"I can agree with that. I know one thing for sure."

"What?"

"If something had happened to you, I would've blamed myself."

"That's nonsense, honey! You didn't put me anywhere I didn't want to be. Don't ever forget that!"

"Maybe not, but still I don't think I could have gone on." A long thoughtful pause followed. "I think we've had enough excitement for a while."

"Yeah, for a while anyway." Beverly took a sip of her sour and winked.

* * *

Later that same night, Dr. Carlos Ramirez sat on the floor of his Annapolis, Maryland home viewing photos of very old and much-damaged documents. The entire east side of his two-bedroom, second-floor townhouse was window from floor to ceiling. From the living room, Carlos could look out over part of the Naval Academy and the Intracoastal Waterway. The room was bathed in ambient light from two antique lamps sitting on each side of the tan leather couch. He was using a flashlight and magnifying glass to study the photos. Each photograph was accompanied by a scientific analysis that verified the age, along with a translation of the writing on each scroll. Much of the documents was damaged beyond repair, but what was legible was truly remarkable. Dr. Ramirez had been hired by a confidential group working through the U.S. State Department to examine the documents and establish authenticity. He had originally turned the contract down, certain the discoverer's story was another hoax, but when the Secretary of State asked him to reconsider, how could he refuse? Carlos kept his growing excitement in check; he wanted to be absolutely sure that what he was looking at was real and not just another artful forgery. There was still a lot of work to do, and he needed help from someone with specific knowledge, but more importantly, he needed help from someone he could trust.

* * *

Lee had been asleep an hour, a very sound sleep.
"Lee, wake up."
He recognized the voice.
"Lee, wake up, it's the phone."
"Answer it," Lee said from beneath the pillow he'd pulled over his head.
"It's on your side of the bed. I can't reach it."
Lee sat up and looked at the phone, hoping it was a dream, but it wasn't. He answered.
"Lee, this is Carlos Ramirez. I know it's late, but it's important…"

THE END

LaVergne, TN USA
15 September 2010
197201LV00001B/1/A